THE
SCAVENGERS

THE
SCAVENGERS
A DEATH & TEXAS WESTERN

WILLIAM W.
JOHNSTONE
AND J. A. JOHNSTONE

PINNACLE BOOKS
Kensington Publishing Corp.
www.kensingtonbooks.com

PINNACLE BOOKS are published by

Kensington Publishing Corp.
119 West 40th Street
New York, NY 10018

PUBLISHER'S NOTE
Following the death of William W. Johnstone, the Johnstone family is working with a carefully selected writer to organize and complete Mr. Johnstone's outlines and many unfinished manuscripts to create additional novels in all of his series like The Last Gunfighter, Mountain Man, and Eagles, among others. This novel was inspired by Mr. Johnstone's superb storytelling.

All Kensington titles, imprints, and distributed lines are available at special quantity discounts for bulk purchases for sales promotions, premiums, fund-raising, educational, or institutional use. Special book excerpts or customized printings can also be created to fit specific needs. For details, write or phone the office of the Kensington sales manager: Kensington Publishing Corp., 119 West 40th Street, New York, NY 10018, attn: Sales Department; phone 1-800-221-2647.

PINNACLE BOOKS, the Pinnacle logo, and the WWJ steer head logo are Reg. U.S. Pat. & TM Off.

ISBN-13: 978-0-7860-4374-3
ISBN-10: 0-7860-4374-1

First printing: April 2020

10 9 8 7 6 5 4 3 2 1

Printed in the United States of America

CHAPTER 1

"Look who's comin' in again," Alma Brown whispered softly to Gracie Billings when the cook walked past her on her way back to the kitchen. Gracie paused and looked toward the front door. It was the second time this week that Jesse Tice had come in the dining room next to the hotel, appropriately named the Two Forks Kitchen. He had become a regular visitor to the dining room ever since his youngest son was killed there some weeks before. Usually, he came in only once a week. "Wonder what's so special about this week?" Alma whispered. They were never happy to see the old man because he made their other customers uncomfortable as he hovered over his coffee, a constant scowl on his unshaven face, while he watched the front door and each customer who walked in. Coffee was the only thing he ever bought. Everyone in town knew his real purpose in haunting the dining room was the chance to see the man who had killed his son. Cullen McCabe was the man he sought. But McCabe was a bigger mystery than Jesse Tice to the people of Two Forks. Everyone knew Jesse as a cattle rustler and horse thief whose three sons were hell-raisers and troublemakers. Cullen McCabe, on the other hand, was a quiet man, seen only occasionally in town, and seeming to have no family or friends.

Alma's boss, Porter Johnson, owner of the Two Forks Kitchen, had talked to Marshal Woods about Tice's search for vengeance against McCabe. Johnson was not concerned about the fate of either Tice or McCabe. His complaint was the fact that Jesse used his dining room as his base for surveillance, hoping McCabe would return. "Doggone it, Calvin," he had complained to the marshal. "I'm runnin' a dinin' room, not a damn saloon. Folks come in here to eat, not to see some dirty-lookin' old man waitin' to shoot somebody."

Marshal Woods had been unable to give Johnson much satisfaction when he responded to his complaint. "I hear what you're sayin', Porter," he had replied. "I reckon you just have to tell Tice you don't wanna serve him. That's up to you to serve who you want to and who you don't. I can't tell folks where they can go and where they can't. As far as that shootin' in here, I told him right from the start that that fellow, McCabe, didn't have no choice. Sonny started the fight and tried to shoot McCabe in the back, but he just wasn't quick enough. I told Jesse I didn't want any more killin' in this town, so I'd have to arrest him if he shot McCabe."

Looking at the old man now as he paused to scan the dining room before taking a seat near the door, Alma commented, "One of us might have to tell the ol' buzzard we don't want him in here. I don't think

Porter wants to get started with him. He's probably afraid he'd start shootin' the place up."

"Maybe we oughta hope McCabe comes back to see us," Gracie said. "Let him take care of Jesse Tice. He took care of Sonny proper enough."

"Meanwhile, I'll go wait on him and take his order for one nickel cup of coffee," Alma said. She walked over to the small table close to the front door. "Are you wantin' breakfast?" she asked, knowing he didn't.

"No, I don't want no breakfast," he snarled. "I done et breakfast. Bring me a cup of coffee." She turned and went to get it. He watched her for a few moments before bringing his attention back to the room now only half-filled with diners. He didn't see anyone who might be the man who killed his son. The major problem Tice had was the fact that he had never actually seen Cullen McCabe up close. When he and his two sons had gone after McCabe, he had circled around them, stolen their horses, and left them on foot. Still, he felt that if he did see him, he would somehow know it was him. When the marshal tried to talk him out of seeking vengeance for the death of his son, Jesse was tempted to tell him that McCabe was a horse thief. He thought that would justify his reason for wanting to shoot him, but he was too proud to admit how his horses happened to get stolen. Every time he thought about the night he and his two sons had to walk twenty-five miles back home, it made him bite his lower lip in angry frustration. When Alma returned with his coffee, he gulped it down, having decided there was no use to linger there. It was already getting late for breakfast, so he thought he might as well go back to join Samson and Joe, who were keeping a watch for McCabe in the River House Saloon.

* * *

It had been several days since he returned to his cabin on the Brazos River after completing his last assignment from the governor's office. The long hard job in the little town of New Hope had turned out to the governor's satisfaction, and Cullen figured it would be a while before he was summoned for the next job. For that reason, he hadn't bothered to check in with the telegraph office at Two Forks to see if he had a wire from Austin. He needed to do a little work on his cabin, so he had waited before checking with Leon Armstrong at the telegraph office. When he was not on assignment for the governor, he usually checked by the telegraph office at least once a week for any messages, and it had not been quite a week since he got back. Halfway hoping there might be a message, he pulled up before the telegraph office and stepped down from the big bay gelding. He casually tossed the reins across the hitching rail, knowing Jake wouldn't wander, anyway.

Leon Armstrong looked up when Cullen walked in and gave him a cheerful greeting. "How ya doin', Mr. McCabe? I got a telegram here for you. Figured you'd be showin' up pretty soon."

"Howdy, Mr. Armstrong," Cullen returned. "Has it been here long?"

"Came in two days ago," Armstrong said as he retrieved the telegram from a drawer under the counter. "Looks like you're fixin' to travel again."

Cullen took only a moment to read the short message from Austin. "Looks that way," he said to Armstrong, and folded the message before putting it in his pocket. "Much obliged," he said, and turned to leave. It seemed kind of awkward that Armstrong always knew Cullen's plans before he did, but since he was the telegraph operator, there wasn't any way to avoid it.

"See you next time," Armstrong said as Cullen went out the door. As curious as he was about the mysterious telegrams the big quiet man received from the governor's office in Austin, he was reluctant to ask him what manner of business he was engaged in. And after the altercation between McCabe and Sonny Tice, he was even more timid about asking. For the most part, McCabe had very little contact with anyone in Two Forks except for him and Ronald Thornton at the general store. McCabe had an occasional meal at the Two Forks Kitchen and made a call on the blacksmith on rare occasions perhaps, but that was about all.

Cullen responded to Leon's farewell with a flip of his hand as he went out the door. All the wire said was that he should come into the capital. That's all they ever said, but it always meant he was about to be sent out on another assignment. So, his next stop would be Thornton's General Merchandise to add to his supplies. As was his usual practice, he had brought his packhorse with him when he rode into town, in the event there was a telegram waiting. Austin was north of Two Forks, while his cabin was south of the town. So, by bringing the packhorse with him, there was no need to return to his cabin. Taking Jake's reins, he led the big bay and the sorrel packhorse up the street to Thornton's.

* * *

Jesse Tice and his two sons came out of the saloon and stood for a while on the short length of board-walk in front. Looking up and down the street, hoping to catch sight of the man who shot his youngest, Jesse figured it another wasted day. Both Samson and Joe were content to participate in the search for the man called Cullen McCabe as long as their watching post was always the saloon. There was not a great deal of gray matter between the ears of either Joe or Samson and what there was seemed easily diluted by alcohol. Neither son carried the same driven desire their father had to avenge their brother. They generally figured that Sonny was bound to run into somebody he couldn't outdraw in a gun-fight and the results would be the same. "How 'bout it, Pa?" Samson asked. "We 'bout ready to go on back to the house?"

"Hold on," Jesse said, something having caught his attention at the far end of the street. At that moment, Graham Price, the blacksmith, walked out of the saloon, heading back to his forge. Jesse stepped in front of Price. "Say," he asked, "who's the big feller leadin' them horses to the general store?" He pointed to Thornton's.

Price paused only long enough to say, "His name's Cullen McCabe." Having no more use for Jesse and his sons than most of the other citizens of Two Forks, he continued on toward his shop. Had he taken the time to look at the wide-eyed look of discovery on Jesse Tice's face, he would have regretted identifying McCabe. As luck would have it, Jesse had asked one of the handful of people in Two Forks who knew McCabe's name. As Price crossed to the other side of the street, he could hear the excited exchange of conversation behind him as the three Tice men realized their search had paid off.

Joe, Jesse's youngest, now that Sonny was dead, ran to his horse to get his rifle, but Jesse stopped him. "Put it away, you damn fool! You're too late, anyway, he's done gone inside the store."

"He'll be comin' back out," Samson insisted, thinking the same as Joe. "And when he does, we can cut him down."

"Ain't I ever learnt you boys anythin'?" Jesse scolded. "And then what, after ever'body in the whole town seen you do it? Take to the hills with a marshal's posse after us?"

"Yeah, but he shot Sonny right there in the dinin' room, and ever'body seen him do it," Joe declared. "Marshal didn't arrest him for that."

"Sonny called him out," Jesse said. "There's a difference. You pick him off when he don't know you're waitin' for him—that's murder, and they'd most likely hang you for it."

Confused now, Samson asked, "Well, ain't we gonna shoot him? Why we been hangin' around here waitin' for him to show up, if we ain't gonna shoot him?"

"We're gonna shoot him," his father explained, impatiently. "But we're gonna wait and follow him outta town where there ain't no witnesses."

"What if he ain't plannin' to leave anytime soon?" Joe complained. "I'd just as soon step up in front of him and tell him to go for his gun—see how fast he is when he don't know it's comin'. Then it would be a face-to-face shootout, and like you said, that ain't murder. Hell, I'm as fast as Sonny ever was," he claimed, his boast in part inspired by the whiskey he had just imbibed. He didn't express it, but he was also thinking about gaining a reputation by gunning down the man who killed Sonny.

Jesse smirked in response to his son's boastful claim. "You don't know how fast McCabe is. You ain't never seen him draw." He had to admit that it would give him great pleasure to have the people of Two Forks see McCabe shot down by one of his boys.

"You ain't seen me draw lately, neither," Joe replied. "I know how fast Sonny was, and I know how fast I am. I'm ready to shoot this sidewinder right now."

"He is fast, Pa," Samson said, curious to see if Joe could do it. "He ain't lyin'."

The prospect of seeing McCabe cut down before an audience of witnesses was too much for Jesse to pass up. Joe was right, he hadn't seen how fast he was lately, and he knew both his boys practiced their fast-draw on a daily basis. There had always been a competition among all three of his sons, ever since they were big enough to wear a gun. Sonny had been the first one to actually call a man out, though, and that hadn't turned out very well. But the fact that Sonny's death didn't discourage Joe was enough to cause Jesse to wonder. "All right," he finally conceded. "We'll go talk to Mr. McCabe. He owes me for three horses he stole. We'll see what he has to say for hisself about that. Then, if you think you can take him, that'll be up to you. If you don't, we'll follow him out of town and shoot him down where nobody can see us do it." They hurried toward Thornton's store, concerned now that McCabe might finish up his business and leave before they got there.

Inside the store, Cullen was in the process of paying

Ronald Thornton for the supplies gathered on the counter when Jesse and his two sons walked in. He had never had a close look at the old man or his two boys, but he knew instinctively who they were, and he had a feeling this was not a chance encounter. He decided to treat it as such until he saw evidence backing up that feeling. He purposefully turned one side toward them while he gathered his purchases up close on the counter, so he could keep an eye on all three. Jesse took only a few steps inside before stopping to stand squarely in front of the door. His sons took a stance, one on each side of him. Thinking the entrance rather odd, Thornton said, "I'll be with you in a minute, soon as I finish up here."

"Ain't no hurry," Jesse said. "Our business is with Mr. McCabe there."

Thornton was suddenly struck by the realization that something bad was about to happen. "Clara," he said to his wife, "you'd best go on back in the storeroom and put that new material away." When she reacted with an expression of confusion, he said, "Just go on back there." Seeing he meant it, she quickly left the room.

Up to that point, McCabe had not reacted beyond pulling a twenty-pound sack of flour and a large slab of bacon over to the edge of the counter, preparing to carry them out to his packhorse. "What is your business with me?"

"Maybe it's about them three horses of mine you stole without payin' me for 'em," Jesse snarled.

"I figured we were square on that count. I paid you the same price you paid for them," Cullen said, guessing Jessie and his boys had most likely stolen them.

"I'm callin' you out, McCabe," Joe blurted, unable to contain himself any longer.

"That right?" McCabe asked calmly. "What for?"

"For killin' my brother," Joe said. "That's what for."

"Who's your brother?" Cullen asked, purposefully trying to keep the young man's mind occupied with something other than the actual act of pulling his weapon. He had faced his share of gunfighters in his time and it was fairly easy to read the wide-eyed nervousness in young Joe Tice's face. The fact that his speech was slurred slightly also suggested that alcohol might be doing most of the talking. Cullen understood the obligation the two brothers felt to avenge Sonny's death, no matter the circumstances that caused him to be shot. There was a chance, however, that he could talk the boy out of a gunfight, so he decided to give it a try.

"You know who he was," Joe responded to Cullen's question. "Sonny Tice. You shot him down in the Two Forks Kitchen."

"So, you're Sonny's brother, huh?" Cullen continued calmly. "Yeah, that was too bad about Sonny. I could see that he wasn't very fast with a handgun. I think he knew it, too, 'cause he waited till I turned around and then he tried to shoot me in the back. He mighta got me, too, but somebody yelled to warn me, so I didn't have any choice. I had to shoot him." He could see that his calm rambling was confusing the young man. He had plainly expected to see a completely different response to his challenge to a face-off. "Yeah, I felt kinda bad about havin' to shoot poor Sonny," Cullen went on. "I've seen it before; young fellow thinks he's fast with a gun and ain't ever seen a man who's a real gunslinger. You must figure you're faster than Sonny was, but I don't know about that. Judgin' by the way you wear that .44 down so low on your leg, I don't see how you could be. How many men have you ever pulled iron on?"

"That don't make no difference," Joe protested. "That's my business." He was plainly flustered by the big man's casual attitude.

"That's what I thought," Cullen said. "This is the first time you've ever called anybody out. Well, we'll try to make it as quick and painless as we can. Let's take it outside this man's store, though." He pulled the sack of flour and the slab of bacon off the counter. "Here," he said, "you can gimme a hand with these supplies. Grab that coffee and that twist of jerky—save me a trip back in here."

Clearly confused by this time, Joe wasn't sure what to do. Accustomed to being ordered around all his young life, he did as McCabe instructed and picked up the sack of coffee and the beef jerky, then started to follow Cullen out the door. Caught in a state of confusion as well, Jesse finally realized that McCabe was talking Joe out of a face-off. "Hold on there! Put them damn sacks down," he blurted, and pulled his six-shooter when Cullen started to walk past him. It was not quick enough to avoid the heavy sack of flour that smacked against the side of his head, creating a great white cloud that covered him from head to toe when the sack burst open. With his other hand, Cullen slammed his ten-pound slab of bacon across Jesse's gun hand, causing him to pull the trigger, putting a bullet hole in the slab of side meat. The hand that had held the flour sack now held a Colt .44, and Cullen rapped one swift time across the bridge of Jesse's nose with it. Stunned, Jesse dropped like a rock.

His two sons stood paralyzed with the shock of seeing their father collapse and Cullen was quick to take advantage of it. "Unbuckle those gun belts, both of you." With his .44 trained on them, they offered no resistance. After laying his slab of bacon on the bar, Cullen took both belts, then picked up Jesse's gun. "Pick your pa up and get him out of here. Take him home and he'll be all right," he ordered, while covering them with his Colt. "There ain't gonna be no killin' here today. And if you're smart, you'll just forget about gettin' even for your brother's mistake. He made a play that didn't work out for him. Don't you make the same mistake." Still numb with shock from the way the confrontation with McCabe turned upside down, Joe and Samson helped their father to his feet. Jesse, unsteady and confused by the blow to the bridge of his nose, staggered out the door with the support of his sons. They managed to get him up in the saddle and he promptly fell forward to lie on his horse's neck. Still covered with flour, he looked like a ghost lying there. Watching the process from the boardwalk in front of the store, Cullen said, "I'm gonna leave your weapons with the marshal and tell him to let you have them back tomorrow." There was no reply from either of the boys and Jesse was still too groggy to respond. Cullen continued to watch them until they rode out the end of the street. It occurred to him then that he hadn't taken their rifles from their saddles. *I hope to hell they don't think about that,* he thought.

"I reckon you're gonna need some more flour," Thornton commented, standing in the doorway of the store. "Maybe some bacon, too."

"Reckon so," Cullen replied. "Flour, anyway. The

bacon looks okay. I'll just cut that bullet hole out of it—might flavor it up a little bit."

"I'll tell you what," Thornton said. "I won't charge you for another sack of flour. That coulda been a bad situation back there, and I wanna thank you for preventing a gunfight in my store."

"'Preciate it," Cullen said. "Now, I expect I'd better get movin'. I'm takin' the road outta here to Austin, and that's the same road they just took to go home. If you don't mind, you can get me another sack of flour and I'll take these guns to the marshal while you're doin' that." He started walking down the street at once and called back over his shoulder, "Sorry 'bout the mess I made in your store."

Still standing in the door, Thornton looked back inside. "Don't worry about that," he said, "Clara's already sweeping it up."

Marshal Calvin Woods was just in the process of locking his office door as he hurried to investigate the shot he had heard several minutes before. Seeing Cullen approaching, he feared it was to report another killing in his town. When Cullen told him what had taken place, the marshal also expressed his appreciation to him for avoiding a shootout with Jesse Tice and his sons. Cullen left the weapons with him, then returned to the store to tie all his purchases on his packhorse. Ronald Thornton stood outside and watched while he readied his horses to ride. When Cullen stepped up into the saddle, Thornton felt prompted to comment, "It looks like Jesse Tice ain't gonna let it rest till he either gets you, or you cut him down."

"It looks that way, doesn't it?" Cullen replied. "I reckon killin' a man's son is a sure way to make him an enemy." He wheeled the big bay away from the hitching rail and set out for Austin.

Thornton's wife was waiting for him when he came back in the store. "Well, you don't know any more about that man than you did before, do ya?" She shook her head impatiently. "You and Leon Armstrong are gonna have to get together to gossip over McCabe's visit to town today, I suppose," she said, referring to the many discussions the two had already had, trying to figure out the man's business. "I'm not sure I like to see him come in the store," she concluded as she pointed to a bullet hole in the floor. "It seems like everywhere he goes, somebody starts shootin'."

"In all fairness, hon," Ronald pointed out, "it's people shootin' at him, and not the other way around."

"I don't care," she said. "It liked to scared me to death. I was sure one of us was gonna get killed and right now I've gotta go to the house and change my drawers."

Thinking it not smart to take another chance on a showdown with Jesse and his boys, Cullen nudged Jake into an easy lope as he set out on the road to Austin. He remembered all too well the day he was forced to shoot Sonny Tice. At the marshal's urging, he had hurried out of town, only to find that the trail to the Tice ranch forked off the road to Austin a couple of miles north of Two Forks. He had managed to pass that trail before they found out he was heading to Austin. It was his intention to do the same today. As he rocked in the saddle to Jake's easy gait, he kept a sharp eye on the road ahead of him. In a short while, he came to the trail leading off to the west and the Tice ranch. He rode past it with no incident, so he hoped that would be the end of it. Time would tell, he told himself, but he was not going to count on it. He had not only killed Jesse's son, but what might be worse for a man like Jesse Tice was the fact that he had made a fool of him twice. There was also the matter of three horses Cullen had taken from the ambush site. *There ain't no doubt,* he told himself, *that old buzzard has plenty of reason to come after me.*

CHAPTER 2

It was time to be thinking about some supper by the time Cullen rode into the capital city of Austin, but he decided it best to take care of his horses first. So, he rode past the capitol building to the stable at the end of the street, operated by a man he knew simply as Burnett. Cullen stepped down from the saddle at the stable door. Having seen him ride up, Burnett walked out to meet him. "Mr. McCabe," he greeted him. "You ain't got no horses to sell this time," he said, glancing past Cullen to see only the one packhorse.

"No, I reckon not," Cullen answered. "Ain't run across any lately. I'd like to leave these two with you overnight. And I'd like to sleep with 'em, if you don't charge too much."

"Sure," Burnett said with a wide smile. "I reckon I charge a little bit less than the hotel does, unless you want clean sheets." He chuckled in appreciation for his humor.

"I 'preciate it," Cullen said. "Maybe you could recommend a good place to get some supper. Last time

I was in town, I ate in the dinin' room of that hotel near the capitol, and it wasn't to my likin'."

"You shoulda asked me last time," Burnett said. "I woulda told you to go to Pot Luck. That's a little restaurant run by Rose Bettis between here and the capitol building. That's where I go when I take a notion I don't wanna cook for myself, the Pot Luck Restaurant."

"Restaurant," Cullen repeated. "That sounds kinda fancy." He thought of the place where Michael O'Brien had taken him to breakfast before and all the diners dressed up in suits and ties. Since Burnett said it was back the way he had just come, he commented, "Sounds like I shoulda noticed it on my way down here."

Burnett laughed. "Nah, Pot Luck ain't fancy. It's anything but. It's just a little place next to the hardware store. I ain't surprised you didn't notice it, but if you're lookin' for good food at a fair price, then that's the place to go."

"I'll take your word for it," Cullen said. He followed Burnett into the stables, leading his horses. He unloaded his packhorse and stacked his packs in the corner of a stall. After checking Jake's and the sorrel's hooves, and finding them in good shape, he asked Burnett what time he should be back before the stables were locked up for the night.

"You've got plenty of time," Burnett assured him. "I don't usually leave here till after seven o'clock. I ain't got a wife to go home to, so I ain't in any hurry to go home." Cullen told him he would surely be back before then and started for the door. "Tell Rose I sent you," Burnett called after him.

Cullen found Pot Luck next to the hardware store and he was not surprised that he had not noticed it when he rode past before. A tiny building crammed between the hardware store and a barbershop, the name POT LUCK RESTAURANT was painted on a four-foot length of flat board nailed over the door. A little bell over the top of the door announced his entry when he walked in and paused to look around the small room, half of which was taken up by the kitchen. A long table with a bench on each side, and a chair at each end, occupied the other half of the room. A man and a woman, the only customers, were seated at the far end of the table. They both stopped eating to stare at the man who appeared to fill the doorway completely. A short, rather chubby woman standing at the stove, whom he assumed to be Rose, turned to greet him when she heard the doorbell. She paused a moment when she saw him before she brushed a stray strand of dull red hair from her forehead and said, "Welcome. Come on in." She watched him as he hesitated, still looking the place over. "Since you ain't ever been in before, and you ain't, 'cause I'd remember you, I'll tell you how I operate. I don't have no menus. I just cook one thing. It ain't the same thing every night, but I just cook one supper—just like your mama cooked for you. Tonight, I'm servin' lamb stew with butter beans and biscuits, and you won't find any better stew anywhere else in town. So you decide whether you wanna eat with me or not." She waited then for his reaction.

"I don't recollect if I've ever had lamb before, but I reckon this is a good time to try it," he decided.

"If you don't like it, you don't have to pay for it," Rose said. "Course, that's if you don't eat it."

"Fair enough," he said.

"Set yourself down and I'll bring you some coffee, if that's what you want." He nodded and she suggested, "You'd best set in the chair at the end, big as you are." He took his hat off, offered a polite nod to the couple at the other end of the table, then sat down in the chair.

The lamb stew was as good as she had claimed it would be and the serving was ample for a man his size. The coffee was fresh and hot and she brought extra biscuits. The price was more than fair at fifty cents, considering prices for most everything were higher in a town the size of Austin. When he was finished and paying her, he asked, "Are you open for breakfast?" She was, she said, opening at six o'clock. "Then I reckon I'll see you in the mornin'," he said. "By the way," he thought to say as he opened the door, "Burnett, down at the stable, sent me here to eat."

The night passed peacefully enough as he slept in the stall with Jake, who snorted him awake at about half past five when the big bay heard Burnett open the stable doors. Knowing Michael O'Brien usually came into his office at eight, Cullen decided he would buy himself some breakfast at Pot Luck before he saddled up for the day. He was sure he would prefer eating breakfast with Rose than going to breakfast with O'Brien at the Capitol Diner, where all the customers were dressed up like lawyers. As it turned out, Burnett went to breakfast with him and they took their time drinking coffee afterward. It was a rare occasion for Cullen, but he had to kill a lot of time before O'Brien would be in. Rose's breakfast was as good as her supper had been, so Cullen knew where he would be eating every time he came to Austin in the future. And that would depend upon whether or not he still had a job as special agent for the governor. He still could not know for sure how long the arrangement would last. Granted, he had received nothing but satisfied responses so far, but knowing it to be an unusual position with no formal contract, it could end at any time.

After leaving Pot Luck, he went back to the stable, loaded his packhorse, and rode back to the capitol building. He was still a little early for O'Brien, but Benny Thacker, O'Brien's secretary, was in the office, so he took a seat in the outer office and waited. He refused the offer of a cup of coffee from Benny, since he had drunk what seemed like a gallon of it at Pot Luck. He sat there for about fifteen minutes, conscious of the frequent glances from O'Brien's elf-like secretary. He wondered why the shy little man seemed to be so intimidated by him. Then he recalled the last time he had been in the office. He had walked in just as Benny was coming out and they accidently collided, the result of which nearly knocked Benny to the floor. Further thoughts were interrupted when O'Brien walked in the door. He started to give Benny some instructions but turned to discover Cullen sitting just inside the door when Benny pointed to him. "Cullen McCabe!" O'Brien exclaimed. "Just the man I wanna see. Have you been here long?" Before Cullen could answer, he asked, "Have you had your breakfast?" He hurried over and extended his hand. When Cullen shook it, and said that he had already eaten, O'Brien said, "Benny could have at least gotten you a cup of coffee while you waited."

"He offered one," Cullen said, "but I've had more than I needed this mornin'. Thanks just the same." Impatient now, he was anxious to get down to business. "Have you got a job for me?"

"Yes, sir, I sure do," O'Brien answered. "But first, let me tell you Governor Hubbard is well pleased with the success of this arrangement." He winked and said, "You did a helluva job in New Hope. He's started claiming that the creation of your job was his idea, even though it was mine right from the start. Nobody had even thought about appointing a special agent who reports only to the governor until I suggested it." Without a pause, he went right into the reason for his summons. "This is a special assignment the governor wants you to investigate this time. So let's go on in and I'll let Governor Hubbard explain the job."

Cullen followed O'Brien into the governor's office and the governor got up from his desk and walked around it to shake hands with Cullen. "Cullen McCabe," Hubbard greeted him just as O'Brien had. "I'm glad to see you," he said. "I was afraid my wire hadn't reached you." He smiled warmly. "I'm glad to see you got it." He motioned Cullen to a seat on a sofa, while he sat down in an armchair facing him. "The job I've called you in for is one of special personal interest to me." He paused then to interrupt himself. "You're doing one helluva job, by the way," he said, then continued without waiting for Cullen to respond. "This is a slightly different situation than the problems you've handled up to now. We've got a little situation about a hundred and twenty-five miles northwest of here between a couple of towns on Walnut Creek."

"Where's that?" Cullen interrupted, not having heard of it.

"Walnut Creek is a healthy creek that runs through the Walnut Valley. It's a branch of the Colorado River. I'm sending you to a little town on the west side of that creek, called Ravenwood. It was named for a man who owns many acres of land next to the creek, Judge Harvey Raven. He gave the land for the town to the county officials, along with about one hundred acres for county government business. Of course, the idea was to make Ravenwood the county seat. The problem, though, was that there was already a town of sorts on the east side of the creek where a lot of settlers had farms and homes. They didn't like it much when the county took Raven's offer. Next thing you know, they started having trouble about the water rights. One thing led to another, and pretty soon there were some shots exchanged between the folks that built up Ravenwood and those that wanted the town left on the east side of the creek. So the east-side folks created their own town and called it East City."

The governor rambled at length about the troubles between the two towns, a characteristic Cullen assumed was common to all politicians, but he wondered what it had to do with him. "What, exactly, is it you want me to do?" he asked when Hubbard paused for breath.

"I'm getting to that," Hubbard said. "The problem lies in East City. It's become a town of saloons, brothels, and gambling halls. The mayor contacted my office. East City's crime is spilling over to the other side of the creek, so the folks in Ravenwood petitioned my office for help, also. I sent a delegation up there to meet with the city officials. They concluded that the town was justified in their complaints, but they couldn't recommend any plan of action to improve the situation. We sent a company of Rangers up there to maintain the peace. They set up a camp and stayed for three days. And for three days everything was peaceful. As soon as they left, East City went back to business as usual."

"Ain't there any law in the towns?" Cullen asked.

"Yes, there is," the governor answered, "in both towns. Ravenwood has a marshal and East City has a marshal and a deputy. The problem is, the East City marshal seems to be in control of the whole town and is nothing more than an outlaw, himself. And the town has become a haven for every other outlaw on the run in Texas. As far as we know, the marshal in Ravenwood is an honest man."

"What do you expect me to do," Cullen asked, "if the Rangers couldn't fix the problem?"

The governor glanced at O'Brien and winked. "What you always do," he answered then. "What you did in New Hope and Bonnie Creek—look into the situation and see if there's anything you can do to improve it."

Cullen shook his head and thought about all Hubbard had just told him. "I don't know," he said, not at all optimistic about reforming two towns. It sounded to him that the governor needed a negotiator, and that label didn't fit him. The next best thing was to make one of the towns a permanent Ranger headquarters, and he was about to suggest that when O'Brien interrupted.

"Just ride up there and look the situation over," O'Brien said. "We trust your eyes more than the Rangers'. If nothing else, you can at least report back with a more detailed presentation of the facts."

Cullen shrugged and shook his head again. "Well, I can do that, I reckon. It's your money. I'll see what I can do."

"Good man," Hubbard exclaimed with a grin. "I knew I could count on you. There's a check for your expenses already in the bank. You can pick up your money today. Think you'll be ready to leave in the morning?"

"I expect I'll leave today, just as soon as I pick up my money at the bank," Cullen said.

"Excellent!" Hubbard responded. "Come, I'll show you where you're going." He walked over to the large state map on the wall and pointed to two small dots that looked to be in the very center of the state. Cullen stood for a few minutes studying the route he would take, noting the rivers and streams. When he was satisfied with the way he would start out, he turned and said he was ready to go. "It's early yet," the governor stated. "If you'll need a little time to get ready to go, maybe you'd like to have dinner with me."

"Thanks just the same," Cullen responded, "but I'm ready to go now, soon as I pick up the money at the bank." He didn't think he'd be comfortable eating with the governor. He imagined it would be more awkward than it had been with O'Brien in the Capitol Diner. He shook hands with both of them and took his leave after they wished him a good trip.

O'Brien and the governor stood at the office doorway and watched Cullen until he reached the end of the hall and disappeared down the stairs. "Might be a waste of time sending him up there," O'Brien commented.

"Maybe," Hubbard said, "but I've got a lot of confidence in that man. Besides, it's a helluva lot cheaper than sending a company of Rangers back there for who knows how long."

CHAPTER 3

After a stop at the bank where his expense money was always deposited in his account, Cullen set out on a road he had taken before when he had been sent to Fort Griffin. Had he been able to start out early that morning, he would have thought about possibly riding as far as Lampasas Springs by the end of the next day. But that would have been pushing Jake and the sorrel a little too hard, so he figured to reach the springs around noon the next day. There was a little trading post a few miles west of there on the Colorado River. It was owned by an old man named Blanchard, if he remembered correctly. It wasn't what a person would consider a going business. Cullen guessed it had seen better days, many years ago. He thought it would be worthwhile to stop by and purchase a few things from the old man.

Once he was on the road, he turned it over to Jake. The big bay gelding knew the gait Cullen wanted to maintain and he trusted his master to know when he needed rest. About twenty-five miles out of Austin, Cullen deemed it time to give Jake that rest when they crossed over a narrow creek. He turned him upstream and rode for about fifty yards, stopping at a spot where there was enough grass under the oak trees to feed his horses. Not really hungry, since he had eaten a big breakfast at Rose Bettis's Pot Luck, he settled for a cup of coffee and a strip of beef jerky.

After a peaceful night, he pushed his horses a little harder in order to reach the springs. He estimated the distance to be about thirty miles. He turned Jake to the west at that point, following a healthy creek to the Colorado River. He expected to find the small trading post still there. As he approached the humble building perched on the east bank of the creek, where it emptied into the river, it occurred to him that it was in a bad state of repair. There were weeds and bushes growing up in the yard and the cabin was dark. It appeared to be deserted. When he rode a little closer, Jake whinnied and was answered with a friendly nicker. Thinking it must have come from behind the store, Cullen became immediately alert. So, instead of continuing to ride straight up to the hitching post in front, he angled Jake to pass by the store. Once he rode even with the front corner of the building, he could see the horse grazing on the other side of it. A red roan, it was saddled with the reins left loosely about the saddle horn. He saw no sign of anyone anywhere around the place. Whoever belonged to the horse had to be inside, he decided, and started to ride on by to find someplace else to rest his horses. He went only a couple dozen yards before he pulled up, wheeled Jake around, and rode back up to the front of the cabin and dismounted. His curiosity had gotten the best of him and he decided to find out who belonged to the horse grazing freely beside the cabin.

With his rifle in hand, he stepped up beside the

door, which was standing slightly ajar, and cautiously pushed it halfway open with the barrel of his rifle. He wasn't sure what he might find, but it wasn't at all what he expected. It was a girl, or young woman, he wasn't sure which. She was crouched in the center of what had been the floor of the trading post, hugging her knees up close to her chin. She looked at him with eyes wide and terrified. Not certain what to make of it, he looked around the empty room to make sure he wasn't about to walk into a trap before he stepped inside. When he saw no sign of anyone else, he pushed the door wide and walked in. Even in the dim light afforded by the open doorway, he could see that the young woman was shivering with fear. "Are you all by yourself, miss?" he asked, but she didn't answer. "Are you all right?" Again, she answered with nothing more than a look of terror. "I'm not gonna cause you any harm, miss. I'll help you if I can, but you'll have to tell me what's wrong. What are you doin' sittin' here in this old shack all by yourself?"

When she finally spoke, it was in a voice barely audible and he had to step closer to understand what she asked. "Did Boot send you after me?"

"No, ma'am. Who's Boot?"

"Boot Davis," she answered, her voice gaining strength when she realized that Cullen was not going to hurt her. "I thought you were one of that sorry crowd he runs with, and you were fixin' to take me back to him."

"Maybe you'd best tell me what's goin' on," Cullen said, "and I'll see if I can help you. You can start with tellin' me your name and how come you're runnin' from Boot Davis."

With his offer of help, she responded hopefully.

"My name's Lila Blanchard. Boot and his no-good sidekick, Charley Turner, jumped me outside the Cork and Bottle Saloon."

"Where's the Cork and Bottle Saloon?" Cullen interrupted.

"East City," she answered. "Kidnapped me is what they did. Boot said he was gonna kill me when he was done with me and I knew he meant what he said. But when him and Charley was passed out drunk, I slipped outta the rope he had me tied up to him with. Then I took off. Boot's horse was still saddled, so I jumped on it and ran."

"So, that's his horse beside the cabin?" Cullen asked, and she nodded. "When was that?"

"Two nights ago," Lila answered. "Him and Charley tracked me to a barn I was hidin' in the next day. But I saw 'em when they rode up to the feller's house that owned the farm, so I lit out again. I don't know if they saw me ride out back of the barn. When I heard you come up, I just knew it was them."

"How'd you happen upon this old place?" Cullen asked, puzzled as to why she chose to sit and wait in an abandoned store.

"I didn't happen on it," she said. "I came here on purpose. I didn't know it was gone." She shook her head sadly. "This was home. This was my daddy's store."

"Your daddy?" Cullen reacted. Then it struck him—Blanchard, she said her name was Blanchard. Howard Blanchard was her father. "Your daddy's gone from here, closed up his store, and you didn't know it?"

"I ain't seen my daddy in four years," Lila said. "He told me, if I ran off with Sid Worthy, not to come back home. Sid said he was gonna marry me, but one mornin' I woke up and he was gone." She shook her head as she relived a mental picture of that morning. "I waited there for three days, waitin' for him to come back, till the feller that owns the hotel told me to come up with some rent money, or I was gonna have to get out."

Cullen didn't have to hear what happened next. It was an all-too-familiar story. "So you moved over to the saloon you mentioned."

"Yes, sir," she said. "I didn't have no choice. I went to whorin'. It was the only way I could feed myself."

It was easy for him to understand the situation that he now found her in and why she sat in the middle of the vacant store, hugging her knees, awaiting her fate. Her one desperate hope had been her father, thinking possibly he would take her in and hide her from Boot Davis. When she found him gone, not even certain he was still alive, she had given up and sat waiting for this Boot Davis fellow to find her and punish her. Cullen wasn't sure what he could do to help the desperate woman's permanent plight, but perhaps he could help her immediate situation. "When was the last time you ate?" he asked, and she said she wasn't sure, maybe she had something before Boot snatched her from the saloon. "Well," Cullen continued, "I'm fixin' to rest my horses and cook some breakfast. Reckon you could use a little, yourself."

"Mister, I surely could!" she fairly exclaimed. "Just the mentionin' of it made my belly bark like a dog." She managed a faint smile for him. "You sure as hell came along when I was prayin' for a miracle." She shook her head in frustration. "And I don't even know your name."

"Cullen McCabe," he said. "Pleased to meet you. Let me take care of my horses first, then we'll cook some breakfast. Reckon you could build a fire in that fireplace? Maybe that pile of wood beside it ain't too rotten to make a hot fire." He reached down, offering his hand. She took it and he pulled her up on her feet. His first good look at her told him she might be young in years, but her face reflected the hard times of the profession she had been forced to practice.

On her feet, she began to show a spark of recovery from the state he had found her in. She went at once to the fireplace in the corner of the room and started to arrange some kindling. "I ain't got no matches," she said, so Cullen went outside to get one from his saddlebags. When he returned with it and handed it to her, she asked, "Is that all you've got? I'd better be careful it don't blow out."

"If it does, I'll go get you another one," he joked, glad to see that she was evidently recovering some spunk. It was a disposition he much preferred to that of a helpless victim. "I'll go take care of the horses now. I ain't much of a cook, but I've got some bacon and flour, and I make a helluva pot of coffee."

"Well, bring it on in here and maybe I can put something together that won't kill us," she said, forgetting the fear that had gripped her senses such a brief time before. She felt safe in his presence, this Cullen McCabe. He was a big man, but that was not the reason. There was a calmness about him, a nonjudgmental patience that seemed to indicate an inner strength.

Lila showed that she had some skills other than those developed in the bedroom as she took what supplies she could find in Cullen's packs to produce a breakfast of bacon and simple pan biscuits. While they ate, they talked about Lila's situation and what she had planned to do if she was successful in avoiding Boot Davis. "I don't know," she confessed. "I was just runnin' for my life, and when I got here and found Daddy gone, I didn't know what to do. Try to go back to the Cork and Bottle, I guess, 'cause I can't make it on my own. I should have done that when I first escaped, but I guess I panicked."

"The Cork and Bottle?" Cullen asked. "Did you say that was in East City, right across the creek from Ravenwood?" She said that it was, so he asked, "Will you be safe there? It looks like you weren't before."

"As safe as I would be about anywhere, I reckon. I was just in the wrong place at the wrong time. Boot weren't after me, especially, he just had his mind set on snatchin' one of us girls. If it'da been Mabel or Wilma comin' from the outhouse, it'd be one of them in this fix, instead of me." She paused to think about that. "I never was the lucky one and I don't know why he kept trackin' me after I got away."

"You think it might be because you stole his horse?" Cullen casually suggested. The expression on her face told him that it had not occurred to her.

"Damn," she finally uttered. "You think they might hang me for a horse thief?"

"Maybe not," he said. "Especially if we take the horse back and tell the marshal you wanna leave it there for Boot to come get it. Then if he does, you can have him arrested for abductin' you."

The possibility brought a smile to her face. "You think I could really do that?"

"I think there would be a good chance of it," he replied. "Hell, if they were to take it to trial, I don't see any way a judge, or a jury, could blame you for what you did."

"Mr. McCabe, it's plain as day to me that you ain't ever been to East City. They don't have no trials with a judge. There ain't no judge in East City. Micah Moran decides who hangs and who don't." She paused to think about that for a moment. "You said, *we . . .* Do you mean you'd take me to East City?"

"Might as well," he replied. "I'm goin' there, anyway, just as soon as my horses are ready to go."

She fairly beamed, newly excited. "I never believed in angels before, but I'm believin' in 'em now. I don't know how I can ever repay you for what you're doin' for me." Her joy was interrupted then when another thought struck her—one she had forgotten for the moment. "You need to know what you might be getting into. Boot Davis and that animal he runs with, Charley Turner, are a pair of mean customers. I wouldn't feel right about this if I didn't warn you about them."

"I 'preciate the warnin'," Cullen said. "Maybe, if we're lucky, we'll get to East City before they figure out where you are. I expect we'll make East City by late afternoon tomorrow. So if you're ready, we'll get started."

Cullen readied his horses, then took a quick inspection of Boot Davis's red roan. The horse was in good shape, about four or five years old, he figured. "You stole a pretty good horse," he told Lila, as he gave her a lift up. "Pretty fancy saddle, too." He didn't say it, but he had no doubt about the zero possibility that Boot would give up on a search for his horse. It would depend on how good a tracker Boot was, and if Lila had taken any pains at all to hide her trail. In her panic to escape, he would bet that she hadn't. There was a chance, however, since she had left the common road to cut over here to the river. Maybe, if Boot was tracking her, he wouldn't have noticed that she had left the road. "Have you looked in his saddlebags?" Cullen asked.

"No," she answered. "I never even thought about it."

He found that hard to believe. "Let's take a look. He might have some jerky or somethin' in there that you could have eaten." He opened one of the pouches. "Extra cartridges for that rifle," he announced, then opened the bag on the other side. "Well, now," he muttered as he held up a sizable roll of paper money. "Look at that."

"My stars!" she exclaimed, surprised, but not very convincingly, in his opinion.

He dropped the roll of money back in the saddlebag. "Looks like he's got enough money there to buy two or three horses like this geldin' you're settin' on. You reckon?"

"I reckon," she replied, certain that he knew she was already aware of the money. "He oughta owe it to me for what he done."

"You might be right," he said, not really caring if she kept the money or not. His only concern was the added incentive Boot Davis and his friend Charley Turner had to track the woman down.

Cullen returned to the common wagon road that led from Lampasas Springs to Ravenwood and East City. Jake and the sorrel had already worked pretty hard that morning, so he planned to push them on no farther than twenty miles or so. That should put them within a day's ride of East City, if his calculations were right. Then, depending upon what he found when they reached the Cork and Bottle, he might have

Lila off his hands. He could not, in good conscience, abandon her to violent men like Davis and Turner, if it turned out that there was no protection for her at the saloon. He might have to talk the matter over with the marshal of East City before he tried to take on his mission of looking into the situation between the two towns.

He decided he had pushed the horses far enough when he came to a place where two streams met to form the creek they had followed for most of that day. From the ashes of several old fires, they could see that it was a commonly used campground. He took a close look at the clearing where most of the fires had been built and picked a spot near the outer edge where there was a little more cover. Then he pulled the saddles and packs off the horses and let them go to water. While he was taking care of the horses, Lila gathered wood for a fire. Once she had it started, she announced that she was going to go downstream to take care of her personal needs. He filled his coffee-pot with water and set it on the fire to warm. He figured he'd let Lila do the cooking. Convinced that Boot would come after her, he was hoping that the two roughnecks didn't know about her father and wouldn't be looking for her on this road any longer. Regardless, he planned to be ready for a late-night visit, just in case. Along with that thinking, he decided to hobble Boot Davis's horse, as well as his sorrel packhorse. He wouldn't bother to hobble Jake. The big bay would not stray far from him. He had just finished with the hobbling when Lila came back to the camp. She was tiptoeing cautiously along the creek bank, carrying her shoes and what appeared to be her undergarments in her hands.

Seeing his quizzical expression, she explained, "I ain't never been on a horse so long in all my life. And, I declare, this last twenty miles, or however far it was, just about wore my bottom out. I had to wade out in the creek and set it down for a while to put out the fire."

Cullen choked back a laugh and asked, "Did it help?"

"I'll say it did," she giggled, "until I got out again."

"Well, if it ain't too tender to set on, you just go find you something soft and set down, and I'll do the cookin'," he volunteered.

"No, no," she protested. "I'll do the cookin'. It ain't gonna keep me from cookin'. I already owe you more than I can ever pay you." She hesitated, trying to decide whether to say more or not, then went on with it. "I don't know if you're interested, but you know the profession I'm in." He knew what she was about to say, but he let her go on. "What I'm sayin' is, that's all I've got to pay you with, and if you're wantin' . . ." That was as far as he let her go before stopping her.

"That's mighty generous of you, Lila, but that won't be necessary. You don't owe me anything at all." He gave her a little smile. "Besides, you ain't really open for business right now, anyway."

"You can say that again," she cried. "My bottom's sore as a boil."

With an extra blanket Cullen carried and a piece of canvas he used for a shelter in bad weather, they fashioned a bed for Lila. Before she crawled into it for the night, they sat by the fire awhile to finish the little bit of coffee left in the pot. "Was you serious when you said we might leave Boot's horse with the marshal?" Lila asked.

"Yeah," he answered, "we could do that—might make it seem like you wanted to do the right thing." When she cocked her head as if skeptical, he asked, "Why? Something wrong with that?"

"No, I reckon not," she replied, but still with a sense of uncertainty. When he prodded her to say what was bothering her, she finally said what was on her mind. "You ever been to East City?" When he reminded her that he never had, she continued. "Marshal Micah Moran pretty much runs that town and he's been known to go awful light on the wild bunch that likes to hang around there. That is, except for the Cork and Bottle. You see, Marshal Moran is half owner of that saloon, and most of the wild bunch know it. That's why I said I was as safe in the saloon as anywhere else. Moran's got a deputy, Ace Brown, and he's the one that takes care of all the marshal's heavy work. Ace enjoys bustin' up drunk cowhands and farm boys, but it don't seem to keep 'em from comin' back for more."

"What about the ordinary merchants in town?" Cullen asked. "The storekeepers, the hotel, livery stable, barbershop, people like that, are they happy with Moran runnin' the town?"

"It might not be just exactly as they'd like it, but there ain't a lot they can do about it. I reckon they do enough business with the cowhands and the farmers to keep 'em from closin' up and movin' across the creek to Ravenwood. That's where the more respectable folks do their business. At least, that's what I've been told. Ravenwood ain't got but two saloons and it's about twice as big as East City. East City's got two

saloons, too, but Cork and Bottle is the biggest." She
rambled on about the two towns, since he seemed to
be interested in her story. When he asked if there was
a town council, or anything equivalent to one, she
said, "Yep, there's a council. There's even a mayor,
Abe Franks. He owns the hardware store."

As the campfire died down, Cullen realized he had
a pretty complete picture of East City, even if it was
from a prostitute's point of view. He figured her to be
fairly accurate in her description because a prostitute
was more likely to be privy to the dark side of the
town. Just out of curiosity, Cullen asked, "Is there a
church in East City?"

"Goodness, no," Lila exclaimed. "Some folks
wanted to build one about a year ago, but Micah said
no. Said it would be bad for business." She paused to
study his face before saying, "There's one in Ravenwood, if that's what you're lookin' for."

"Just wondered," he said. "Was it just the marshal
that said no to the church, or did the mayor and the
town council decide against it?"

"It was just the marshal that said it," she answered
with a shrug. "But that's all it takes. The council and
the mayor pretty much go with what he says. Tell
you the truth, most everybody who thought about
buildin' a church gave up on it before they got told
they couldn't have one. They already knew what the
marshal would say."

He thought that over for a few moments before
getting up from the fire. "I reckon it's about time to
turn in. I'm gonna take a little look around before I
do, though—won't be gone long." He left her to crawl
into her bed while he whistled Jake up from the edge
of the creek. With only a bridle but no saddle, he

jumped on Jake's back, his rifle in hand. He thought it a good idea to ride a wide circle around the camp just to make sure Boot and his partner hadn't gotten on their trail.

He rode Jake for about half a mile back down the road they had come up. There was no sign of anyone else behind and he figured, if they were being followed, they would most likely be that close. Otherwise, they couldn't watch the camp from much farther away. He left the road then and rode a circle around his camp, maintaining the same half-mile distance. *A nice summer night,* he thought. *I'd appreciate it if we didn't get visitors to spoil it.*

CHAPTER 4

Twenty miles behind Cullen and Lila, her two pursuers sat by the fireplace in Howard Blanchard's abandoned store. Unaware that the woman they chased was only twenty miles ahead, Boot might have decided to press their horses to continue had he known. The fact that the trail they now followed was leading back to East City was enough to satisfy him that Lila was heading back to the Cork and Bottle. He was determined to punish her for the trouble she had caused him, not to mention the fact that she had stolen his horse and his money. "Damn her!" he blurted in anger as he thought about it. "If we hadn't gone back to town to look for her, we'da most likely caught her right away."

"You're the one said she'd run straight back to the saloon," Charley reminded him, "even when I showed you them tracks headin' toward the Austin road. If we'da followed them tracks, we wouldn't be settin' here in this old shack right now."

"Ain't that what I just said?" Boot complained. "I'm gettin' tired of hearin' about you seein' them tracks." He paused to spit in the fire. "I swear, I thought she'd surely circle back and head for town." He wiped his mouth with the back of his hand. "I'm the one that found them tracks that led over here to this shack," he felt the need to remind him.

"Reckon how she knew about this cabin?" Charley wondered aloud.

"I don't know," Boot responded. "I'm more curious to know who them other tracks belong to. There was at least two other horses leavin' tracks around this place and they sure as hell all left here in the same direction."

"Just because we found tracks don't mean them others were here at the same time Lila was," Charley suggested. "And even if they was, there weren't but two of 'em." He shrugged. "Mighta just been one feller and a packhorse."

"I swear, I'll kill that woman if she's run my horse to death," Boot grumbled. He could picture the terrified woman galloping along that road. "There's close to three hundred dollars in my saddlebags and it better be there when I catch up with her."

"Hell, she ain't had no place to spend it," Charley chuckled as he got to his feet. "I'm goin' to bed, if you ain't gonna do nothin' but bellyache all night."

"Yeah, and you can go to hell, too," Boot complained. "It ain't you that lost your horse and three hundred dollars." That triggered another complaint in his mind. "I've half a mind to shoot Art Becker when we get back to East City. That damn horse he lent me ain't worth spit. I don't believe it was ever saddle-broke. I think it'd be better off pullin' a wagon."

"I declare, Boot," Charley japed. "Who else you gonna shoot? Ain't nothin' wrong with that gray. Besides, you picked him out. Art told you to take your pick of

all them he had in the corral." He unrolled his blanket
roll and spread it in a corner away from the fireplace,
the fire in the small store having heated up the room
more than enough.

It was late afternoon when Cullen got his first look
at East City. The first business they came to, on the
south end of the one street, was the stable, owned
by Art Becker, according to Lila. She pulled the
roan up beside Cullen and they walked the horses
slowly up the street. Seeing them pass, Art walked
outside to watch them, surprised to see Lila returning
to East City riding the red roan he recognized as
Boot Davis's. He had wondered why Boot had borrowed a horse from him. Curious as he was about that,
he was even more interested in the big fellow on the
bay, riding beside Lila. There was going to be hell to
pay when Boot found out about her ridin' to town on
his horse. *Things might get pretty interesting,* he thought.
Something must have happened to Boot, for there
was no way he was going to let Lila Blanchard ride
his horse. His thoughts came back to focus on the
stranger riding the bay, and he wondered if he had
something to do with it.

When they had already passed by the stables,
Lila asked, "Should I have left Boot's horse at the
stable? You didn't pull in, so I didn't say nothin' till
we went by."

"No, let's go find the marshal and let him decide
what to do with the horse," Cullen directed. "We
wanna be on the up-and-up about the horse. Then
you might wanna make your charges against Boot

Davis for abductin' you and threatenin' to kill you.
You think?"

Lila hesitated, thinking about the marshal and his
posse, as he called the rough gang of riders who answered to his commands. Boot Davis was a member
of Micah Moran's "posse." "I don't know," she started,
then hesitated again before coming out with it.
"Boot's one of Moran's posse. Maybe it would be
best to just forget about the kidnappin' and rapin',
and just go on back to the way things were before he
snatched me."

"You sure about that?" Cullen asked. It wasn't really
necessary to hear her answer; he already knew she
would not protest her treatment. She was afraid of the
consequences if she attempted to make any charges.
Not waiting for her answer, he said, "Well, we'll go
find the marshal and turn that horse over to him."
He turned to look her in the eye. "You take that
money you found and tuck it in your bodice. As far as
you know, there wasn't any money. You understand?" She responded with a look of fearful uncertainty, so he said, "You're liable to need some extra
money someday, if you decide to leave this town.
And Boot damn sure owes you something." Seeing
the jail ahead on the right, he said, "Let's go in and
talk to the marshal."

"You won't find him in there," Lila said. "This time
of day, he'll be settin' at the back-corner table in the
Cork and Bottle. That's where he always is. Ace
Brown's in the jail, though, if he ain't out walkin'
around town. He's Micah's deputy."

"I think we need to talk to the marshal. Let's go to
the Cork and Bottle. I see it up ahead." He gave her
another look in the eye. "You just remember, you ain't

the one that's done something wrong, so don't be afraid to tell him what Boot did to you." She still looked uncertain. He was afraid she was going to cave in if confronted by Boot.

Cullen tied the horses at the rail and walked Lila to the door. There was a modest crowd at the saloon, for it was still early. But there was an immediate quiet when they walked in. As Lila predicted, the marshal was seated at his regular table, talking to another man. They paused as well when Lila walked in with her formidable-looking escort. Cullen figured the word must have gotten out that she had stolen Boot Davis's horse and left town without telling anyone what she was going to do. The marshal looked Cullen up and down while giving Lila only a quick glance, but he waited for Cullen to speak. His companion did not, however. "Lila, where the hell have you been?" Tom Loughlin, the marshal's business partner, asked.

When Lila hesitated, easily intimidated by the two of them, Cullen answered for her. "I came across Lila a couple dozen miles south of here. To answer the question, where's she been, she's been runnin' for her life. Two of your regular customers kidnapped her when she went to the outhouse a few days ago, and she's been tryin' to get back ever since."

"Is that a fact?" Micah Moran spoke then, staring hard at Cullen. "And just who the hell are you?"

"My name's Cullen McCabe," he answered. "I'm just glad I found her. She didn't have any food and was scared she might run into those two no-goods that abducted her. She was tryin' to get back here to turn the horse over to you."

"That's a mighty interestin' story, ain't it, Tom?" Moran glanced at his partner, then back at Lila, who appeared to be trying to make herself as small as she could. "And who are these two fellows you say carried you off?"

When faced with the two owners of the saloon, one of them being the town marshal, Lila lost any determination she had mustered before. She began thinking about where she would be if they tossed her out to fend for herself. Seeing her hesitation, Cullen answered for her. "Boot Davis and Charley Turner." He saw the immediate alarm in her face.

"Is that what you say, Lila?" Moran demanded.

"It was Boot and Charley," she said. "But I don't think they was out to cause me any real harm. They just had too much to drink and was just foolin' around. They'da probably brought me home before long. I reckon I shouldn'ta got scared and run away from 'em."

Moran nodded, satisfied. "That sounds about the way I figured it to be," he said. "They're both pretty good boys. I think sometimes you women get 'em to thinkin' crazy things, specially when they're too drunk to know what they're doin'. I'll talk to 'em." He turned his attention back to Cullen then. "How 'bout you, Mr. Cullen McCabe? You make it a practice to ride around lookin' for whores to rescue?"

Cullen answered the sarcastic remark with a knowing smile. "Only occasionally, Marshal, when I meet one that's been mistreated by a couple of no-good drunks." He locked eyes with the sneering marshal as both men sought to determine the strength of the other.

"Now that you've brought Lila back where she belongs, I expect you'll be wantin' to get on to wherever you were headin'. Right, McCabe?"

"Oh, I don't know," Cullen replied. "I'm not in any hurry, and I've never been in East City before. I might wanna stick around for a little while, just to see what kinda town you've got here."

"Maybe I can help you with that," Moran said. "It's the kind of town that comes down hard on anybody makin' trouble. Me, or my deputy, will be glad to take care of any troublemakers. Now, don't get me wrong, strangers are always welcome in East City, as long as they obey my rules. But, if I was to give you any advice, I'd suggest you might wanna be gone from here before Boot and Charley get back. I don't hold for back-shootin' and murder, but if a man gets called out for a face-off, that ain't against the law. At least, not in this town."

"I 'preciate the advice, Marshal. It's good to know where you stand. I assure you, I'll keep that in mind, and I guarantee you I ain't gonna call anybody out while I'm in your town." He smiled again. "But I still think I'll stick around a little while, just to see what's here."

He turned to look at Lila, who lowered her gaze, not wanting to look into his eyes. When another woman walked over and took her by the arm, Lila glanced up at him and mouthed a silent thank-you. She quickly lowered her gaze again as the woman led her over to the side of the big room, where a third woman stood watching. After some quick conversation, all three turned and went up the stairs to the second floor. Cullen was sure Lila was finding some comfort from her fellow prostitutes, who no doubt were greatly interested in her plight. His attention was called back when Moran asked him a question.

"If I was to look through my notices when I go back to the office, am I likely to find some paper on you?"

"I'd be surprised," Cullen replied.

Another thought struck the marshal then. "You lookin' for a job?" He had appraised many gunfighters over the years, and it was easy to assume he was looking at another one. This man calling himself McCabe, was a big man, and he wore a Colt sidearm riding in easy reach on his hip. Due to the size of the man, and the effortless way he carried it in one hand, the Winchester 73 went almost unnoticed. Moran thought he might be able to use a man like that, so he said, "If you're lookin' for a job, I might have one for you."

"Doin' what?" Cullen asked.

"Whatever needs takin' care of," Moran answered.

"That could mean just about anything," Cullen said. "I'll think it over while I take a look around town. I'm on a little vacation right now, and I don't know much about this part of Texas. Just thought I'd see what's here."

"The offer might not be open for long," the marshal said, "so you'd best decide quick."

"Fair enough," Cullen said. "I'll do that." He started to leave but paused to ask, "What about that horse Lila rode in on? I'll be glad to take it to the stable for you."

"Yeah, take it to the stable," Moran said, not sure when Boot would be back in town. "Tell Floyd I said to pour you a drink on your way out."

"Thanks, I will," Cullen replied, and stopped at the bar before leaving.

"I heard," Floyd Chandler said before Cullen could relay Moran's offer. "What's it gonna be?"

"One shot of rye whiskey," Cullen answered, and

watched as Floyd filled a shot glass. "Who's the fellow sittin' at the table with the marshal?"

"He's the owner," Floyd answered. "That is, he's the half owner, Tom Loughlin. Marshal Moran owns the other half of the business. Tom's the one who operates the business part of the saloon."

"Yeah? Who's the boss?" Cullen asked before he threw the shot back.

"Marshal Moran," Floyd said with a wry grin.

"That's what I figured. Thanks for the drink." He walked out of the saloon, then took the reins of the three horses and led them back to the stable he had passed on his way in.

Art Becker walked out of the stable to take in the evening air while the sun was still barely visible above the horizon. Looking uptown toward the saloons, he saw Cullen walking toward the stable, leading the horses, one of which he was certain belonged to Boot Davis. His initial thought was that the big man was another outlaw showing up to join Micah Moran's "posse." This especially, since he just came from the Cork and Bottle Saloon. Art stood there waiting, and when Cullen approached, he greeted him. "Good evenin', can I help you?"

"Evenin'," Cullen returned. "I'm gonna be in town overnight, so I'd like to leave my horses with you. These two are mine. The roan belongs to somebody else."

"Boot Davis," Art quickly interjected.

"That's what I was told," Cullen continued. "Anyway, I don't intend to pay for the roan. You don't think there'll be any problem gettin' money for his board, do ya?"

"Nah, there won't be any problem," Art replied, thinking there never was any problem because there never was any pay for boarding Boot's horse. This was a special privilege dictated to him by Marshal Moran. "You just stayin' one night?"

"Don't know for sure," Cullen answered, "but right now that's my thinkin'. I've never been in East City before, so I thought I'd look around, long as I'm here. Any place in town to rent a room and maybe get a decent supper? I noticed that two-story building on the other side of the Cork and Bottle has a sign that says it's a hotel. Is it as bad on the inside as it looks on the outside?"

Cullen's questions caused Art to wonder if maybe he had misjudged him. "Did the marshal recommend the hotel?" Art asked, surprised that he had not, since that was the usual accommodation for his posse.

"No," Cullen answered. "I reckon it never occurred to me to ask him where to get a bed for the night."

Art studied the tall, solemn stranger for a moment before deciding to take a chance on giving him an honest answer. "Mister, if you're really interested in a clean bed and a decent meal that ain't likely to give you belly cramps, stay clear of the hotel. That ain't nothin' but a whorehouse, even though they do serve a little food, if you've got stomach enough to handle it. Moran owns it. He just stuck a sign on it that says 'Hotel.' It ain't got a real name."

"Much obliged," Cullen said, and nodded his head in honest appreciation of the warning.

Confident from Cullen's reaction to his comments, Art ventured to say more. "Like I said, if you're lookin' for a clean bed and a decent meal, there's a lane leadin' off the road to a roomin' house just north of town. It sets back a ways from the main road. There ain't no name on it, just walk on in the parlor and ask for Hortense. She'll fix you up for the night, or for a month. And I know she's got an empty room, 'cause that's where I stay, and the room next to mine ain't got nobody stayin' in it."

"That sounds to my likin'," Cullen said.

"Good. I was just gettin' ready to go to supper. You can go with me and talk to Hortense about a room for the night. We'll take care of your horses right quick, and you can leave those packs in the stall if you want to. It ain't far to walk from here. There's a little path that's a shortcut. We've got time before supper's over." He grinned at Cullen, feeling he had read the somber man correctly, and extended his hand. "Art Becker's my name."

"Cullen McCabe," he said as he shook Art's hand. In spite of what he had been told, he was beginning to think there were honest people in East City. The whole town wasn't evil, and thinking that, he asked, "How long have you been here, Art?" Art boasted that he had been there since before it was called East City. So Cullen figured there had to be more good people who were there before Micah Moran moved in to take over the town.

After the horses were taken care of and they had moved the packs from Cullen's sorrel, Art showed him a footpath behind his stable that followed the creek to Hortense Billings's rooming house. It was a shortcut that saved following the main road around to get there. Hortense was in the kitchen, helping her cook get the food to the table when Art called her.

Wiping her hands on her apron, she walked out into the hallway. "What is it, Mr. Becker?" Cullen stepped into the hall behind Art then, causing her to pause.

"I got a fellow here lookin' for some supper and a room for the night," Art said.

"Oh?" Hortense responded, arching her neck to look around him for a better look at the stranger.

"I realize this ain't exactly a good time to pop in on you," Cullen volunteered. "I mean, right at supper-time without any notice, but I just now got into town. You most likely didn't plan for an extra mouth at the table, so I've got some jerky and coffee in my packs back at the stable I could make do until breakfast." His comment caused both Art and Hortense to laugh.

"I ain't ever seen Annie run short of food, no matter who showed up," Art declared.

"That's right, Mr. . . ." She paused to get his name. ". . . McCabe," she continued when he supplied it. "I'm sure there's enough, so nobody will go without. I'll show you to your room. You won't need those at the supper table," she added, glancing at the rifle in his hand and the saddlebags on his shoulder. She turned and headed to the stairs, signaling him to follow. He couldn't help marveling at her immediate acceptance, considering the reputation of the town and the population of outlaws there. He figured it had to be that she trusted Art's recommendation.

As Art had told him, the room Hortense led him to was neat and the bedclothes smelled clean. He left his rifle and gun belt on the bed and threw his saddlebags in the corner, then went down to the dining room to find four guests, including Art, seated at the table. They all paused to give him their attention while Hortense introduced him. He received polite nods from all as he sat down in the one empty chair. "I think you'd best move your plate to the end of the table, Mr. McCabe," Hortense said after he had settled in the chair. "I'm afraid you'll have your elbows in Mr. Skelton's plate, if you don't."

Only slightly embarrassed, Cullen said, "I reckon I figured that was your place at the head of the table."

"No, indeed," Hortense responded. "I can squeeze in anywhere. Mr. Billings used to sit in that chair before he passed away."

Not sure how to reply to that remark, he said, "If you say so, ma'am," then got up and moved to the head of the table. Everyone at the table smiled and nodded their agreement with his relocation, especially Mr. Skelton, Cullen assumed. Once the new guest was settled in his chair, everyone got back to the meal before them, and the conversation began once more. Much of it was aimed at Cullen in the form of questions, which he tried to answer in terms as vague as possible. In general, he told them that he was looking over a big section of the state to evaluate the prairies most suitable for raising cattle. It was the first thing he could think of.

"I ain't the smartest feller around," Roy Skelton saw fit to comment. "But it seems to me it oughta be pretty simple to figure that out. You need grass and water. Ain't that about it?"

"That's about right," Cullen answered the old gentleman, already wishing he had come up with some other explanation for his presence there. "Course, the company I work for is wantin' me to find water and grass where there's room for some more big ranches. I declare, Mrs. Billings," he said, anxious to change the subject, "Art surely wasn't lyin' when he said this was the best food in the territory."

Sensing his reluctance to talk about himself, Hortense replied, "Well, thank you, sir. I'll tell Annie what you said. Now, I expect we'd better let you eat before it gets cold."

He appreciated her comment, coming as it did when he was beginning to think he had made a mistake in taking a room there. It might have been better to have camped outside of town, where there would be no questions. Since he was looking for answers, himself, he walked back to the stable with Art when supper was over, under the premise that he wanted to check his horses' hooves.

After spending some time with Jake and then his packhorse, Cullen climbed up into the hayloft, where Art was forking down some new hay for Jake's stall. "Hortense doesn't look that old," Cullen said. "How long has it been since her husband passed away?"

"Been 'bout three years, now," Art replied, scratching his head to help him remember.

"What took him?" Cullen asked.

Art paused before answering, thinking how best to put it. "Ignorance, I reckon you'd have to say." When Cullen raised his eyebrows at that, Art explained further. "He told one of them low-down gunslingers of Moran's posse not to use such foul language in front of his wife. Well, that caused the half-drunk louse to make a downright filthy remark to Hortense to see if her husband had the guts to do anything about it. Billings shoulda known he didn't stand a chance against that gunman, drunk or sober. Hortense tried to get him to walk away, but he was too stubborn to turn tail. So you know the rest." Cullen said that he did.

Art had some questions for Cullen as well. "I saw you when you rode into town this evenin', you and one of those whores that work at the Cork and Bottle. That ain't none of my business, and you can tell me to go to hell, but she was ridin' Boot Davis's red roan. I couldn't help wonderin' if Boot is no longer with us, not that that would be any great loss."

Evidently, Art didn't know that Lila had been missing or that Boot went after her. "I don't have any idea if Boot has passed away," he said. "I've never had the pleasure of makin' his acquaintance. But I can tell you how I happened to be in the company of that prostitute. I found her alone about sixty-five miles south of here, just her and that red roan." He didn't tell Art the whole story, explaining why Lila was so far from East City. "I was comin' this way, anyway, so I brought her along with me, and that's the end of that story."

Art considered that, but he was still not satisfied that he had all the details. "But how did Boot's horse get way down there where you said you found it?" Cullen figured it shouldn't have been tough to figure out, but he spelled it out for him. "Oh," Art said, finally getting the simple picture. "Boot grabbed the whore, she got away from him, stole his horse, and ran off with it. You came up on her and brought her back here." Cullen nodded, amazed that it took so much explanation. Understanding finally, Art nodded, too. "You know, McCabe, you ain't done nothin' but help a woman in a fix and return a horse to where it came from." Having allowed that, he felt the need to offer advice. "I don't know how long you intend to stay here in town, but it might not be a good idea for you to be here when Boot gets back. He's liable to think you had somethin' to do with her running off. And I can tell you, Boot ain't a very peaceful man, and if Charley Turner is with him, there's bound to be trouble."

"'Preciate the warnin'," Cullen said. "You strike me as an honest man. Who else can an honest man trust in this town?"

The question caused Art to hesitate before answering. Then he decided there was nothing suspicious about it, so he answered. "What you're wantin' to know is who ain't in cahoots with Marshal Moran and his gang of outlaws. Right?" When Cullen nodded, Art continued. "Well, there's a lot of honest, hard-workin' folks settled around East City. But the folks who've been here in business the longest are me; Joe Johnson, down at the general store; Abe Franks at the hardware store; Cary O'Sullivan at O'Sullivan's; Martin Pearson at the feed store; Stewart Ingram, the postmaster; and Buck Casey, the blacksmith. We make up the town council with Abe Franks as the mayor. So that's who you can trust, if that's what you're drivin' at." He paused and shook his head. "But it's a town council in name only. We don't decide a damn thing. Micah Moran decides what we can and can't do."

"Much obliged," Cullen said, since that was exactly what he wanted to know. East City was as close to a lawless kingdom as he could imagine, with Micah Moran sitting on the throne. The town council was a council in name only, and as such, would never have a prayer of building a respectable town. It occurred to him that the governor had sent him up here when he pretty much knew the situation already.

CHAPTER 5

After a solid breakfast at Hortense Billings's table the next morning, Cullen announced to those seated at the table that he was going to walk around town to see what East City was all about. "Should I save your room for you?" Hortense asked. "Or are you going to be moving on today?"

"To tell you the truth," Cullen answered, "it's been a long time since I've had a nice bed and been able to enjoy some real cookin'. I think I'll stay with you for a few days, if that's all right with you." She was pleased to hear his answer and assured him that he was welcome. "Good," he went on. "I'm gonna take a look around Ravenwood while I'm out in this part of the state, too. But I'm so comfortable in your house, I think I'll still stay here, since Ravenwood is right across the creek." That really seemed to please her.

"Glad to hear it," Art Becker said, just coming in the back door. He was just getting back for his breakfast after leaving earlier to open his stable. "I took a look in his stall," he joked. "Your horse is still there."

"Well, that surely is good news," Cullen came back at him and laughed with him.

"Heard you say you're gonna cross over to Ravenwood," Art said. "Goin' over to rub elbows with the fancy folks, are ya? Over there in the county seat," he went on.

"If it's that fancy, I think I'd best clean up a little bit before I go. And maybe I'll visit the barbershop, too."

"If you want a shave and a haircut, you'll have to get 'em across the creek," Art said. "We ain't got a barber over here where the poor folks live."

"Maybe that's what I'll do, then," Cullen said. "I'll be back for supper this evenin'," he said to Hortense, and took his leave.

"Pork chops tonight," she called after him. When he had gone, she turned to Art and asked, "Who is that man? You know darn well he didn't come here to look for grazing land for cattle."

Art didn't answer until he heard the front door close. "I don't know, Hortense. You might be right about that, but he seems to be on the up-and-up, and he doesn't appear to have any connection to Micah Moran and his bunch. That right there makes him all right in my book."

"He doesn't say much," Hortense commented, "but he's polite enough. I expect he'll move on in a day or two."

"He's liable to move quicker'n that," Art said, "when Boot Davis gets back in town and finds out McCabe brought his horse with him and a whore in the saddle." He saw at once that Hortense had no idea what he was talking about, so he had to tell her the story. It only added to the mystery Hortense already saw in her new tenant and caused her to wonder if Art might be justified in his concern for Cullen.

* * *

Cullen saw immediately that Michael O'Brien and Governor Hubbard had been right on the money when they said the difference in the two towns was like night and day. As he slow-walked Jake down the main street past the courthouse, he saw that Art had been right as well when he said there was a barber in Ravenwood. He spotted it right next to the post office, so he figured he'd go through with what he had threatened in East City and pay for a shave and a haircut. He figured it to be a good investment, because usually the barber knew about everything going on in town most of the time.

"Mornin', stranger," Rodney Blake greeted him when he walked in the door. "What can I do you for?"

"It's been a while since I've bought a shave and a haircut," Cullen said. "I feel like doin' it today."

"Well, you've come to the right place," the barber said. "Don't believe I've seen you in town before. You passin' through, or are you gonna stay with us awhile?" Without waiting for an answer, he stuck out his hand. "My name's Rodney Blake, and I'll be glad to fix you up fit for the church social, or the soiled doves over at the saloon. I can shape that mustache up for you."

"Just shave all the mustache and chin whiskers off and cut my hair off a little shorter, and I'll skip the church and the saloon." He shook the extended hand and said, "Cullen McCabe," then sat down in the barber chair. By the time Rodney had finished, Cullen knew about all the latest news and activities in the town—where to get the best dinner and Rodney's choice of saloons between the two in town. As a final touch, and before Cullen had a chance to stop him, Rodney splashed a high-smelling solution on his face.

Twitching his nose like a bloodhound on a hot trail, Cullen paid the barber, settled his hat on his shorter hair, and went outside to take a look at the town. Before he untied Jake, however, he walked over to the horse trough on the corner of the street and washed his face as vigorously as he could in an effort to rid himself of the aftershave. Satisfied that he wouldn't attract horseflies then, he climbed up into the saddle and slow-walked Jake up the street, looking at the shops and the people coming and going. He decided it was in direct contrast to the streets of East City. Ravenwood appeared to be a normal town, and from the looks of it, probably on the way to becoming a sizable city. *Peaceful* was the word he thought of to describe it. He decided to stop in a large store bearing a sign that identified it as HORMEL GENERAL MERCHANDISE.

James Hormel glanced up toward the front of the store when he heard the screen door open. He paused to take a longer look at the imposing stranger before greeting him. "Good mornin'. Something I can help you with?"

"Yep, I need to buy me a new razor," Cullen replied. "I had to go to the barber this mornin' to get a shave."

"Come on down to this end of the counter and I'll show you what I've got," Hormel said. "Might have something you can use." Cullen followed him to the end of the long counter where Hormel opened a drawer holding several different razors. "Something like this?" he asked. While Cullen picked up the razor and examined it, Hormel continued talking. "Don't believe you've been in before."

"That's a fact," Cullen said. "Never been in Ravenwood before. Looks like a quiet little town. Did I hear about some kinda trouble you folks were havin' a while back?"

"Trouble?" Hormel asked, surprised. "What kind of trouble? The only trouble we ever have is when some of that outlaw riffraff on the other side of the creek crosses over to raise a little hell." When he saw the interested look on Cullen's face, he quickly explained. "Ravenwood's a peaceful little town and we're on our way to becoming a city. I'm on the city council and we're working to make Ravenwood the best place in Texas to settle. We have a little trouble now and then when some of those drunken outlaws come over here. But we've got an honest, hardworking marshal that tries to keep the peace."

"Have you ever tried contacting the governor's office for some help?" Cullen asked, already knowing the answer, but he wanted to hear Hormel's version.

"Oh, we complained to the state, all right," Hormel answered, rapidly warming up to the subject. "They sent two men up here to meet with Mayor Raven and the council, and said they'd go back and report to the governor about the problem. A couple of weeks after that, they sent a whole company of Rangers up here to camp on the other side of the creek. They stayed for three days. I reckon they figured that fixed all the problems, so they left and we're back with the same old problems with that damn Sodom across the creek."

"I'll take the razor," Cullen said, having heard what he needed to confirm what the governor had told him. He dug into his pocket for some money.

"Don't let my ranting give you the wrong impression of Ravenwood," Hormel quickly implored. "Are you thinking about settling in Ravenwood?"

"Just passin' through," Cullen said.

After he left the store, he decided he'd pay a little visit to some of the other businesses, so he would have the opinion of more than one man. Before he was through, he had spent the rest of the morning talking to other merchants, almost everyone but the staffs at the saloons and the hotel. He decided he might as well eat, since it was past noon already, and he had plenty of expense money. Before that, however, he decided to check out the Whistle Stop Saloon, the one the barber had recommended.

There was a small crowd of customers in the Whistle Stop. Cullen walked over to the bar, where half a dozen drinkers were lined up. He stepped in beside a fellow wearing a Stetson Boss of the Plains hat atop long hair that hung to his shoulders. "What's your pleasure, stranger?" Toby Futch, the bartender, asked. His greeting caught the attention of the long-haired man and he turned to take a look at the stranger, but said nothing.

Cullen ordered a single shot of whiskey, a little drink before he went in search of dinner, he told Toby. And when Toby poured it, Cullen was curious enough to ask, "Why do you call this place Whistle Stop? There ain't any railroad around here, is there?"

Toby chuckled, accustomed to the question from strangers. "Ain't got nothin' to do with the railroad. The boss named it that 'cause this is the place to come to wet your whistle." He paused to chuckle again. "There's some talk about the railroad comin' through here, though. Ain't that right, Marshal?"

The man with the hair to his shoulders, turned to Cullen again, this time far enough for Cullen to see the star on his vest. "That's what they say, all right."

Giving Cullen his full attention now, he asked, "What brings you to town, stranger?"

"Just curiosity, I reckon. I've never been in your town before, so I thought I'd stop long enough to see what's goin' on here. My name's Cullen McCabe."

"Tug Taggert," the marshal said. "What line of work are you in? You don't look like a cowhand, or a farmer, either."

"I've got a little place south of Austin, but I've been up north of here visitin' some friends. I'm on my way back home and I decided to take a look at Ravenwood. So far, it looks like a right friendly town."

"We're tryin' to keep it that way," Taggert said.

"Well, I've had my one drink, so I think I'll look for some dinner," Cullen announced. "Any recommendations?"

"It's hard to beat the dinin' room over at the hotel," Taggert said.

"I'll take your word for it," Cullen said. "Much obliged."

Outside, Cullen stepped up into the saddle and took the short ride past the courthouse to the hotel beyond and left Jake at the hitching rail by the outside door of the dining room. He was met by Marcy Manning at the door and asked to leave his firearms on a table nearby. After he left his Colt and his Winchester on the table, Marcy showed him to another small table close to the kitchen door. The beef stew was good, and the coffee was hot, so he took his time to enjoy the meal. He intended to make more stops, although he felt that he had a pretty good picture of the town. He had seen nothing that would lead him to believe Ravenwood was the major cause of the trouble between the two towns. East City was just a town of outlaws, run by outlaws, and he wasn't sure he could do anything to change that. Michael O'Brien told him to just ride up there to look at the situation, and that's what he was doing. He might as well start back to Austin in the morning.

He finished his dinner, collected his firearms, and prepared to head back across the creek to East City when he heard the sound of gunshots. He couldn't be sure, but he thought they might have come from inside the saloon he had been in earlier. With an eye toward caution until he figured out the source, he waited to hear if there were more shots. Less than thirty seconds later, he heard two more. Louder and sharper, he figured they were shot outside the building. Then he saw the source. Two men moved out in the street in front of the saloon, blazing away with six-guns at someone taking cover behind a wagon. When he got a glimpse of the man behind the wagon, he grabbed his rifle and ran toward the Whistle Stop, leaving Jake there at the dining room hitching rail. It was Marshal Tug Taggert and he was not in the best position to defend himself. The two gunmen he faced were obviously hoping he would raise up from behind the wagon to take a shot at them. It wasn't going to be much longer before he would be in the open because the two horses hitched to the wagon were frightened and already rearing frantically. "Come on outta there, Marshal!" one of the shooters taunted. "Stick your head up for me!" He fired three more shots into the side of the wagon.

So intent upon keeping an eye on the marshal, neither man was aware of the big man carrying the rifle running toward them. "Drop your weapons!" Cullen ordered as he approached, which stopped both men from firing momentarily. "Drop 'em right there and stick your hands up in the air! Now!"

"Go to hell," one of them snarled, and spun around to face Cullen. The slug from Cullen's rifle tore into his side before he had turned halfway. In the brief instant while the other man stood stunned to see his partner drop, Cullen cranked another cartridge in and was set to fire. The shooter wisely dropped his pistol and held his hands up.

Stunned as well, Marshal Taggert stepped out from behind the wagon, his handgun aimed at the remaining outlaw. "Get on your knees!" he ordered the gunman, then took a quick look at the man Cullen shot before picking up their weapons. Then he looked at Cullen and confessed, "Damned if you didn't save my bacon! There ain't no doubt about that. It was my fault I let 'em pin me behind that wagon. Mister, I forgot your name, I owe you for sure."

"Cullen McCabe," he reminded him. "I'll help you herd this one to the jailhouse."

Unnoticed by the participants in the gun battle, or Cullen, either, the confrontation was being watched by a man on a horse. Two stores down from the saloon, he sat, holding the reins of two more horses with empty saddles. When it was plain that the shootout with the marshal had failed, he wheeled his horse and loped off toward the end of the street, leading the two extra horses. Thinking the shooting was over, anxious spectators came streaming out of the saloon to see the carnage. Taggert grabbed one of them by the arm. "Go fetch Doc McNair. Tell him there's a wounded man outside the saloon. I gotta get this one locked up." On the way to the jail, Taggert told Cullen what had happened to set up the ambush he blindly walked into. "One of 'em shot a feller they were playin' cards with and shot at me when I started after 'em. I was lucky to jump behind the bar to keep from gettin' hit. Then they ran out the door and I ran after 'em, but I found out too late that they were standin' out there, waiting for me to run out the door." He prodded his prisoner in the back with his six-gun. "Ain't that right? That crooked marshal over the creek sent you two to shoot me."

"That's you that's sayin' that," his prisoner snarled. "We weren't tryin' to kill you. We was just protectin' ourselves."

"We'll see if Judge Raven thinks that," Taggert said. Then it occurred to him to ask, "Where'd you leave your horses?"

"We walked over here," the prisoner spat defiantly.

"So there were three of you assassins," Taggert said. "And your brave partner ran off with the horses when the shootin' started. What's your name?"

"I ain't got one," his prisoner replied. "We was poor where I came from, so my mammy couldn't afford a name."

"Why, you're a regular clown, ain't you?" Taggert responded. "I expect you musta been a bastard and that's why you ain't got no name. But everybody in my jail has to have a name, so I can tell the hooligans apart, so I'll have to give you one. I think I'll call you Cow Pie. You like that name all right?"

Cullen stayed there until the marshal had his prisoner, who still refused to give his name, locked up in a cell on the lower floor of the courthouse. When they walked back outside, Taggert extended his hand. "Man, I appreciate the way you stepped in back there. Everybody else was just stayin' under cover. The city council just voted me the money to hire a deputy, but he ain't startin' till the first of the month. Fine young man—name's Beau Arnett—comes highly qualified. For a while back there behind that wagon, I was wishin' he'd started the first of this month. So I'm damn glad you decided to take a look at Ravenwood." Still gripping his hand, he blurted a question. "Who the hell are you, anyway?"

"I told you, Cullen McCabe."

"I don't mean your name. Hell, I got that. What I mean is, who are you, really? I ain't never seen anybody handle a Winchester rifle like you did when that feller tried to shoot you. He didn't even have to draw, he already had his gun in hand, and he didn't get turned halfway around before you hit him."

"I was just lucky, I reckon, and he wasn't that fast." He shrugged as if to say he had no explanation for it.

Taggert just stared at him for a long moment, a smile on his face indicating he didn't believe him. "All right," he finally said. "Whatever you say, but the least I can do is buy your supper. Whaddaya say?"

"Thanks, Marshal, I appreciate the offer, but after I make a few stops, I've gotta get back to East City. I'm rentin' a room in a boardin'house over there and I told 'em I'd be back for supper."

"East City!" Taggert exclaimed. "I hope you're talkin' about that little boardin'house owned by Hortense Billings." Cullen said that he was and Taggert went on. "Damn, McCabe, you'd best keep your head down over there. If word gets out over there what you done tonight, it won't be safe for you to go to the outhouse. I ain't got a doubt in my mind that Micah Moran sent those two jaspers over here to get me. He's liable to find out that it was you that saved my bacon. The third man, who was holdin' the getaway horses, musta seen you."

"He probably didn't get a real good look at me, but I'll be extra careful," Cullen said, and started back to the dining room to get his horse.

Taggert stood in front of the courthouse, watching Cullen walk away. *I don't know what line of work you're in, but I'll bet my bottom dollar it has something to do with that rifle you're toting*, he thought.

Cullen was thinking about the rugged-looking marshal with the shoulder-length hair hanging like a curtain from under the Stetson hat. He got the impression that he was an honest, hardworking lawman. He liked him. He was the kind of man East City needed, if they could ever successfully rid the town of Micah Moran and his "posse."

CHAPTER 6

Right across Walnut Creek from each other, the two towns were about a mile and a half apart, as the crow flies. There was a road that linked them and there was once a bridge across the creek, but someone had destroyed the bridge. Cullen had discovered it when he crossed there that morning. Now, as he approached the crossing on his way back, he was thinking that someone on the Ravenwood side must have done away with the bridge. And he found that he couldn't blame them. If Tug Taggert knew about Hortense Billings's boardinghouse, he must know other people in East City who are honest hardworking people. There was only one solution for the problems between the two towns and that was to clean Micah Moran and his rotten crowd out of town. It was a simple answer, but he wasn't sure it could be done without a Ranger company permanently stationed there. *That will be my recommendation to Governor Hubbard*, he thought. And with that in mind, he reaffirmed his plan to start back to Austin in the morning.

It was nearing dusk by the time he rode up out of the creek and followed the road into town. As he approached Art Becker's stable, he thought he spotted something odd swaying in the gentle breeze moving the trees beyond the corral. He didn't think he had noticed it before, but he didn't focus on it. When he approached the stable door, he glanced toward the corral again and realized what he had seen. It was a body, hanging from a limb of a large oak! A woman's body! He turned Jake's head toward the tree to get a closer look. It was Lila Blanchard! Hearing a sound behind him, he turned to see Art Becker running toward him. "Hung for a horse thief!" he cried out obviously upset. "It's that whore you brought back here! They hung her for a horse thief, said she stole Boot Davis's horse. Didn't matter she brought it back. Micah Moran said she stole the horse and horse thieves get hung in this town. He won't let nobody cut her down, said to let her hang there, so everybody gets a chance to see her and learns a lesson."

Cullen felt the blood run hot in his veins as he stared at the pitiful corpse when it swayed slowly back and forth with every little change of the breeze. The murder of this innocent young woman was one of the lowest acts of pure evil that he had ever seen. After a long moment, he asked, "Who strung her up?"

"Boot and Charley actually tied the rope around her neck and hauled her up on that limb," Art said. "But it was Marshal Moran that told 'em to do it."

"Did she tell him about gettin' kidnapped and raped and Boot Davis sayin' he was gonna kill her when they were finished with her? And the part where she had to run for her life?"

"Well, I wasn't there when Boot and Charley showed up at the Cork and Bottle this mornin'." He paused to point out, "That ain't my favorite saloon. But it likely wasn't more'n half an hour after you left. Well, like I said, I wasn't there in the saloon, but Wilma Wiggins was. She's one of the women that works there. She said Lila told Moran all about that business with Boot and Charley. Boot said she was a damn liar and she oughta be hung for stealin' his horse. So the marshal told 'em to go do it."

The more Cullen heard of the vicious act on this poor defenseless victim and her killers' callous disregard for human life, the madder he became. This was no longer an investigation for the governor. With this evil act, it was now a personal matter, and he was resolved to see that the perpetrators were made to pay for their deeds. Not planning now to return to Austin in the morning, he pulled his horse up close to Lila's body and put his arm around her. With his other hand, he drew his skinning knife and hacked the rope in two, easily holding the frail corpse in one arm. Seeing what Cullen was doing, Art hurried over to help lower the body gently to the ground. "Whaddaya gonna do?" Art asked, anxiously.

"I'm gonna bury her," Cullen replied. "I think she deserves that."

"Cullen," Art implored, "there's gonna be hell to pay if Moran finds out you cut her down. You'd better bury her somewhere back in the woods before somebody comes along here and sees us. I'll help you dig a grave, but let's get the hell out of the open before we get caught."

"This ain't got nothin' to do with you, Art. You've got no part in it. I'm the one who cut her down and I'm the one who'll bury her. And I want Micah Moran to know it. He can come talk to me about it, if he doesn't like me doin' it."

"Oh, he's gonna be hoppin' mad, all right," Art responded. "Only, I doubt he'll come talk to you. More'n likely, he'll send his deputy, Ace Brown, to come after you—him or Boot and Charley—maybe all three." He wasn't sure Cullen realized he might have signed his death warrant with that skinning knife. And chances were his body, shot full of holes, would be swinging from that limb where Lila's body had been.

"I 'preciate you offerin' to help, Art, but all I want from you is the borrow of a shovel to dig the grave. I'm hopin' nobody notices that Lila's gone from this tree tonight. If you say it happened right after I left here this mornin', I expect everybody's already done all their gawkin' at her. I reckon what I'm tellin' you is there's gonna be a war, and I don't want you or Hortense Billings to get involved in it. So, I won't be stayin' in the boardin'house. I'll go pick up my possibles from there after I take care of Lila. Then, if it's all right with you, I'll sleep with my horses tonight in your stable. Like I said, I think we'll be all right for tonight, and tomorrow I'll be outta there. Is that okay?"

"Yeah, sure it is," Art replied. "But if you're plannin' on being here in the mornin' when they do find out that body's gone, you ain't gonna stand much of a chance alone."

"I'm willin' to risk it," Cullen said. "Now give me a hand with her body. It's already gettin' stiff and I'm gonna lay her behind my saddle, if she ain't too stiff to ride there." They saw right away that wouldn't work, so Cullen ended up holding her across his thighs. Her back pressed against the saddle horn helped secure her. Art went to the barn and returned with a shovel, which Cullen stuck down beside his saddle sling.

Before Cullen pulled away, Art felt the need to

explain something. "Cullen, I might be wrong, but I think you're an honest man. And I wanna let you know I am, too. I reckon I spend more time with Micah Moran's gang of outlaws than anybody else in East City. But that's because I ain't got no choice. I own the stable, and they keep their horses here. I hear a lot of their talk, but I sure as hell ain't one of 'em. So I just want to let you know I ain't gonna say who cut Lila down."

"Hell, I know that," Cullen said. "I already figured that out."

Then Art stood back to watch Jake walk slowly away with the dead woman cradled by the big man and the shovel sticking up like a cavalry flag. He almost called out to tell him he was going the wrong way, since he was heading toward town, but he held his tongue. He shook his head and headed back toward the barn.

Less than fifteen minutes later, one of Moran's posse, Stan Molloy, came riding up, leading two rider-less horses. "Here," he yelled to Art, "take care of these horses!" He jumped down and started to run toward the Cork and Bottle.

"Who do the other two belong to?" Art shouted after him, even though he knew Molloy and two others, Johnny Barr and Sam Polek, rode out that morning, talking about going to Ravenwood.

"Just do what I said and take care of 'em!" Molloy shouted back, in too great a hurry to stop to talk, and luckily, too great a hurry to notice there was no one hanging in the tree.

Art was thankful for that. *Maybe it was on the side of his bad eye*, he thought. Molloy, an especially belligerent individual, wore a patch on his left eye, the result of a knife fight some years before.

* * *

Micah Moran was angry and confused at the same time. Stan Molloy was standing in front of his table, shifting nervously from one foot to the other. "Why do you think it was McCabe?" Moran asked.

"It was him, all right, the same feller I saw walk outta here yesterday when he brought Lila back on Boot's horse."

"But you're tellin' me he was helpin' the marshal, and he shot Johnny and Sam?"

"He shot Johnny, but he didn't shoot Sam," Molloy insisted. "Then him and the marshal arrested both of 'em and hauled 'em off to jail, I reckon. I didn't hang around to see."

"Where the hell were you all that time they were gettin' shot at?" Moran demanded.

"I was two or three stores down from the saloon, holdin' the horses, just like we decided. Johnny and Sam wanted to be the ones that went in the saloon to pick a fight. And I was ready to bring their horses as soon as they shot the marshal, so we could make a quick getaway. It all happened too quick. I didn't have no time to help 'em, far away as I was. Besides, they was supposed to shoot the marshal in the saloon, but I reckon they missed 'cause most of the shootin' was in the street. And that McCabe jasper was waitin' out in the street for 'em. I swear, Micah, it looked more like they was set up, waitin' for us, than the other way around. I got outta there fast, but I didn't know if they saw me or not, so I took off out the north end of town 'cause I didn't wanna lead 'em here. Found me a spot to hide out till I was sure I could come back."

It was a very worrisome report on the planned

assassination of Marshal Tug Taggert. Moran had decided to make that move several days before all this mess with Boot Davis and Lila Blanchard was on everybody's mind. As he thought back, he remembered that Ned Larson was one of the ones who thought it a smart plan. "Might even get one of our boys to run for marshal," he had said. And Cullen McCabe was there. How'd he know to be there? And now, he had lost two good men.

Thinking at first that he should find a quiet secluded spot to bury the unfortunate prostitute, Cullen changed his mind, somehow certain that Lila would approve. Instead of the creek bank, then, he guided Jake to walk slowly behind the backs of the buildings on the one street. It was almost a hard dark by then, so he thought his odds were good that he wouldn't be disturbed in his labor. The sounds of raucous laughter and loud conversation, mixed with the notes of a tinny piano, came to him as he guided Jake to a stop between the Cork and Bottle and the hotel. He let Lila slide down to the ground, then he dismounted, grabbed his shovel, and started testing the ground between the two buildings, hoping to find a spot that wasn't too hard. There didn't seem to be any place better than another, so he went to work on a spot close to the backs of the buildings. It was not easy digging. He wished he had a pick as well, but after breaking through the sunbaked surface, he began to make real progress. It took him an hour to dig a grave that suited him. When it was finished, he laid Lila gently into the grave and uttered a sincere apology for the rough burial. He was still of the opinion that she would approve of this as a chance to come back at Micah Moran and his posse. He could not help feeling that he had a part in her death, for he had brought her back to this hellhole. She had been convinced that she would be safe at the Cork and Bottle, thinking Moran would protect her from Boot Davis. Standing over the mound of dirt, in the darkness of the alley, he promised her that Moran and his kind would not get away with her murder.

As he prepared to leave, he was suddenly overcome with memories of the personal tragedy that resulted in his appointment to serve as the governor's special agent. Fleeting sketches flashed across his mind's eye of his wife, Mary Kate, and their three children: Lucy, nine; Cullen junior, seven; and William, five. Their lives were snuffed out, and their home burned to the ground, by ruthless men such as those surrounding Micah Moran. He had hunted those men down and hung every one of them, but it brought no peace to his mind. It left him with only an empty feeling with no concern if he lived or died. He knew it was this state of mind that the governor saw as an ideal qualification for his job.

His mind came back to reality when he felt a nudge against his back. He turned and gently rubbed Jake's face. The big bay gelding always seemed to know when his partner was visiting that dark place again. "All right, Jake," he said softly, "let's take Art's shovel back. I'm gonna put you in your stall, then I'll go pick up my things from the boardin'house."

Although it was late and well past suppertime, he found there was a plate of food warming for him in the oven. He was met in the hallway by both Hortense and Annie when he came in the front door. "There's supper for you in the oven," Hortense said. "Mr. Becker said that you wouldn't be able to get here till later."

"And we didn't want you to go to bed hungry," Annie said. It occurred to him that it was the first time she had ever spoken directly to him. The serious, almost solemn, attitude they appeared to have made him wonder how much Art might have told them. He would have preferred for them to know nothing about his activities on this evening, so they would be innocent if Moran came to ask questions about him.

"I'm sorry to cause you extra trouble, but I surely do appreciate it," he said. "Did Art tell you that I won't be stayin' here tonight? I just came back to get my things and to pay you what I owe you."

"You shaved your mustache off," Hortense suddenly stated, surprising him. He had forgotten it, himself.

"Yes, ma'am, and cut my hair off, too," he replied.

"You don't have to pay me for the one night. You were just our guest for the night," Hortense said. "Now, come on in the kitchen and sit down before that food dries out." He followed them into the kitchen and sat down at the table. Annie got his plate out of the oven and Hortense sat down across from him. "You know," she said, "as late as it is, you don't have to leave tonight. You might as well stay here."

He was sure now that Art had told them the whole story, and he appreciated their attitude, but he didn't want to take any chance of endangering them, or the other boarders. "Art tell you what I did?" Both women nodded.

"I'm sorry he did," Cullen said. "I don't want you folks gettin' mixed up in any trouble I've caused with the marshal and that gang of his. I'm hopin' he ain't got any idea that I'm stayin' here at your place, so I wanna get out before he finds out."

"I reckon that's the smartest thing you could do," Annie said. "But like you said, Moran probably don't know you're here. So, you oughta be able to stay here tonight and leave town in the morning. I'll fix you some food to take with you and you'll be long gone before anybody knows you've left town." Hortense nodded in agreement with her.

"I'm not leavin' town," Cullen said. "I'm just leavin' your house."

"Are you crazy?" Annie exclaimed. "They're gonna know you cut that woman's body down! You were the one who brought her back to East City!"

"Annie's right," Hortense said. "You might be making a terrible mistake if you hang around this town. They'll blame it on somebody and you're the obvious one. Why are you gonna stay?"

"I've got my reasons," he answered, and got up from the table. "Now, since you ain't afraid to have me sleep here tonight, I'll go upstairs to bed now 'cause I'll be gettin' up early in the mornin'."

"I will, too," Annie said, "so I'll have somethin' for you to eat."

"'Preciate it, but you don't have to get up for that."

"I know it," Annie replied. "But if breakfast in the mornin' is liable to be your last meal, I wanna make sure you get a good one." He left them, still shaking their heads over his stubborn suicidal tendency.

"She's gone!" Charley Turner blurted as he stormed in the Cork and Bottle. "She's gone!" he declared loudly again as he headed straight to the table where Boot Davis was eating breakfast with two other members of the marshal's posse, Shep Parker and Shorty Miller.

"Who's gone?" Boot asked, not really caring.

"Lila Blanchard, that's who," Charley answered him, immediately capturing their attention. "She's gone outta that tree. Somebody's cut her down and hauled her off."

"What about Becker?" Boot asked. "He musta seen who done it."

"You'da thought so," Charley replied. "But he claims he don't know who did it, said they musta done it in the middle of the night. He didn't even know she was gone, till I told him."

"Micah ain't gonna like this," Shep said. "He told ever'body to leave that body swingin' till he said to take it down."

"Hell, I don't like it," Boot snorted. "I've had enough trouble 'cause of that whore. He turned to a table across the room where the two remaining prostitutes were having breakfast. "Mabel!" he roared. You know anything about this?"

Had he taken a closer look at the two women, he might have seen the shocked surprise in both their faces. "No, Boot, it's news to us. We don't know nothin' about it. Do we, Wilma?" Wilma immediately shook her head. When Boot looked away, the two women immediately started speculating on the mystery, themselves.

Hearing the chatter going on between them, Boot barked, "You sure you women ain't planned a funeral somewhere?" When they both shook their heads, he threatened, "If I find out you did, there's gonna be two more funerals." He was distracted then when Leroy Hill came in the back door.

Unaware of the conversation going on in the saloon while he was outside relieving himself of some of the coffee he had consumed that morning, he made a comment. "Hey, I was just out back gettin' rid of some coffee, and I saw somethin' I never noticed before." More interested in the disappearance of Lila Blanchard's body, nobody paid much attention to Leroy's news. He continued, anyway. "I'm standin' there, doin' my business, and I looked over toward the back corner of the saloon, in the middle of the alley. And, I swear, there's a grave back there. At least it looks like a grave. Maybe it's just a pile of dirt. Anybody else ever notice that before?" He was aware then that he suddenly had everyone's attention and he was soon amazed when everyone, including the two women, got up from their chairs and rushed toward the back door. Astonished by the extreme interest they all had to confirm his story, he had no choice but to follow them.

When he saw them standing around the grave and the intensity of the conversation going back and forth across the mound of dirt, he grabbed Shorty by the elbow. "What the hell's goin' on?" Leroy asked.

"Lila," was Shorty's one-word answer before he turned his attention back to what was being said by Boot and Charley.

Still in the dark, Leroy turned to Wilma for explanation. "Looks like Lila's come back to haunt Boot," she whispered. Then she went on to enlighten him on the events of the morning, so far, which properly stunned him, just as they had everybody else. "Of course, that might not be a grave, at all," Wilma continued.

"Might just be a pile of dirt, but I believe it's Lila come home, a-layin' under that dirt."

"Well, I'll be . . ." Leroy started, then moved up beside Boot. "Whatcha gonna do, Boot? What you reckon ol' Micah's gonna do when he finds out somebody cut that whore down and brought her right back to bury her behind his saloon? You gonna dig her up?"

"Yeah, I'm gonna dig her up," Boot answered him. "I wanna make sure that's her in the ground and not somebody just tryin' to jape us. And after that, I'm gonna find that devil that brought her back to East City, ridin' on my horse. I've already got some business to settle with him. Now, I think I've got more." They were interrupted then by a call from the back of the saloon.

"What's goin' on back here?" Micah Moran demanded. "Floyd said somebody cut that woman down." They turned to see the marshal with his deputy right behind him. Boot was quick to explain why they were gathered around the mound of dirt. He told Moran he figured it was the man who brought her back to town, and he intended to settle with him. "I thought he left town," Moran said. "He wasn't here last night, was he? Anybody see him?" No one had. "I think I made it pretty clear to him day before yesterday that it wouldn't be healthy for him to be here when you and Charley got back." He turned to gaze down at the grave again. "Somebody go get a shovel. There's one by the back door." Leroy went at once to fetch it.

Seeing two shovels by the back door, Leroy brought them both and he and Shep went to work on the mound of dirt. Since it was not a very deep grave, it didn't take long before they began to uncover the body. The interested spectators gathered as closely around the grave as they could while staying out of the way of the men with the shovels. "Stop!" Mabel finally yelled when the shovels were beginning to rough up the body. She got down on her knees at the edge of the grave and started clearing the dirt away from the body, until gradually it became fully exposed.

"What's that she's holdin'?" Leroy asked, and they all crowded over the grave to see.

"It's a rope," Shorty said. "It's the noose that was around her neck." He looked back at Moran. "She's holding the rope she was hung with in her hand. Kinda like she's tellin' us to go to hell, ain't it?"

Moran stood rigid, his fists tightly clenched. Somebody in this town was throwing this hanging back in his face. "I wanna get the people who did this," he growled softly. Then raising his voice, he ordered, "Couple of you men pull her outta that hole and fill it up. I'm gonna find out who's responsible for this and we'll have us another hangin'."

"I don't believe there's anybody in this whole town who's got the guts to cut that body down, even in the middle of the night," Boot insisted. "It's gotta be that jasper that brought her all the way back here, and I aim to find out where he hightailed it to when he left here. It was me who got my horse stole. And maybe he brought my horse back, but he didn't bring my money back that was in my saddlebags." At the mention of the money, Mabel and Wilma exchanged a quick glance, having found the roll of money Lila had hidden. "He's holed up somewhere," Boot went on, "and I aim to find him. What was his name again?"

"McCabe," Moran said, "Cullen McCabe. Where the hell could he hide around here without somebody seein' him? I expect he left here and went to Raven-wood."

"Ain't no place he could hide in East City," Charley said. "He wasn't in the stable when I found Lila gone just now. And Becker said he didn't leave his horse there last night. So, hell, he's gone."

"What about that Billings woman?" Ned Larson asked, having just come from the saloon to see what was going on. "She's got a house full of lily-white churchgoers. He mighta took a room there."

"I didn't think about that," Boot said. "That's right, that might be the place he'd get himself a room, since he was too proper to stay in the hotel and it's a little ways outta town. I think I'll take a little ride over there and see if Mr. Cullen McCabe has a room there."

"Why don't you invite him back here to have a drink?" Leroy joked. "He might wanna join up with us."

"You want me to go over there and arrest him, Boss?" Ace Brown asked. "He might put up a fuss and I'll have to shoot him," he said with a wink for the marshal.

"No," Moran said, after a moment's consideration. "Boot's right, he deserves first crack at him. Charley, you better go with him, in case Boot ain't as fast as he thinks he is. I want that lowlife dead." He was still burning inside because of the gall of McCabe to cut that body down after he had ordered it to be left there. "Leroy, you and Shorty take that carcass away from my building and get rid of it somewhere."

"Looks like somebody don't care much for hangin' whores, don't it?" Ned Larson commented to Moran while they watched Lila's body being lifted out of her temporary grave. "I reckon I'll go back in and get some breakfast now."

Moran watched Larson when he turned and walked back toward the back door. He was still steaming over the gall someone had to cut Lila down. *I wouldn't be surprised if you had something to do with it,* he thought. There was no basis for thinking the thought, other than his usual suspicions regarding Ned Larson. Ned had his own gang of rustlers before coming to East City to join up with him. He brought three of his old gang with him, and it seemed to Moran that on too many occasions, he had felt it necessary to remind Larson that he was the boss. Moran felt secure in the knowledge that he had the loyalty of nine hardened gunmen, while Larson had only three. The number of gunmen had been reduced to seven, but as long as the odds stayed in his favor, Larson was obliged to toe the line with the rest of his men. But still a mystery to him was this new arrival, the stranger, Cullen McCabe, and whether he had some connection to Ned Larson.

At the back corner of his corral, unnoticed by the group of men gathered behind the saloon, Art Becker watched the party of outlaws through a cavalry field glass. It afforded him an excellent view of the grave robbery. "That son of a gun," Art muttered in admiration as he focused the lens on his glass. "He buried her right behind ol' Moran's saloon. I'd give a dollar to hear what they said about findin' Lila back home."

Knowing they wouldn't waste time and energy to dispose of Lila's body, Art continued to watch to see who got the job. When two of the men loaded her on the back of a horse and started up the creek, he was sure they would go no farther than they thought necessary to dump the body. Thinking the woman deserved a decent grave, and knowing Cullen wouldn't want her left to the buzzards, he determined to follow their trail and put her in the ground.

CHAPTER 7

"I was wondering how long it would be before that sorry bunch of outlaws would show up here," Hortense Billings said to Annie as she watched the two riders coming up the lane from the road. She opened the front door and walked out on the porch. Annie followed her, and the two women stood there to await their unwelcome guests. "It's the one they call Boot and that no-account that's always with him," Hortense commented.

"Reckon we shoulda brought the shotgun with us?" Annie was inspired to ask, since a more dangerous pair was hard to imagine.

Boot and Charley rode right up to the edge of the porch, plodding through a flower bed in the process. Seeing the stern show of defiance exhibited by the two women, Boot curled his lip into a sarcastic smile. "Well, good mornin', ladies, nice of you to come to welcome us."

"What do you want, Boot Davis?" Hortense demanded, which inspired Boot to chuckle. "State your business here," Hortense demanded again.

"Why, I'm surprised you know my name." It pleased

him to find that she did. It gave him a small sense of
fame. "Me and Charley just decided we'd ride over
and take a look at your roomin' house, in case we
might wanna rent a room with ya."

"Well, I reckon you picked a bad time to come,"
Hortense responded. "I ain't got any vacant rooms
right now. You can try me again next month."

"Just ain't my lucky day, is it?" Boot said with a
grin. "But I think me and Charley might as well look
the place over, long as we're here, get an idea what
you got to offer. You say you're full up. I reckon your
new boarder, Cullen McCabe, musta took your last
vacant room." He paused to watch her reaction to
his statement. "Let's go see his room." Both riders
stepped down.

"I've not invited you to step down," Hortense said.
"I've not got any vacancies, and I don't expect to have
any anytime soon, so you just wasted your time comin'
here. I've got no guest by the name of Cullen McCabe.
Why don't you try down at the hotel? Maybe he took
a room there."

The sarcastic smile returned to his face in response
to her cynical remark. "I reckon I'm gonna have to
see for myself." He drew his .44 from his holster and
came up the steps to the porch. Charley followed his
lead and they confronted the two women, now standing side by side, arms folded boldly before them, their
backs to the door. Apparently amused by the defiant
stance of the two women, Charley grabbed Hortense
by her throat and forcefully pulled her out of the way.
Annie immediately came to her aid, only to receive a
blow on the back of her head from Boot's handgun.
Prepared to meet the troublesome McCabe, the two
of them stormed into the parlor to find Roy Skelton

coming to see what the noise was about. Startled to find himself face-to-face with the two desperadoes, Roy could only stand gawking. "Where's McCabe?" Boot demanded.

"He ain't here," Skelton replied. "Is there somethin' I can help you with?" he asked, for want of anything better to say at that moment. Boot's response was a hand in the middle of Roy's chest, shoving him out of their way. Then they proceeded to stalk into the hallway and up the stairs, kicking every door open as they searched the length of the corridor.

"I reckon he's right," Charley said when they went back downstairs, passing Skelton, who was still standing gawking. "He ain't here." Boot drew his arm back, as if to strike him, causing the frightened man to stumble back against the wall. Laughing at the old man's reaction, they went out the front door to the porch, where Hortense was down on her knees trying to comfort Annie.

"You filthy vermin," Hortense spat at Boot. "You could have killed her."

"Weren't nothin' but a little tap on the head," Boot replied. "Maybe it'll knock a little sense in her head— yours, too. I don't take no sass from women. That'd be a good thing for you to remember." They went down the steps and climbed on their horses. "You're lucky I didn't find McCabe in there," he said as he wheeled his horse away from the porch. "If I hadda, I'da burnt this damn house to the ground."

They turned their horses back through the flower bed to the lane leading to the road. They had ridden no farther than the sharp turn in the lane when they pulled up suddenly, met by a solitary figure seated motionless on a bay horse in the middle of the lane.

Even though they had never seen him before, both men knew at once that it was Cullen McCabe. The shock of the man they hunted suddenly appearing before them caused them both to hesitate. "You lookin' for me?" Cullen calmly asked. There was another moment of indecision on the part of the hunters before they went for their guns. Two quick shots from the Winchester he was holding knocked both men out of their saddles, shot through the chest.

Back on the porch, the two women heard only two shots, for the two assailants were dead before their six-guns cleared their holsters. Hortense helped steady Annie, who was still a little shaky from the blow to her head, as they peered out toward the lane. They were joined a few seconds later by Roy Skelton and they all stared at the two horses with empty saddles, standing in the lane. They could not see the cause of the empty saddles due to the trees that stood between them and the curve of the road. "Cullen McCabe," Hortense whispered softly, without seeing past the horses. A moment later, he appeared around the curve in the path and continued on up to the house.

"Are you folks all right?" Cullen asked after he guided Jake around the flower bed. He noticed some blood on the back of Annie's neck. "Are you hurt, Annie?"

"I got a headache," she replied. "But what happened to those two devils makes it feel a lot better."

"I'm sorry about this," Cullen said. "I didn't want my troubles to involve you folks here. I didn't think they'd look here for me." Seeing Roy on the porch, he had to ask, "Anybody else hurt?"

"No, there ain't nobody else here now, and won't be till suppertime," Hortense said.

"Well, I'm gonna load those two on their horses and take 'em away from here, so Moran won't know where they got shot. Maybe it'll keep him from sendin' somebody else out here lookin' for me."

"Don't worry about us," Hortense said. "It'll be what it's gonna be. Those murderin' hooligans killed my husband and you just made the first payment on what they've got comin' to them."

"I expect you're gonna need some dinner in a couple of hours," Annie said. "I don't cook much in the middle of the day 'cause there ain't usually anybody here but us women and Roy. Sometimes, Art Becker will come over in the middle of the day for dinner, but most of the time he waits for supper. So, if you get hungry, I've got a pot of soup beans on, and I'll bake some biscuits to go with 'em."

"That sounds hard to pass up," Cullen said. "I'll have to see where I am about that time. If I do show up, I'll come in the back door and hope nobody sees me." It was a tempting thought, since there was no place else for him to eat in East City, and his pack-horse and all his supplies were in Art Becker's barn. "I'd best go take care of those two on your front path before somebody spots them."

It took a bit of effort to lift Boot Davis up to lie across his saddle. Charley Turner, being a smaller man, was a little easier. Once he had each would-be assassin lying across his saddle, he used some rope Charley carried on his horse to tie the hands and feet of both men together under their horses' bellies. He wanted to make sure the bodies didn't fall off before he transported them to where he wanted to leave them. Boot and Charley had never seen him before today. He, as well, had never seen them. As he tied

Boot's hands to his feet, that occurred to him, but he had been certain it was Boot because he was very familiar with the red roan he rode. His biggest regret was that the first blood-letting was at the boardinghouse, but on second thought, he realized it was a logical place for Moran's men to look. He had told Art Becker that there was going to be a war. What Art didn't know was that it was not simply an act of revenge for the brutal murder of Lila Blanchard. His plan now was to destroy Micah Moran's evil headquarters for outlaws. It was not going to be easy, with the cards stacked as they were in the outlaws' favor. But he had nothing to lose but his life, and that had been worth less than a nickel from the day his wife and family were taken from him. With that thought in mind, he said, "Let's go to town, boys, your boss is probably worried about you."

"Everything goin' all right, Mr. Johnson?" Deputy Ace Brown asked casually when he walked into Joe Johnson's general store. "I like to keep a sharp eye out, make sure you merchants ain't got no troubles," he said as he casually walked past Johnson to a barrel of apples at the end of the counter. He spent a few moments pawing the apples, trying to find the best ones. When he was finished, he held his selection up and said, "That's a beauty." Then he took another one and said, "Need one for later on." He turned and went back out the door. "Keepin' the peace," he said as he left the store.

"Deputy Brown stopping by to buy some apples?" Doris Johnson asked, flippantly, as she came in the back door.

"Yeah," Joe answered, disgusted. "You know, I would be happy to give an apple to an honest deputy marshal, but I swear that worthless son of a gun just comes in any time he pleases—thinks it's his privilege." She nodded slowly, knowing the anguish burning inside him. They talked often of the unfortunate situation they were forced to endure and talked about closing the store down and moving to Ravenwood, or some other town—anywhere away from East City. But it always boiled down to the fact that they couldn't afford to move and start over again. They weren't the only honest merchants talking about leaving East City, and that only seemed to make their future even more insecure. In the beginning, there was business in their store from the ranches and farms on this side of the creek. But since the takeover of the town by Micah Moran and his gang, most all of those customers crossed over the creek to Ravenwood to do their trading. Over there, you were less likely to get shot by a stray bullet from some drunken cowhand or suffer rude behavior before your wife and children.

"Well," she concluded, "I'm going back in the kitchen. It's almost time to fix a little dinner." A few moments after she uttered the words, the sudden sound of gunshots reached her ears. She turned to face her husband.

"Sounds like they came from the end of the street," Joe said, accustomed to sudden unexplained gunfire. He walked to the front window in time to see two horses galloping down the middle of the street with two bodies lying across the saddles. "Damn!" he exclaimed, causing Doris to run to the window beside him. When the horses had galloped past, they went outside to see Ace Brown running out in the street, waving his arms frantically, trying to stop them. He succeeded in causing the horses to swerve to avoid him, finally stopping them, one on each side of the street in front of the Cork and Bottle.

"It's Boot and Charley!" Ace shouted to the men pouring out of the Cork and Bottle. He grabbed the bridle of Boot's horse and yelled for one of the men to grab the other one. Shep Parker caught the frightened horse.

"Are they dead?" Micah Moran demanded.

"They're dead, all right," his deputy answered. "Shot through the chest, both of 'em. I reckon they musta found McCabe."

"Cullen McCabe," Moran uttered to himself. It was his work, all right. He didn't need any witnesses to tell him that. There was no one else it could have been, and Moran suspected there was motive behind McCabe's arrival in his town. He didn't just wander through to see a common whore back to town. He came here with a purpose, and that purpose was to take over control of the town. Moran was sure of it, and it was the first open challenge he had faced for control of his town, and he was determined to smash the attempt right away. "Ace!" he yelled at his deputy, "come here!"

Ace handed the reins he was holding to Shorty Miller and ran across the street to answer the call. "It's Boot and Charley, Boss," Ace said. "You want me to arrest that McCabe feller?"

"He's the one who done it, don't you think?" Moran replied, sarcastically.

"Yeah, that's what I think," the dull-witted deputy answered. "Sure looks like he got the best of 'em, though, don't it?" When Moran failed to give him any more instructions, Ace said, "I'll saddle up and ride out to that Billings woman's roomin' house. That's where Boot and Charley went lookin' for him, right?"

"That's right," Moran said. "But I doubt he's settin' out there waitin' for you. Those shots sounded like they came from the top of the street. You find him! He can't be far. Track him down, wherever he went. Trackin', that's what you're supposed to be good at. I want to hang that snake."

"I'll get him," Ace said, duly excited about the chance to succeed where Boot and Charley had failed.

"That's what I pay you for," Moran replied. "Kill him, if you have to, but if you can arrest him, I'd like that better. Then we can have another hangin' for the good folks of East City to see what happens when they don't toe the line."

When Ace ran back to the marshal's office to get his horse, Leroy Hill walked over beside Moran. "You reckon me and a couple of the boys oughta go with him to get that feller?"

"No, he oughta be able to arrest one man by himself. I want you boys to search the town in case he didn't run. He might be hidin' in one of the stores, like Johnson's or O'Sullivan's. Matter of fact, I'd search O'Sullivan's first. That's where Johnson, Becker, Franks, and the rest of that town council do their drinkin'. He might be hidin' in one of those rooms back of that saloon. I don't know how Boot and Charley got themselves shot. Looks like they rode right into an ambush. Ace ain't got a lotta brains, but he knows to watch where he's goin'." He glanced at Ned Larson, who said he would go with Steve Tatum and Billy Fish to search the town. The thought returned to him that it was Ned who had suggested that

Boot and Charley should go to Hortense Billings's boardinghouse to look for McCabe. Then there was the shooting in Ravenwood yesterday when McCabe took out two more of his men. That made four men in two days. How did McCabe happen to be there? Did somebody tell him they were going after Tug Taggert?

There was another factor in Moran's thinking, but he wasn't willing to admit it. He preferred to have his men close around him. He was still convinced that McCabe and whomever he was working for were set on taking over his town. And the first thing they would be thinking would be to get rid of him. He didn't know who McCabe was, or where he came from. It wasn't a name he had heard of before, but he had to be a stud horse to take Boot and Charley down. Anybody could hide in ambush and pick a couple of riders off at a distance. But Moran knew that the odds of shooting two riders from a distance and placing two shots squarely in the middle of their chests, were too high to be believed. Boot and Charley had to be facing McCabe, and at a short distance apart. For that reason, Moran wasn't sure he wanted to chance giving McCabe the opportunity to ride in and openly challenge him to a face-off for control of the gang he had assembled. Loyalty was not a common thing among outlaws, and it could be bought for the price of a bullet. Even Leroy felt superior in intelligence when compared to Ace, and Leroy was as simpleminded as could be. But Moran was confident in Ace's fearlessness, strength, and natural ability. "And, Leroy," he called after him, "make sure you check Becker's stable. He stayed there before, he mighta come back there, thinkin' we wouldn't look for him there."

* * *

The stampede of the two horses down the main street of East City had the effect that Cullen intended, but he didn't linger to witness it. Knowing there would be a hasty assembly of an outlaw posse on his tail, he waited only long enough to see that the two horses ran straight down the street. The question now was, in which direction to run? While he thought about it, he guided Jake off the road and rode toward the thick growth of trees that hugged the banks of the creek. The spot he picked to wait in was close to the footpath Art Becker had made between the back of his stable and Hortense's boardinghouse. Remembering the invitation she had given him, to come to dinner, he hoped maybe Art might pick that day to have dinner, too. With the commotion he had just caused in town, he figured there was a chance he would. And if he did, Cullen would see him walking along the path, and Art could tell him how Moran was reacting to the trouble he had started. He also had to consider the possibility of a posse of lawless gunmen searching the woods between town and the boardinghouse. In that event, he would cross the creek and hightail it for Ravenwood. It was unlikely the outlaw posse would be bold and reckless enough to follow him there. From his visit in that town the day before, it appeared to be built by solid merchants and an honest marshal and was more than double the size of East City. For the time being, he prepared to wait and see just what his options would be. As he had told Art, this was a war he had started. The trouble was, the other side was the one with the army.

As close as he was to town, he could hear faint noises of heated activity from there and he could imagine that a posse was getting ready to ride. He regretted the fact that one of the first places they were likely to head for was the boardinghouse. He felt a strong obligation to defend it, but that could mean it would be shot to pieces with the likelihood of the women being killed. Their chances were better to escape harm, if Moran's men were allowed to search the house and move on to look elsewhere for him. Thinking about that, he walked down by the creek where Jake was nibbling on some green lily pads at the edge of the water. He gave the bay a few strokes on his neck and said, "I might have started something bigger'n I can handle, boy. Right now, I'm thinkin' about those soup beans and biscuits Annie said she was gonna cook for dinner." He was startled then by a noise up the bank. He pulled his rifle from the saddle sling and made his way carefully up the bank to a position where he could see the footpath. He relaxed as soon as he saw Art hurrying along toward the boardinghouse. His legs plowing through some patches of overgrowth bushes was the source of the noise Cullen had heard.

"Jumpin' Jehoshaphat!" Art bellowed when Cullen suddenly stepped out from behind a thick laurel bush. "You gave me a start." Cullen apologized and Art said, "I'm just glad you're out here in the woods instead of at the house. That's what I was comin' to see and I was gonna tell you to get goin', if you hadda been. Moran's already sent Ace Brown to hunt you down. Leroy Hill was already at the stable lookin' for you. I told him you don't keep a horse there, that I ain't seen you since that first day. I didn't tell him that you've still got a packhorse there." He paused to take a breath before continuing. "It's a good thing we put your packs and stuff in the barn." He paused again in his excitement before asking, "Were you involved in a shootout in Ravenwood yesterday mornin'?" Without waiting for Cullen to answer, he continued. "After you carried Lila's body off last night, Stan Molloy came in. He was leadin' two horses with empty saddles. He didn't waste no time at the stable, just mumbled somethin' about a shootout in Ravenwood and told me to take care of the horses. Then he hotfooted it up to the Cork and Bottle. Did you have any part in that?"

"I happened to be there when it happened," Cullen said. "Two men were tryin' to shoot the marshal outside a saloon, but he came out of it all right and arrested both of 'em." He paused to consider that. "So there were three of 'em, and it looks like they were sent after the marshal, by Moran, no doubt." More interested at the moment about what might be happening on this side of Walnut Creek, he changed the subject. "Ace Brown," Cullen asked, "you say he's already lookin' for me? I reckon he's headed to the boardin'house."

"Yeah, he's gone to Hortense's house 'cause that's where Boot Davis and Charley Turner went lookin' for you." He paused again to comment on that. "You caused quite a stir with that trick and I'm afraid it's gonna cause you more trouble than you can handle. Boot and Charley were a couple of tough customers, especially Boot. I expect there's two or three in that gang of murderers that might wanna make a reputation by killin' the man who gunned down Boot Davis and Charley Turner."

"I expect you're right. The man who shot Cullen

McCabe would make a name for hisself, all right."
Cullen froze when he heard the comment from
behind them. A moment later, Leroy Hill stepped out
onto the path from behind a tree, his six-gun leveled
at Cullen. "I reckon this is my lucky day, ain't it,
Mr. Cullen McCabe?" He glanced at Art then. "You
just step aside, Becker. I knew you was lyin' when you
said you didn't know where he was. I oughta shoot
you down for lyin', and I might, anyway, if you make
the first wrong move." Back to Cullen, he said, "I'll
thank you to drop that Winchester on the ground."
Having no choice but to comply, Cullen dropped his
rifle, wondering why the man hadn't simply shot him.
As if reading his thoughts, Leroy told him why. "If it
was up to me, you'd already be dead. But the marshal
said to arrest you, so we can have a public hangin'. So
you get to live a little bit longer, unless you try somethin'. You do that and you're dead, don't matter what
the marshal said. Now, Becker, ease that gun you're
wearin' outta that holster with nothin' but two fingers
on the handle. Then, before it clears leather, you grab
it by the barrel with your other hand and hand it to
me, handle first." Art did as Leroy directed, and Leroy
quickly took the pistol and stuck it in his belt. "Now
set your ass down on the ground there."

With Art's weapon in his belt and Art on the ground,
Leroy was ready to deal with Cullen. "You ain't said
much, Mr. Cullen McCabe. You ain't as slick as you
thought, are you?"

"I reckon I figured you were all as dumb as Boot
Davis," Cullen said. "I guess I was wrong." Having
been caught like this, he could only hope Leroy would
make a mistake.

"You're damn right you was wrong," Leroy replied.

"You saw how ol' Becker, there, handed over his six-shooter, now let's see if you can do the same thing. You're a pretty big man, but not so big when you're lookin' at the business end of this .44 I'm holdin', ain't that right? So you keep that in mind when you pull that gun up. Nothin' would give me more pleasure than to shoot you down right here."

"All right," Cullen said. "You're callin' the shots. But whaddaya holdin' a gun on him for? Hell, he's on your side."

"The hell he is," Leroy responded. "He led me straight to you."

"He wouldn't be standin' here if I hadn't stopped him. He said he was cuttin' through here on his way to dinner. But ain't no skin off my back if you shoot Moran's stable man. How do you like that, Becker? You thought Moran was your friend." As Leroy had ordered, Cullen started to pull his Colt, but hesitated. "You said pull it out with just two fingers," he said. "I ain't sure I can pull it out with two fingers. Is it all right if I use one finger and a thumb?"

The question confused the simpleminded outlaw. "What are you talkin' about? Pull it out just like he did. Do it with your left hand."

"With my left hand, all right, nice and slow, with one finger and one thumb, just like Art did," Cullen said, and exaggerated the slowness in his movements.

"That's right," Leroy said, "nice and slow. Now grab that barrel with your right hand and hand it to me." He was beginning to wonder if McCabe was as slow in the head as Ace Brown.

Cullen lifted the Colt with deliberate motions, then slowly grasped the barrel with his right hand and eased the weapon toward Leroy. Impatient to the point of frustration with the seemingly thickheaded slowness of the big man, Leroy grabbed the gun and attempted to snatch it out of Cullen's hand. But Cullen held on to the barrel and grabbed Leroy's gun hand, forcing both his hands outward. "Let go!" Leroy blurted. "Damn it, let go, or I'll shoot you down right here!" Realizing at once that he was not able to match Cullen's strength, Leroy held on, knowing now that he was fighting for his life. In a panic, he pulled the trigger on the only pistol that was cocked. It sent a bullet harmlessly into the ground near his feet.

The two combatants were locked in a standoff with Leroy weakening rapidly. In desperation, he aimed a knee at his taller opponent, which Cullen blocked with his thigh. Still, Leroy held on, fighting for his life but realizing he was helpless to free his hands. He managed to continue to struggle until Cullen said, "Becker, pick up my rifle and shoot this piece of crud."

Leroy's eyes spread wide open in fright, held in the powerful grip of his antagonist. Art, having sat stunned throughout the whole contest between the two men, was jolted out of his trance. He got up from the ground, went over, and picked up Cullen's rifle. Knowing then he was about to die, Leroy sank to the ground, releasing his hold on both pistols. On his knees he looked up at the sinister man over him, his eyes pleading like a steer about to be slaughtered. It was especially hard for him to die this way. Never having been thought of as a gunman in the class of Boot Davis, or even Shep or Shorty, he had always talked big. But he was never taken seriously by the other men. This, then, would have been his chance for some respect, had he been able to bring Cullen McCabe in to be hanged. Micah would have had to see him in a different light. Another failure. He felt like crying when he heard the sound of Art cranking a cartridge into the Winchester's chamber.

Cullen held his hand out. "Give it to me," he said. "I knew you couldn't shoot one of your own. I reckon I shoulda shot you when you came walking down this path." Art immediately handed the rifle to him in shocked confusion over Cullen's sudden change. Looking down at Leroy, Cullen asked, "Have you got a horse back there somewhere?"

"Yes, sir," Leroy answered, completely submissive in defeat as his executioner stood towering over him, "back at that sharp turn in the path." Thoughts flashed through his simple brain of his father, who warned him that he was taking the wrong path in life. That path, his pa told him, ended up in hell. *You was right, Pa*, he thought, *it led straight to hell*. When he looked up again to see Cullen staring down at him with the barrel of the rifle only a couple of feet from his head, he spoke softly. "He's a pretty good horse, but you ain't gonna get too much for him. He's gettin' some age on him."

"You think he's young enough to tote you back to your boss to give him a message?" Cullen asked. Leroy didn't answer immediately, he couldn't. Thinking Cullen was playing some sadistic game with him, he continued to stare up at him without responding to his question. He couldn't help thinking about a mental image of Boot Davis and Charley Turner when they came back to town lying across their saddles. That was the kind of message Cullen McCabe sent. "Well, do ya?" Cullen prodded when Leroy failed to respond.

"Oh yes, sir, I surely do," he blurted then, suddenly

realizing that Cullen was talking about letting him go free. "I can take a message for ya!"

"All right, get on your feet," Cullen ordered, and waited until Leroy got up before continuing. "Now, walk back down the path to get your horse." Oblivious to the wet stain that had spread on the front of his britches, Leroy turned and started down the path, with Cullen and Art right behind him. As Leroy had said, his horse was tied in the bushes, just beyond the curve. Cullen untied the reins and held on to them. "Get on him," he ordered, and Leroy eagerly obeyed. Cullen emptied the cartridges out of Leroy's gun and handed it to him. "Can I count on you to give Micah Moran a message?"

"Yes, sir, you surely can!" Leroy answered at once.

"All right, the message is this: The days of East City as the city of outlaws is over. The town is sick of it and so is the state of Texas. If Moran is smart, he'll get out of town now and take the rest of you saddle tramps with him before a company of Rangers sets up camp here permanently. And you might as well tell him not to waste his time comin' back here lookin' for me. I won't be here. You got that?" He turned to address Art. "And the same goes for you, Becker. I won't be here by the time you come back."

"Yes, sir," Leroy answered. "I'll tell him." He hesitated a few moments when Cullen handed him the reins. "I reckon I oughta say I'm obliged to you for lettin' me go."

"Make no mistake," Cullen said. "I let you go because I need to send a message. The next time you come at me with a gun in your hand, I'll kill you. You understand?"

"Yes, sir," Leroy replied. Cullen gave the horse a

slap on his croup and he was off at a lope down the narrow footpath.

Cullen turned to find Art staring at him curiously. "Who the hell are you really?"

"You know who I am," Cullen replied. "The same fellow I was yesterday, Cullen McCabe. I had to put on a little show for that jasper. I'm hopin' he thinks you weren't in cahoots with me at all."

"I don't know about him, but you had me convinced that I was in the same boat with him." He shook his head in relief. "What about all that talk you said about the town and the state of Texas sayin' Moran and his posse had to get out of town? When is all that stuff supposed to happen?"

"I don't know," Cullen replied, "maybe right after you folks in this town decide you've had enough of their kind. I can't see why it's taken you folks so long to decide. I don't even live here, but the hanging of a common whore was enough for me to know I'd had enough of that gang of outlaws. If there's no will to fight, maybe the best thing for the honest people in East City is to cut bait and run. Then maybe the army will bring some cannons in here and level the damn town."

"You can't expect us to fight a gang of murderin' outlaws like Moran's posse," Art felt compelled to say. "Joe Johnson, Abe Franks, Buck Casey, Cary O'Sullivan, Stewart Ingram, and me; we're the major merchants left in this town. What chance would we have against that gang? You had me nervous as hell back there when you told me to shoot Leroy. I'll be honest with you, I don't know if I coulda done it. I mean, with him just sittin' there helpless. I guess I could have if he was shootin' at me." He shook his head, unsure of the consequences that might follow the confrontation with Leroy Hill. "I don't know what Moran might do if he tells him what you said to tell him. It might go hard on all of us honest folks."

Cullen studied the contrite man for a few seconds before replying. "Maybe you're right, Art. I've got no right tellin' anybody what they oughta do. I reckon I'm to blame for any trouble you folks might have. I'll do what I can to make it a one-man fight between me and Moran. At least I'll stick around to see it through. I owe you that. But right now, we'd best get off this path, in case we get some more company right away."

Art had one more thing to say. "I just wanted to tell you that I'll still help you all I can. In spite of what I said, I know it's time to stand up to Moran. I just don't know if we can. But I ain't got no family to worry about, so I oughta be able to step up if I'm needed. Tell you the truth, though, I can't figure out why you're standin' up to Moran. I mean, you bein' a stranger and all, just passin' through, was what you said. Most strangers would just move on, but you're stayin' to risk gettin' shot in the back for your trouble. You're already a marked man for shootin' Boot Davis and Charley Turner. And that was on top of cuttin' Lila Blanchard down from that limb. Did you really ride through this part of the territory lookin' for good grass and water for cattle?"

"Somebody has to do it for the big cattle operations," Cullen said. "It's pretty important to those people not to have a whole town full of cattle rustlers on their doorstep."

"I reckon that's right," Art said after giving it some thought.

"I appreciate your offer of help, Art. I figured

you had some grit." He started to go after his horse but hesitated long enough to say, "I'm sorry 'bout threatenin' to shoot you."

"I'll let it pass this one time," Art joked. "What are you fixin' to do now?"

"Why, Annie said she was gonna cook soup beans and biscuits. And since all my cookin' things are in your barn, Annie's biscuits sound pretty damn good right now."

"Ain't you forgettin' I told you Ace Brown was going to Hortense's?" Art reminded.

"I didn't forget," Cullen said. "But it's bound to be just a matter of time. Might as well go ahead and see what the deputy has in mind."

CHAPTER 8

"I ain't leavin' this place till one of you tells me where Cullen McCabe is," Deputy Ace Brown threatened. "And if one of you don't start talkin' pretty soon, I'm gonna have to get a little rough. Now, where the hell is he?"

"Are you hard of hearing?" Hortense responded. "None of us know where Cullen McCabe is. We told you that. He's not rooming here and he's not eating here. He wouldn't likely be here this time of day, even if he was one of our guests. Why can't you understand that?"

Her retort earned her a hard backhand that knocked her back against the wall. Annie rushed to keep her from falling. "You understand that?" Brown roared. "If I don't get some answers pretty quick, there's gonna be worse than that."

"What kinda law officer do you call yourself?" Roy charged. "Hittin' a defenseless woman. You ain't nothin' but a damn coward!"

Brown turned to scowl at the old man. "You're right. Ain't no need to hit a woman when there's a broke-down old man to hit." Then he gave Roy a rap beside his head with the barrel of his pistol that caused the old man to drop like a sack of potatoes. Both Annie and Hortense went to his side. Ace stood over them, trying to decide what to do to get the information he needed. He was convinced that they knew where McCabe was hiding and there was no limit to what he would do to make them tell. "You folks don't know what it's gonna cost you to keep your mouth shut, do ya? Well, now I'm gonna show you." He holstered his pistol and drew a long hunting knife he wore. Then he reached down, grabbed a handful of Annie's hair, and jerked her head back. With the keen edge of the knife firmly against her neck, he announced, "Now, if nobody don't open their mouth, I'm gonna open her throat." He pressed the knife just enough to draw blood, causing Hortense to try to get to her feet and come to Annie's defense. He waved his knife back and forth, taunting Hortense. "Come on, girlie girl, and I'll chop up both of you." He was determined to accomplish what Boot Davis and Charley Turner could not, and he felt no remorse in the killing of both women and the old man, if that's what it took. Still holding Annie by her hair, an insolent grin spread across his face as he motioned toward Hortense with his knife. "Come on, you old hag." Fighting mad now, Hortense gathered herself, set to spring at him, regardless of the cost. The report of the Colt .44 from the kitchen door behind her, caused her to fall to the floor again.

Not sure what had happened at first, Hortense looked up to see Ace Brown stumble awkwardly, and she flinched again when a second shot ripped into his abdomen. Ace dropped his knife and released Annie to clutch his belly with both hands. Trying his best to stay upright, he staggered out the front door in an attempt to escape. But he made it no farther than the edge of the porch before stopping to support himself on a porch post. Following behind him, Cullen raised one boot and kicked him off the porch to land flat on his face a few feet from his horse. Cullen stood at the edge of the porch for a few moments more, watching him to make sure he was finished before turning back to see if Roy and the women were all right. He saw then that Art had come in behind him and was helping the women to their feet. Cullen walked back inside and extended a hand to Roy, who took the help gratefully, as Cullen pulled him up.

"Is everybody all right?" Cullen asked.

"I ain't never felt better!" Annie declared loudly. "You're a welcome sight, I swear."

Less exuberant, but grateful just the same, Hortense said, "We'd best take a look at that cut on the side of Roy's head. He got hit pretty hard. Are you all right, Roy?"

"I reckon I'll live," Roy answered, and wiped a trickle of blood off his face. "I tell you, though, for a minute there I was seein' stars."

With nothing he could do to help at the moment, Cullen stood watching while they recovered from what might have been a fatal visit from Ace Brown. "I'm sorry I didn't get here sooner," he said.

"You got here soon enough," Annie insisted, wiping the blood from her throat. "That crazy blankethead woulda ended up killin' all of us." She dabbed at her throat again to make sure it had stopped bleeding. "Well," she announced, "I reckon you're all wantin' soup beans and biscuits, now that we've worked up a little appetite. I swear, the marshal's deputy got here right after I pulled them biscuits from the oven, but I'll bet they're still a little bit warm."

They all gaped at her as if she was crazy, but Hortense, better than anyone else, knew she was just Annie. "I guess we do need to eat, but some of us might have lost our appetites."

"Not me," Art confessed, although a little reticent to admit it after Roy and the women had just suffered Ace Brown's traumatic visit.

"I'm gonna take care of the deputy," Cullen said. "Then I'm gonna take a little look-see back toward town to make sure he was alone. Art, I could use your help in loadin' the deputy on his horse." He paused before walking out the door to say, "I'd appreciate some of those beans and biscuits, though. I ain't sure when I'll get a chance to eat again." He didn't express it, but he was concerned by the tendency for Moran and his gang to assume that Hortense's house was his home base. He wanted to change their focus on the boardinghouse, if he could, but he was not yet sure how he could do that.

He walked down the front steps, pushed Ace's horse away from the body, and waited for Art to get there. "He's a pretty hefty load, all right," Art commented. "You wanna throw him across the saddle?"

"No," Cullen answered, having just decided. "I wanna sit him in the saddle, let him ride home the same way he came."

Skeptical, Art said, "He won't hardly stay in the saddle before he gets out of the yard."

"I'm aimin' to tie his feet in the stirrups and tie his

hands to the saddle horn. He might sway from side to side, but I don't think he'll fall off."

"Oh," Art responded, "I reckon that might work." He still seemed skeptical. "We'll see after we get the hard part done—liftin' his big ass up on his horse."

They picked up Ace's body, Art by the shoulders, and Cullen by the feet. Then they lifted the corpse high enough for Cullen to shift the lower body over to rest on the saddle and let the feet drop on either side of the flea-bitten gray gelding. Then Cullen helped Art to lift the upper body up to a sitting position in the saddle. "Can you hold him up like that till I tie him on?" Cullen asked. Art said that he could, so Cullen took the rope from Ace's saddle, pausing to take a look at the project before deciding how best to do what he wanted. Once he made up his mind, he tied one end of the rope around Ace's foot in the stirrup, then pulled it under the horse's belly and took a few turns around Ace's other foot. Then he pulled the rope up across Ace's thighs, took another turn under the horse's belly, coming back to the saddle. After binding the body's hands together, he tied them to the saddle horn. "You can let go of him now," he said. "He might sway like hell, but he won't fall off."

"If you say so," Art replied with a grin for Cullen's handiwork. "Whaddaya gonna do with him?" He figured Cullen had something in mind to have gone to so much trouble when the normal thing would have been to simply take the body off in the woods somewhere.

"I'm gonna help him find his way back home. I know his boss will wanna hold funeral services for such a loyal servant of the people of East City."

Art stayed there and held the gray's reins while Cullen went behind the house to get Jake. He was glad that Cullen didn't take long because he would almost swear that Ace locked eyes with him when he glanced up once. Art honestly believed that the evil in the man lived on after his body was done. It was a feeling he wouldn't share with anyone, and he was damn glad to hand the reins to Cullen when he came back. He stood there a few minutes longer to watch Cullen lead the gray down the path with Ace's body swaying like a rag doll. "I swear," Art said softly, turned around, and went into the house.

With no thoughts of the kind that troubled Art, Cullen was more concerned with the boardinghouse becoming the center of Micah Moran's attempts to get to him. What he feared might happen was the possibility that Moran would send a party of men in big enough numbers to attack the house and burn the occupants out. Even if Hortense survived, she would be without means to support herself, and he knew the blame would lie at his feet. These were the thoughts that troubled him as he led the flea-bitten gray back toward town, even though he knew the way he was returning Ace Brown's corpse was a message to Moran and his posse.

When within a short distance of the south end of town, he had still seen no sign of any other riders watching the trail. It didn't surprise him, for he had a gut feeling that Moran expected Ace to get the job done. As Art Becker had told him, Ace was Moran's bulldog, and no one was better at plugging a skull or breaking a back. Moran used Ace like a weapon and everyone in East City was aware of it. For his purposes on this ride to town, Cullen left the main road and circled the town. There were two reasons for coming into town from the north end. One was his hope to draw Moran's attention away from Hortense's boarding-house, which was south of town. The second reason was the fact that Art Becker's stable was the first business you came to on the south side of town. If he turned Ace's horse loose on that end of town, the horse could well wander straight to the stable and Cullen's planned show for Moran would not be as effective. And he hoped he could send a message that all assassins would be returned in the same state as Boot Davis, Charley Turner, and Ace Brown. Added to the two men captured in Ravenwood, that would be a loss of five of his notorious "posse." He had hopes that it would stop Moran's attempts to kill him, maybe even lessen his men's willingness to go on these attacks.

When he was about a hundred yards from O'Sullivan's Saloon, he looped the gray's reins over the late Ace Brown's hands. Then he gave the horse a swat on his croup that caused it to lope for a few yards, but it slowed to a stop, causing Cullen to repeat the process. Again, the horse loped for a short distance before slowing to a walk. But this time, the horse continued walking, evidently realizing it was back in familiar territory. It had no doubt carried Ace up and down this street countless times. Cullen watched for a while as the horse padded slowly along the street, wandering from one side to the other. As interested as he was in Moran's reaction to his deputy's return, Cullen decided it best not to linger in broad daylight, so he wheeled Jake and started back the way he had come.

* * *

As the meandering horse plodded slowly by O'Sullivan's Saloon, a cowhand from one of the ranches east of town staggered out the door, having spent all he had on whiskey. "Howdy, Ace," he offered. Receiving no return greeting from him, he took a step back to stare at the man on the horse, swaying drunkenly back and forth, side to side, forward and backward. "Damn," he uttered, "he's drunker'n I am." He continued staring, then added, "Unless I'm a helluva lot drunker'n I think I am."

Farther down the street, Shep Parker walked out of the Cork and Bottle, starting to cross the street to Johnson's general store. He stopped suddenly when he caught sight of the horse meandering aimlessly, still some distance up the street. The rider flopped on the horse's neck, then bent backward while leaning toward one side. It took a moment before Shep realized what he was staring at. When he did, he turned and ran back to the Cork and Bottle. "Micah!" he yelled as he ran in the door. "You've gotta come look at this!" When Moran hesitated and started to ask why, Shep blurted, "It's Ace! He's back!" Not waiting for Moran then, he turned and ran back in the street to catch Ace's horse. Catching the urgency then, Moran, as well as Shorty, Leroy, and Stan, who were playing cards with him, jumped up and ran out to see what Shep was yelling about.

In the middle of the street, Shep was in the process of catching the horse by its bridle. Expecting to see Ace Brown triumphantly parading a captured, or a deceased, Cullen McCabe, they were stopped, stunned

by the sight of the body flopping back and forth in the
saddle. After a moment, Shorty and Molloy hustled
out to help Shep while Moran and Leroy remained,
still staring at the grotesque spectacle. Leroy couldn't
help but picture himself in that saddle, sagging from
right to left like a drunk. Had it not been for the fact
that McCabe wanted a message delivered to Moran,
he was sure he might have returned much like Ace.
He had not delivered that message to Moran because
he didn't want him to know about his encounter with
McCabe on the footpath through the woods. There
would be too many questions about why he was
spared, when no one else who went up against him
was. Moran was already suspicious about Ned Larson
and his friends, even to the point of thinking Ned and
McCabe were partners in a scheme to take over leadership of the gang. Leroy couldn't afford to let Moran
know he had talked to McCabe. As tightly wound as
he was, Micah might be inclined to lump him in with
Ned's boys. He was still uncertain about Art Becker,
not fully convinced that he was not in league with
McCabe, in spite of what McCabe had said. But that
issue would just have to stew in its own pot. Leroy
couldn't say anything to Moran about it without
having to tell him how he knew it.

Moran said nothing while his men untied the ropes
holding Ace on his horse. Once they got him on the
ground, Moran told them to take him away somewhere
and put him in the ground. "What about his horse
and saddle and all his other stuff?" Molloy asked.

"You can cut cards for all his gear," Moran responded. "Just get him to hell away from here." There

was already a small crowd of spectators gathering to gawk at the dead deputy, and the spectacle of his less-than-glorious return could only be a negative reflection on the marshal and his posse.

It didn't help his disposition when Ned walked up to stand beside him to comment. "Looks to me like it's the same result every time somebody goes lookin' for McCabe," he said. "They always come back full of bullet holes. Even when you sent somebody over to Ravenwood to go after that marshal, McCabe was there to welcome them."

"Yeah," Moran said. "Does look that way, don't it? Makes you wonder if there ain't somebody tippin' him off—like maybe they're thinkin' about takin' over this town."

"Oh, I doubt that," Ned responded. "There's too many of us for that."

"There ain't as many as there was a couple of days ago. We've lost five good men in the last two days. At least, I have, and three of 'em were damn good men, Boot Davis, Charley Turner, and now Ace Brown." He paused, then said, "You ain't lost none of those boys you brought with you."

"No, I reckon I ain't," Ned replied. "It's all a matter of luck, I s'pose."

Moran didn't comment further on the subject, but he couldn't discount the fact that, up until Cullen McCabe arrived on the scene, he had an edge over Ned with nine men, compared to Ned's three men. Now that edge was closer with his advantage only four to three. It didn't help matters any that Tatum, Fish, and Ledbetter still had a tendency to keep a bit apart from Moran's men. He hadn't thought much about it until this business with McCabe began. He had to admit that Ned mixed in with him and his men when eating, drinking, and playing cards, but that didn't mean he wasn't trying to deceive them. *You might think you're the man to run this outfit,* he thought, *but you've got another think coming. I'll be keeping my eye on you.*

CHAPTER 9

After delivering Ace Brown's body back to town, Cullen decided he would risk returning to the boarding-house to get some of that food Annie had cooked. His main concern at the present time was the safety of Hortense and her boarders. It was unfortunate that all the attention was drawn to Hortense's plain little two-story house. But it was just bad luck that every killing involved the house, and there seemed to be no way he could divert it. No matter his concern, Hortense, Annie, and the four men who roomed there insisted they were not about to leave their home, come hell, high water, or Micah Moran. "Let them come looking for you," Hortense said. "I won't give 'em any trouble. They can look all they want and maybe it won't take too many more times to show 'em they're wasting their time." All Cullen could do was to try to be ready to intercept anyone else who came looking for him before they got to the house.

When he had finished a healthy serving of Annie's soup beans and biscuits, Cullen went back along the footpath with Art. Art had finished his dinner long before Cullen got back from the north end of town, but he waited for him to return. He hoped to hear about the reaction of Moran and his gang when Ace came riding back to town. Cullen wanted to get some of his supplies and cooking utensils from Art's barn, since he was going to have to set up a camp somewhere not too far from Hortense's place. So he walked with him, leading Jake along behind them. Art had told him before that Moran's men came and went all the time in his stable, and they were never too guarded in their conversation. He often overheard them talk about things they were planning to do. Once, he claimed, he had ridden over to Ravenwood to warn Marshal Taggert about a planned robbery of the bank over there. "If they'da found out I told the marshal, that woulda been the end of this child, and that's a fact," he said.

"What happened?" Cullen asked, surprised that Art had the guts to do that. "Did they try to rob the bank?"

"They rode over there, fixin' to rob it, but when they rode by the bank, Marshal Taggert and about a dozen men with rifles were camped out on both sides of the street. I heard Johnny Barr say it looked like a real hot party they had waitin' for 'em. They just kept on ridin' and came back to East City. From what I could hear, ol' Moran was mad as hell about it."

"I expect he was," Cullen said. "When we get back to the stable, you might find out if Leroy believed me when I said you were on his side. He's dumber'n a stump, but he might notta been fooled. I reckon we'll find out. I'll be hidin' behind the corral, anyway, and if there's any trouble, I'll come as fast as I can. I would like to know if he gave Moran my message. I'm hopin' he'll think there's gonna be more than just one man comin' after him."

"Are you thinkin' about tryin' to clean up the whole town?" Art asked, the thought just having occurred to him.

"I think it needs doin', don't you?" Cullen replied.

"How are you gonna do it, kill all of 'em?" Art asked, but didn't wait for an answer before saying, "You ain't got a chance in a million of doin' that. There's too many of 'em and all of 'em have been to the dance before."

"I reckon you're right," Cullen admitted.

"I know I'm right," Art insisted. "I'm glad you changed your mind."

"I didn't say that. I just said you're probably right."

"I swear, Cullen," Art blurted, exasperated by the man he had taken a liking to and would like to see ride away from East City still alive. "All this started by the hangin' of a whore you didn't really even know."

"You could say that," Cullen remarked. "We're close enough now. I'll stay here with Jake by these bushes. If it's all clear, gimme a signal out the back door of the barn, and I'll come in and get my possibles."

"If there's nobody there, I'll wave like this." He demonstrated. "If you need to wait a little, I'll give you this sign." He held one arm up with his fist balled. With the signals understood between them, Art hurried off to the stable. Cullen stood in the shade of the trees by the creek, watching the back door of the barn. It seemed Art had barely time to get inside when the door opened partway and he saw the all clear signal. He led Jake a little closer to the barn, looped his reins on a bush, and trotted to the barn. Inside, he found Art waiting for him and the two of them went to the tack room where Cullen's packs were stored. "You want me to bring your pack-horse outta the corral?" Art asked.

"No, I'll leave him here as long as I'm in town," Cullen decided. "I'll just take what I need to get by on in this sack. Jake and I don't wanna be worryin' about a packhorse." The words had just left his mouth when he suddenly held a finger to his lips, having heard the sounds of someone approaching the stable.

"I'll go catch 'em so they don't come in here," Art whispered. "Most likely somebody ready to leave their horses for the night." There was a small window in the tack room wall over a workbench. Taking a cautious peek, he could see the open door of the stable. "Yeah," he whispered again, "it's Shep Parker and Shorty Miller. They're just leavin' their horses." He hurried out into the stable and Cullen could hear him greeting them.

"Shep, Shorty," Art sang out. "You fellers fixin' to call it a day?"

"And not a minute too soon," Shorty answered him. "I need a good drink of likker. You ain't got any, have you, Art?"

"Nope, don't carry no whiskey," Art responded, aware that Shorty was joking. "I know better'n to give the Cork and Bottle any competition."

"Especially right now," Shep commented, looked at Shorty, and they both shook their heads.

"Micah's a little testy right now, is he?" Art asked.

"I reckon you could say that, right enough," Shep replied. "Weren't you here when Ace Brown came back, tied to his horse?"

"I reckon that musta happened while I was gone

home to get me some dinner," Art allowed. "You mean Ace Brown got shot?"

"He damn sure did," Shorty answered.

"Is that a fact? Do you know who done it?"

Both outlaws snorted in response and Shep answered the question. "The same jasper that's doin' all the killin' around here, that McCabe devil. But Micah's ready to smoke him out in the mornin', and it ain't gonna be just one or two going after him. We're all gonna be on this hunt." He got a sharp nudge with an elbow from Shorty, warning him not to say too much. "Ah, hell, Art's all right. Who's he gonna tell? Right, Art?"

"Right as rain," Art said, "and the horses don't talk much, either." He went suddenly tense when Shorty spoke again.

"I need to get my other bridle out of the tack room," he said. "This 'un's irritatin' my horse's mouth. I meant to swap 'em this mornin' and didn't do it."

Doing his best to stay calm, Art blurted, "I'll go get it for you!"

"Ain't no need to do that. We've gotta take our saddles back there, anyway."

"I just thought I'd save you the trouble, so you could get to that drink of whiskey right away," Art sputtered fearfully, while trying to control his panic. He almost choked then, when he saw Cullen calmly walk out of the tack room and up the alley between the stalls. All they had to do was turn around and they couldn't miss seeing him. Knowing Cullen was counting on him to hold their attention, he kept talking. "I ain't doin' nothin' right now. I'd be more'n tickled to tote them saddles to the tack room."

The offer caused them to hesitate only a moment, and Art was relieved to see Cullen disappear into the stall across from the tack room. "That's mighty neighborly of you, Art," Shorty said, "but I wanna find that bridle." He grinned and added, "Maybe you'd better carry Shep's. He's older'n I am and startin' to look a little feeble." It earned a painful expression and a filthy remark from Shep. They picked up their saddles and bridles and headed for the tack room.

Kneeling up close to the side of the stall, his Colt in hand, Cullen could hear the two outlaws talking in the tack room. "I don't know if it's a good idea to talk much in front of Art," Shorty remarked. "I mean, about what Micah's plannin' to do, and stuff like that."

"I reckon," Shep allowed. "But I ain't worried so much about Art. I don't think he pays attention to half of what we say." He dropped his saddle in a corner of the room. "Did Micah say anything to you about watchin' your back when you're with any of the boys that came in with Ned?"

"Yeah," Shorty answered. "I ain't surprised none, either. I've been lookin' for some kind of trouble ever since Ned and his boys joined up with us. Him being used to callin' the shots, and all. It won't surprise me if him and Micah get to buckin' up against each other. And you know Micah, he ain't gonna tolerate no trouble from anybody. He's already got to thinkin' Ned knows more about this McCabe jasper than he lets on about, like how come McCabe always knows when we're comin' after him."

"It does make a body wonder, don't it?" Shep responded. "But I don't know if Ned's that dumb. If

Micah finds out he knows McCabe, it's gonna be Katy bar the door, and that's a fact."

Finished stowing their tack, the two outlaws left the tack room with not even a glance toward the empty stall across from it. They gave Art a casual wave of the hand on their way out of the stable, unaware of the inspiration they had generated in the mind of the man still kneeling in the stall. The greatest obstacle he had been facing was the fact that he was so badly outnumbered in his fight with the marshal and his posse. There was no way he could face the whole lot of them in a shootout. But after hearing Shorty and Shep discussing their problems, he saw a way to reduce the odds. Why not let the outlaws help his situation by killing one another? The only knowledge he had of Micah Moran and his posse was what he had learned from Art and a few others in town. But it was easy to figure him as a gang leader wary of any challenge to his leadership and quick to put down any threat of defiance. The thing to do now was to think of a way to plant the thought of an actual threat into Moran's head without his knowing where it came from. *I'll have to think about it*, Cullen thought, holstered his Colt, and left the stall.

He met Art on his way out of the stalls. He was coming from the stable door after having gone outside to make sure Shep and Shorty were on their way to the Cork and Bottle. "I swear, a feller could have himself a nervous breakdown if he hung around with you very long," Art declared. "First, Leroy Hill, then this with Shorty and Shep. All they had to do was for one of 'em to turn around."

"I figured I could count on you to hold their attention," Cullen said. "Now, tell me about the fellow they were talking about in the tack room. Ned was his name."

"Ned Larson," Art stated. "Whaddaya wanna know about him?"

"Anything you can tell me," Cullen replied. So Art told him everything he had learned about Ned Larson. And by the time he had finished, Cullen had a pretty good picture of the man. "So he had his own gang of rustlers over in east Texas," Cullen remarked. "Now, he's ridin' as just another hand for Micah Moran."

"That's right," Art said. "And I've heard a little of that talk from some of the other men. They say it was Ned who told Micah to send Ace out to Hortense's house to get you. And they're curious as to how you were in Ravenwood waitin' for Polek and Barr. The bad thing about that is it makes it a big deal about which one of 'em finally gets you. And they figure one of 'em is, sooner or later. You oughta think about that, Cullen."

"You're right, but I'm thinkin' about something else right now." He was trying to come up with a way to make Moran certain that Ned Larson was working with Cullen McCabe to take over his men. "I'd best move along now before somebody else comes in and catches me in town. That wouldn't be good for either one of us. I need to go scout me out a place to set up a camp. I don't wanna get too far from the boardin'-house, in case there's some trouble there." He paused at the back door of the barn when an idea struck him. "Do you go to the Cork and Bottle when you want a drink?"

"Lord, no," Art exclaimed at once. "I don't ever set foot in that place. If I want a drink, I get it at O'Sullivan's, where the rest of the honest men drink."

His answer gave Cullen pause for a few moments, then he asked another question. "Talking about the honest men, and honest businesses, Moran and his men have to go to the other businesses to buy whatever they need. Where would that be? The general store, maybe?"

"I s'pose so," Art replied, wondering what Cullen was getting at. "Even a damn outlaw has to go to the store. He just don't always pay for what he buys," he felt inspired to say, "but the store's the only place to get cigars and tobacco, whatever he needs."

"What's the fellow's name that owns the general store?" Cullen asked. "Is he the kind of man that ain't afraid to take a little chance to try to rid East City of some of its undesirable people?"

"Joe Johnson?" Art responded. "Well, yeah, I reckon he might be. Like the rest of us, he figures it's only a matter of time before all the honest men are gonna be forced to leave."

"I've got something in mind I'd like to try, but I need your help and I need Johnson's help." He laid out the plan he had in mind and Art readily agreed to do his part, since there wasn't a lot of risk involved. He wasn't sure about Johnson, however, but said he'd sound him out on it. "Might not work at all," Cullen said, "but you never know."

As Moran had threatened, he ordered all his posse out of bed and mounted before breakfast the morning after Cullen and Art agreed on a plan. The fact that every one of the marshal's posse would be out of town, with the exception of Stan Molloy, made it more convenient for Art to present Cullen's plan to Joe

Johnson. Moran named Molloy as his new deputy and left him with the responsibility to keep his one eye on the town. Art was just doing his morning chores at the stable when the gang of men arrived to saddle up. As soon as they left, he trotted down the footpath to alert Hortense and the others that Moran was coming to call. Micah Moran was not with the posse when they came to the stable, but Leroy Hill was assigned the extra chore of saddling the marshal's horse. Art was sure he would get to the boarding-house in time to warn them, due to the fact that the footpath was a shortcut, plus the time it would take to pick Moran up.

"All of 'em?" Hortense exclaimed, and she and Annie exchanged concerned glances. "They're coming here looking for Cullen again?" When Art nodded emphatically, she continued. "Why can't they get it in their thick heads that Cullen doesn't have a room here?" She looked at him for an answer, but when he didn't have one, she said, "Well, since the marshal, himself, is coming to call on us, we'll have to be as polite as we can, and let him search the place. Maybe, if he sees for himself that McCabe ain't here, he'll leave us alone after this." She shook her head, exasperated, and pointed toward the table. "You'd better sit down and eat your breakfast while you've got the chance. Everybody else has finished."

They rode into the yard like a cavalry patrol. Moran rode up to the front porch while his men split up and rode around both sides of the house to meet again behind the house. Moran didn't bother to knock and walked right in the front door, where he was met by

Hortense in the parlor. "Well, good morning to ya, Marshal. What's the occasion for the visit on this fine summer morning? If you've brought your posse for breakfast, I'm afraid it'll be a little wait. When you're bringing this many for a meal, I need some notice, so I can prepare enough food." She heard a couple of his men coming in the back door then, led by Ned Larson. One of the men exchanged words with Art, who was still finishing his breakfast.

"I expect you know why I'm here," Moran said. "I'm lookin' for Cullen McCabe, and if I have to, I'll have my men tear this house to the ground to find him."

"There's no Cullen McCabe rooming in this house," Hortense said. "He stayed here one night, three nights ago, but he said he was just passing through, so I imagine he's long gone from East City." She paused when Ned, Shorty, and Duke Ledbetter came in from the kitchen. "But you're welcome to search the whole house, if that's what you want. Mr. Becker has just come back from his stable to eat his breakfast. The only other guest here is Mr. Skelton. He doesn't work anymore. Mr. Pearson and Mr. George have gone to work. You may have met them on your way in from town. So you can go right ahead and search the house."

Moran turned toward the three men standing there. "Anything?" he asked, knowing there was nothing.

"Some of the boys are still tearin' that little barn apart," Ned answered. "Ain't a sign of him anywhere. If he was stayin' there, he didn't leave a trace of it. Leroy and Billy checked the outhouse. He ain't hidin' there. We even looked down at the hog lot, just in case he was visitin' his relatives."

"Go ahead and search upstairs," Moran said, "and

damn it, I mean search, any place a man could hide. Look for clothes or a bedroll."

"They know, of course, that my other men guests have clothes and personal items in their rooms. I hope your men will remember that when they're searching." Moran ignored her remarks and simply signaled his men to go upstairs with a nod in that direction. "Maybe you would like a cup of coffee while your men are searching the house," Hortense offered politely.

"Yeah, I'll take a cup of coffee," Moran replied, and followed her to the kitchen.

They found Annie standing by the stove, holding a poker in her hand. She gave Hortense an inquisitive look when Moran came in behind her. "Marshal Moran would like a cup of coffee," Hortense announced, "while his men are searching the house for Mr. McCabe." When Annie looked dumbfounded, Hortense said, "You remember Mr. McCabe, that big, polite man who stayed with us one night."

"Yeah, I remember him," Annie said, her voice lacking the syrupy sweetness that Hortense affected. She looked at Moran and said, "Set down at the table, yonder, and I'll pour you a cup. There ain't nothin' left to eat, though."

"I'll just take it right here," Moran said, well aware of the show the two women were trying to put on for him. "That way, there's a lot less chance of somethin' droppin' in it by accident." He watched her while she poured it, then took it from her.

Art Becker came into the kitchen then. He had been outside watching Moran's men search. He was not quick enough to disguise the look of surprise he displayed when he saw Moran in the kitchen drinking coffee. "Well, I reckon I'd best be gettin' back to the stable, now that I've had my breakfast. Anything you need from me, Marshal?"

"Maybe you can tell me where your friend Cullen McCabe is. I've got a powerful interest in that mystery man. He rode into my town and folks started dying of lead poisonin'. And it's my job to keep the citizens of East City safe from men like him."

"I swear, Marshal, he ain't no friend of mine," Art declared. "Where'd you ever get an idea like that? He kept his horse in my stable one night, and ain't paid me for it yet. No, sir, I don't know nothin' about his whereabouts. I expect he's long gone from East City. There's too many folks lookin' for him." He turned back toward the door. "I'd best get to work," he said, and was gone.

The search went on for over an hour with no sign that the man they searched for had been there. With no alternative but to admit the hunt was in vain, Moran finally ordered it to stop. "All right, we might as well mount up and get on back to town. We're wasting our time here." The men gladly climbed on their horses, thinking more about getting back to the Cork and Bottle and the breakfast they had given up for this worthless raid. Moran put his empty cup on the corner of the table and looked Hortense in the eye. "If he shows up here again, I'm gonna expect you to let me know. It ain't safe for you if he's in this house. That man's murdered three good men right here in this town. He won't think nothin' about killin' a woman."

"I'll keep that in mind," Hortense said, her eyes meeting his gaze defiantly. He turned and walked out. The two women went to the window and watched until the marshal and his posse of hoodlums rode out of sight.

They turned to see Roy Skelton come in from the outhouse. "Least, they didn't beat none of us up this time," he said.

Hortense looked at Annie, who was still holding the poker in her hand. "Whaddaya still hanging on to that for?"

"'Cause, I was fixin' to lay him among the sweet peas, if he tried to lay a hand on me," she said. Her treatment on previous visits from members of Moran's posse was still fresh in her mind.

"I believe you would have," Hortense said. Then she went over to the corner of the table, picked up the empty coffee cup, and held it up for Annie and Roy to see. Then she threw it against the iron stove as hard as she could, smashing it in pieces. "Nobody in this house will ever have to worry about drinking after that lowlife," she declared.

"Amen," Annie seconded. "I'll sweep it up."

CHAPTER 10

Leroy Hill walked up to the counter in the general store and threw a quarter on it. "Gimme a couple of plugs of that chawin' tobacco," he said.

"Which brand do you want?" Joe Johnson asked. "I got two, and I don't remember which one you usually get." He started to call out the brand names, but Leroy interrupted.

"Gimme the one with the picture of an apple on the package," Leroy said. Since he couldn't read or write, calling out the names wouldn't help. Then, when Joe turned back to the shelves, Leroy stuck a dirty paw in the jar of hard candy on the counter and helped himself to a handful. Moran had ordered the men to pay for their incidental needs in order to show some sense of lawfulness. But to a natural-born thief like Leroy, that order didn't apply to whatever you could steal without being caught at it. He stuck the candy in his pocket, unaware his theft was observed by Doris Johnson, who was standing in the back corner, arranging a display of bandannas. She shook her head in disgust for his sneakiness but said nothing. Just like the apples the late deputy Ace Brown used to help himself to, it was the cost of doing business in East City.

Joe turned around and placed two plugs of chewing tobacco on the counter and picked up the money Leroy had left there. "Will that be all?" he asked, and glanced back at his wife, who was still shaking her head. He nodded, signaling to her, and she started walking casually toward the counter. "I remember how you like that hard candy there," Joe said, pointing toward the jar, which was considerably less than full, and Doris had filled it that morning. "You need some more? Ain't but a penny for three of 'em."

"Nah, I reckon not," Leroy replied. "I reckon the stuff they put in my chawin' tobacco is enough to satisfy my sweet tooth." He started to leave, but Doris stopped him.

"Is this something you dropped out of your pocket?" She made a show of bending down to pick up a piece of brown paper that looked to be torn from a paper bag. "Might be something important." Leroy glanced at it, already certain it was not something he had dropped. Knowing he couldn't read, Doris said, "Let's see what's written on it." Then she read, "'Ned, what are we waiting for?' And it's signed, 'McCabe.'" She looked at Leroy, who was staring back at her with eyes and mouth wide open. "Well, I guess you didn't drop it. Ned Larson must have dropped it when he was in here before. I'll just hang on to it and maybe he'll be back in sometime soon."

"No, no, ma'am!" Leroy blurted, excitedly. "I'll take it to him. Just give it to me." He snatched the paper out of her hand, turned at once, and hurried to the door.

Behind him, Joe and Doris exchanged uncertain

glances. "Well, that went just like we hoped it would," Joe commented. "We'll tell Art that the fish took the bait, but I reckon we'll have to wait and see if it does what he thinks it will do."

"I'm a little afraid Ned Larson might take it out on us, if that simpleton gives him that note," she said, her face now a frown.

"I don't see how," Joe tried to reassure her. "We just found the note. Anybody coulda dropped it in here." He shrugged. "Besides, ol' Leroy, there, is gonna take that message straight to Micah Moran. Leroy's one of Moran's boys. That's why we were lucky he came in the store. We couldn't have picked a better one." He looked at her and grinned. "I especially thought that was a nice touch you made with part of a footprint on that note."

"Well, I had to make it look like it had been dropped on the floor." She could tell by her husband's attitude that he was feeling good about the part they were playing in the scheme to split the marshal's posse into opposing sides. The trick they were hoping to pull might not work as planned. Even if it didn't, it gave him a sense of fighting back. And like the other honest merchants in East City, it was a feeling they needed. She hoped with all her heart that, somehow, the miracle would happen. She shrugged and smiled. "Wouldn't it be something, if this fellow, McCabe, just happened to be the spark this town needed?"

The spark Doris Johnson had referred to was never so bright as the one that lit a raging fire in the veins of Micah Moran. When Leroy had charged into the Cork and Bottle, where Moran was sitting with a couple

of the members of the posse, he went straight to the
marshal, holding the message out to him. Puzzled,
Moran took it from him and glanced at it. In less
than a second after, his teeth were clenched in anger,
the note crumpled in his closed fist. Looking around
him at the lounging men, he seemed to be suspicious
of every one of them. Then he got to his feet, knocking his chair over in the process. His heavy eyebrows
lowered over his dark eyes like storm clouds building,
and he grabbed Leroy by the arm. "Come on," he ordered, and walked him toward the privacy of the
storeroom in the back of the saloon.

Closing the door behind them, Moran spun Leroy
around and demanded, "Where did you get this?"
Leroy wished at that moment that someone else had
found the message. Judging by Moran's rage, he
thought he was being blamed for its existence. As
quickly as he could manage to get the words out, he
told him that it had been found on the floor of the
general store, that Mrs. Johnson thought he had
dropped it, but he certainly didn't. When he got to
the part where she read it and said she'd keep it and
give it to Ned, Moran said, "You done the right thing.
It's good you brought it to me. You tell anybody else
about it?"

"No, sir," Leroy responded. "I came straight to you."

"Good," Moran said again, his mind already working. With confirmation for what he had recently come
to suspect, he was deciding what steps to take first.
Ned must die, and he would take special delight in
personally taking care of that. But first, he had to
know if any of his men were thinking of siding with
Ned. He had to assume that Ned's three men were all
in the takeover with Ned. He had to know whom he

could depend on in the final shootout. His initial feeling was that it would be a shootout between two gangs, Larson's and his. That reasoning was backed up by the actions of Cullen McCabe. The initial thought he had on the killings of his men pointed that way. For it seemed obvious that McCabe's job was to trim the numbers down to Ned's advantage. Moran had been right all along. Ned Larson was the dangerous one, but McCabe still had to be accounted for. He was Ned's assassin. Moran knew that it was critical that he and his men make the move before Ned did. And it had to be done fast, judging by the note crumpled in his hand. Already, this assassin, McCabe, was asking when they would strike. He opened his fist and straightened the paper out so he could read it again. The time to act was now. With that decision made, he said to Leroy, "I'm goin' up to my room. I want you to go get Shorty, Shep, and Molloy, and bring 'em up to my room. Don't tell anybody why you're doin' it. Understand?" Leroy said that he did. "I don't want any of Ned's boys to know we're onto 'em. All right, get goin'." He followed Leroy out the door of the storeroom and went directly to the stairs, feeling now that a bullet could come his way at any time. He wasn't worried about a direct face-off with Ned or any of the other three, because he knew he was faster with his six-gun. He knew it, and they knew it, and it was one of the reasons he was never challenged as the boss.

As instructed, Leroy walked over to the table where Shep and Molloy were sitting, nursing a bottle of corn whiskey. He told them that Micah wanted them up in his room right away, and not to ask any questions, just go on upstairs. Shorty, however, was sitting at a table with Steve Tatum and Billy Fish. Leroy paused to consider that, but decided he'd best do as Micah ordered. So, he walked up behind Shorty and leaned over his shoulder to whisper in his ear. Feeling him suddenly hovering over him, Shorty jumped, thinking it was one of the saloon women. When he saw who it was, he blurted, "What the hell are you doin', Leroy? Get offa me."

"I was tryin' to tell you somethin'," Leroy said.

"Well, tell me, then," Shorty replied. "Don't be blowin' in my ear like that. Hell, I thought it was Wilma wantin' to take me upstairs."

"Hell, I don't think Wilma ever gets that desperate," Billy joked. It was good for a laugh, but it only frustrated Leroy.

"Damn it," he said, "Micah wants to see you upstairs right now." He turned then and headed for the stairs without waiting to see if Shorty was coming after him.

"Yeah, you better get up there," Steve was quick to join in the japing.

One who was not, Ned Larson thought it was kind of odd that Moran wanted a meeting with only "his boys." So he called after Leroy, "Leroy, does he want the rest of us up there?"

Leroy paused long enough to answer. "Nope, he just said them three."

"Well, what's it all about? Did he say?" Ned asked. Leroy replied that he didn't. It struck Ned as more than strange. Anytime before this, if there was something to talk over, it was always with the whole gang, not just the men he had brought to the posse. Feeling a need for caution now, he told the three remaining, "Somethin's goin' on with Micah, and I ain't sure it's gonna be good for the four of us. Might be nothin', but he's been actin' jumpy as hell ever since that

McCabe jasper showed up. So I'm tellin' you boys to pay attention to what any of 'em might be up to." His warning was received with expressions of total astonishment from the three men who had ridden with him in east Texas. There had always been a feeling of competition between Ned and Micah, but never to the effect that there was any question regarding who was calling the shots for the combined gangs. When Ned saw the obvious puzzlement in their faces, he said, "Just keep your eyes open and be ready for anything. I got a feelin' somethin' ain't right with Micah." A witness to all this, bartender Floyd Chandler was not quite sure what was going to happen. He felt he owed his allegiance to Micah, since he was his employer, but there was nothing he could do to warn him without risking getting shot, himself.

In the private meeting upstairs, there was a similar reaction of confusion as Micah Moran smoothed out the crumpled piece of paper bag with the message written to Ned on it. "Now you know why that damn McCabe knew when anybody was comin' after him. He's in cahoots with Ned and them boys all along, and him and Ned's figurin' on takin' over after he shoots me in the back."

The four men gathered in the room were shocked speechless at first. This possibility of revolt came as a complete surprise, for any sense of competition among them was restricted to Micah and Ned. The rest of the men got along fine, as long as all were enjoying the power they held over an entire town. After a few moments of silence, Shep was the first to comment. "Damn, Micah," he drawled, "we ain't had no idea that them boys weren't nothin' but straight shooters." He turned to look at the others. "Ain't that right, boys?" They all nodded in agreement. Back to Micah then, he asked, "What are we gonna do?"

"I reckon the first thing I wanna know is which one of us are you boys backin', me or Ned Larson?"

"Hell, Micah," Shorty spoke up at once. "You oughta know you don't have to ask us that question. We've been ridin' with you from the first, and we're settin' in pretty good shape right here in East City. And we wouldn't be if it wasn't for you. Ain't that right, boys?" His question was met with enthusiastic grunts of agreement.

"All right," Micah said, "that's what I wanted to know." Still he wanted to be sure. "Ain't none of 'em said anything about this to any of you? Billy or Duke? They always think any idea Ned has is the best one." All four shook their heads in answer. "Good, then it's time we stomp this snake before it has a chance to strike."

"You just tell us how you wanna play this hand," Molloy said. "You're the boss." The other three nodded in agreement.

"Well, I've been studyin' this possibility for a little while, even before we found this message," Moran said. "I'm thinkin' that it's Ned that's wantin' to take over this posse, but maybe Steve and Billy and Duke might just be satisfied to ride with whichever one of us comes out on top." Moran had concerns about the loss of too many of his men, thinking it might weaken his hold on the town. Otherwise, he wouldn't have bothered to take the risk. He would just give his boys the word and they would go downstairs blazing away and take all of them down. He decided to call Ned out to face him in a showdown, thinking that would demonstrate to all the men, his and Ned's, that he was an honorable man. He didn't consider it a risk on his part, since he already knew who was the fastest draw.

His decision made, he gave his final instructions. "We'll go back downstairs now, and I'll return Ned's message to him. Then I'm gonna challenge him to face me to decide who's the boss of this posse. An election by bullets, that's the only fair way to do it. I want you boys to fan out, so you can keep an eye on the other three. Make sure none of 'em wants to help Ned out."

"All right, everybody keep alert till we know what Micah's up to," Ned cautioned when he heard them coming back downstairs.

Micah paused briefly when he noticed a difference in the positioning of Ned's three men. While Ned sat at a table, facing the stairs, Billy and Steve were leaning casually on the bar, while Duke sat at another table off to the side of Ned's. Behind the bar, Floyd was all the way back to the far end. It struck Micah as an odd arrangement for four men at their ease and having a drink. All the more evidence in a plot against him, as far as he was concerned.

Ned Larson watched with considerable interest as the men descended the stairs and casually fanned out in the barroom, none of them taking a seat. "What's goin' on, Micah?" Ned asked. "You boys havin' some kind of secret meetin' upstairs?"

Moran didn't answer until he came down the stairs. "Oh, we was just havin' a little discussion about the way things have been goin' lately. Then we decided to bring you this little message you musta lost somewhere." He held the piece of paper sack up for him to see, watching him closely for his reaction. "Reckon you musta dropped it last time you was in the general store. And whaddaya know? Leroy found it layin' on the floor."

"What are you talkin' about, Micah?" Ned reacted, obviously puzzled.

"Here," Moran said to Leroy, "hand this to him. Then maybe he'll remember it.

Leroy took the note and gave it to Ned, who quickly glanced at the writing on the piece of brown paper, torn from a bag. Then he read it again more closely. "What the hell?" he uttered in disbelief. "I never saw this message before. I didn't drop it."

"You didn't?" Moran asked, obviously sarcastic. "Maybe the person who was supposed to give it to you dropped it before you got a chance to see it. That was kinda unlucky, weren't it? For you and your friend McCabe. He's wantin' to know what you're waitin' for. I'd kinda like to know that myself."

"Whoa! Wait a minute!" Ned exclaimed. "I don't know what the hell's goin' on here. I don't know McCabe. I ain't ever seen him but once, that day he came in here, and I sure as hell ain't ever talked to him. You're the only one who's ever talked to him." He looked around frantically, looking for some explanation. "Hell, Micah, anybody coulda wrote that message. Leroy's the one who brought it to you. How do you know he didn't write it?"

"'Cause Leroy can't write," Moran answered smugly. "Seems to me you got caught in the trap you was settin', and I expect you're gonna have to answer for it. And right now is as good a time as any."

"Now, hold on, Micah, this is all a mistake. I don't know nothin' about this McCabe message." Then another thought struck him. "Maybe he did try to get it to me, but maybe what he was doin' was callin' me out. Look at it, he says 'what are we waitin' for?' He might be tryin' to say he's wantin' to see if I'll shoot it out with him."

"Well, now, that is another way to look at it, ain't it?" Moran allowed, enjoying Ned's obvious squirming at this point. "Ain't it funny, though, I mean how he knew your name was Ned, and why he didn't pick me to draw against? He knows I'm the boss, and he knows my name 'cause I told him my name. You musta told him you was plannin' to be the boss of this gang."

Desperate now, for he knew he could not beat Moran in a fast-draw competition, Ned looked to his men for support. "Billy, you know there ain't nothin' goin' on between me and McCabe. Right? All of you know that. Right?"

"Nothin' I know about," Billy answered, not sure how far Moran was planning to go with this showdown and whether or not he, Steve, and Duke should be worried as well.

Of the three from the east Texas gang, Duke Ledbetter had known Ned the longest, and he had never thought of him as anything but fair, so he felt a responsibility to speak up for him. "I don't think Ned's mixed up in nothin' with Cullen McCabe. That damn message is a trick you're usin' to turn us against him."

"And I reckon you ain't mixed up in nothin' with McCabe, neither," Moran said. He glared back at Ned then. "Time for talkin's over. Get on your feet, Ned, or take it settin' in that chair."

Everyone in the saloon became tense at that. What had been one gang, one posse, suddenly became two opposing sides. Floyd ducked down behind the bar. Wilma and Mabel scrambled in behind him. The man with the most to lose was Ned Larson. To go up against Micah Moran was akin to suicide, and Ned knew that better than anybody. His options were to turn belly-up like a whipped dog and beg for his life, or to pray for that one moment in time when he bucked the odds. He decided it was better to go out like a man, than to live with the shame of cowardice. He got to his feet. "All right, Micah, but you're dead wrong on this."

"If I am," Moran said, "then you'll be the one standin' when the smoke clears." Ned walked out in the center of the room, poised to duel. Moran stepped over to square up with him. "When you're ready," he said, and stood waiting.

After a few seconds that seemed like minutes, Ned made his move. He succeeded in clearing his .44 from his holster, but Moran's bullet struck him in the gut before he could raise the weapon to fire. Seeing Ned double over, dropping his pistol, Duke drew his six-gun, only to be cut down by Shep Parker, who had anticipated such a reaction. The chain reaction continued when Steve Tatum shot Shep and was promptly cut down by a second shot from Moran.

Billy Fish promptly extended his hands in the air when he saw four guns pointed at him. Stunned by what had just happened, he tried to make sense of it, but was unable to understand how it could have come to this. Ned had warned them that Moran was acting very strange recently, but Billy could not have imagined it would come to this. Of the three of them who had followed Ned here to join Micah Moran's band of outlaws, he alone was standing. And Ned was curled up on the floor, moaning as he lay dying. "I don't know where that message came from," Billy finally managed. "Didn't none of us know anything about

Cullen McCabe. If Ned hadda been talkin' to McCabe, he woulda told us about it."

"What about the note?" Molloy asked him.

"I don't know," Billy replied, and dropped his hands. An instant later, he was struck by four bullets, fired almost like one single shot. He dropped on the floor beside Ned, shot dead.

"Damn," Molloy swore. "When he dropped his hands, I thought he was goin' for his gun." He grinned and reached up to adjust his eye patch.

"I reckon we all did," Shorty said, "since he's got four bullet holes in him. Maybe we shoulda waited to see what he had to say. He always seemed like he was one of us. I didn't ever have no trouble with Billy."

"I swear," Leroy remarked, "I wouldn'ta thought any of them boys was thinkin' about double-crossin' us, especially Billy."

"It's better this way," Moran was quick to reassure them. "We'da never been able to trust him anymore. We couldn't ever be sure that he wasn't in it up to his eyeteeth, just like the rest of 'em. We'll see what happens around here now, see if we hear anythin' more outta McCabe since he ain't got Ned and the other boys to count on."

"If he's got any brains a-tall, he'll just move on and try to find him another strawberry patch to land in," Leroy said. He couldn't help thinking about the message McCabe told him to deliver to Moran, that the days of East City as a place for outlaws were coming to an end. He said a company of Rangers might be permanently based there. Moran would be plenty hot if he heard that. Leroy wished he could tell him what McCabe threatened, but he couldn't without having to explain how he got the message to deliver.

"Might as well get these bodies outta here," Moran ordered. "Strip 'em down and get everythin' that's worth anythin', and we'll divide it up later."

The sudden eruption of gunfire that rang out from the Cork and Bottle caused a wave of concern among the honest citizens of East City. It was not at all unusual to hear a random shot here and there in the town run by outlaws. But this burst of gunfire was enough to worry everyone with a business to operate, with three exceptions. When Art Becker heard the uproar inside the Cork and Bottle, he hurried up the street to Joe and Doris Johnson's general store. "Did you hear that?" Art blurted when he ran in the door. "It sounds like hell broke loose in that saloon."

"We'd have to be deaf not to," Doris replied. "I wonder what happened in there."

"I know what happened," Art declared. "Leroy delivered that note to the marshal, just like Cullen McCabe said he would. I'm just waitin' to see how many got shot."

"I hope Moran doesn't come down here to give us some trouble, if Leroy told him this is where he got that message," Doris said. "He's such a simpleton, there's no telling what he might have said."

"I wouldn't worry about that," her husband reassured her. "With that footprint on it, it looked obvious that somebody dropped it on the floor. And Leroy saw you pick it up off the floor."

"Joe's right," Art said, and walked out to the boardwalk out front to watch the front door of the Cork and Bottle. Joe followed him out. They found they were not the only curious citizens. Looking up the street, they saw Abe Franks in front of the hardware store. Beyond him, there were several people outside O'Sullivan's Saloon, including Cary O'Sullivan. Looking down the street, they saw Buck Casey, the blacksmith. All eyes were staring toward the Cork and Bottle, and all faces carrying the look of deep concern.

Seeing Art and the Johnsons standing in front of their store, Abe Franks walked down to join them. "Now, what do you suppose they're up to?" Abe called out as he walked up. "Anybody know what that shooting was all about? It sounded like a war broke out in there."

Joe and Art exchanged uncertain glances, wondering if they should confess to their involvement. It was Joe who spoke first. "You think we oughta tell the mayor?"

When Art didn't respond right away, Abe asked, "Tell me what?"

Art gave Joe another glance and they both shrugged, so Art said, "I reckon it's safe to tell the mayor what we *think* just happened in the Cork and Bottle." He turned directly to Abe and continued. "We think the shootin' we just heard was the thinnin' out of Marshal Moran's posse goin' on. What we're watchin' for now is to see how many bodies we can count and who's left we gotta put up with." When Abe asked what led him to that conclusion, Art glanced again at Joe and Doris. They both nodded their approval, so Art went on to tell Abe of the hoax the three of them had concocted, with Leroy Hill the scapegoat: "And from the sounds comin' out of that saloon," Art concluded, "it just mighta worked like McCabe said it would."

"McCabe?" Abe questioned. "What's he got to do with it?"

"It was McCabe's idea," Art answered.

The mayor clearly didn't understand. He knew very little about the man called McCabe. Like most of the other folks outside the Cork and Bottle, he had heard the name, but mentioned only as a stranger who brought the whore Lila Blanchard back after she had run away. "McCabe?" Abe repeated. "I thought he was another one of that herd of gunmen who drift through here. Brought that prostitute back for Marshal Moran to hang for a horse thief, is what I understand. And Moran put the word out that McCabe is responsible for the parade of dead men on horses we've had riding through our town. We certainly don't need another gunman to join the outlaw we've got for a marshal."

Johnson looked to Art again to explain, since Art had spent considerably more time with the mysterious Cullen McCabe. Truth be told, Joe and Doris weren't totally sure they were not dealing with another devil, come to destroy their town. "McCabe ain't a gunman. He works for some big cattle company—in Fort Worth, I think," Art said. "He's just passin' through this part of Texas, lookin' over the grass and water possibilities." Even as he said it, he found it hard to believe the story he was telling. "Anyway," he continued, "he didn't bring Lila Blanchard back to be hanged. He found her between here and Austin, down and out, without no food. She had run away from a kidnapper who was fixin' to kill her—took his horse to get away from him. Cullen brought her back here, and the horse, too. Hangin' her for a horse thief was Moran's idea."

"Huh," Abe snorted, still not convinced that Art's judgement of the man was accurate. "What about the dead men roped to their horses to parade down the street? One of 'em was the deputy marshal, for goodness' sakes."

"I don't know, Abe," Art declared. "Ain't nobody come forward and said they saw McCabe shoot anybody." He knew for a fact that he did, but he saw no point in admitting that. "I'll tell you the truth, Cullen McCabe is on our side, and he's willin' to help us drive the outlaws outta East City."

Abe was still unconvinced. He had seen too many outlaws on the run come riding into town and going to the Cork and Bottle. "I hope you're right, Art, but I can't understand the man's motive for helping the people of East City. What does he expect to gain by it?"

The debate was interrupted then when a horse and wagon pulled up to a stop in front of the Cork and Bottle. Art strained to see who was driving the wagon. "Leroy Hill," he announced aloud. "Looks like he helped himself to my wagon and a horse." It was not unusual that he did. Most of the posse used his stable as if it belonged to them. He turned toward Joe Johnson and winked. "Looks like they need a wagon to tote 'em up to the graveyard." They stood there and counted the bodies being carried out and loaded on the wagon, calling off the number as each corpse was piled on. When the count reached the number five, that was the end of it. When they were finished, Shorty Miller climbed up on the wagon seat with Leroy, and they moved away toward the graveyard. "Five of 'em!" Art exclaimed. "And that last one looked like it mighta been Ned Larson—hard to tell from here."

"I didn't see any of them that looked like Micah Moran," Abe said. "There's five less, but we've still got Moran to deal with, so I don't think we're that much better off."

"I reckon it's gonna take a miracle for us to ever get rid of all the outlaws and have a peaceful town," Joe offered. "The biggest mistake we made was moving over here on this side of the creek. We shoulda stayed over there in Ravenwood, but I can't afford to move back now. We need to build another bridge and learn to get along with Ravenwood, and that ain't gonna happen unless we get an honest lawman over here."

"I've got a little more hope than I had before," Art claimed. "I'm thinkin' that shootout in the Cork and Bottle just now looks like a step in the right direction." He grinned at Joe. "That miracle you're wishin' for might be ridin' a bay horse named Jake."

CHAPTER 11

During the time when Micah Moran was eliminating Ned Larson as his chief competition, Cullen was in the process of establishing a camp for himself. The foliage along both sides of Walnut Creek was thick enough to provide reasonable coverage for just one man and one horse. After looking at several possible choices, he decided to make his camp where a tiny stream emptied into the creek. There was not a great deal of grass for Jake, but it was adequate for the short time he planned to stay there.

Since he now had the means to do so, he decided to build a fire and make some coffee to drink with some beef jerky from his packs. It was time to think about his next step, but he wasn't really sure what it should be. It would depend a great deal on whether or not Art took that message to Joe Johnson, and whether or not Johnson had the nerve to pass it along to one of Moran's men. Then it would depend on whether or not it got to Moran. If it did, he could only imagine how he would react. Based upon his initial impression of the marshal, he would bet he would react violently. He knew he should be extra cautious about going back to Hortense's boardinghouse, but it was the best way to check with Art Becker for a report on the bait they sent Moran. *What the hell*, he thought, *nobody lives forever*, and decided to risk a visit to Hortense's supper table. With that in mind, he put his coffeepot and jerky back in his war bag, thinking he'd wait and get a good supper at the boarding-house. There was still a little time before the usual suppertime at the house, so he decided to use it to take a thorough scout around it before riding in. He had to be concerned with the possibility that Moran had men watching the house in the event he did show up again.

He rode Jake slowly along the west creek bank until he was within about one hundred yards of the little shed that served as a barn for Hortense's guests. He stopped there and took a long look around before turning his horse a little farther west to take a wide circle around the house. As he started to cross over to the east side of the creek, he pulled up suddenly when he caught sight of movement through the bushes along the footpath on that side. Deer or horse, he couldn't be certain. He backed Jake up to make sure he wasn't spotted, then focused his gaze on a spot farther along the path where the bushes weren't so thick. In a few seconds, he saw him. Neither deer nor horse, it was Art, on foot, coming home for supper.

He was tempted to call out to him and tell him he came close to being shot for a deer, but he wasn't ready to reveal his presence just yet. First, he wanted to make sure Art wasn't being followed. So he re-mained where he was for a few minutes more, until he felt reasonably sure no one was trailing Art. When he was satisfied that no one was behind Art on the

THE SCAVENGERS 151

path, he crossed over to that side of the creek and continued his careful circle around the house. He took extra caution when he crossed over the lane leading to the road from town, in front of the house, because of the likelihood that a spy would approach from that direction. When he completed his circle, he left Jake by the edge of the creek and walked to the back door.

"Got enough for one more?" he asked when he eased the kitchen door open far enough to stick his head in, causing Annie to start. He apologized immediately. "Sorry, I didn't mean to startle you like that."

"Cullen McCabe!" Annie exclaimed. "You almost made me dump these potatoes on the floor. What are you doin' sneakin' in the kitchen door like that?" As soon as she said it, she followed it with, "I reckon you ain't likely to come marchin' in the front, though, at that. Well, come on in, I've got plenty of food."

"I apologize again, and I will surely appreciate eatin' some of your cookin'. Of course, I'll pay for it, since I'm not a payin' guest anymore."

"You can take that up with Hortense, but I doubt she'll charge you. You know you're always welcome here. I was just fixin' to put it on the table. You need to go on in there and hear all about the big gunfight in town today."

"Much obliged, Annie," he said, and walked into the dining room to find Art, Martin Pearson, and Franklin George telling Hortense and Roy Skelton all about the incident at the Cork and Bottle that day. They were all startled to see Cullen come in the door.

"Cullen!" Art exclaimed. "You're just the man I wanna see! It went just like you said it would. There's five less of those vultures. We counted the bodies when they carried 'em out." He went on to tell Cullen the whole story on how the message got in the hands of Micah Moran. "Course, Moran came out on top. That is, aside from the fact he lost five of his posse. But they killed Ned Larson and the three men that came with him from his old gang. Moran didn't lose but one of his, Shep Parker."

Martin Pearson spoke up then. "The one called Molloy, that tall, lanky one with the eye patch, he came by the feed store just before I left for supper. He said he was the new deputy, takin' Ace Brown's place and he'd be keepin' an eye on the town from now on." He paused then said, "The one behind his eye patch, if he's anything like Ace Brown was."

It was the news Cullen wanted to hear. His plan had worked better than he had expected. But when Art asked him what he was going to do now, he could only answer, "I don't know yet." It was a problem cut in half, but it was still a helluva problem. Micah Moran alone was a dangerous undertaking. Micah Moran and three gunmen was even worse. He didn't like the idea of turning to the role of assassin to solve the town's problem with a series of sniper shots. That might solve the immediate problem, but there was the chance that it would simply leave East City open for another outlaw to move in and take over where Moran left off. And that was a definite possibility, thanks to East City's reputation as a haven for outlaws. What was needed was a tough, honest marshal to take the responsibility for keeping the law.

When he didn't say more about his plans, Art had to say, "I figured you'd be movin' on to wherever you was goin' when you first got here. For somebody just passin' through, you've done a helluva lot of damage to Moran and his gang. But you've got a bigger target on your back now than you did before. Course, he don't know it was your idea that caused him to kill half his own gang of murderers. But he's convinced it was you that done in Brown, Boot, and Charley. And Molloy told him it was you that done for Johnny Barr and Sam Polek over in Ravenwood."

"I still ain't figured out why you hung around here in the first place," Roy Skelton felt the need to comment.

Because Micah Moran hanged a whore, Art thought, but didn't say it. Instead, he answered for Cullen, "Because he got a taste of Annie's cookin' and he's wantin' more of it."

"And, if you all don't get to the table pretty quick, she's gonna take it back to the kitchen," Hortense said. That was all the incentive needed.

While the discussion at the supper table was in progress, another matter was being discussed in town at the Cork and Bottle. "Why the hell didn't you come to me with this before now?" Micah Moran demanded when Leroy finally decided to tell him Art Becker was in with McCabe. He didn't mention the message he was released to deliver.

"Well, Micah, I swear I meant to, but I didn't think it mattered that much at the time," Leroy whined. "To tell you the truth," he continued, making up the tale as he went along, "I was plannin' to shoot the lame brain. But then I remembered you'd rather have him arrested, so you could hang him. That's why I followed Becker down that path. I figured he was in with that McCabe feller, and sure 'nuff, he led me right to him." He paused then to see if Moran was buying it, but the marshal was still fixed upon him with a steady gaze. So he sought to embellish his tale a little more. "I figured that was how McCabe knew everythin' that was goin' on—Boot and Charley, Ace, and even Sam and Johnny over in Ravenwood."

"Well, why the hell didn't you shoot both of 'em while you had a chance?" Moran demanded.

"I was comin' to that part," Leroy said, wondering how he was going to explain it. Then he was inspired to say, "Like I said, that path back by the creek is so narrow that I couldn't draw a bead on McCabe because Becker was in the way. And I knew it was important to get McCabe. You see, if I'da shot Becker, then McCabe woulda got away, so I needed to shoot him first." Comfortable in his story now, he plowed forward. "Well, I left the path and cut around to get me a spot where I could get a clear shot at both of 'em, you know, like from the side. Only problem is I slipped on some moss or somethin' when I stepped on a rock and I made a helluva noise when I fell. It was enough to spook McCabe and Becker. By the time I got back to the path, they was long gone." He looked at Moran, trying to determine whether or not he believed him. Contrite now, he made his confession. "I didn't come tell you right away 'cause I was ashamed I had a chance to get McCabe and I messed it up."

Moran listened to Leroy's confession with some degree of fascination. All in all, he bought the simple man's story, but it occurred to him to ask one question. "When McCabe was right behind Becker on that narrow path, why couldn't you shoot Becker, then shoot McCabe when Becker dropped?"

Leroy hesitated. That might have been the thing to do. He didn't think of that. Struggling to think of an answer to Moran's question, he decided to just tell the truth. "I swear, that woulda been the way. I just didn't think of that."

Moran shook his head, not at all surprised by Leroy's answer. It was another example of how simpleminded he was. He had gotten one piece of information out of the concocted tale Leroy had spun, however. Art Becker was another source of McCabe's information. He told himself that he should have suspected the owner of the stable all along. The men had become so familiar with him until they were prone to talk rather loosely around him. His first thought was that it was time for another hanging in East City. Concerned about the temper of the community, since being shocked by the sudden civil war in the Cork and Bottle, he decided he would make a show of a trial before the hanging. His intent was to make the citizens of East City believe there was a sense of responsible law and order. Then he would hang Becker on a pole in front of the jail as a lesson to anybody else who might be thinking about helping Cullen McCabe.

"How 'bout it, Micah?" Stan Molloy asked. "You want me to go arrest Art Becker?"

"Ain't no hurry," Micah said. "He ain't goin' nowhere. He's most likely gone to supper right now. He don't close the stable till later, you can pick him up then. Hell, I'll go with you to make sure his friend McCabe ain't with him. Right now, I'm gettin' hungry. Go tell

Lizzie I want my supper." Molloy turned at once to go to the kitchen to deliver Moran's order.

It was already getting dark when Art left the supper table and started walking back to the stable. It would soon be hard dark on that footpath, with the over-hanging limbs of the trees closing over him like a giant tent. *I must have stayed later than I thought,* he told himself. *I might as well just lock up and turn right around and come home.* That thought was immediately dis-missed when he came out of the trees back of his corral and saw a lamp glowing inside the barn. *One of Micah Moran's gunslingers wanting some special favor,* he thought. It had to be someone from town because there were no horses out front. They must be on foot.

He walked around to the front of the barn and walked in to find Micah Moran and Stan Molloy wait-ing inside. "Well, Marshal Moran and Deputy Molloy," Art said as cheerfully as he could affect. "What can I do for you fellers?"

"You can start by puttin' your hands up," Moran an-swered casually. Art, confused, just stood there gaping at the marshal. "Don't make me tell you again!" Moran bellowed, and whipped his .44 out and leveled it at Art.

"Whoa, Marshal!" Art blurted. "What's goin' on? What's this all about?"

"Take his gun," Moran told Molloy.

"He ain't wearin' one," Molloy replied.

"Well, put those irons on him," Moran ordered, and Molloy pulled Art's hands down behind his back and put the handcuffs on him. "Well, Mr. Becker," Moran declared in his most official-sounding manner, "you're under arrest. We're gonna give you a fair trial, then we're gonna hang you for your crimes against the town of East City." In total shock, Art's knees buckled and he would have fallen had not Molloy held him up. "You can make it a little easier on yourself if you tell me where I can find your partner in crime, Cullen McCabe."

Fighting to hold on to his emotions, Art managed to respond after a few moments. "Marshal, you're makin' a mistake."

"I don't make mistakes," Moran said. "Tell me where that damn coward is hidin'."

"I swear, I don't have no idea where Cullen McCabe is, and that's the truth. He left his horse here one night, and he stayed at the house where I stay one night. Then he left. I don't know where. He might have a camp somewhere, or he mighta gone to some other town. I just don't know. I swear to God!"

"Is that a fact?" Moran responded. "What would you say if I told you one of my men, Leroy Hill, saw you and McCabe havin' a secret meetin' on that little path behind your corral? What would you say to that?"

"I'd say he was a liar," Art blurted, desperately realizing he was done for. The little weasel, Leroy, must have cooked up some story in order to put the finger on him as McCabe's friend.

"Take him to the jail and lock him up," Moran said to Molloy. Back to Art then, he said, "I'm gonna let you set in that jail for a day or two while you remember where McCabe is hidin' out. Then we'll have a trial for you."

"What about my stable?" Art pleaded. "I've gotta take care of the stock, feedin' and waterin'. Most of 'em belong to you and your men. I'll have to take care of those horses."

"Oh, you won't have to worry about that anymore," Moran said with a smug grin. "I'll be takin' possession of this stable in the name of East City. I'll put somebody in to run it and you won't have the worry of it anymore." Cocking his head toward the door, he motioned for Molloy to take Art outside. "Go and lock him up," Moran ordered. "I'll close the doors and put out the lantern. We don't want nothin' to happen to our horses in our stable."

"Start walkin'," Molloy ordered, and gave Art a shove in the back to get him started. Still in a state of shock, Art almost stumbled, finding it difficult to understand the gruffness in Molloy's tone. Before this, Molloy and all of the other men in Moran's band of outlaws had treated him almost as though he was one of them. It was still hard for him to believe this was happening to him, but after Molloy locked him in the one cell in the tiny jail building, it struck home.

"Stan!" Art cried out when Molloy started to leave. "Stan, you know me. I didn't do nothin'. Hell, Cullen McCabe is as much a stranger to me as he is to you. And I sure ain't done nothin' to get hanged for. Talk to Moran for me. I don't deserve this."

"If you gotta take a dump, do it in that bucket yonder. That's what it's for. I'll get you some water afterwhile. If I don't come back tonight, I'll get you some in the mornin'. I don't know 'bout breakfast, I reckon Lizzie will cook you somethin'." He paused to grin at Art. "You're my first prisoner since Micah made me his deputy. Won't be for long, though— couple of days and we're gonna hang ya."

"Will you talk to Micah for me?" Art pleaded, but

Molloy ignored the question, went out the door, and Art could hear the sound of the padlock snapping shut on the jailhouse door. He had never felt such despair in all his life, locked in a cell, inside a dark little building, and no one knew where he was. It was hard not to blame Cullen for his predicament. He wished now that Cullen had never set foot in East City. He wished the big somber drifter had left Lila Blanchard to shift for herself and never wound up in East City. Gone was the glory he had felt after he and the Johnsons had pulled off the hoax that resulted in the elimination of half of the outlaws who held the town hostage. Life wasn't good before McCabe drifted through town, but it was something he had been used to. And now, his business was lost, and he was lost. He never suspected something as devastating as this could happen to him. With light only from the one window in the front of the jail, and the one small window in the back of his cell, Art sat down on one of the bunk beds. With all hope gone, he dropped his face into his hands and prayed.

While Art languished in the sorrowful ending of his evening, the friend he now regretted he'd ever met was saying good night to Hortense Billings. "That was a mighty fine supper Annie cooked up, but I still think I oughta pay you for it."

"No such a thing," Hortense insisted. "Supper was on me tonight. If you wanna come back tomorrow, you can pay me for that supper."

"I'd like to do that," he replied. "But I don't reckon it's a good idea for me to keep showin' up around here. I'm afraid Moran and his boys might come down hard on you, if they found out."

"Who's gonna tell him?" she responded. "Nobody in this house is gonna tell him. I don't think he'll make another search. He didn't find any trace that would make him think you were here. And you said you scouted around the whole place before you came in tonight. You can do that again tomorrow before supper. I'm gonna have Annie cook enough to feed you and my other guests. So if you get hungry come on back tomorrow."

"That is mighty temptin'," he admitted. "I might do that, but only if I pay you for it." Before finding out how successful their hoax on Moran had been, he would not even have considered it. But now that the marshal's posse had been cut in half, he agreed with Hortense. Moran would not likely come with all his men for another search. The possibility was stronger that he would send only one or two men to try to watch the place. And Cullen was confident that he could handle two men. But he was not ready to sleep in the boardinghouse and risk the chance of triggering a shootout in the middle of the night. He was concerned that the two women, as well as the other guests, might be caught in the cross fire.

He said good night and walked back to the creek where he had left his horse. Depending on when he got back this way tomorrow, he just might stop in for supper again. He planned to make another visit to Ravenwood in the morning. He wanted another talk with Marshal Tug Taggert. "Besides that," he said to Jake, "I think you're about ready for a portion of oats, and I can get 'em over there without worryin' about somebody takin' a shot at me."

CHAPTER 12

He woke early the next morning and decided to wait to eat breakfast in Ravenwood at the hotel dining room. The meal he had eaten there before was good enough to tempt him to come back again. Feeling no guilt at all for not cooking his own breakfast, he decided that was why the state gave him expense money. He stepped up into the saddle and headed Jake north along the creek, with the idea of approaching Ravenwood from the south. Although breakfast was what he was craving at the moment, he pulled Jake up in front of the marshal's office. There was a lock on the door as well as a handwritten sign that read, GONE TO BREAKFAST. *Well, that suits me just fine,* he thought, remembering that it had been Taggert who recommended the hotel dining room. He figured he might find him there and kill two birds with one stone.

"Yours will come later," he told the bay gelding, remembering that he had promised Jake some oats this morning. He looped the reins over the hitching rail and entered the dining room's outside door. Without waiting to be reminded, he left his weapons on the table provided for that purpose, and while he was doing so, he scanned the busy dining room. He spotted the marshal seated at a table near the back of the room. However, there was another man with him. Since he wanted to talk to the marshal privately, he decided he'd better wait and catch him after breakfast. While he was standing there making up his mind, Marcy Manning saw him and hurried over to welcome him.

"Well, you came back to see us," Marcy greeted him. "I've forgotten your name, but I certainly remember you."

"Cullen McCabe," he reminded her. "If I recollect, yours is Marcy, right?"

"That's right, Mr. McCabe. Let's see where I can seat you." She turned to look over the busy room in time to see the marshal with his hand in the air, signaling her. "Looks like Marshal Taggert has spotted you." She turned back to Cullen and laughed. "Would you like to sit at his table, or do you need to run for it?"

He smiled in appreciation for her humor and said, "I'll risk eatin' with the marshal." Instead of waiting for her to escort him over, he walked on back to the table. "Marshal Taggert," he greeted him.

"Cullen McCabe," Taggert returned. "Have a seat. Are you lookin' for some breakfast?"

"I am," Cullen replied, and pulled a chair back. "I don't wanna interrupt anything," he said, and nodded to the young man sitting with the marshal. Like Taggert, the young man wore a badge.

"Not at all," Taggert assured him. "We're just havin' a little breakfast. Meet Beau Arnett. He's my new deputy, the man I was tellin' you about last time you were in town." Cullen reached over and shook hands with Arnett. Looking toward the young man, Taggert continued. "Beau, this is Cullen McCabe, the man I told you about before. If it hadn't been for McCabe, I wouldn't be settin' here eatin' breakfast with you." He paused to chuckle. "And ol' Cow Pie, back yonder in the cell, wouldn't be there. On the other hand, you mighta been the marshal right now, instead of the deputy, if McCabe, here, hadn't stuck his nose in marshal's business."

"I'm pleased to meet you, Mr. McCabe," Beau said. "Marshal Taggert told me how you stepped in to help him out of a bad spot. I'm glad you did because I've got a lot to learn from him about this job."

"It's Cullen, Beau. I expect it's a job where you never do get to where you know it all, although I expect the marshal is gettin' pretty close."

"Yep," Taggert cracked. "And that's about the time when you start makin' dumb mistakes, like gettin' yourself trapped behind a wagon with two scared horses fixin' to bolt." Conversation halted for a moment then when a young girl came to the table with a cup of coffee and asked Cullen what he wanted to eat. He told her that what they were eating looked pretty good, if the eggs were scrambled. She nodded and turned to go. "And put that on my bill, Polly," Taggert called after her. She turned back and confirmed it with a nod. "Don't even start," Taggert interrupted when Cullen was about to protest. "I told you I wanted to buy your supper when you were here the other day, but you were in a hurry to get back to East City."

Beau Arnett's eyebrows raised slightly at the mention of East City. "Are you stayin' over in East City, Mr. McCabe, I mean, Cullen?"

"Well, I'll have to say I'm stayin' close to East City," Cullen answered. "Campin' on the creek near there,

as a matter of fact. I reckon I'm just about as close to
Ravenwood as I am to East City."

"What brings you over to this side of the creek
today?" Beau asked.

"Breakfast, for the most part," Cullen answered.
"That and I brought the marshal some information
he might or might not have gotten." Taggert's eyebrows went up at that, and he asked what information
that might be. "Well, I don't know if you know the
names of the men involved in that shooting." He
could tell by Taggert's expression that he did not, so
he continued. "The man you have in jail now, the one
you named Cow Pie, the name his mama gave him is
Sam Polek. The one I shot was Johnny Barr, and the
one who got away with their horses is Stan Molloy."

"That is some information I didn't have," Taggert
said, seeming to be more than pleased and definitely
interested in what else Cullen might have to say. He
took a piece of folded paper from his pocket and a
stub of a pencil and wrote the names down as Cullen
called them out again. "Judge Raven is gonna think
I've done some real detective work when I give him
these." He wet the pencil lead with his tongue then
crossed the *t* in Stan Molloy's name. "Good information, but I think Cow Pie suits that one in the cell
better."

The conversation took a brief pause when Polly
Peters brought Cullen's breakfast and placed it before
him. All three concentrated on the food for a few
moments before the talking resumed. "I'm just a little
curious," Taggert said. "How did you find out about
this? That don't seem like somethin' everybody in
town would know."

Cullen hesitated. It was something he had never done before, and he was just naturally more comfortable keeping it to himself. But he decided it probably was best to level with the marshal, since he had decided Taggert was an honest lawman. "I reckon it's time I told you why I'm really in your territory. I don't usually bring it up, if it ain't necessary, and up till now it ain't been." He reached into his inside vest pocket and pulled out a small canvas bag he usually carried in his saddlebags. He pulled a paper out of the bag, unfolded it, and handed it to Taggert.

Taggert glanced at it, and seeing a lot of writing on it, handed it to Beau. "I don't read all that well," he said.

Beau took the document and read over it quickly, then looked up at Cullen before turning toward Taggert. "This says that 'one Cullen McCabe is a special agent of the State of Texas, reporting directly to the governor and only the governor.' And it's signed, 'Richard B. Hubbard, Governor, State of Texas.'" He held it up for the marshal to see. "And it's stamped with the official seal of the state of Texas." Both Taggert and Beau looked from the document to stare at Cullen.

It was the first time he had ever told anyone of his special assignments by the governor's office. And from the reaction he read in the two faces gaping at him, he wasn't comfortable with it now. While he thought of what he should say next, he reached in another pocket and pulled out a piece of velvet material. He unwrapped it to reveal a shiny badge. "They gave me this, too, but I don't ever wear it. I wrapped it in this piece of cloth to keep the shine on it."

"I knew it!" Taggert finally shattered the brief silence. "I knew damn well you weren't no ordinary drifter passin' through town. You came to do somethin' about that rotten den of snakes across the creek, didn't you?" Without giving Cullen time to answer, he went on. "They send a company of Rangers here for three days, and they can't do a damn thing to clean up that mess. So they send one man back to do it?"

"Well, not really," Cullen answered. "I reckon you could say the governor sent me here to take a look at the situation to see how best to maybe clean the lawless crowd outta there for good. My job was to look both of the towns over and make my recommendations, but I turned up some things I reckon I didn't see comin'. So I had to get involved a little more than I'd planned to. There are some good people over there in East City, and I think they're ready to forget about havin' their own town, separate and apart. I think they're ready to build that bridge back across Walnut Creek and be part of Ravenwood."

"There ain't a chance in hell of that happenin' with that damn army of gunmen runnin' the town," Taggert declared. "There's too many of 'em for the Rangers to handle, and so far, the army don't seem interested in our little problems."

Cullen nodded his understanding and said, "Well, there ain't quite as many of 'em anymore."

Interested then, Taggert asked, "That so? What happened to 'em?" He had a feeling he knew the answer to his question, having seen Cullen use a Winchester before.

"There were a couple of different incidents that took place," Cullen said. Then he went on to bring

Taggert up to date on everything that had happened since his first day in East City. Taggert listened with rapt attention as well as a mixture of wonder and disbelief.

When Cullen had finished, Taggert had questions. "So you're tellin' me that Micah Moran ain't got but three men left outta that gang he had?"

"That's the number of men he has since last night, all that's left of the main core of his gang. The trouble is, I expect him to be hiring every lawless drifter that passes through town, the same way he built up his gang before. Another problem I have is I don't know how many customers he's got stayin' in that whorehouse he calls a hotel. They go and come so often till it's been hard to put a number on 'em. Art Becker, the fellow I told you about, he owns the stable, and he says most of the horses there belong to the gang and the customers in the hotel. If I knew there weren't but four of 'em left for sure, I'd ask you if you'd like to help me, and we'd ride in there and arrest 'em or shoot 'em, and that would take care of the problem. But once we got rid of Moran and his men, we'd have to have an honest lawman in there right away to take his place. And we have to make sure the town council is gonna back us. Otherwise, the same old scum will creep right back in. The trouble is, every outlaw in Texas and Oklahoma knows about East City."

"I see what you're sayin'," Taggert said. "It ain't as simple as it sounded at first. I don't know what our city council would say about me gettin' involved in a war across the creek. So I reckon that'll have to be discussed in a meetin'. Might be best if we hold on a little longer till you know a little bit more about how many they've got in that hotel."

Beau Arnett had held his tongue throughout the discussion between Cullen and Taggert, keenly interested in the dilemma that was East City. When it seemed that Cullen and the marshal had talked it out, he made a statement. "It sounds to me that when the time is right to drive those outlaws out of East City, it's gonna be a helluva fight. I just wanna let you know I'd like to be a part of it. And when the time comes to find a lawman to hold the job over there, I don't think you'll find a better man than me."

His statement surprised Cullen, but not Taggert, who could not suppress a smile. He had already seen the drive and the confidence in his newly appointed deputy, and he had to agree with him. He would have thought that Beau might have applied for the job in private with Cullen.

"That's good to know," Cullen said, not quite sure if Taggert would actually encourage such a plan, especially since he would be losing a deputy he just acquired. "I'll pass it along to the governor."

"You know, we hear sounds of gunshots over here from time to time when the wind is right," Taggert said. "I mighta heard that shootout you just told us about. Made me wonder what kinda devilment was happening over there. Never struck my mind to ride over there to see what it was. I'm the marshal of Ravenwood. My job is to keep the peace in this town. I don't have any jurisdiction outside of town."

Cullen thought Taggert felt the need to offer excuses for why he hadn't attempted to do something about Micah Moran. "You were right to take care of your own town. It's best to wait until I contact you for help, after I find out for sure what we're up against. When the time's right, I can officially give you the clearance to participate in a raid on East City." It was not true. Cullen didn't think he had any authority to give the marshal clearance to go to war with the town across the creek. When the time was ripe for it, he wouldn't hesitate to enlist Taggert's and Beau's help in taking Micah Moran down, and to hell with getting legal permission. "I'll keep in touch to let you know what's goin' on over there," he said, as he drained the last swallow from his coffee cup. "Thank you for the breakfast. Good to meet you, Beau." He extended his hand. "I've gotta stop by the stable. I promised Jake I'd buy him some oats this mornin'."

True to his promise, he rode down to the stable where he met the owner, a friendly, mild-mannered man named Jim Farmer. He reminded Cullen of Art Becker, the two could have been brothers. Farmer recognized Cullen as the man who stepped in to back up Tug Taggert when the marshal was under attack. When he found that Cullen was just looking to buy some oats for his horse, Farmer insisted there would be no charge. "Least I can do for the man who kept our marshal from gettin' shot," he said. When Cullen made a mild protest, Jim chuckled and said, "If you wanted a whole sack of oats, that'd be different." Satisfied there was nothing more he needed in Raven-wood, Cullen thanked Jim Farmer for the oats and headed back to his camp on the creek bank south of Hortense Billings's house.

As a precaution, he guided Jake into the trees lining the banks of the creek well north of the spot where he had made his camp. That way, anyone who might be watching wouldn't see him enter the trees right at the camp. He walked Jake slowly along the wide creek, in the shade of the oak trees, until reaching the point where he had left their cover on his way to Ravenwood earlier that morning. About to turn the bay down to the water's edge, he suddenly jerked the horse to a stop. A slight movement he glimpsed through a band of laurel bushes told him someone was at his campsite! Not expecting it, he automatically drew his rifle from the saddle sling and quickly looked all about him, fearing he might have ridden into an ambush. He slid out of the saddle and knelt on one knee, still looking all around him, trying to present as small a target as possible. Still, there was no attack, no shots fired from any direction, so he left Jake where he was and cautiously moved closer to his camp until he could see one man sitting beside the ashes of his campfire, his back turned toward him. Puzzled, for there was no sign of a horse or packs of any kind, he decided he had taken all his precautions because a homeless drifter was snooping around his camp. He promptly stood up and pushed through the bushes and walked down to the water's edge. Hearing him then, the man stood up and turned to face him. Surprised, Cullen blurted, "Roy! What are you doin' out here in the woods?"

"Waitin' for you," Roy Skelton answered. "I was hopin' you'd show up sooner or later."

Immediately alarmed, Cullen asked, "Why, what's wrong?"

"It's Art," Roy replied. "They got him locked up in the jailhouse, and that ain't all. They're fixin' to have a trial for him, then hang him!"

"What?!" Cullen exclaimed. "What for?"

"For helpin' you kill Boot Davis and them others is the word Micah Moran is spreadin' around town. Franklin George came from O'Sullivan's to tell us about it. We didn't know what was wrong when Art never came back from the stable after supper last night. I thought you needed to know," Roy went on. "I didn't have no idea where you were, so I was hopin' you'd come back here. I didn't know where your camp was, so I just walked up and down both sides of the creek. I figured wherever it was, you'd be by the water somewhere. And I found this old campfire, so I sat down and waited. I was hopin' it was yours. Didn't think there'd be anybody else campin' here."

"I'm glad you stayed here," Cullen said, his mind racing. "You did the right thing." He had never expected Moran to take out his vengeance on Art Becker, since Art appeared to have been accepted by Moran and his men as a harmless individual. But once again, Moran had ignited a spark of rage in Cullen's veins, much like the spark he caused with Lila's hanging. This time it hit even closer to home. Art was not only a friend now, but Cullen felt totally responsible for any harm that might befall Art as a result of his actions. All the possible plans of action he had talked over with Tug Taggert that morning were cast aside. If Micah Moran was trying to draw him out of hiding, he was finally successful, for Cullen was damned if he would let Art Becker hang. "They said they would have a trial first?" Cullen asked again to be sure.

"That's what Franklin said. He said Molloy came in O'Sullivan's and told everybody there. He's Moran's deputy now, since you shot Ace Brown. I think Franklin said the trial was this afternoon, and the hangin's gonna be in the mornin'."

There were many dark images swirling through Cullen's brain, memories of devasting tragedies that tore his life to pieces. Painful memories of the half-burned bodies of Mary Kate and the three children among the charred timbers of his cabin came back from the darker regions of his brain, where he tried to keep them. He thought of the men who had destroyed his family, dead now by his hand. But men like that were spawned every day, born to torment and kill, just like the men who reigned over East City. He thought again of the meeting he had with Taggert and his young deputy that morning, and that he had told them to wait to see what would happen after Moran's posse was so severely crippled. None of that talk mattered anymore. This fight had become even more personal. He would deal with it, himself.

He must have been in an angry trance because he suddenly realized Roy was staring at him with mouth and eyes wide open. "Whaddaya gonna do?" Roy asked.

It was enough to bring his mind back to the business of making war. "I'm gonna do what I can to make sure Art doesn't hang," he told him. "Let's go back to the house now. I'll pick up my horse on the way." Roy followed him up the bank and into the larger trees to the place where Jake stood, waiting patiently. Cullen stepped up into the saddle, then he took his foot out of the stirrup and asked, "You wanna step up behind me?"

"No, thanks," Roy replied. "You go ahead. I'll just walk back to the house. It ain't that far."

"Suit yourself," Cullen said, and gave Jake a nudge

with his heel. He wanted to get back first thing to make sure there was no one harassing Hortense and Annie, for the same reason they arrested Art. At this point, he was less inclined to take elaborate precautions, as he had before. Had it not been for the threat of harm to the two women, he would have hoped to find some of Moran's crew lurking about the boardinghouse. Even as he thought it, he cautioned himself not to let his anger override his good judgment. When he reached the house, he found there had been no need for caution, anyway. There were no unwelcome guests anywhere about.

"Cullen!" Hortense cried out from the kitchen door, having seen him ride up from the window. "They've got Art! They're gonna hang him, like they did that whore!"

"I know," Cullen said as he dismounted. "Roy told me."

"Where is Roy?" Annie asked, pushing by Hortense in the doorway, suddenly afraid that something might have happened to him.

"He's comin' along behind me. He oughta be here in a minute or two," Cullen said. "Have any of Moran's men been pokin' around here?"

"We've not seen 'em, if they have," Annie answered. "Whaddaya gonna do?" she asked, much of the same opinion as Roy—that it was because of Art's willingness to help Cullen that Art had been arrested.

"I'm gonna go get Art out of that jail," Cullen declared. Seeing the sinister spark in the solemn man's eye, none doubted him, and no one asked him how he was going to do it.

"Will you bring him back here?" Hortense asked, concerned for Cullen and Art, but also thinking about the almost certain possibility of Micah Moran and his three henchmen showing up there to look for them.

Cullen had thought of that same probability and he told her that Art would not be staying at the boarding-house. "I'm not sure where we'll end up, maybe the stable, maybe the woods. I'll cross that bridge when I get to it. The main thing I'm interested in right now is keepin' Art's neck outta that noose."

The two women nodded in unison. Always the more practical of the two, Annie asked, "Do you need somethin' to eat?"

"No, ma'am," he said. "I'm not hungry." The two women walked out with him while he stepped up into the saddle. He turned Jake toward the footpath that led to the stable and left the yard at an easy lope.

Roy walked up from the creek in time to see him ride away. "Where's he goin'?" he asked when he reached the two women.

"He said he's gone to get Art outta that jailhouse," Annie answered him.

"Lord of goodness," Roy sighed. "I hope he knows what he's about. He ain't got much chance ridin' into that devil's town and ridin' back out alive."

"I don't know," Annie declared. "I'm thinkin' we oughta be feelin' sorry for the marshal and his men."

As for the man they worried for, he had every intention of riding out alive, and with Art alive, as well. He made his plans as he rode along the narrow foot-path that served as Art's shortcut between his stable and his "family" at the boardinghouse. Knowing for sure he was a walking target anywhere he showed up in the town of East City, whatever he did had to be done after dark. The one thing he counted on was the accuracy of Roy's and Hortense's accounting of the story. If there was a chance they decided to hang Art today, instead of tomorrow, then he was too late to do anything to stop it. It might already be over. The notion of having a fake trial was just for Moran and his trash to enjoy themselves, as well as an attempt to persuade the honest folk of East City that he wanted to give every man a fair trial. Cullen had a pretty good idea about who the judge would be, His Honor, Micah Moran, and the bar would remain open throughout the trial. The more he thought about it, the madder he got, so much so that he had to calm himself down again to decide what his plan of action should be.

His hands shackled behind his back, Deputy Molloy on one arm and Shorty Miller on the other one, Art was led across the street from the jail to the Cork and Bottle. Already being harassed by his two guards, he did his best to walk straight and keep his eyes on the ground in front of his feet. "You gonna plead guilty or innocent, Becker?" Shorty japed. "If you get down on your knees and beg like a little dog, you never know, ol' Micah might let you take a shot in the head, instead of swingin' on that rope." He cocked his head and grinned. "Make it a little quicker," he added. Art made no reply. As far as he was concerned, he was already dead.

"Tell the marshal where Cullen McCabe is and he might let you go back to runnin' your stable," Molloy said, knowing that was what Moran would really like to know.

Art remained mute. He knew that was no option.

He was dead regardless of what information he coughed up. Moran owned half of the saloon and the hotel next to it. With Art's death, Moran would own the stable, too. With one more little detour for their amusement, the two guards walked Art toward a set of deep wagon tracks that still held rainwater from two days before. With his guards walking on either side of the widest rut, Art was forced to walk up the middle of the rut. Try as he might to tiptoe from one of the muddy sides of the rut to the other, he was unable to keep from sloshing through the muddy water. His dilemma was enough to delight his guards, leaving them still laughing as they delivered him to the makeshift courtroom.

To complete his farce, Micah Moran was seated at a table alone, facing two rows of barroom chairs set up for the "jury" and any spectators brave enough to come to witness the trial. There was an empty chair beside his table that was supposed to be the witness stand. Of the spectators, Art saw only two friendly faces, Abe Franks and Joe Johnson. He could guess that they were there under duress—the purpose, to make a show of involving the town council. The other spectators were a couple of drifters who stayed for an overnighter in the hotel next door to the saloon. "Everybody come to order," Moran announced. "This court is in session. We're tryin' Art Becker for his part in the murder of Boot Davis, Charley Turner, Ace Brown, and Shep Parker. How do you plead, prisoner?"

"You know how I plead, Moran," Art responded with as much defiance as he could muster. "This is all a bunch of horseshit. I never killed nobody and I never helped Cullen McCabe kill nobody. And ain't nobody seen McCabe kill those fellers, either."

"Is that all you've got to say for yourself, just a

bunch of lies?" Moran barked. "We'll see what the witness says. Call the witness." At that command, Leroy Hill came up and sat down in the chair next to the table. He was still holding a glass of whiskey. Moran continued, obviously enjoying himself with the charade. "Did you, or did you not, witness the prisoner havin' a secret meetin' with Cullen McCabe on that little path behind the stable?"

"Yes, sir, I did," Leroy answered, and took a drink from his glass of whiskey.

"Well, tell the court what you saw," Moran commanded.

"Him and McCabe havin' a meetin' on the path," Leroy replied.

"Damn it," Moran railed, "tell us about it!"

Not really happy to talk about that meeting on the footpath when he had tried to capture Cullen McCabe, Leroy took another belt from the glass of whiskey. "Well, sir, I was suspicious about Becker, so I tailed him when he went home to eat. And sure as shootin', he met that feller McCabe before he got halfway to that boardin'house where he lives. I was tryin' to get a clear shot at McCabe, but Becker kept gettin' in my line of sight, so I had to hold fire and McCabe got away."

"The main thing is you saw the two of 'em plannin' a murder, right?" Moran asked.

"That's right, Micah, I mean Your Honor," Leroy said, and immediately got out of the chair. He walked back toward the bar to the cheers of the two spectators from the hotel.

It was too much for Art to remain quiet. He jumped to his feet and yelled out at Leroy. "You lyin' little weasel, why don't you tell the honorable judge

there the truth? About how you came sneakin' out of
the bushes when I ran into McCabe on that path,
and about how he took your gun away from you. And
had you cryin' like a baby before he let you go with a
message to take back to Micah Moran." Talking as fast
as he could, that was as much as he could get out before
he was jerked off his feet and given a hard backhand
by Molloy.

"All right, Becker," Moran said. "You're so damn
anxious to talk. Why don't you tell the court where
Cullen McCabe is hidin' out? You do that and tell me
who else is in cahoots with McCabe, and I'll lighten up
on your sentence."

Art didn't respond right away. He could not help
thinking about talking himself out of a hanging. But
he didn't actually know where Cullen was camped. He
might buy some mercy by revealing Joe and Doris
Johnson's part in the hoax that led to Ned Larson's
killing. He glanced over at Joe Johnson, seated next
to Abe Franks, and met Joe's nervous gaze back at
him. It was easy for Art to imagine that Joe was having
the same thoughts as he was. He looked back at Micah
Moran, sneering at him, and knew that no matter
what he confessed to, Moran was going to hang him.
"I ain't got no idea where Cullen McCabe is hidin',
and I don't know anybody that's helpin' him," he
stated. He dropped his gaze to his shackled hands,
still cuffed but now resting in his lap. If he had looked
again at Joe Johnson, he would have seen the rigid
emotion drain from his face.

"You ain't leavin' me no choice," Moran said, disappointed. He had predicted to his men that Art would
squeal like a stuck hog to save his neck. "The court finds
the defendant guilty as hell, and the sentence is hangin'

by the neck till dead." Then he added, almost cheerfully, "Hangin's tomorrow mornin' after breakfast." He took a drink of whiskey to make the verdict official, then ordered, "Drag him outta here!"

Johnson attempted to make eye contact with Art when Molloy and Shorty stood him up and hustled him out the door. He was hoping to silently convey his appreciation for protecting him and his wife, but Art never lifted his head. The two town council members got up to leave, but Moran stopped them before they reached the door. "You see that, Mr. Mayor? I tried to give him the chance to clear himself and help the town. You merchants have to see that it ain't always easy to keep murderers like Cullen McCabe out of our town. Sometimes a hangin' or two is what it takes. If you know anything about this McCabe gunman, it's your duty to let me know before he kills any more innocent citizens."

"Marshal," Abe answered him, "we don't know a thing more about Cullen McCabe than you do. He just showed up one day with that woman you hung before. We figured he was just another drifter passing through town. And I sure as hell don't have any idea if McCabe killed any of your men or not." He started to turn to leave, but paused to say, "And I don't think for a minute that Art Becker had anything to do with it. In my opinion, you're hanging an innocent man." Abe had no real occasion for direct contact with Cullen. But he knew about the farce Joe and Doris had pulled off with the note Art brought them. That was because they had confessed it to him. He also knew they held McCabe in high regard. As far as Joe Johnson was concerned, he had nothing to say.

Moran was not pleased by their lack of cooperation

in the capture or killing of Cullen McCabe, but there was nothing more he could do to persuade them. After hearing Abe's comments on the trial, he was tempted to hang him alongside of Becker. "Well, maybe Becker will have time to think about it tonight before we hang him in the mornin'," he said, straining to hold his temper.

Outside, as they walked back toward O'Sullivan's for the drink they both decided they needed, Johnson said to the mayor, "Abe, how long are we gonna take this before we do something about it?"

"I don't know," Abe answered honestly. "Not much longer, I guess, but I don't know what else we can do about it. We've asked the Rangers for help and contacted the governor's office directly and you can see how much help they've all been." They walked a little farther, both thinking about their situation, then Abe spoke again. "I guess we can hope they'll have another argument between themselves and finally kill each other off." The mayor paused at the door to O'Sullivan's. "Do you think that McCabe fellow is still around, or do you think he's figured he's done enough and moved on?"

"I don't know, Abe," Joe said. "I suppose Art coulda told us more about that, if they hadn't arrested him." He shook his head and thought aloud, "It was kind of nice having our own gunman for a change." They went inside, knowing Cary O'Sullivan would be interested to hear how the trial went.

CHAPTER 13

As Cullen had anticipated, there was not much activity in the stable. Every one of Moran's men were no doubt at the Cork and Bottle. He was sure that's where Art's trial was being held. But he took the precaution to leave Jake in the trees by the creek while he slipped up behind the barn and entered the same way he had on a previous visit. Most of the stalls were already filled and the horses fed, another sign that Moran's men had taken care of their horses early, so they wouldn't have to come back after the trial. This worked in Cullen's favor, for he figured he could be a little bold in his plan. He left the stalls and went to check the front door to the barn. Finding it locked, he was double sure he wouldn't be disturbed, so he went back out the back to get his horse. Leading Jake inside the back door, he put him in one of the few empty stalls and pulled his saddle off as a precaution. If for some reason, someone had to return to the stable that afternoon they would not likely notice an extra horse in the stalls, unless maybe the horse was saddled. After he made sure Jake had water, he took a bucket he saw hanging on a nail and fetched some grain for the bay to eat. Thinking about the oats Jake had in Ravenwood that morning, he said, "Don't you go gettin' used to eatin' grain twice a day."

After Jake was taken care of, he looked in the other stalls to pick a horse for Art to ride. The horse he selected was a blue roan, almost totally black. The owner had left the saddle on the rail between the stalls. All set then, as far as their riding horses were concerned, he looked in the rest of the stalls, looking for his sorrel packhorse, but with no luck. So he went out to the corral where he found four horses, his sorrel among them. "Reckon you weren't good enough to rate a stall. I hope they fed you." He decided to take the sorrel inside and put it in the stall with Jake, thinking they knew each other well enough. Once that was done, and the sorrel was fed, too, he went to get his packs and packsaddle from the barn where Art had put them.

Thinking he had done all he could in preparation for the jailbreak he was planning, there was nothing left to do but wait. With that in mind, he went to the tack room and searched the workstand under the window, where Art kept some hand tools. In one of the drawers, he found what he was looking for, Art's cavalry field glass. Then he climbed up into the hayloft and went to the open door. With no way to determine how long the trial would last, or even if it had already started, he sat down beside the door and watched what he could see of the street.

He had not been at the door long when he spotted the two men walking Art out of the saloon, heading across the street to the jail. With the use of Art's field glass, he could see the two guards talking every step of the way. Art, on the other hand, looked lost and despairing. It was enough to fire Cullen's rage once more and he felt his hand tighten on the glass he held. In the middle of the street, they stopped and the two guards pointed toward something while their mouths continued jabbering away, broken by fits of laughing. Using the glass, Cullen followed the line pointed out until he spotted what they were pointing to. It was a rope, with a noose formed on one end, dangling from a large pole in front of the jail, a pole Cullen had never seen there before. The sight of it infuriated him and he had a strong urge to limber up his rifle. The shots would be easy at that distance. It was hard to sit there and watch, but he reminded himself that his objective was to get Art out of town in one piece. So he waited, and watched the two men walk Art to the jail and take him inside. Less than two minutes passed before the two guards came back outside. One of them closed the padlock on the door, then they returned to the saloon. *Hopefully for the rest of the night,* Cullen thought, but that was not to be the case. About an hour later, he saw one of the original two men come out of the saloon, carrying what looked to be a cup of coffee and something wrapped in a cloth. It surprised him to see they were feeding Art his supper.

Inside the jail cell, Art Becker sat, dejected and fearful, afraid to meet his rendezvous with the noose Molloy and Shorty had taken such great delight in pointing out to him. Edgy as he was, he jumped, startled when he suddenly heard Molloy unlock the big padlock outside. Expecting more harassment, he was surprised to see the coffee and ham biscuits Molloy brought with him. He made no move to get up from the bed he was sitting on until Molloy motioned for him to come to the front of the cell. "I brung you some supper," Molloy said. "Come here and get it."

Expecting a trick of some kind, Art came to the front of the cell when Molloy pushed the coffee and a couple of ham biscuits through the bars. Still expecting a trick, Art reached out very carefully and took them. Then he stepped back quickly, still wary of Molloy's intent. "Ain't no trick to it," Molloy assured him. "We weren't gonna let you go hungry on your last night alive. Micah ain't as hard as he lets on. He was really hopin' you'd help us find McCabe, so he wouldn't be murderin' nobody else. That would be better for the whole town. I'm pretty sure I could get him to let you go free, go back to runnin' your stable, just like it was, if you'd tell me where we can find Cullen McCabe. Whaddaya say?"

"I told you I can't tell you where he is, because he's gone," Art said, not believing the seemingly compassionate outlaw for even a moment. "He didn't say where he was goin', most likely it's way to hell away from this damn town."

All trace of compassion evaporated from Molloy's face and he spat, "You're makin' one helluva dumb mistake, Becker. What the hell's he holdin' over you?"

"Molloy, you know damn well, just like I know, Micah Moran ain't gonna let me go, even if I did know where McCabe is. He figures he owns my stable now. He's gonna hang me in the mornin', no matter what I say."

"You got that right!" Molloy responded, irritated that Art hadn't been fooled by his charade. "And me and the boys are already bettin' on how many times you kick your feet before you croak."

"I'll tell you somethin' that you can tell that lowdown

skunk you work for," Art said, fully angry now. "I wrote that message that Leroy found and took to Moran." When Molloy looked as if he wasn't sure what he was talking about, Art clarified it. "You know, that one from McCabe to Ned Larson, that asked Ned what they were waitin' for."

"How do you know about that note?" Molloy demanded.

"I just told you, you damn fool. I wrote it and dropped it on the floor in the general store. And you toads believed it and started shootin' each other, just like the fools I knew you were—gunned down half of your own gang. You and your friends think about that while I'm swingin' on that rope." In spite of his certain fate, Art experienced a feeling of triumph over his executioners. It felt good, a welcome uplift in his spirits and he favored the gaping Molloy with a wide satisfied smile. "Thanks for the coffee and biscuits," he said. "I didn't expect 'em." So mad he couldn't say anything at that moment, Molloy turned on his heel and charged out the door. Several minutes later, Art heard the sound of the padlock closing. He smiled to himself when he realized the brainless brute had been so mad that he forgot to lock the door and had to come back to do it.

"What do you mean, he wrote the message?" Micah Moran demanded. "How did he even know about that message? Somebody musta told him about it!" He looked accusingly around the table at the three remaining men in his gang. "One of you shot your mouth off. Who was it? You might as well own up to it.

Who was it? I'll go over to the jail and he'll tell me who it was."

"Maybe he was just guessin' about that message, Boss," Leroy said.

"No, hell, he weren't," Molloy insisted. "He told me everything that was on it, the part about 'what are we waitin' for' and all. I believe he wrote it."

Moran was burning inside. He had worked to build up a gang big enough that no law agency wanted to challenge him. And he had thought Larson was the man he needed with the three men he brought with him, killers all. He forced himself to think rationally. Becker might have written that message, but Moran was certain that McCabe was behind it. McCabe was still the man he wanted. Calming himself to regain his self-control, he looked around the table at the concerned faces of the remnants of his once-powerful posse. He would rebuild, he told himself. "Never mind what Becker said," he finally told them. "It doesn't make a lot of difference, anyway. It was just a matter of time before Ned made his move to take over. I told you, I'd been seein' signs of it for a while. Better to have it settled and out of the way sooner than later. We'll watch Art Becker swing in the mornin' for his part in this trouble, then I'll rebuild my posse back to where it was. But in the meantime, we're gonna flush out Cullen McCabe if we have to burn the town down to find him."

Surprised that he had any appetite, Art ate the last of the second ham biscuit and swallowed the last gulp of coffee. He didn't know if he had been wise in spilling his guts about the message he had caused to be delivered. But it made him feel good to think he had taken down Ned Larson and his men, not to mention Shep Parker. He had kept Joe and Doris out of it and taken the entire blame. The only thing that could have made it better would have been the chance to tell it to Micah Moran in person. He hoped his part in that shootout might inspire Abe Franks and the rest of the council to stand up to Moran and his gunmen.

There was nothing for him now but to wait for morning and face whatever was waiting for him on the other side. He had thought about trying to break out of his cell. He had plenty of time to try because Molloy didn't sleep in the marshal's office. He stayed in the hotel, close to the drinking, gambling, and prostitution. But after testing every foot of the cell walls, he couldn't find any weak places where he might force the bars apart far enough to squeeze through. If he had his steel pry bar that he kept in his stable, he might have been able to spring the cell door loose. But with no tools, he was pretty much a possum in a cage.

He wasn't sure he wanted to go to sleep, even if he thought he could, not wanting those last hours to slip by unnoticed. So he sat up on the bunk and waited. He could hear the raucous sounds of drunken laughter and loud swearing coming from the saloon across the street. After a while, the moon must have lifted up over the horizon because he could see splinters of light showing through the cracks of the shuttered window in the marshal's office. It was not enough to light his dark prison. After a little longer in his solitude, the feeling of triumph he had enjoyed began to fade away and he started to sink into his prior mood of despair. He realized that he was not ready to die and there was nothing he could do to prevent it. He put his head down into his hands and prepared to pray, only to be jolted by the sudden sound of splintering wood, followed by another one of equal clamor. Then the heavy front door, metal hinges and all, was wrenched from the doorframe. Backlighted by the bright moonlight, the doorway was filled by a powerful image that could only be Cullen McCabe! Too stunned to speak, Art stared in shocked amazement. "Are you ready to get out of here?" Cullen asked, his voice calm in contrast to his actions. He lifted his boot again and gave the sagging door a kick that sent it slamming against the wall and out of his way.

"Cullen!" Art blurted. It was all he could say for a long moment. "Cullen, I shoulda known you wouldn't let me die in here!" he finally managed. Then he brought his mind back to the barricade still to be overcome. "The cell door," he exclaimed. "You gotta find somethin' to pry it open." All of a sudden so close to freedom, he became fearfully worried that his escape might be blocked by the locked cell door. "You need a pry bar!"

"Let's try this," Cullen said, still calm in contrast to Art's excitement. He walked over to a large key hanging on a nail on the wall, then came back and unlocked the cell door. Art rushed out of the cell and stood shaking with the excitement of his escape. He only nodded rapidly in answer when Cullen asked if he was all right. "Good," Cullen said, and went to the front door to take a quick look out across the dark street toward the lights of the Cork and Bottle. Satisfied the patrons of that saloon were making too much noise to have noticed the uproar he had created with his rather unsubtle entrance into the jail, he turned back to the business at hand. "Let's find you a weapon," he said, and began searching through the desk drawers, since the gun cabinet on the wall was empty of everything except a box of cartridges. In one of the bottom drawers, he found what he was looking for, a handgun and holster. "Here, put this on. If we're lucky, we won't need it." He took the box of .44 cartridges from the gun cabinet and started toward the door. "You ready?"

"Damn right!" Art blurted. "I couldn't get no more ready!" He followed Cullen out the door, surprised to see the two saddled horses plus Cullen's packhorse waiting at the hitching rail. Still finding it hard to believe his escape to be so easy, at least for his part, he couldn't help taking nervous glances toward the saloon, expecting shots to fly at any moment.

Noticing Art's worried looks toward the Cork and Bottle, Cullen sought to calm him. "They're makin' such a noise in the saloon I coulda blasted that door with dynamite and they wouldn't have heard it. As long as they're havin' such a good time over there, I think it'll be all right if we go back to the stable before we leave town, and you can get any clothes and things you're gonna be needin'. I've already got everything we'll need to camp with for a while."

"Where are we goin'?" Art asked as he stepped up on the black horse. Before Cullen could answer, Art said, "This is Ned Larson's horse. I always figured Larson had to have him a black horse to match that Morgan Moran rides."

"Is that a fact?" Cullen replied. "I doubt he'll miss it, but Marshal Moran might still try to hang you for a horse thief." Then, answering Art's question, he said, "I don't know for sure where we're headin'. I'm just

thinkin' about gettin' you away from here right now."
He climbed on Jake and wheeled him away from the
rail, heading for the stable.

With no one in the street and the town buttoned
up for the night, with the exception of the two saloons
at the opposite ends of the street, they rode quietly
away from the jail. When they got to the stable Cullen
told Art they'd best tie their horses out behind the
barn. Then, while Art picked up the personal articles
he kept at the stable, reluctant to leave them behind,
Cullen went through the stable and opened all the
stalls, chasing the horses out the front of the stable. It
was hard for Art to watch. Cullen had to remind him
that the horses weren't his to lose, even as he opened
the corral gate. "I reckon," Art replied. "I just spent so
many years tryin' to make sure this didn't happen."

"It might buy us a little more time," Cullen said.
"I'd like to make sure they scattered, but I reckon if
we try to stampede 'em, they *would* hear that in the
saloon. If we had the time, we'd cut all the cinch straps
on these saddles, but I reckon it would be best for us
to get goin' while everything's still quiet."

Art tied his raincoat and the few personal items he
wanted to take with him onto Cullen's packhorse.
Then they rode away from the stable on the narrow
footpath that led to Hortense Billings's house. Both
of them agreed that they should take the time to let
Hortense and the others know what had happened,
and Art could pick up some extra clothes. Cullen was
sure they would want to know that Art was still alive.
In the deep darkness under the trees, Cullen let Art
lead them, since he knew the twists and turns in the
path so well.

With no idea what the hour was, only that it was

late, they arrived at the boardinghouse to find it totally dark, everyone having gone to bed. It didn't stay that way for long. Hortense's two hound dogs came out from under the back porch to alert the house. Art tried to quiet the baying hounds, but he was not in time to prevent a couple of lamps from flaring into light in two separate windows. As Cullen and Art dismounted, the lamps left the windows and showed up together in the kitchen. The door opened slightly, and Annie demanded, "Who's out there?"

"It's me and Cullen," Art answered her. "We figured we didn't have nothin' else to do, so we thought we'd pay you ladies a visit." Cullen, as well as Annie and Hortense, was surprised by his show of carefree bravado.

"Did they knock you in the head?" Annie demanded. "That bunch of scum will sure as hell be out here lookin' for you. This is the first place they'll look."

"We know that," Cullen assured her. "We planned to stop just long enough to let you folks know that Art's gonna miss his appointment with that necktie party in the mornin'. Then we'll be on our way." He knew that what Annie had just said was very likely what would happen. Moran and his crew would be here to look for them. It had troubled him as he thought about that possibility on the ride from the stable.

Having been awakened by the sound of the dogs barking under his window, Roy Skelton came down to stand in the kitchen door behind Hortense and Annie. "I swear," he exclaimed upon seeing who the women were talking to. "Danged if he didn't do it, just what he said he would do!"

It was a little longer before Pearson and George joined them, their rooms being on the front of the house. Like Roy, they wanted to hear how Art had escaped. He was about to give them a blow-by-blow accounting of it, but Cullen cut him short, and pushed to get started. "I don't know how long it's gonna be before they discover you're gone, and how long it's gonna take them to round up their horses. So, to play it safe, we need to get away from here right now." He turned to Hortense then. "When they show up here, don't give 'em any trouble. If they wanna search the house, let 'em. Don't give 'em any reason to get rough. I'm sorry to have to leave you like this, but it's better than havin' a shootout here."

"I understand," Hortense said, "and I think I like our chances better that way. Have you got anything to eat?" Cullen said he had some jerky, flour, and coffee in his packs, and maybe, if they were lucky, they might find some rabbits, squirrels, or a deer to hunt. "I've got bacon in the smokehouse. You'd best take some with you." He tried to refuse it, but she insisted. "Won't take me a minute," she said, and ran immediately to the smokehouse.

Art, basking in the glory of his escape, appeared to be disappointed when Cullen said it was time to ride, but a grin reappeared on his face and he said, "They locked me up in the jailhouse and went to the saloon. Afterwhile, Cullen come up and kicked the front door off its hinges and unlocked the cell door. We went to the stable and let all the horses out. End of story."

Cullen tied the side of bacon onto the packhorse, and they rode out of the backyard, heading for the creek and the prairie beyond.

"Oh shit!" Stan Molloy blurted when he approached the jail and saw the gaping black hole where the heavy oak door was supposed to be. "Oh shit!" he repeated, and ran the rest of the way, drawing his .44 as he ran. Just before reaching the step up to the door, he stopped running and took a more cautious approach. The full moon was now higher in the sky and more directly over the center of the roof. Consequently, there was just enough light falling on the doorway to permit him to see only a few feet inside the office. Fearing an ambush waiting for him inside the jail, he pressed his body against the wall to the side of the doorway and tried to peek inside. He was still unable to see anything inside the room. "Becker!" he called for no reason other than he didn't know what else to do. When there was no answer, he knew he was going to have to go inside. He couldn't go back to the Cork and Bottle and tell Micah Moran he didn't check inside because he was afraid he'd get shot. At this point, he wasn't sure that Becker was gone. He might still be in the cell. He had to be sure, so he knew he had to go inside. There was a chance that he might get shot. But if he didn't go in to check, he was sure to get shot when he reported that to Moran. With no concern for the time he might be wasting, he called again. "Becker! You in there?" He waited for a minute or so, then reached in his pocket for a match. He struck it on his belt buckle and carefully held the burning match at arm's length before him. When nothing happened, he followed it inside the building to discover it was empty, no Becker inside the cell, and the cell door standing open with the key in the lock. When the flame started to flicker down, he pulled out another match and lit it off the first one. Then he used that match to light the lamp on the desk. Fearing the wrath of Micah Moran to come down on them all, he took the lamp in hand and walked inside the open cell. Standing in the middle of the cell, he turned around in a circle, as if hoping to see Becker hiding somewhere, in a room where there was no place to hide.

Fearing the worst, he left the lamp on the desk, still lit, and walked back across the street to the saloon, pausing a moment when a horse trotted in front of him. It didn't strike him as odd, his mind occupied with how Moran was going to react to the news he was bringing. He continued on to the saloon, his mind so locked on the escape that he paid no attention to the two horses walking between the saloon and the hotel.

Inside the saloon, Micah Moran was sitting at a table talking to Jeb Dickens and Riley Pitts, two bank robbers on the run from Arizona Territory. The hour was late, and Moran had been drinking since supper, but he had no desire to retire for the night. He would sleep late in the morning. And when Molloy had asked what time he wanted Becker out for his hanging, Moran had told him whenever he got up and had his breakfast. "There ain't no hurry," he had told Molloy. "Let him stew a little longer over gettin' his neck stretched. Besides, I wanna make sure the town council gets a chance to see it. I wanna make sure everybody's come to work in time."

Sitting at the table now with the two young men from Arizona, Moran was already in the process of re-building his posse of outlaws. Jeb and Riley had just come from Tucson, where they were chased by a posse of angry vigilantes. Having heard of East City, Texas, as a haven for outlaws on the run, they headed there straightaway. It had turned out to be a lucky decision,

they thought, for they found that Micah Moran was
hiring new members for his outlaw posse. A fair monthly
payment, plus occasional opportunities to pull a job
and receive a portion of the profit. Added to this was
the benefit of various goods and services at the expense of the merchants in town, a room in the hotel
with hot-and-cold-running prostitutes. And your boss
is the town marshal.

"So, whaddaya say, boys?" Moran asked. "You wanna
ride with my posse?"

They didn't have to think about it, or even look at
each other before replying. "Yes, sir," they said almost
in unison. Then Riley, who was Jeb's elder by two
years, spoke for them. "Yes, sir," he repeated. "And I
don't mind tellin' ya, you got yourself two good men.
Me and Jeb has been makin' a livin' offa cattle ranchers, sheepherders, banks, and anyplace that had a
payroll. Ain't that right, Jeb?" Jeb nodded, grinning
proudly.

Unimpressed, but in desperate need of gunmen,
Moran asked, "You ever kill a man? Either one of you?"

There was no hesitation on Riley's part. He answered
right away. "Yes, sir, we've been shot at plenty, and
there's been times when we had to kill a man before
he killed us." He looked at Jeb again for confirmation, and as before, Jeb nodded profusely.

"How many times have you had to kill?" Moran
asked, already of the opinion neither of them had
ever killed.

"I don't know," Riley fumbled. "Once or twice, I
reckon. You remember, Jeb?"

"Once or twice," Jeb repeated.

Although certain now that he was talking to two

greenhorn would-be outlaws that may have robbed a candy store in addition to that one bank they were now on the run from, Moran was not in a position to be choosy. He needed men. He could cull them out after he was fully strong again. "All right, boys, welcome to my posse. The first thing you've gotta know is, I pay the bills, so my word is law. Any of my men will tell you that. Understand?"

"Yes, sir." Almost in unison again.

Moran picked up the whiskey bottle in the center of the table and filled three glasses. "Let's have a drink on it." They tossed the whiskey back and slammed the glasses back hard on the table. "Tomorrow mornin' you'll get a chance to see what happens to those who cause me trouble."

Sitting at another table closer to the door, Shorty and Leroy sat, working on another bottle of whiskey. Both of them were interested spectators of the hiring of the two new men. "Damn if those two ain't the greenest gourds I've ever seen," Shorty commented. "I hate to think we've got so desperate that I'd have to depend on one of them to back me up."

"Yeah," Leroy said. "Look at ol' Micah givin' 'em the evil eye. Two months ago, he'da run 'em outta here to go back to the farm." Further discussion was halted when Stan Molloy suddenly burst into the front door, looking as if he had seen a ghost. "What's the matter with him?" Leroy uttered as Molloy stopped and looked around until he spotted Moran, then went straight to him.

"He's broke out!" Molloy blurted. "Becker's gone!"

"What the . . ." Moran uttered as he came to his feet. "What are you talkin' about?"

"He's gone!" Molloy repeated. "He ain't there no more!"

"What do you mean?" Moran pressed. "You mean he's dead?" His first thought was that Art had somehow killed himself, because there was little chance that he had found a way to break out of a locked cell inside a building locked from the outside.

"I mean he's gone!" Molloy insisted, frustrated that Moran didn't seem to understand simple English. "I went to check on him and the door was open and the cell empty!"

Moran's face flushed red, but he said nothing. Instead, he ran immediately to the door, thinking his deputy must be drunk or crazy or both. He had to see for himself, and right away, that Molloy was wrong, too drunk to know what he had seen. Moran had suffered too many defeats in the few days since Cullen McCabe had entered his world. His patience was at an end when it came to the somber stranger who continued to thwart his every move. With his gun drawn, he ran out the door. Alarmed as well by Molloy's frantic announcement, Shorty and Leroy jumped to their feet and followed Moran out the door, weapons ready to fire. Confused by the sudden charge out the door, the two newly recruited members of the posse looked at each other in astonishment, then jumped up and followed the others.

The first thing Micah Moran noticed, when he ran out on the dark street, was the sight of a couple of horses, standing unattended, casually watching the men pouring out of the saloon. His mind occupied with Molloy's announcement, he didn't bother to wonder about their presence in the street. Before he was halfway across the street, he could see the lamp

sitting on the desk through the open doorway. Just as
Molloy had, he went inside to see for himself and
was back standing in the damaged doorway when
Shorty and Leroy arrived. "He's right," Moran confirmed. "The dirty rat is gone." He stepped outside
and looked up and down the street. It occurred to
him then. "Where the hell did all these stray horses
come from?"

The five men gathered at the door of the jailhouse
all looked around, too, aware of the unusual number
of horses as well. "I know where one of 'em came
from," Leroy suddenly announced. "That's my buckskin yonder. Somebody's turned the horses outta the
stable!" He started toward the horse, but the buckskin
decided it was enjoying its freedom and turned to trot
off toward the other end of the street. Leroy ran after
it. Shorty and the other men started looking for their
horses, but Moran yelled at them to go to the stable
first to see if they were all out, or just the ones they saw
in the street. Leroy was already too far up the street to
hear the order, but the other men headed for the stables. Jeb and Riley led the pack, eager to please their
new boss. When they reached the stables, they found
the corral gate open and the barn door open as well.
There were a couple of horses milling around the
front of the stable. They were quickly herded back
in and the men prepared to go back to catch the rest
of them.

"Grab some rope," Shorty yelled. "I didn't see no
bridles on them other ones." Already in a panic to save
their horses, the other men ran in the barn to fetch
rope from their saddles.

Equally as frantic to retrieve his horse, a four-year-
old Morgan gelding named Satan, that stood fifteen

hands high, Moran caught Riley Pitts by the arm when he ran by him. "Are you any good with that rope?" When Riley said that he was born and raised on a cattle ranch, Moran said, "Good, you stick close to me." The marshal was no good with a rope, and he was desperate to find that Morgan. Even though Cullen had not thought it worth the risk to make enough noise to stampede the horses out of town, his emptying of the stable proved to be more effective than he had anticipated. It gained several hours for him and Art, since the horses scattered about town before finally ending up along the creek bank. By the time they were all rounded up, it was only a half hour or so before sunrise.

Some of the early risers in town, like the black-smith, Buck Casey, were treated to see the curious horse roundup by Moran's men on foot, as they herded the horses toward the stables. At the precise time they drove the horses by him, Buck was standing on the one step before the jailhouse, staring with wonder at the smashed-in door. He had already gone inside when he saw the jail was open and found that the prisoner was gone, and he was anxious to spread the word about his discovery. Knowing Art Becker could not have done this by himself, it was not diffi-cult to guess whose work it was. *Cullen McCabe* was the name that came to him. *Art had escaped!* He was eager to tell Abe and Joe, especially. He started to return to his shop when he saw Micah Moran walking behind the herd of horses. Thinking he might risk getting shot, Buck still could not resist asking the question. It was in his nature. "Mornin', Marshal." He nodded back toward the jailhouse door. "Does this mean the hangin's canceled?"

Moran jerked his head around sharply to stare menacingly at Buck. "No, damn it," he answered. "It means it's delayed." He continued walking toward the Cork and Bottle, but stopped before taking more than a dozen paces to turn back and say, "And you'd best get started to repair that door. So anybody that wants to can kick it in," he added sarcastically.

"Yes, sir, Marshal, I'll get right on it," Buck responded. *I hung that door on those hinges, myself*, he thought, *so anybody couldn't have kicked it in. It took a hell of a man, who was mad as hell, to kick that door in.* He headed back to his shop, wondering how long it would be before Joe Johnson opened the store. He couldn't wait to tell him the news. The dark sky was already starting to lighten up with the promise of the sun's appearance. Buck looked toward the distant hills on the eastern horizon and thought, *Looks like it's going to be a good day.*

It was certainly an interesting day, at least for two young outlaws on the run from Arizona Territory. The reason they had made East City their destination when they had fled was stories they had heard of Micah Moran and his outlaw posse. The picture they had formed of the outlaw empire was vastly different than the scene they witnessed today. To begin with, the marshal's posse had been reduced considerably, down to the marshal, and in their young eyes, three washed-up-looking saddle tramps, one of whom had only one eye. Never having met Boot Davis, Charley Turner, Ace Brown, or any of the other hardened gunmen who rode with Moran until recently, their picture of the posse was not intimidating.

"You know what, Riley?" Jeb saw fit to remark. "Micah Moran needs me and you a lot more than he realizes. And from the looks of those three he's got left, that ain't much of a posse. I think we mighta landed right where we wanted to."

Riley grinned back at him. "I can't say as I disagree, partner, and the sooner he finds out, the better."

CHAPTER 14

It was a good day, indeed, that greeted Art Becker as he awakened after a couple of hours' sleep. He rolled over and sat up to discover Cullen kindling a fire. "Mornin'," he said.

Cullen looked over at him. "Mornin'," he returned. "I'll get some coffee workin' here in a minute, then I'll fry up some of that bacon Hortense gave us. How 'bout it? Think you could use a little coffee?"

"I surely could," Art answered. "And I don't care if you make a good cup of coffee or a sorry one, it'll be the best cup of coffee I've ever had in my whole life. When you kicked that door in, it sounded like the whole jailhouse blew up. But it turned into music like the angels sing. I ain't never been so glad to see anybody as I was when you came through that door."

"Damn," Cullen replied, "I reckon I better pay attention to what I'm doin'." He could well appreciate Art's good spirits, considering what he had expected to happen to him on this morning. He had no real notion of how far ahead of Micah Moran and his posse he and Art had gotten during the remainder of the night just passed. But he had decided to stop by this little stream that made its way down a narrow ravine in a line of low hills. It offered good water and there was plenty of grass for the horses. He had decided that, as well as the horses, he and Art needed to rest. And if they were not as far ahead of their pursuers as he hoped, and had to defend themselves, the top of the ravine would be a good place to do it.

"What can I do to help you?" Art asked.

"Well, I ain't exactly cookin' up a big breakfast here," Cullen replied. "I'll let you cook your own bacon. How 'bout that? And I've got some hardtack in one of those packs we can fry in the bacon grease. It won't be like you'd be gettin' back at Annie's table, but maybe it'll keep the sides of your stomach from rubbin' together."

"That suits me just fine," Art said as he caught the cup Cullen tossed to him. He watched his mysterious rescuer, compelled to wonder why this complete stranger had risked his life to save his. "You know," he felt the need to say, "I don't know if I thanked you for gettin' me outta that jail. But if I didn't, I wanna thank you now."

"Well, you're welcome, but if it wasn't for me, you wouldn't have been in that jail. So I sure couldn't let you hang just because that little rat I shoulda shot surprised us on the path back to the house. The question right now is what to do next." He was thinking about where to leave Art while he returned to finish what he had started.

"Whatever you say, partner," Art said. "I would like to get my stable back, but I reckon we'll be on the run for a spell, till Moran gives up on findin' us." He filled his cup with coffee when the pot finished boiling. "I hate to give up my room at Hortense Billings's board-in'house, though. I don't know when I'll ever get back there, maybe never." He took a sip of the hot coffee. "I reckon it won't do no harm to talk about it now, since I might not ever go back, but I've got a soft spot in my heart when it comes to Hortense. I was even thinkin' I might wanna see if she'd consider hookin' up with me." He looked up at Cullen and added, "You know, marriage."

Cullen was surprised to hear that affirmation come from the mild-mannered stable owner. He hadn't noticed any obvious signs of Art's affection for the spunky landlady in the short time he had spent at her house. He was not sure how to respond to his confession. Finally, he spoke his mind. "You know, Art, you're talkin' like you ain't ever goin' back to East City, like you and me are gonna have to leave the territory for good. I'm plannin' to go back. I've got unfinished business to take care of in your town. And what I'm hopin' is that, since you showed 'em the guts you had to take Moran's boys down, maybe it'll encourage Abe Franks, Joe Johnson, Buck Casey, and some of the others to fight to get rid of Moran for good. I'm thinkin' you and the others aren't quite ready to give up on East City." He paused, then added, "I think that would be a pretty good pairin', too, you and Hortense."

"You think so? She might take a broom to my backside, if I was to ask her." He paused to picture it, then returned to the subject of taking back their town. "I don't know, Cullen. I ain't sure we're strong enough to go up against Moran, even if he ain't got all the men he used to have. They're still cold-blooded gunmen and I ain't even there to help 'em. I don't see any chance of it."

"I'm not talkin' about Franks and the others doin' it all by themselves," Cullen tried to explain. "I'm plannin' to draw Moran out to settle it. I don't expect the townspeople to take that gang on themselves. And I don't expect to drag you into any shootouts with those gunslingers, either. Right now, we have to decide where you can go to be safe for the next few days. Do you know anybody in Ravenwood?" He could see that his statement had Art confused.

"Well, yeah, I know Jim Farmer," Art said. "He owns a stable over there. I used to be partners with him before I got the bright idea to build my own stable in East City." He grunted an amused chuckle and said, "You can see how that turned out."

"You still get along with Farmer?" Cullen asked, thinking the split might not have been a friendly one.

"I reckon," Art answered.

"Think maybe he'd let you stay in his stable for a little while, till things in East City get under a little better control?"

"I expect so," Art said, scratching his head while he considered it. "If he don't, my sister will let me stay at the house. She's his wife. But I'd just as soon stay in the stable."

Cullen didn't say anything for a few moments while he paused to wonder if he really had heard what Art had just said. "Jim Farmer is your brother-in-law?"

"He married my sister, Rena," Art stated simply. "I reckon that makes him my brother-in-law." Cullen couldn't help shaking his head when he thought about his meeting Jim Farmer. At the time, his first thought was that Farmer reminded him of Art, even to the extent they could have been brothers.

"Good," Cullen said. "We're goin' to Ravenwood right after we eat this fine breakfast." Art looked disappointed, and it occurred to Cullen that the mild little man wanted to stay with him when he went back to East City. Cullen didn't want to risk Art's life again with any meeting he might have with Moran or any of Moran's men. He worked better alone when it came to what he planned to do, anyway. Foremost in his mind was to check to see if Hortense and her little family were not being threatened by Moran. He was bound to go there to search for him. Thoughts of his family came back to haunt him. He feared a fate for Hortense and Annie like the fate of his Mary Kate and the children. There was a good possibility that things would get pretty nasty before he was through with East City, and he didn't want to have to worry about Art's safety, too. Of concern also, however, was Art's newfound courage. Cullen did not want to discourage him, or make him feel he was not thought of as dependable. So he said, "I'll look around to see how things are settlin' down over there. It's easier for one man to scout out the place. Then I might need you to help me if it comes to goin' up against the posse. Whaddaya think?"

"You can count on me," Art said at once. "If it comes to the town squarin' off against Moran and his gang, I wanna be in on it."

"I knew I could count on you," Cullen said. "When I need help, you're the first one I would think of."

That seemed to satisfy Art, and he settled back to eat his bacon and the hardtack Cullen had fried. After a while, he began to think about everything that had happened in the last few days, especially to him, and he was prompted to ask a question. "Cullen, somethin' I ain't figured out, why are you takin' on East City's fight with Micah Moran? You didn't know anybody here before you rode in with Lila Blanchard. And you said from the first, you ain't plannin' to stay. How come you're riskin' your life to help us?"

"I don't know, Art, sometimes I do crazy things, I reckon. I ain't got anything better to do right now."

"I reckon you're the first crazy man I ever had any use for," Art declared. "I'd hate to see you get yourself shot while you're in one of your crazy spells."

When breakfast was finished, they saddled up and set out for Ravenwood. They would have to ride back a few miles in a more northeastern direction, since they had ridden west of the town the night just passed. Cullen was not overly worried about the chance they might meet Moran and his posse coming after them. But he decided not to double back on their own trail, just in case Moran was a better tracker than he figured. He doubted Moran could track them during the night, at any rate.

"I declare, Art Becker," Jim Farmer acknowledged when he walked out of the stable to meet the two riders approaching. He grinned when he saw his brother-in-law. "Reckon had I better notify Marshal Taggert that one of them outlaws from East City is in town?" He chuckled and winked at Cullen. "I was thinkin' it was about time you gave up on that devil's playground across the creek and came back to work with me."

"Howdy, Jim," Art returned. "I'm glad to see you're still in business since I left."

"Hell, business has picked up since you left," Jim joked. He nodded to Cullen, then said to Art. "I see you met up with the feller who saved Tug Taggert's bacon." Art gave Cullen a look of surprise. He knew only that Cullen had shot one of Moran's men in Ravenwood, but he didn't know anything about saving the marshal's bacon. Before he could comment on it, Farmer continued talking. "You gonna be able to visit Rena while you're here?"

"I expect so," Art answered, "since I'm plannin' on sleepin' with my horse for a couple of days or more in your stable. That is, if you don't charge too much."

Jim looked genuinely surprised when he heard that, but he continued to jape with his brother-in-law. "Is that a fact? I reckon I'd best clean up the bridal stall and throw down some fresh hay." Cullen was glad to see there appeared to be no friction between the two ex-partners. Jim turned his attention to Cullen then. "Glad to see you back in town, even with the company you're keepin'." He winked at Art. "What brings you two back to Ravenwood?"

"I reckon I'll leave Art to tell you that," Cullen answered.

When Jim looked at Art then, Art chuckled and said, "I just broke outta jail and Cullen thinks I oughta lay low for a while."

"What were you in jail for?" Jim asked. "Anything serious?"

"Well, I reckon you could say so," Art answered with a wide grin on his face. "They was plannin' on hangin' me this mornin'." Confused, Jim automatically looked at the black horse Art had ridden in on. Reading his thoughts, Art said, "No, it ain't for stealin' the horse. They don't even know about that yet, I don't reckon."

Cullen couldn't help noticing that Art was enjoying his new notoriety and before he started to fill Jim in on all the events that led to their appearance at his stable, he interrupted. "Well, I'll leave you two to catch up with everything. If it's all right with you, I'll leave my packhorse here with you, Art. I'll get my war bag with the few things I'll need and I'll head out."

"What's your hurry?" Jim asked, totally unaware of the urgency of their appearance in Ravenwood. "You'd be welcome to take dinner with us at the house. My wife would be tickled to have you join us." He paused to issue a chuckle. "I don't know about her brother, though."

"'Preciate it," Cullen said, "but I expect I'd best not linger—as good as it sounds. Art, I'll be in touch as soon as I see how things are gonna go." He untied his war bag from the packhorse and tied it onto Jake, then he promptly climbed on the bay. "Much obliged," he said, wheeled the horse, and started off down the street at a comfortable lope.

In spite of his intent to mount an early search party for the escaped prisoner and his conspirator, Micah Moran found himself still delayed in East City. It had taken well into the morning to round up all the stray horses and drive them back to the stable. Even then, they were not at all certain that they had recovered all of them. His posse were all stumbling around, nursing hangovers from a night of celebrating the hanging to come, as well as a night with no sleep at all. Moran, himself, was not exempt from the suffering his men were experiencing, having imbibed too heavily, too. But he was driven by the burning desire to kill Cullen McCabe. The recapture and hanging of Art Becker would be satisfying, but secondary to the death of McCabe, preferably by his hand. He had overheard grumbling between Shorty and Molloy, that it was useless to saddle up and go after Becker and McCabe. They thought they were too late to catch them now and tracking would be unlikely. But Moran was convinced that Becker and McCabe would go straight to Hortense Billings's house from here to pick up anything they needed for their escape. "I reckon we're ready to ride, Boss," Stan Molloy said, interrupting Moran's thoughts.

"Get the men in the saddle, then," Moran replied. "We'll head to that woman's boardin'house on that little path behind the stable."

"You reckon we oughta load up a couple of pack-horses?" Molloy asked. "How long you reckon we'll be gone?"

"No," Moran answered, not willing to wait another minute longer. "We need to get to that boardin'house as soon as possible while the trail's fresh. If we don't find 'em hidin' out around there somewhere, we'll try to pick up their trail from there. We'll send back here for supplies then."

"Right," Molloy responded, although with very little enthusiasm. He then risked Moran's ire by making another comment. "When you come to think of it, with Becker and McCabe on the run, they're just gettin' rid of our problem for us. With McCabe gone, things will just get back to normal. Whaddaya think, Boss? Ain't that about right?"

"Get ready to ride," Moran answered. "We've already lost too much time. You and Shorty ain't got sense enough to know that the folks in this town need to see Art Becker swingin' from that pole. That's what it takes to keep 'em in line." Molloy turned and started toward the four men gathered at the front door of Art Becker's barn, their horses saddled and waiting. Having second thoughts, Moran stopped him. "You tell them to get ready. You're gonna stay here and keep the peace in town till we get back," he ordered. It had struck him that, as a matter of insurance, one of his men should always be there to be seen by the merchants. And Molloy, being the deputy, was the logical choice to stay. "And you be damn sure everybody sees that you're watchin' the town."

"Right, Boss," Molloy responded, this time with considerably more enthusiasm. "I'll get 'em ready to ride." Nothing could have made him happier at this particular moment with his head pounding like someone was inside it, trying to get out, and a load of liquid contents in his stomach that threatened to erupt at the same time. Already planning his day, he told himself that as soon as the posse pulled out, he was going to get a dose of the hair of the dog that bit him. Then he would get Lizzie to cook something for him to see if he could hold it down. Then he was going to get some sleep. With all those thoughts in his head, he walked up to the four men waiting at the barn. "Micah said, get on your horses."

"I swear," Leroy complained, "oughta let 'em go and be done with 'em."

"You can tell Micah that," Molloy said. "He might let you stay here and keep an eye on the town with me."

"Whaddaya mean, with you?" Shorty asked. "You ain't stayin' here."

"I hate to let you boys down," Molloy japed, "but we can't leave the town without any protection. Micah says I gotta stay and protect the town. Makes sense 'cause I'm the deputy marshal. Folks respect me. They wouldn't pay you no mind." He stood back and laughed at the two of them as they reluctantly climbed up into the saddle.

Standin' a little apart, saying nothing, but listening to the conversation going back and forth between the three older members of the posse, Riley Pitts and Jeb Dickens climbed on their horses, as well. "These jaspers act like a couple of old men," Riley said aside to Jeb. "We can damn sure outdrink 'em, and I expect we can outshoot 'em, if it comes to that. All we need to do is get a chance to show Micah what we can do." Jeb nodded his agreement. When Micah climbed up on the big Morgan named Satan, he signaled for Shorty to lead out to the path. That was in case McCabe might be waiting somewhere on the narrow little footpath in ambush. Shorty had always assumed he led because Micah thought he was the best tracker. Jeb and Riley moved their horses in line as close to Moran's as they could.

Molloy stood watching them ride away until he could no longer see them. Then he turned and headed as fast as his aching head would permit to the Cork and Bottle. When he went inside, he found Tom Loughlin, Micah's partner in the saloon, seated at a table with a couple of cowhands from one of the ranches east of town. Molloy figured they were most likely out of money and were trying to talk Loughlin into granting them some credit. There were no other customers in the saloon, which suited Molloy just fine. He went to the bar and told Floyd to pour him a stiff drink. "I thought you boys had drunk all the whiskey you could hold for a week," Floyd cracked as he poured the whiskey. "What you doin' back here? I thought you were goin' after Becker."

"Micah and the rest of 'em went after Becker and McCabe. I'm stayin' here to look after the town, and I ain't in no mood to put up with any trouble."

"Well, I don't know if drinkin' more of that corn whiskey is gonna do you any good. Maybe you oughta get Lizzie to make you some coffee instead, maybe a little somethin' to eat along with it, if you can hold it down."

"I was thinkin' about doin' that, but I need a little hair of the dog first," Molloy insisted. "Pour me another one."

"All right, but if you ask me . . ." That was as far as he got before Molloy cut him off.

"Damn it, I didn't ask you," he blurted. "Just pour the damn drink!" Floyd said no more, shrugged, and poured the glass full. Having seen Molloy's short temper before, he didn't say anything further. The belligerent deputy took his glass of whiskey and sat down at a table a few feet from Loughlin and the two cowhands. He didn't bother to acknowledge Tom. None of the posse had much to do with Micah's partner, even though he had a half ownership in the saloon. He had been the one who originally bankrolled the building of the Cork and Bottle. It was a feeling among the posse that it would only be a matter of time before Micah decided to retire him with a bullet in his head. After taking another stiff drink of the corn whiskey, Molloy decided he'd better get some coffee and food inside him. "Floyd!" he roared out. "Go tell Lizzie I need somethin' to eat, and I need some coffee to go with it." His words were followed out of his mouth by the contents of his stomach which splattered across the entire surface of the table. Molloy wiped his mouth with his sleeve and swore. "Damn," he blurted, "and tell her to bring a mop and a bucket to clean this mess up."

Tom Loughlin, as a rule, made very little noise in the saloon he owned half of. Like everyone else in town, he was in fear of Micah Moran. And he especially avoided contact with the outlaws that frequented his saloon. But this disgusting exhibition was too much to ignore, so he commented, "Lizzie's busy getting ready for dinner, Molloy. I think it would be a good idea if you went up to your room and slept it off." He glanced at the two cowhands sitting with him before adding, "You'll be driving off our customers."

Molloy was in no mood to be corrected. "Our customers? You mean Micah's customers, don't you? You snivelin' old bastard, I'll let you know if I wanna hear anything outta you. Lizzie!" He shouted as loud as he could. "Get your lazy behind out here and clean this up." His howling brought Wilma and Mabel from the back room to see what the fuss was about. Seeing them, Molloy shouted, "You two come clean this up."

"Clean it up, yourself," Wilma responded. "You did it."

"Why, you low-down slut, I'll make you lick it up," Molloy threatened, and got up from his chair.

"I think that's about enough outta you," one of the cowhands sitting with Tom spoke up then and got to his feet. "You'd best do like everybody's been tellin' you and go on to your bed, wherever that is."

"Well, now," Molloy said. "You reckon you're man enough to make me?"

"I reckon I am," the young man said. "But it wouldn't be a fair fight. You're too drunk to stand up on your own. You'd best get on outta here. You'll feel better after you sober up."

"Is that so? You're pretty good about tellin' people what they oughta do, ain'tcha? I see you're wearin' a gun. You any good with it?"

"It don't matter if I am or not. This ain't gonna come to any gunplay," the cowhand quickly replied. "I don't use my gun for nothin' but killin' snakes."

"That's too bad," Molloy said, "'cause I use mine for yellow-belly cowboys." He drew his six-gun and shot him in the stomach. Stunned, the young man bent double and collapsed and Molloy turned to aim his .44 at the unfortunate cowhand's friend, who immediately put his hands in the air.

Tom Loughlin stood up at once and stood in front of the frightened cowhand. "He ain't lookin' for no trouble. Put it away!"

They stood for a long moment, glaring at each other, Molloy's .44 still leveled at Loughlin. At the bar, Floyd stood rigidly fixed, not certain what to do. There was a double-barreled shotgun within his easy reach, only a few feet away, but he was hesitant about going for it. Molloy was obviously deciding whether or not to shoot the half owner of the Cork and Bottle. No matter if the posse held low regard for Micah's partner, he couldn't let a drunken outlaw shoot him down. He was saved from reaching for the shotgun when Molloy lowered his gun. "Get him outta here before I cut you down, too," he ordered the wounded man's friend. He looked at Loughlin and said, "You're lucky I ain't in a bad mood." Then he pushed him aside and stalked into the kitchen to confront a frightened cook.

Loughlin exhaled a sigh of relief as the tension that had gripped the almost-empty saloon eased with Molloy's departure. He turned to the wounded man's friend, who was stunned speechless. "You'd best take your friend to get some help," Loughlin said. "Mabel, get him a bar towel to help stop that bleeding." Back to the dumbfounded cowhand, he said, "There ain't no doctor here, but if he can stay on a horse, there's one across the creek in Ravenwood. Here's a couple of dollars to pay the doctor." With Floyd, Mabel, and Wilma's help, they managed to get the wounded man into the saddle, leaning forward on his horse's neck, and they started for the road leading to Ravenwood.

"I don't know, Tom, you think he'll make it?" Floyd asked.

"I doubt it," Loughlin answered. It was not the Cork and Bottle's policy to pay the doctor's bill for patrons shot in their establishment. But he was especially sickened by Molloy's blatant murder of a customer. He and Micah had discussed the savage disregard his men had for human life before, but Micah had maintained that the nature of his posse was what maintained the peace in East City. Loughlin planned to talk to Moran about this incident when he returned. He turned to Floyd and repeated, "I doubt it." They could still hear Molloy grumbling in the kitchen while Lizzie tried to sober him up.

CHAPTER 15

Lying on his belly, on a sandy rise on the west bank of the creek, Cullen McCabe watched the column of outlaws emerge from the trees along the narrow footpath and ride out into the yard behind the house. From his position, not quite fifty yards away, he could see each rider clearly. And with his rifle ready, he could easily pick one or two of them off before they took cover. He hesitated to do that, however, thinking he was reluctant to ignite a gunfight that might cause Moran to take cover inside the house. And that might result in injuries to Hortense and Annie, if only for the purpose of retaliating for the loss of his men. It was perfectly clear to him that the solution to East City's problems was the complete extermination of Micah Moran and his rats. And at this point, he would not hesitate to start the process, but the safety of Hortense, Annie, and Roy was too important for him to make his fight here. So he decided he would hold his fire as long as there was no threat to any of those three.

As Micah Moran rode around Shorty, pulled his horse up before the kitchen door, and dismounted,

Cullen watched the rest of the men file into the yard behind him. He counted four men riding with Moran. Art had told him that Moran had only three men left, so that meant he had picked up another man already. Then he remembered that Art had described Moran's new deputy as a one-eyed man who wore an eye patch over his left eye. From his sandy rise by the creek, he could easily see there was no man wearing an eye patch. That had to mean that Moran had picked up two new men, and he had left the one-eyed deputy in town. He had to consider the possibility that Moran might have picked up more than the two he could now account for. It wasn't likely, however. He would have probably brought everybody except the one man left to cover the town.

He watched while Moran and his men searched around the house. Finding no trace of him or Art, Moran sent two of the men to search inside the house. Cullen guessed Moran didn't go in, himself, because of the risk of someone hiding behind a bed, waiting to ambush him. The temptation to thin out one or two of the notorious posse was strong, but Cullen couldn't risk it. Moran was bound to hold Hortense and Annie as hostages and shoot Roy. So all he could do was sit and watch, waiting to fire only if he was forced to. After what seemed a long time, the posse mounted up again and left, following the tracks he and Art had left when they rode away during the night before. When he was sure the posse was going to continue their tracking, he whistled Jake up from the trees behind him and rode across the creek to the house.

"Good Lord in heaven!" Annie cried out when she

saw Cullen ride up from the creek. Out the kitchen door she ran, in a panic, thinking he wasn't aware that Moran was just there. "Cullen," she exclaimed, "they was just here lookin' for you!"

"I know, Annie, I saw 'em. They're gone now, tryin' to follow our trail away from here." Considering the possibility they might decide not to follow their tracks very far, he said, "I just wanted to make sure you folks were all right and then I'm gone."

"We're all right," Annie said. "But you'd better not stay here long. They might be back."

"I know. I'm leavin' right away. Thought you and Hortense would like to know that Art is all right. He's stayin' in Ravenwood with his brother-in-law."

"His brother-in-law?" Annie responded. "Art ain't never said anything about a brother-in-law." She thought another couple of seconds and said, "He ain't ever said anything about havin' a sister."

"Well, he's safe where he is," Cullen said. "I'll be on my way. Just wanted to know you were all right." He turned Jake back toward the footpath and disappeared into the trees.

Behind Annie, Hortense came to the kitchen door and asked, "They come back?"

"No," Annie said.

"Well, who were you talking to?"

"Cullen."

"Cullen?" Hortense responded. "What were you talking about?"

"Art," Annie answered. "He said Art's all right. He's stayin' with his sister."

"Sister?"

* * *

Some doubts returned to his mind as he rode the narrow footpath back to town. He had made his decision to mount a one-man war on Moran and his posse primarily for a personal reason. The trial and planned hanging of Art Becker, after the brutal hanging of an innocent woman, had turned this assignment into a personal war. He wasn't sure how O'Brien and the governor would react to his method of eliminating the problem he was sent to investigate. But he saw it as the only way to put a halt to it right away. Moran was already hiring new men to ride with him. And now, as he approached the rear of Art's stable, he was thinking of the opportunity to eliminate Moran's deputy.

When he rode around to the front of the stable, he reined Jake to a halt when he saw a man on a horse, leading another horse with a second man on it. The man being led was evidently hurt, for he was lying on the neck of his horse. They were heading for the road to Ravenwood. His first thought was the man had been shot, and it didn't surprise him. Evidently, it was business as usual in East City. He wondered if Moran's new deputy apprehended the shooter. If he did, he had no jail to put him in. Then he corrected himself, for the deputy could lock him in the cell.

After the two riders passed, he nudged Jake again and headed for the Cork and Bottle, thinking that to be the place he would most likely find the deputy. He figured the most dangerous part of this trip for him was the ride up the street to the saloon because he would be shot on sight by anybody who worked for Moran. However, he went unnoticed by the few people in town with the exception of Buck Casey, who walked out to the front of his shop to watch him ride by. "Cullen McCabe," Buck muttered to himself, astonished to think he would show up in town after he was positive it was McCabe who busted the jailhouse door. He was further amazed when he saw Cullen pull up before the Cork and Bottle and dismount. "Lordy, Lordy," he muttered. "I think I need a drink." He pulled his blacksmith's apron off and hustled over to the Cork and Bottle.

Cullen, his rifle in hand, paused for a brief second at the door to survey the room before entering. The only people he saw were the bartender, talking to Tom Loughlin standing at the end of the bar, and two women seated at a table in the center of the room. When he stepped inside, all four faces turned to stare at him and all conversation stopped. From the kitchen, he could hear the drunken rambling of a male voice. He took a few more steps to stand closer to the center of the saloon, then stopped again to listen. There was still not a word spoken by any of the four he saw, only the continuous rambling of the man in the kitchen. "Who's in the kitchen?" Cullen asked.

Answering immediately, Wilma said, "Stan Molloy." Then she emphasized, "*Deputy* Stan Molloy."

Cullen nodded, then called out, "Molloy! Get out here!" There was no response right away, so he called out again.

This time the one-eyed deputy walked out of the kitchen and demanded, "Who the hell is hollerin' my name?" Then he stopped short when he saw the imposing figure standing in the middle of the room.

"Cullen McCabe," Cullen answered. "You lookin' for me?"

Dumbfounded, Molloy did the only thing he knew to do and reached for his gun. The .44 slug from Cullen's rifle struck him in the middle of his chest, causing him to take a couple of steps backward. His gun, only halfway out of his holster, dropped back in it as his knees buckled and he sank to the floor. Cullen's rifle immediately swung around to cover Floyd and Loughlin. "Lizzie, don't!" He heard the cry from Wilma behind him and turned to discover the skinny little cook standing at the kitchen door, holding a shotgun. "He's the man who brought Lila home," Wilma said, and Lizzie immediately put the shotgun down on the floor.

Cullen nodded to Wilma, then, with his rifle still leveled at Floyd and Loughlin, he asked, "Who else is here?"

"No one else," Loughlin answered.

"He's all right, McCabe, he ain't like Moran and his crowd." Cullen whipped his rifle around to discover Buck Casey standing at the front door. He raised his arms to show Cullen he wasn't armed.

Cullen recognized him as the man he had seen in front of the blacksmith shop. Responding to Buck's statement, he turned back toward Loughlin and said, "You need to find you a better partner, if you're plannin' on stayin' in this town."

"I run this place the best I can," Loughlin felt compelled to answer. "I can't help it if we attract so many of the least desirable customers."

Buck came on in the saloon and walked up to Cullen. "I'm Buck Casey. I got a little blacksmith shop you just passed on the street back there. I'm on the city council. Tom Loughlin's all right. I don't know how he got himself in a business deal with Micah Moran. He don't like to talk about it. Does he, girls?" He paused to grin at Wilma and Mabel. Back to Cullen then, he chuckled and said, "I'm the feller

Moran told to fix that door you kicked in last night. You must have a kick like a mule."

"Glad to meet you, Buck," Cullen said, then asked, "What makes you think it was me?"

Buck answered with a wide grin, "Ever'body in town knows who kicked that door open. Couldn'ta been nobody else."

Cullen knew who Buck was, but he had never talked to him. According to Art, Buck was one of the honest men in town, and Cullen was glad that he was because he felt he was a little careless in smoking out Stan Molloy. *Coulda got shot in the back twice*, he thought, *once by a skinny little woman with a shotgun, then again by a blacksmith standing at the door.* He was going to have to be more careful from now on and the first thing he wanted to know was how many he was up against. He figured Buck could tell him. "I saw Moran and his men out at Hortense Billings's house a little while ago. He had four men with him. Do you know if he's picked up any more that I oughta be watchin' over my shoulder for while I'm in town?"

"Nope," Buck answered. "Four's all he's got, now that you put the 'Out of Order' sign on ol' Molloy. He wouldn'ta had four, but there were two young fellers in town that were wantin' to join up, I reckon. 'Cause they rode out with Moran and Shorty and Leroy. But tell me where Art Becker is. Is he all right? I was tickled pink when I got to my shop this mornin' and got a look at that jailhouse."

"Art's all right," Cullen said. "He's in a place where nobody will likely bother him." He decided not to tell everybody exactly where Art was. He remembered that Moran had once sent three men to Ravenwood in an attempt to kill the marshal. "He's gettin' kinda itchy about takin' your town back to the honest folks," Cullen said. He hoped that might encourage Buck and other council members to scrape up some grit. He needed the whole town in on this deal to throw the outlaws out of East City for good. "Art's waitin' for me to give him the word when you folks are ready to fight. He wants to be in the middle of it." He could tell that Buck was thinking hard about what he was saying. What he needed was to get most of the other people committed to saving the town as well. "I wanna go talk to the mayor while I'm in town right now. I need to see where he stands before I take on the rest of Micah Moran's gang. I don't know how long they're gonna try to track Art and me before they come back to town. From what I saw out at Hortense's, they weren't packed up to stay out long, and I don't think Moran will stay away from town very long anyway."

"Ain't you gonna hang around town awhile longer?" Buck asked. "I'd be proud to buy you a meal at O'Sullivan's."

"Well, I appreciate that, Buck, but I don't aim to hang around here very long. I've got a target on my back for any one of Moran's men that sights me. And I ain't bulletproof, so I have to be able to pick my fights."

"I understand," Buck said, but Cullen doubted that he did. He suspected that Buck thought he was going to challenge all five of them to face him in the street for a shootout. "I'll drag ol' Molloy outta here for you, Tom," Buck said to Loughlin, who was still studying the strange man that was Cullen McCabe.

"I'll give you a hand," Cullen said to Buck, and they each grabbed a wrist and dragged Molloy's body out the front door. They left it on the boardwalk in front of the Cork and Bottle, so Moran could see it first thing when the posse returned. Then Buck, already invested in the overthrow of Marshal Micah Moran's regime, walked with Cullen when he led Jake up the street to the hardware store.

Abe Franks looked up when he heard them come in the door of his store. He knew without being told that the big man with Buck was Cullen McCabe. He was not sure if he wanted to talk to the mysterious killer of some of the key members of Micah Moran's posse. In spite of Art Becker's and Joe Johnson's high regard for the dangerous drifter, Abe was not sure that McCabe was not just another lawless gunman. And that his interest in East City was the same as the devil running it now. From the looks of it, it would appear that Buck Casey had also jumped on the Cullen McCabe bandwagon.

"Hey, Abe," Buck sang out. "Cullen, here, is wantin' to talk to you about somethin'."

Abe put down the new saw he was removing from a wooden crate and walked up to the front counter to meet them. "I heard a rifle shot a little while ago," he said. "Did that have anything to do with you?"

"As a matter of fact," Cullen answered, sensing the mayor's caution in talking to him. Before he could say more, Buck interrupted.

"Yes, sir," Buck started, "that shot you heard created a vacancy in the deputy marshal's job. Stan Molloy has officially retired." He chuckled at his humor. It served to convince Abe he had been right in his opinion of Cullen.

"That's puttin' it kinda bluntly," Cullen was quick to say. "I reckon anybody given the choices I was given would most likely make the choice I made."

"That's right," Buck said. "Molloy went for his gun and Cullen cut him down."

Abe cast a frown at Buck, much as he would a precocious child, before addressing Cullen. "Is that what you specialize in, Mr. McCabe? Are you a fast-draw expert?"

From the mayor's curt manner, it was obvious to Cullen that Franks saw him as merely one more lawless individual seeking to take advantage of a town already a haven for outlaws. "I don't fancy myself as anything more than a man who's seen enough trouble in your town to know that there ain't but one direction it can go in. And if the people in East City don't do something about it pretty quick, it's gonna be too late to save your town." He let that sink in before adding one more comment. "And I don't figure I'm a lot quicker to draw my handgun than the next fellow, so I've got a lot more sense than to try to find out. Molloy got shot because he didn't have enough sense to know he couldn't beat a rifle already out and cocked."

His statement gave Franks pause to reconsider the manner of man he faced, but not completely. "As a stranger just passing through East City, it strikes me as odd that you seem so interested in our town's troubles. Are you thinking about settling here, if we are successful in ridding the town of Micah Moran and his kind?"

"No, sir, I'm not. I've got some property south of Austin that requires my attention. I'll be headin' back there pretty quick now." He didn't go into any detail, since his property was a small cabin in various states of repair, that he worked on between assignments from Austin. "It just appears to me that now's the time to do something. The big posse that Moran had has been cut down to him and four men."

Abe interrupted then. "You mean that *you* have cut down to four men."

"I'm afraid I have to give most of the credit for that to Moran, himself. He's the one who took Ned Larson and his boys out of the picture."

Still eager to be part of the discussion, Buck was quick to inject, "Don't forget Boot Davis, Charley Turner, Ace Brown, and Stan Molloy," he said. "That's four of a kind that's hard to beat in any poker game. Don't try to tell me you didn't take care of them."

Wishing he had left Buck back at the Cork and Bottle, Cullen replied, "Most of that business was a matter of luck." Back to Franks, he said, "The main thing is that it's time to strike Moran when he's at his weakest, and that's right now before he has time to build up his gang."

Skeptical at first, Franks could not help softening his attitude toward the solemn man, thinking he might have no selfish motive after all. So he allowed himself to talk earnestly about the town's problems for a few minutes. "Even if Moran and his men were gone, what would keep the next outlaw gang from moving in to pick up the pieces where Moran left off? Then it would start all over again."

"You need a strong, honest man to fill the job of maintaining the peace, just like they have across the creek in Ravenwood," Cullen said. "I don't reckon I have to tell you that."

"And that would be you, right?" Abe was swift to jump on that, his skepticism returning in a heartbeat.

Cullen shook his head and favored him with a tired smile. "No, Mr. Mayor," he said patiently. "Like I told you,

I don't plan on staying here. I've got other business to tend to somewhere else. But I know where you might find the kind of man you need to protect your town."

That tweaked Abe's interest. "Oh? Where's that?"

"Marshal Tug Taggert just got a new deputy, a fine young fellow. He's strong and won't stay a deputy very long. His name's Beau Arnett. He'd be a good one for you folks."

"How in the world do you know that?" Abe responded.

"I was over there a couple of times. I met him, young fellow, seems to have the right attitude for what you're lookin' for. And Marshal Taggert thinks he's highly qualified." That was all the explanation Cullen offered.

In spite of his natural caution, Abe allowed his mind to think about that idea for a moment. The thought of East City operating in a peaceful existence, like Ravenwood, was something he had given up in despair long ago. "You think this Beau Arnett would be interested in taking the job of marshal here in East City?"

"Don't know for sure," Cullen answered, "but he said he was interested." He realized he was making a recommendation on nothing more than a gut feeling about the young man, but he believed it would be a good match. "Seems to me you folks over here oughta get together with the folks in Ravenwood again, patch up any differences you've had, make the two towns one big city. It would be good for both of you, and it would sure as hell pick East City up."

Abe considered all that had been said in the short time Cullen had been in the store, especially the idea of combining with Ravenwood to become one city.

The two parts of town could be joined by one big bridge and commerce could travel back and forth. In another moment, however, reality returned and he said, "Sounds good, I reckon, but the fact is, we ain't rid of Micah Moran yet." He looked at Cullen directly and confessed, "It might seem a simple solution to a man like you, but the men who would have to confront Moran and his gunmen are men like Joe Johnson and me—hardly gunmen."

Buck interrupted again. "Don't forget about me. I ain't afraid to go up against 'em. And Art Becker, he's already showed a lotta grit. Hell, I say we tell Micah Moran his day in East City is over and it's time for him to pack up his posse and get outta town."

"Use your sense, man!" Abe responded. "That would be the quickest way to get shot down. Do you think Moran will even debate the issue? Him and his four gunmen would put that protest down before you got it out of your mouth. We need the backing of the army, or the Rangers to set up here to enforce our demands."

"We tried that already," Buck reminded him, "and look how that went."

"That was because when the Rangers camped here, all they were doing was policing the town against any lawbreaking," Abe said. "We weren't actively trying to force the marshal out of East City for good. When the Rangers felt like Moran and his deputy were keeping things peaceful, they left. And they're not likely to come back anytime soon to help us run the marshal out of town. If we try to go up against Moran without help from the state, it'll just be a shootout between Moran and his four gunmen against any of our merchants who feel brave enough to do it."

"What do you say to that, McCabe?" Buck pressed.

"I expect he's probably right," Cullen said. "I'm afraid you might lose some of your honest people in that kind of gunfight." The expression on Buck's face told him how disappointed he was to hear him seeming to back off. But Cullen realized that the businessmen of East City would risk suicide in demanding a showdown with Moran and his kind. He knew then that he was going to have to carry the fight alone to keep Abe and his fellow storekeepers from being killed. He wasn't even sure now that it had been a good idea to talk to Franks, after all. In spite of making a great effort to hide it, Abe had clearly let his mind wander to a vision of a town without Micah Moran. Cullen was afraid the reality of his situation might serve to discourage the mayor more when it came to taking steps to uproot the marshal.

Evidently of the same mind as Cullen, the mayor said, "I think it would be best to call a meeting of the town council tonight to discuss our problem and find out how many are ready to take action." This he addressed to Buck.

Thinking he might have done more harm than good, Cullen said good day to the mayor and left his store. Buck followed him outside. "Whaddaya aimin' to do now?" he asked.

"I'm aimin' to get outta town right now," Cullen said.

"Ain'tcha gonna wait for Moran to come back?" Buck asked, obviously disappointed to hear Cullen was leaving. "Or at least come to the council meetin' tonight."

Obviously, Buck was still thinking that he was going to stand in the middle of the street and challenge

Moran and his four men to face him in a gunfight. "There's some things I need to check on out of town. In the meantime, don't you go gettin' yourself in a fix you can't get out of when Moran and his men come back here. He ain't gonna be too happy when he finds Molloy by the front door. He's liable to shoot the first person he sees. So go to that meetin' and find out if the others are ready to fight."

"We're ready to take our town back," Buck stated confidently. "We'll give Moran the word that his time here is finished. At the meetin' tonight, we'll decide how best to make him understand we mean it."

"Buck, make sure you tell everybody to come to that meetin' with a weapon." He stepped up into the saddle and left Buck standing there, watching him ride away.

Still a little disappointed that Abe didn't put his complete trust in McCabe, Buck's lips parted in a mischievous grin, thinking about Moran's reaction when he saw what McCabe had done to the jailhouse door. *Maybe, if I hurry before it gets too late, I can fix up another surprise for him*, he thought.

As Cullen had speculated, Micah Moran and his four men were not prepared to pursue Art and him for very long. With Shorty acting as scout, they had no trouble finding tracks leading away from the boarding-house. The trouble for Shorty was too many tracks, coming and going on a trail back along the creek. He was able to follow some of those tracks only to have them end in the small clearing where Cullen had made a camp. "He was here, all right," Shorty said, in an effort to justify his skill as a tracker.

"Yeah, but he ain't here now," Moran said, visibly irritated. "So, where'd he go from here?"

"I don't claim to be no tracker," Riley was prone to say, as he studied the tracks leading in and out of the campsite. "But it looks to me like these tracks was left by one horse. There oughta be more tracks if there was two horses."

"Well, that's right," Shorty said. "That's what I was fixin' to say."

"Looks to me like maybe Riley oughta be our tracker," Moran cracked. "We'll just have to turn around and go back to where this trail split off that other one before the creek."

They went back and picked up the original trail and followed it until it left the creek and headed west, staying with it until they lost it where it crossed a wide stream. "We shoulda thought about bringin' somethin' to eat," Leroy commented, when after a considerable amount of searching, they had still not found the place where Cullen and Art had left the stream. "We're liable to be out here a helluva long time before we catch them two."

With his patience already in short supply, and hungry as well, Moran reined his horse to a halt in the middle of the stream and sat gazing out toward the west. Then he looked up the stream and considered another possibility. What if McCabe just continued riding up that stream for a long distance before leaving it and then cut back to return to the camp they had discovered close to the boardinghouse? They had never caught McCabe at Hortense Billings's house, but he was convinced that it was McCabe's base. That thought caused him to speculate further. What if McCabe, having sent him and his men off on a fruitless chase, was taking that opportunity to double back to East City and make his move against the one man left to maintain his hold on the town? What kind of condition was Molloy in, if that happened? He was still half-drunk when they left that morning. It was clear to Moran that McCabe's sole purpose in showing up in East City was to kill him and take over his operation. He decided at that moment. "We're goin' back!" He announced it loud and clear. No one asked why— they were all hungry and still hungover. Still thinking it a possibility that McCabe might have gone back to Hortense's house, he said, "We'll head straight back to that boardin'house. We'll get something to eat there."

CHAPTER 16

"They're back," Annie sang out when she saw Micah Moran's dark Morgan gelding come up from the creek. The two new members of his reduced posse appeared right behind him. "Don't look like they had a successful hunt," she reported as she threw the dishwater out, having just cleaned up after the midday meal.

"I sure hope they didn't catch up with Art and Cullen," Hortense said when she walked to the kitchen door to look over Annie's shoulder. "They might have killed them."

"No, ma'am," Annie insisted. "They didn't catch 'em. If they had, they'd be leadin' their horses back with 'em."

"I guess you're right," Hortense decided. "I wonder why they came back here, instead of going back to town?"

"They're comin' back to pay us another visit," Annie said. "They've gotta make sure Cullen and Art didn't double back on 'em. Better tell Roy. He's asleep on the front porch. He ate so many biscuits with that ham gravy on 'em that they weighed his eyelids down."

"I'll tell him," Hortense volunteered, and went back down the hall toward the front door. Hearing Roy talking to someone, she paused to listen.

"I ain't lyin'," she heard Roy say, so she continued on to the front porch to find Shorty Miller and Leroy Hill seated on their horses, facing the porch. They had evidently been sent to cover the front, in case Art and Cullen were inside the house.

"Don't you lie to me, you old buzzard," Shorty threatened him. "We know they doubled back here."

"I told you, I ain't lyin'," Roy insisted. "They ain't here."

"You heard what he said," Hortense stated. "They ain't here. If you had the brains God gave a jackrabbit, you could see there ain't any horses back of the barn. Or did you think they walked back?"

Leroy favored her with a slow grin. "You're a sassy little spitfire, ain't you? For all I know, you mighta cut their horses up and cooked 'em for supper. Now I expect the marshal is gonna want us to search your house again to see if those jaspers are hidin' under a bed somewhere. Most likely under your bed, sweetie pie. Wouldn't you say, Shorty?"

"Wouldn't surprise me a-tall," Shorty replied. "She's built like she could give a feller a good ride."

"You watch your mouths," Roy reacted. "You saloon trash ain't fit to talk to a lady. Cullen McCabe, or Art Becker, ain't neither one of 'em here. I done told you that, so get your sorry carcasses off the property and leave honest folks alone."

"Did you hear what that old buzzard said to me?" Shorty responded.

"I sure did," Leroy said. "He talks like he thinks he's better'n us, don't he?"

"Sounded like it to me," Shorty said. "I know I feel like he's insulted me. I think he's called me out to a face-off. You got a gun, old man? Go get it and we'll settle this little argument right quick." Looking confused, not sure if Shorty was serious or just amusing himself at his expense, Roy could not respond. After a few seconds, when he still didn't, the smile faded from Shorty's face and he threatened, "You get your gun, or I'm gonna shoot you down where you stand."

Roy froze for a few minutes, unable to move, as Hortense watched in horror. When the two outlaws continued to stare at the unfortunate old man, he slowly started to turn toward the door. "Don't you dare go get that gun!" Hortense scolded. "You go in the house and stay there!" Then back at Shorty and Leroy, she railed, "You filthy animals, treat an old man like that, go away and leave us alone. Cullen and Art aren't here."

"I told you, old man," Shorty said, ignoring her. He drew his .44 and put a shot in the back of Roy's leg as he was going in the door." Roy went to his knees and fell in the doorway, accompanied by the laughter of both outlaws. Hortense went to his aid at once, pulling him inside the house and slamming the door shut behind her.

Hearing the shot, Moran kicked his horse hard and charged around the house but pulled up sharply when he found Shorty and Leroy, still sitting on their horses and seeming to be in a laughing fit. "What the hell was that shot?" Moran demanded.

"Ain't nothin', Boss," Leroy replied. "Shorty was just helpin' that old man into the house."

Moran was not amused. "You damn fool. If McCabe is hidin' around here somewhere, he sure knows we're back now."

"Sorry, Boss," Shorty apologized, "I didn't think about that."

"Maybe if he is hidin' somewhere, and he heard that shot, maybe it'll make him come out to see what happened," Leroy suggested.

"More likely make him run again," Moran said. "You two go on in the house and search it again, just in case they did come back here." They got off their horses and went into the house and he rode back around to the kitchen door, where Jeb and Riley were waiting. Annie was no longer standing at the kitchen door. He dismounted after telling his two new men to stay there and keep their eyes and ears open.

He found Annie in the kitchen, helping Hortense in an effort to stop the bleeding in Roy's thigh. He could hear the sounds of Shorty and Leroy upstairs making their search of the bedrooms. From the thuds of crashing furniture their less-than-gentle touch was evident. Concerned with Roy's suffering, Hortense ignored the obvious destruction overhead. Moran paused only a moment to consider the wounded man before going over to the stove and the coffeepot sitting on the edge of it. He picked it up and shook it back and forth before opening the lid to make sure it was empty. When he saw that it was, he banged it back down on the edge of the stove. "My men and I haven't had anything to eat. You're supposed to be in the business of sellin' bed and board, so we're gonna need something to eat."

Both women looked up at him, amazed he could be so insensitive to the suffering his men had caused.

Annie was the first to respond to his request. "You're too late. We done served the midday meal."

"That's all right, you can start cookin' supper. My men and I are hungry."

Hortense looked up at him, her face tense and strained with anger. "It's not time to fix supper yet. Can't you see we're busy here trying to treat this poor man those animals of yours shot just to amuse themselves?"

Moran's dull expression never changed as he bluntly responded, "It doesn't take but one of you to wrap a rag around his leg. The other one can get up from there and find us somethin' to eat. Start with makin' a pot of coffee."

"I'm sorry," Hortense replied. "We're not open for business right now. You'll have to go into town to find something to eat."

There was no hint of emotion in the baleful face that looked down at her as she knelt beside Roy. Consequently, she had no chance to protect herself when he suddenly struck her with a brutal backhand that knocked her flat on the floor. Shocked, Annie cried out in anger, "Stop! You dirty coward! I'll get you some food. Just wait a minute!" She reached for Hortense. "Are you all right, honey?" Hortense, too stunned to answer, could only stare at her while she tried to recover.

"Make the coffee first," Moran said, still with no evidence of emotion.

"You're lucky you caught me without my poker," Annie informed him, "or you'da been thinkin' about somethin' besides coffee."

He drew his hand back, prepared to strike her, but hesitated when Hortense came to her senses enough to cry out, "Don't hit her! We'll get your damn food for you. Give us a minute to take care of his wound."

"He can wait till later," Moran said. "What you're gonna do now is fix me and my men somethin' to eat. Tie that rag around his leg. He'll die of old age before that bullet in his leg kills him, and I'm hungry now."

"You go ahead and make some coffee," Hortense said to Annie. "I'll help Roy into the parlor, then I'll help you cook up some bacon and eggs, with some pan biscuits. That'll be the quickest." To Roy, she said, "I'm gonna help you into the parlor and you can rest on the sofa, then I'll see what we can do for that wound after they leave."

"I'm sorry, Hortense," the suffering old man murmured. "I'm sorry, I ain't no help to you."

"You just try to rest," she said as she walked him into the parlor, letting him use her as a crutch. "I'll check on you to make sure that bleeding has stopped." When she came back, she saw that Moran was still standing in the kitchen, watching the progress of his breakfast. "I'll roll out some dough," Hortense said to Annie, "and you scramble up some eggs."

"It's mighty lucky we've got some eggs," Annie said, "with this many poppin' in on us all of a sudden. Wonder how come they didn't just ride on back to get some of that good food at the Cork and Bottle? I hear Lizzie is just a wonderful cook," she added sarcastically.

"If you'd keep your jaw from flappin' so much, you'd get the cookin' done a lot quicker," Moran said, watching their every move to make sure there were no shenanigans with his food.

"If you would go wait outside, I'd get the cookin' done a helluva lot quicker," Annie informed him.

He gave her a long hard look before saying, "You know, I don't like you a helluva lot to begin with. You and that smart mouth of yours are liable to get you more trouble than you wanna handle. Hey!" he barked at Hortense when she suddenly left the room. "Where are you goin'?" She said she was just going to check on Roy to make sure his bleeding was under control. "Well, get back here quick," he ordered.

"How's he doin'?" Annie asked when Hortense returned.

She replied that he was doing about as well as could be expected for an old man with a bullet wound. "I'll keep checking on him, maybe take him a cup of coffee when that pot finishes boiling." They continued with their food preparation under the watchful eye of Micah Moran, while upstairs the noisy searching of every inch of the house went on. Thinking she heard a whimper from the front room, she said, "I'd best take another quick look at Roy," and left the kitchen again. When Moran again asked where she was going, she told him she'd be right back. He said nothing in response. She returned in a minute and reported to Annie. "He's just in a lot of pain, but there's nothing we can do with this going on."

Moran walked out of the kitchen. Hortense and Annie looked at each other, both hoping he would stay out of the kitchen until they were finished cooking. They were startled a few moments later by the sound of a gunshot inside the house. Both women started toward the door only to be met by Moran returning from the parlor. "He ain't in pain no more," Moran announced matter-of-factly. "Now you don't have to run back and forth and you can get the cookin' done."

Shocked by his casual demonstration of callous concern for the life of the gentle old man, both women went weak-kneed, holding on to each other for support to keep from collapsing. Even Annie's tough shell was cracked by the cold-hearted act of casual execution, leaving her unable to speak. It seemed to the two women that it was an eternity between the sound of the shot and that of Shorty and Leroy hustling down the stairs. It was actually only seconds before they rushed into the kitchen. "What was that?" Shorty blurted.

"Nothin' but that old man in the parlor," Moran answered. "You and Leroy drag him out on the porch. We're fixin' to have somethin' to eat in a little bit, if these women will shake their behinds 'stead of standin' around like a couple of tombstones in a graveyard." He cocked an eye at Annie and said, "Which is where they might end up, if they don't."

Cullen was still some distance from the boardinghouse when he heard a shot ring out. There was no doubt where it had come from, so he nudged Jake for a little speed. He had taken the main road from town, instead of the shortcut along the footpath. It was a little longer that way, but he figured if Moran and his men were coming back, he would be at a disadvantage on the footpath. He might shoot the man in the lead, but then he would still have four others shooting at him.

When he came to the lane from the main road that led to Hortense's house, he turned onto it in time to hear a second shot, and he decided this one came from inside the house. When he came to the curve where the lane wrapped around a grove of oaks, he guided Jake into the trees and dismounted, He thought it a good idea to scout the house first, instead of riding straight in. As soon as he moved halfway through the trees, he saw the two horses standing at the front porch. "Damn," he muttered, "they did come back here." With two in the front, that meant the other three were at the back of the house, or maybe all inside. His concern now was the cause of the shooting he had heard. His concern was immediately answered when the front door swung open and Shorty and Leroy came out, dragging a body. He couldn't get a good look at the victim, but it was not one of the women, so it had to be Roy. He felt a sharp pang of anger when he watched the two outlaws drag Roy out on the porch and leave him there. Wishing he could release his anger, he pulled his rifle up and dropped the front sight on Leroy's chest. *I should have killed him when I caught him back on that footpath,* he thought. He lowered his rifle, unable to risk any endangerment of the women's lives. The fight would have to be fought somewhere other than here. Since there was pretty good cover where he now stood, he decided to wait them out right where he was, until they moved on.

There was much to think about. They had killed Roy. Possibly they had killed Annie and Hortense as well. The thought of it caused his veins to throb with anger. He had no way of knowing. And what if Moran was still there when Martin Pearson and Franklin George came home for supper? He needed to get Moran and his men out of that house, but didn't know how to do it without putting the women's lives in danger. The afternoon was wearing on; soon it would be suppertime. He would have to start watching the lane behind him to keep Pearson and George from walking into a hostage situation. Fortunately, the front door opened before either of the two boarders came home, and Shorty and Leroy came out of the house and got on their horses. They rode around the house and soon Cullen saw all five of them ride out of the backyard and onto the footpath to Art's stable.

He waited until they were completely out of sight before he left the cover of the oak trees and rode up to the front porch. With a worrisome feeling of dread, he quickly dismounted and hurried up the steps. There on the porch, he saw the body. The poor unfortunate man had been shot in the forehead. In a hurry to find Annie and Hortense, he didn't look at Roy's body close enough to notice the wound in the back of his thigh. The first thing he saw when he walked into the parlor was the bloody stain left on the sofa. Anxious more than ever now, he rushed down the hall to the kitchen to be met by Hortense with a double-barreled shotgun aimed at him. "Hortense!" he yelled. "It's me, Cullen!"

Rigidly determined before he yelled, she started to collapse when she saw it was him. He caught her by the arm to support her with one hand while he took the shotgun from her with the other. "Cullen," she gasped, "I thought it was that monster coming back. I swear I was gonna kill him if he did."

"If that shotgun didn't kill him," Annie said as she stepped out from behind the door, gripping her trusty poker, "I was gonna finish the job." He helped Hortense over to sit at the table. Annie, the stronger of the two women, went back to the stove. "I was just fixin' to make us some coffee when we heard you come in the front door. There was still some in the pot, but I'm makin' us some fresh. Me and Hortense both need a strong drink and since we ain't got any whiskey, we're settling for coffee. Didn't want what was left in the pot. I made it too weak," she said, paused, and added, "And there was spit in it."

"I'm just happy to see both of you still kickin'," he said. "I'm awful sorry about Roy." He was even more sickened about it when they told him how he came to be murdered. Cullen took a closer look at both of them then, noticing the welt and broken skin on Hortense's face and thinking it could have been a lot worse. When he looked hard at Annie, something looked different about her. He wasn't sure what it was until he looked closer. "Broke?"

"Reckon so," she said. "Feels broke." She reached up and gently touched her nose with a fingertip. "The marshal rapped me with the barrel of his pistol when I told him I'd fed men like him before."

Already regaining strength as a result of Cullen's presence, Hortense perked up enough to elaborate. "That's not exactly the way she said it. Moran said something about proving we could whip up something in a hurry to feed his men. And Annie said, it wasn't the first time she'd had to slop hogs." They both giggled when she told it. "It was a bloody mess on her face till she cleaned it up. I thought he had killed her."

"Takes more'n that to kill this ol' she-bear," Annie boasted. "That jackal better hope he don't ever come around here again. Me and Hortense are gonna get us a gun belt, and we'll be ready the next time he shows his face around here."

"I'm hoping you won't get the opportunity," Cullen said. "I was hoping they wouldn't come back here after they broke off their search for Art and me."

"I think they came here 'cause they were hungry," Annie said, "and they didn't wanna eat that slop Lizzie cooks up at the Cork and Bottle."

"Maybe so," he allowed. Her mention of the name brought to mind the image of the skinny little cook standing behind him with a shotgun that looked bigger than she. Thinking of her, and looking at Annie, caused him to wonder if all women cooks were naturally ornery. "I expect I'll go on into town to see what the marshal and his posse are up to tonight. But first, I'll take care of poor ol' Roy." He shook his head. "I swear, there just ain't no excuse for men like Moran to live on this earth. I'll find Roy a nice spot under the trees."

"We're gettin' ready to fix supper," Annie said. "You can eat somethin' after you bury Roy." When he hesitated, thinking he didn't want to waste too much time before going into town, she prodded him to stay. "You need some good food, and I've got some beans soakin' on the side porch since breakfast. They'll be ready to cook with some ham right about now. I'm fixin' to roll out some biscuits and blackstrap molasses." She paused then and gave Hortense a wink. "You know, when the marshal and his hogs wanted somethin' to eat, I reckon I plum forgot about those beans and ham."

"I expect it would be downright impolite to say no to that invitation," Cullen said, surprised that they all three could find humor after what the women had just suffered through. *Just the joy of survival I suppose,* he thought as he went out the back door to get a shovel and pick from the barn.

Martin Pearson showed up when Cullen had a hole dug about half the size he wanted. After the women had told Pearson what had occurred there that afternoon, he came out to find Cullen and pitched in to help. Hortense told him that she and Annie decided to have a little ceremony over the grave the next day. They finished up the grave and laid Roy in it, then covered him up. Martin said he would carve a tombstone for him out of some pine boards in the back of the barn.

"That was a powerful waste of time, weren't it?" Jeb Dickens said, his voice low so as not to be overheard by the other posse members. He pulled his horse over closer to his friend Riley Pitts.

"You got that right," Riley responded. Expecting to ride on a real posse to catch up with the two men Micah Moran was obsessed with killing, all this posse did was ride around in circles. The net result of the chase was a poor meal at that boardinghouse and a lot of bellyaching about how hungover everybody was. And now, back in East City, they rode down the middle of the street, past the jail with its broken door. Someone was sitting in one of the two rocking chairs on the front porch of the Cork and Bottle. In the shade of the porch roof, it was hard to tell who it was until they were pulling up to the hitching rail. It turned out to be Stan Molloy, Moran's one-eyed deputy. He looked like he was sitting in the chair, but he didn't appear to be actually relaxing comfortably.

Asleep or passed out, he showed no sign of awareness that the posse had ridden right up to the hitching rail.

"Molloy!" Moran yelled at the corpse as he dismounted, but there was no response from Molloy.

"He's drunker'n a skunk," Leroy said to Shorty, "stiff as a board."

"He's gonna sober up pretty damn quick when he finds out Micah's back," Shorty replied. They both stood by the rail to watch what was going to be an entertaining event. Moran was already steaming mad as a result of their wild-goose chase.

"Molloy!" Moran yelled again as he went up the two steps to the porch but stopped suddenly when he was close enough to see Molloy's bloodstained shirt. Furious now when he stared at the empty eye socket staring back at him, he kicked the chair over and stormed into the saloon.

"I swear," Leroy muttered. "He ain't drunk. He's dead."

"McCabe," was all Shorty could say.

They went up on the porch to look at the body. "He don't look right," Leroy said.

"He looks dead," Shorty replied. "That's what he looks like, and I reckon we'd best haul his ass off the porch. Micah's already about to blow the roof off."

Still thinking Molloy looked different, Leroy studied the corpse carefully. "He's wearin' that patch on the other eye. Maybe that's why he didn't see McCabe comin' after him." He looked around at the other three. "I reckon we oughta dig a hole for him." No one seemed eager to volunteer.

"Hell, me and Jeb'll do it," Riley spoke up. "We gotta take the horses to the stable, anyway, so we'll throw him on a horse and plant him down by the stable somewhere.

"Before you do," Shorty said, "I wanna take a look at that eye. Molloy was mighty particular about anybody seein' what was behind that patch—always said it was his evil eye and if he ever looked at you with that eye, you'd be a dead man."

"Did you believe that?" Leroy asked.

"Hell, no," Shorty replied. "Are you japin' me?"

"I did," Leroy admitted. "Leastways, I didn't see no sense in puttin' it to the test."

Shorty struck a match and held it close to Molloy's face. "I swear," he uttered, "ain't nothin' but a hole—ain't no eyelids or nothin'."

At the jailhouse, diagonally across the street from the saloon, Buck Casey stood at the back corner of the building, chuckling to himself. He saw the five returning possemen when they rode by his shop, so he immediately hurried over behind the jail, eager to see their reaction to the deputy's welcome. After his meeting with McCabe and Abe Franks, Buck had hurried back to the Cork and Bottle, thinking to arrange a little surprise for the marshal. Unfortunately, Molloy's body was already getting stiff, so he couldn't work with it as well as he had planned. After some strain on his part, he had managed to get the corpse in a position that appeared to be sitting. When he had done the best he could with it, he stepped back to admire his work. *Well, you ol' devil spawn,* he thought, *you're just as ugly dead as you were alive.* He paused to take another quick look in the window to make sure no one was aware of his preparations. Looking back at the corpse, he muttered, "Needs somethin'." Then he decided and moved Molloy's eye patch over to his good eye.

Observing the reaction to his handiwork now, he felt it had been well worth his effort, as well as the risk of having been seen while in the process. The reactions of the members of the posse were what he had hoped for, especially Micah Moran's. He imagined he could almost feel the marshal's rage at this distance. He watched until the two new members of the posse carried the body off the porch and hefted it up on one of the horses, then led the horses to the stable. He chuckled the whole time, giving no thought as to whether or not his prank might cause additional harassment by the marshal.

CHAPTER 17

"What the hell did you volunteer us to bury this one-eyed drunk for?" Jeb asked as they led all of the horses down to the stable.

"Hell, I figured I'd rather take care of the horses and ol' Molloy than stand around that saloon listenin' to Moran rantin' and ravin' about the way the folks in this town don't respect him. Always ends up blamin' Cullen McCabe for everythin' that don't go the way he wants it to."

"Well, he's right, ain't he? He had a damn good thing goin' here before McCabe showed up. That's what Shorty says," Jeb said.

"I ain't sayin' that ain't so," Riley protested. "I'm just sayin' I'd just as soon let Moran get some of that anger out when I don't have to listen to it."

"Well, I don't feel like diggin' no hole to put this dead dog in," Jeb complained.

"Hell, I don't either and I ain't plannin' to. They ain't gonna know where we buried him, or even *if* we buried him. We'll ride up the creek a ways and dump him in the woods far enough to where you can't smell him when he ripens up."

They found an old stump hole a good way up the creek that was almost deep enough to take half of Molloy's body. So they dumped him in headfirst. "At least, we left him with his better-lookin' side showin'," Riley commented.

When they started back to the Cork and Bottle, Jeb said, "I'm gonna go to the store before he closes up. I need some smokin' tobacco."

"I'll see you back at the saloon," Riley said. "I need a drink of likker after all that work we done diggin' that grave." They parted when they reached the street.

When Jeb got back to the saloon, Moran was still fuming over the loss of another one of his men, his anger intensified by the condition in which he had found his deputy. The display that someone had arranged for him was more infuriating than the actual loss of his man. It was an insult to his authority to be made fun of in a town he owned. Jeb walked inside just in time to witness the dressing-down of Floyd, Wilma, Mabel, and Lizzie for having no notion that someone was having their fun with Molloy's corpse right under their noses. As was customary, Tom Loughlin had retired to his room upstairs beforehand. "The whole town has got to thinkin' they don't have to toe the line," Moran fumed. "We might have to do a little reeducating in this town. They've forgotten who runs it."

When there was a brief pause in Moran's promises of threats to come against those who would befriend Cullen McCabe, Jeb spoke up. "They're havin' a town meetin' tonight at O'Sullivan's. Was you plannin' to be there?"

Moran didn't answer right away, pausing as if he

had been dealt another clue of a merchant uprising. "How do you know that?"

Jeb told him that he had gone into Joe Johnson's store for some smoking tobacco. When he was looking around the shelves for anything else he might want, he overheard a man Johnson had been talking with tell Johnson there was a meeting of the town council that night.

"And he said O'Sullivan's?" Moran asked, interested at once.

"O'Sullivan's," Jeb repeated. "That's what he said."

"I wasn't notified of any meeting," Moran fumed. "I'm the town marshal, and I wasn't notified about a town meetin'." He looked around him defiantly. "Well, I'm damn sure goin' to that meeting!" He looked back at Jeb. "What time?"

"The feller didn't say," Jeb answered. "After everybody closes their stores, I reckon."

"Who was the man who told Johnson about the meetin'?"

"I don't know," Jeb replied. "I ain't been here long enough to know anybody's name, but he favored the feller that runs the blacksmith shop."

Buck Casey, Moran thought, *the joker.* That's probably who it was, all right. He remembered Buck's rather flippant attitude when he saw him in the street after the jailbreak, when they were rounding up the runaway horses.

After supper, Abe Franks left his house and went to O'Sullivan's Saloon for the hastily called meeting of the town council. When he got there, he saw that Cary

O'Sullivan had pulled several tables together to form one big one for the members to sit around. Buck Casey and Joe Johnson were already there and Martin Pearson arrived shortly after Abe. Cary offered beer to anyone who wanted it and everyone did, so Cary's bartender, Freddy Lee, brought a tray to the table. As he was coming back to the bar, Stewart Ingram, the postmaster, walked in and snagged a beer from Freddy as he went past the bar. "Just like the mail," Buck Casey couldn't resist saying. "Always late."

After Ingram was settled, Abe looked around the table and commented, "Well, that's everybody but Art Becker and I reckon everybody knows why he isn't here." There were ordinarily seven members at these meetings. The odd number made it easier to have a majority if there was a vote on something, but without Art, they were six in number.

"Does anybody know where Art went when he broke outta jail?" Joe Johnson asked.

"No, nobody, but maybe Cullen McCabe," Buck Casey said, "since he's the one who broke him out."

"I'd like to know that, myself." The statement came from the front door. They all turned to see Marshal Micah Moran walk in the door, accompanied by Leroy and Shorty. The tension at the table immediately increased. Moran marched back to the council table, his forceful stride like that of a man in charge. "Evenin', gents. I apologize for bein' late, but I wasn't notified about a town council meetin' tonight. And I know it wouldn't be an official meetin' if the town marshal wasn't here. Right?" He glanced back at Shorty and Leroy. "You boys go on over to the bar and have a drink while me and the council are talkin' about things." He pulled a chair back from the table and sat down. "Well, now, Mr. Mayor, I reckon you can call the meetin' to order, now that everybody's here." He graced the surprised merchants, who were momentarily struck dumb, with a smug smile.

Not at all prepared to deal with the marshal when he called the meeting, Abe Franks tried to maintain some decorum, nevertheless. "There were a couple of reasons you were not notified of this meeting, Marshal. In the first place, you were out of town until this afternoon, late. And we didn't think you would be interested in attending, anyway, since there was no plan to discuss any matters of law enforcement. We, as merchants, wanted to discuss matters related to merchandising and ways to do more business with the people living around us in the county. I imagine that would be something you hold no interest in."

"Is that so?" Moran responded. "Well, that's where you're wrong, Mayor. I'm interested in everythin' that goes on in this town. And if I'm gonna do my job of keepin' the peace, I damn sure better know about everythin' you shopkeepers got on your minds." He paused to sweep the nervous faces with a threatening stare. "And I mean everything," he emphasized. "'Cause I'm the only thing keepin' you men safe in your stores and your families safe in your homes." He paused again to see if the mayor, or anyone else at the table, had anything to say about that. When no one offered any comment, he continued. "All right, good, we'll get on to another matter we need to discuss. We just had us a serious jailbreak and a convicted criminal was broke outta jail, and he's still on the run. You need to know that helpin' Art Becker in any way is a hangin' offense, and if I find out anybody is helpin' him, I'll stretch his neck for aidin' and abettin'." He waited a few moments to make sure everyone understood that. "Now we need to talk about that gunslinger, Cullen McCabe. Is there anyone at this table who doesn't think McCabe killed my deputies and possemen?" Again no one spoke. "I didn't think so."

Abe interrupted then. "I think, to be fair, we have to admit that no one here actually saw McCabe kill anybody."

"Is that so?" Moran scoffed. "Maybe you think they all committed suicide."

Buck Casey couldn't resist. "That might be what happened," he commented. "'Cause anybody goin' after McCabe is the same as committin' suicide." His remark was followed by a few quiet chuckles.

Obviously heating up a little, Moran said, "You're a funny man, ain't you? Like to make a lotta jokes, right? Maybe like that little joke you pulled with the body of Deputy Stan Molloy?"

"I'm afraid you've got me there, Marshal. I don't know what you're talkin' about," Buck maintained. "Did somethin' happen to Deputy Molloy? I mean, after he got shot in the Cork and Bottle? I'll admit, I did see that. That was another one of them suicides we were talkin' about. Damn fool Molloy drew on Cullen McCabe—death by suicide." That crack brought a few more chuckles.

Moran's brow knotted in an angry frown as his eyes fixed on Buck. Over at the bar, two interested spectators watched, scarcely believing what they were witnessing. "That fool's talkin' hisself into a pine box,"

Shorty said, "and I mean right now in a minute. What the hell's wrong with him?"

"Blacksmith," Moran stated as he stared threateningly at Buck. "I don't like jokes and I don't like jokers. They're the same as cockroaches to me, and when I see one, I stomp the life out of it."

"It ain't gonna be long now," Leroy said, a grin already forming on his face.

The mayor interrupted again at that point, afraid Buck was going to provoke Moran into a killing. "I think we're getting too far off our agenda. Let's get back to the business we came here to discuss tonight." He read the storm warnings in Moran's eyes, and wanted to strangle Buck, but he decided he'd better address the issue at hand, since Moran had unwittingly introduced it. "All right, next on the agenda, since the marshal wants to discuss law enforcement, we'll take that up now. Did you all bring weapons as requested?" He waited then while every member of the council, including himself, placed a pistol on the table in front of them. A look of pure astonishment appeared on Moran's face when he realized there were six guns to compete with his one. He instantly thought of Shorty and Leroy at the bar, now his only way to reduce the odds.

The two possemen were as stunned as their boss when the council produced their weapons. A moment later, they were even more at a loss when they heard the solid contact of a double-barreled shotgun on the bar behind them. "Just relax and enjoy your beer, boys," Freddy Lee advised.

"What the hell is this?" Moran demanded. Accustomed to a cowering look in the face of each merchant he directly confronted, he now looked around the table, confused by the determination he saw in every face.

"Just a way to make sure the votes are counted correctly on any issues we vote on tonight," Abe informed him. "Marshal Moran introduced it, so shall we go ahead and discuss the issue of law enforcement? How many say aye?" All five of his fellow councilmen replied with *aye*. "I say aye as well," Abe continued. "None opposed, so let's get on with it." Not sure what was going on, Moran held his tongue for a few minutes.

"Mr. Mayor," Cary O'Sullivan spoke up. "I make a motion, or whatever you call it, to decide the term of the present town marshal."

"I second the motion," Buck Casey said. "And I think it's time we voted on whether or not we wanna keep Micah Moran as the town marshal. Based on his performance in keepin' outlaws out of our town, I'd like to call for a vote on whether or not to keep him in his present position."

Unable to believe what he was witnessing, Moran sat dumbstruck as the men he had totally intimidated for two years casually voiced their opposition to him. His natural inclination was to draw his .44 and end this travesty of a hearing. But the presence of six weapons at point-blank range against his one was enough to still his hand. When he glanced back at the bar, he readily saw that Shorty and Leroy were of no use as backup to him, due to the shotgun leveled at them in the hands of the smiling bartender. He realized his helplessness without his small army of possemen. Still, he was certain that if he got out of this meeting he had so unwittingly attended, he would

once again retain his advantage. Even with just four
men left, he knew he could strike whom and when he
wanted. And after a couple of the suddenly high-and-
mighty town council members were found dead and
burned out, the rest of this cowardly group of storekeepers would be begging him to save them.

"I propose we should terminate Micah Moran as
marshal of East City, and anybody he's named deputy
after the sudden demise of Stan Molloy. I propose his
termination be effective as of right now with a sever-
ance pay of one dollar." Buck smiled smugly at Moran
during the whole time of his proposal.

"Are there any seconds to that?" Abe asked.

"I second it," Joe Johnson spoke up. "And I want to
propose an addendum to the motion, that Moran and
his gang have until midnight tonight to get out of East
City and never come back." The motion was called to
a vote by a show of hands. Again, it was unanimous.

"While we're at it," Martin Pearson said, raising his
hand, "I propose we officially revoke the sentence of
death for Art Becker that was the result of a kangaroo
court run by outlaws." Again, there was unanimous
passage of the motion.

"Well, Marshal, or should I say, mister?" Abe addressed the baffled outlaw. "You've heard the ruling
by the town council, so come midnight tonight, you
shall be gone from this town." He paused, then said,
"Sooner would be better."

Still stunned by a revolt by the men of the town,
men who had cowered before him until the curse of
Cullen McCabe had been cast upon him, Moran
could not find words adequate to speak his rage. He
sat, stone-faced for a long moment before responding. Then he finally rose to his feet, preparing to

speak before he left. "You damn fools. Don't you know who you're messin' with? I don't know who put this horseshit into your dumb skulls. Nobody tells me to get out of a town that I, by God, own! All you've done here tonight is make it hard on yourselves from now on. Nobody elected me marshal when I came here. I made me the marshal and that's how it's gonna be from now on. Only, it ain't gonna be as easy on you as it was."

"I figured you wouldn't have sense enough to get the hell out of this town when they gave you a chance to." Moran turned when he heard this and found himself facing Cullen McCabe. Cullen was not alone. Art Becker was with him, as well as a tall stranger, all three with weapons drawn—Cullen's rifle leveled at Moran. When they walked on into the saloon, the young stranger moved to disarm Shorty and Leroy while Cullen continued on to the table in the back.

"Have a seat right over there at that table," Beau Arnett told the two at the bar. He pointed to a table against the wall. "Take your beer with you and sit there quiet till I tell you you can go."

"Who the hell are you?" Shorty demanded defiantly.

"I'm the man who's gonna raise a knot on the side of your head if you don't do what I tell you," Beau answered.

"What the hell is he doin' here?" Moran demanded of Abe when Cullen walked back to the table.

"Maybe you'd better ask him," Abe answered, not sure, himself, and wondering now if the meeting had gotten out of his control.

"You shoulda got out of town when the council told you to," Cullen said. "Now, you ain't got no choice.

You and your friends are goin' to jail to await trial for the murder of Lila Blanchard and Roy Skelton, and the attempted murder of Art Becker—plus holding an entire town hostage. Add robbery to that. I reckon that's enough right there to get you a ride on a noose. So take your left hand and ease that .44 outta your holster real slow. And if you're thinkin' about takin' a chance with it, please do. It would save us a lot of trouble."

Moran was trapped. He knew he was a dead man if he tried to make a move with Cullen's rifle already aimed at him, as well as six handguns, all pointed in his direction. He eased his pistol out and Cullen took it from him. Still not ready to go willingly, Moran said, "You ain't no lawman. You can't arrest me."

"I'm not arrestin' you, he is." He nodded toward Beau Arnett. "This is Deputy Marshal Beau Arnett," Cullen said for the benefit of those men seated at the table. "I'm just helpin' him."

"You can't hold me for trial," Moran insisted. "There ain't no judge in East City." Abe didn't comment, but he was thinking the same thing.

"That didn't stop you when you held that trial for Art Becker, did it?" Cullen charged. "But that ain't the case here. You're gonna be held in the Ravenwood jail and tried by Judge Harvey Raven."

Equally as worried as Moran, Shorty called out, "They ain't got no authority on this side of the creek, Micah. That's another county. This deputy can't arrest nobody in East City."

"That's right!" Moran exclaimed. "He's got no jurisdiction over here. Me and my boys can walk right outta here."

"That's where you're wrong, Moran," Cullen said.

"The deputy and Judge Raven both have been granted special jurisdiction by the governor, himself, to rid this town of you and your lawless crowd." He paused to give him a little smile. "Besides, even if they didn't have the authority to arrest you, I'd shoot you down like the mad dog you are before you reached the door." Thinking of Lila and Roy and Art, he meant what he said. As far as the part about special jurisdiction from the governor, that wasn't entirely true. He had exaggerated his authority to Tug Taggert in order to get the loan of Beau for the arrest. Thinking of possibly killing two birds with one stone, he was hoping to place Beau in the position of marshal of East City. He was convinced he was the right man for the job.

"What about the other two?" Joe Johnson asked, thinking of Jeb Dickens and Riley Pitts. "They just joined up with Moran. I don't know if they've done anything to arrest 'em for, unless we can arrest 'em for just ridin' with him."

"I reckon that might be up to the town council," Cullen replied. "If nobody knows of anything they've done against the law, I'd be inclined to let 'em go with a warning, as long as they agreed to leave town and never come back. What do you say, Deputy?"

Beau responded in the manner Cullen hoped he would. "I was thinkin' along those lines, myself. From what you've told me about those men, I'd be satisfied to let 'em go, if they understand they'll be arrested on the spot, if they show up in town again. You say they're young men. Maybe this might serve to show them the folly of riding on the wrong side of the law."

Cullen watched Abe for his reaction to Beau's response. He was satisfied to see Abe nod his head in agreement with Beau. "All right, Deputy," Cullen suggested then. "Late as it is, I reckon we could hold these three in the jail here overnight, if that's all right with you." Beau said that sounded like a good idea, but he was surprised that Cullen kept asking his opinion on each step taken with the prisoners. He was prepared to do whatever Cullen said.

"Buck, over there, is the blacksmith," Cullen went on. "He ain't got around to fixin' the front door, but the cell room will hold 'em till mornin'. I'll volunteer to guard 'em, then you can take 'em across the creek in the mornin'. Of course, I'll be glad to help you with that chore, too, if you want me to."

"Hell," Buck spoke up. "I'll volunteer to guard 'em, too."

"Me, too," Art Becker volunteered. "I'd enjoy settin' all night with those sidewinders."

Cullen could well understand why both men would enjoy the satisfaction of watching Moran and his two killers sweat it out in the tiny jail cell room. It would help him out as well. "If you both will stay and make sure they don't get out of that cell, Beau and I could pay a visit to the Cork and Bottle to see if we can have a word with those two young boys Moran just hired. While we're there, we'll see if Lizzie will fix 'em a farewell breakfast in the mornin' before we start."

"Too bad I didn't bring but one set of handcuffs," Beau commented. "But I reckon we could use some rope to tie those two fellows with. I've got some rope on my saddle."

"I'll get it for you, Deputy," Buck quickly volunteered, thoroughly enjoying the arrest of Marshal Micah Moran. "Which horse?" Beau told him he was riding the gray.

Once the prisoners were secured, they were marched out of the saloon and down the street to the jail, accompanied by all seven of the town council, plus a few curious townsfolk. On the way, there were a couple more volunteers for guard duty. It was a joyous night for East City, and most of the town's residents weren't even aware of it.

Hearing the sound of people in the street, Jeb Dickens walked to the door of the Cork and Bottle to see the cause of the noise. He wasn't sure he was seeing correctly at first, since he had been drinking ever since supper. "Riley," he called out after a few seconds, "come look at this."

"What is it?" Riley called back, not eager to get up from his chair.

"Come here!" This time it was a command. "It looks like a lynchin' party and it looks like Micah and Shorty and Leroy are the guests of honor!"

That was enough to bring Riley out of his chair right away. He rushed to the door, thinking Jeb might be too drunk to see straight. "Damn it all . . ." he uttered. "It is Micah! They're takin' him to jail!"

"And Shorty and Leroy with 'em!" Jeb exclaimed. "What do we do—go help 'em?"

"Are up crazy?" Riley responded. "It looks like half the town's marchin' 'em down the street, and they've all got guns."

Their excitement caught the attention of everyone else in the saloon and soon Floyd, Wilma, and Mabel were at the door to see what the two young outlaws were looking at. "Lord have mercy," Wilma muttered.

"Micah Moran goin' to jail, I wouldn'ta believed it, if I wasn't seein' it with my own eyes."

"Cullen McCabe," Mabel stated simply.

"Which one?" Riley asked, having never actually seen the man who was Moran's nemesis.

"The big one, holdin' the rifle," Mabel answered. She looked at Wilma and asked, "You know what's happened, don't you? This town's finally got up the nerve to take it back from Micah. I swear, I never thought I'd see the day."

"What's gonna happen to us?" Wilma worried. "You s'pose they're gonna shut this place down and run us outta town?" No one could answer for sure, but she suggested somebody should go upstairs to let Tom Loughlin know what was going on, but no one wanted to leave the door at that moment. The mob in the street had reached the jail by then. "They're puttin' 'em in the jail. If they're gonna hang 'em, don't look like they're gonna do it tonight."

The two newest recruits in Moran's posse continued to stare at the small mob in front of the jail, still trying to decide what they should do. "What about us?" Jeb wondered. "We ain't been here but a couple of days, but they know me and you are ridin' with Moran. You suppose they'll be comin' after us next?"

Riley was already thinking the same as Jeb. "I don't know," he answered. "But I ain't gonna be here when they do. I think it's time to light out for somewhere else. It damn sure looks to me like these folks here have decided to clean this town up."

Jeb wasn't sure. "You don't think we oughta try to help Moran get outta that jail? This was the deal we were hopin' for when we came here. To take over a whole town."

"Hell, no," Riley replied. He looked his friend in the eye. "Has Micah Moran done so much for you that you think you owe him?"

Jeb shook his head. "Well, not so far he ain't."

"That's right, and we'd best get outta here while we've still got a chance. Come on!" He grabbed Jeb by the sleeve and pulled him after him as he headed for the back door of the saloon. What few belongings they possessed were upstairs in the hotel next door. So they ran in the back door of the hotel, past a couple of prostitutes sitting on a sofa in the parlor. Taking the stairs two steps at a time, they wasted no time in picking up their saddlebags.

Bounding back down the steps, they ran past the prostitutes again. One of the women, a short, plump blonde named Effie, was prompted to ask, "What in the world has got into you two boys?" When told to go to the front door and see for herself, she and her friend did so. But when they turned to ask the two retreating possemen what was happening over at the jail, Jeb and Riley were already out the back door.

Running for the stable, they still had concern that there might be somebody guarding it, since they couldn't know how well organized this obvious uprising of the town's honest folks might be. They found, however, that there was no one. After their horses were saddled, they decided to take one of the packhorses. Then, thinking they might as well take their pick of the other horses there, they took their saddles back off and each of them picked out a better horse to ride. Riley was quick in choosing Micah Moran's black Satan. "I've been admirin' that horse ever since we've been here. Ol' Micah ain't gonna miss him where he's goin'."

"Where we headed?" Jeb asked, still not sure they were doing the right thing.

"I don't know," Riley answered, "just away from this place."

"And head in which direction?" Jeb countered. "There ain't nothin', no town of any size, within a hundred miles of here. We've been on the run ever since we left Tucson. And I've been thinkin' about the setup Micah had here and how it all came undone when Cullen McCabe showed up. That ain't but one man we need to take down—Cullen McCabe—and if he's done for, there ain't a nickel's worth of grit in the rest of the whole town. And think about those two buzzards, Shorty and Leroy. They ain't no competition for you and me, especially if we kill Cullen McCabe. He's the devil drivin' Micah loco. We get McCabe and we'll be Micah's top dogs. Then when he builds his posse back up, we'll be right there as his right and left arms."

"I don't know, Jeb," Riley said. "A lot of what you're sayin' makes sense, if it would work out in our favor."

"I'm sayin' there ain't much risk in it for me and you, if we hide in this stable and wait to see who shows up here tonight. Think about it. McCabe's gotta put his horse somewhere, if he's gonna be here all night. And I expect he will 'cause they put Micah and them in the jail. He walks in here with his horse, he's dead. Couldn't be much easier. He ain't no different from any other man, he's just got the rest of 'em spooked."

"I don't know, Jeb," Riley repeated. "It sounds pretty good. I reckon it could happen like you say, but I still got a natural feelin' in my gut that says run while you can."

CHAPTER 18

In the only way left for him to rebel, Moran suddenly sat down in the street before the jailhouse steps. He refused to get up and walk into the jail. When Beau told him to get up on his feet, Moran replied. "Go to hell. I ain't goin' in that jail."

"Couple of you men, give me a hand here," Beau said, since Cullen showed no signs of responding to the petulant outlaw. Buck Casey and Martin Pearson stepped forward right away, and with Beau's help, they carried Moran inside the jail and pitched him roughly on the cell floor. Preferring not to be thrown around like a sack of potatoes, Leroy and Shorty walked in with no show of resistance.

Once the cell door was locked, Art Becker could not pass up the opportunity to ride Moran a little. "Hey, Moran, how's it feel to be on that side of the bars? There was some water in one of those buckets, if you get thirsty tonight. And I know I left a little bit of pee in that other bucket. I doubt anybody bothered to empty 'em after I left here. Be sure you don't get 'em mixed up."

When the prisoners were locked inside, Beau told

them they could back up to the bars, one at a time, and he would free their hands. Shorty and Leroy stepped up dutifully and Beau untied their ropes, but Moran remained where he had landed on the floor, still defiant. Beau waited for him a few seconds, then said, "I think you'll be a helluva lot more comfortable if your hands aren't behind your back all night, but I ain't got time to waste on you. Too bad one of your friends in there with you can't untie your hands, since you're the only one in handcuffs."

Not unexpectedly, Buck Casey saw fit to comment, "I reckon you're gonna find out if Shorty or Leroy is your best friend when you gotta use that pee bucket."

Evidently, that problem hadn't occurred to him, for he barked, "All right, all right, I'll back up to the bars." He struggled to his knees, then was helped onto his feet by Leroy to suffer the further indignity of standing against the bars to have his hands freed.

With the prisoners secured and the volunteer guards in place, Cullen and Beau were ready to go across the street to the Cork and Bottle. There was no way of knowing what to expect from the two remaining members of Micah Moran's outlaw posse. So they decided it best to approach the saloon cautiously. With weapons drawn, they split up and moved quickly toward the building. When there were no shots fired, they continued up on the porch, past Stan Molloy's rocking chair, to stop at the door. Cullen pushed it halfway open to take a look before entering. There was no one in the saloon but Floyd and the three women, all with their eyes focused on the door.

"If you're lookin' for Riley Pitts and Jeb Dickens," Floyd said, "they lit out for parts unknown when they saw what was happenin'." He looked around him.

"The place seems right empty with all Moran's boys gone. Always nice to see you, though, McCabe. Can I pour you a drink?"

"Reckon not. Thanks just the same," Cullen answered. Hearing a footstep on the stairs, he turned immediately, his rifle aimed that way, ready to fire, until he saw Tom Loughlin on the steps. "Beau," Cullen said, "this is Tom Loughlin, he's the owner of this saloon." To Tom, he said, "You might wanna get to know Beau Arnett, here. You might be seein' more of him around town." Cullen knew it was premature, and he was betting strictly on a hunch, but he felt strongly that Beau could wind up with the marshal's job in East City.

"McCabe," Loughlin said. "Are you closing us down?"

"Me? No, I ain't closin' you down," Cullen responded. "I've got no authority to close anybody down. That's up to the town council to decide, or the marshal, when they get one." He glanced at young Beau Arnett, then added, "I expect they won't waste any time appointin' a new one. It'd be my guess they ain't thinkin' about closing you down, now that Moran's gone, as long as you're figurin' on runnin' an honest business, like O'Sullivan does." He took another quick look up toward the top of the stairs. "No, sir, what I'm interested in right now is whether or not two young outlaws are sittin' in one of those rooms upstairs waitin' to put a bullet in me."

"Floyd told you the truth," Loughlin said. "Those two young men fled the building when they saw what was happening."

"Well, they finally made one smart decision, didn't they?" Cullen responded.

"You don't want to take a look upstairs, just to be sure?" Beau asked.

"No," Cullen answered. "I've got no reason to doubt Mr. Loughlin's word, but you go on and take a look if you think we oughta be more thorough." He was convinced the two had run when they had the chance. Beau, however, was not, so he went upstairs to make sure. While Beau was upstairs, Cullen's gaze fell upon Lizzie. "I don't believe I ever thanked you for not shootin' me in the back with that shotgun the last time I was in here." Lizzie shrugged in response.

"I was the one hollered at her not to shoot," Wilma said.

"And I wanna thank you for that," Cullen said. Back to Lizzie then, he said, "One of your former employers and his two friends are in that jail across the street. I'm wonderin' about the chances you might cook 'em a little breakfast in the mornin' before we transport 'em to Ravenwood."

The skinny little woman curled up one side of her lip, much like an ill-tempered hound dog. "I didn't much like cookin' for 'em when they was here," she said. "Who's gonna pay for 'em?"

"Who paid for prisoners' meals before?" Cullen asked. When she said the town council, Cullen said, "That's who will pay for 'em again. You can ask Deputy Arnett what time he wants 'em fed. I expect he'll work with you on the time. It ain't much of a trip to Ravenwood." He paused when he saw Beau coming back downstairs.

"I reckon Mr. Loughlin is a man of his word," Beau said. "Nobody upstairs, but I figured it couldn't hurt to check." He studied Loughlin for a few long seconds, then was tempted to ask, "How did you happen to go into business with Micah Moran?"

"I've been asking myself that question for the last two years," Loughlin answered. As far as Cullen was concerned, the man need say no more. He imagined Loughlin might be one of the happiest people in East City to see Micah Moran arrested.

When Cullen and Beau returned to the jail, they told all the volunteers that they could go on home now and leave the guard duty to them. "We're gonna bunk right in here with 'em to make sure they stay put," Cullen assured them.

"Be sure you do," Joe Johnson said. "'Cause if they get out, they're liable to kill every one of us."

Overhearing his remark, Moran called out from the cell, "You can count on it, Johnson."

"You men have made a big step tonight toward buildin' a fine, peaceful town that has a lot better chance now of attracting families and businesses," Cullen reminded them. "That's worth takin' some risks for and that's what you did. Beau and I will see that they all get to the jail in Ravenwood. And the court will decide what happens to 'em from there, but they're gone from East City for good. The next thing is to put an honest man in the position of marshal, a man like Beau, here, who ain't afraid to inform troublemakers they ain't welcome in East City."

When he finished giving his little speech, his volunteers started drifting away, most of them back to O'Sullivan's to celebrate what Buck Casey called East City Independence Day. One of the ones who lingered a bit longer was Art Becker, who told Cullen that he was going back to his stable to see what kind of shape Moran's men had left it in. "You and Beau

are gonna sleep here tonight. You want me to take
your horses to the stable with me? I'll feed 'em some
oats if I've got any left and water 'em good, so they'll
be ready to go in the mornin'."

"We'd appreciate that, Art," Cullen said. Then he
had another thought regarding the two young outlaws, Pitts and Dickens. He was sure they had run for
it. There wouldn't be any reason for them to hide out
in the stable, waiting to ambush him or Beau when
they brought their horses in. On the other hand, they
might be as crazy as Moran. And poor Art, Cullen had
already caused him to come close to being hung. "Tell
you what, I'll go with you and help you take care of
'em. Okay with you, Beau? I won't be gone long."

"Okay with me," Beau replied. "Take your time. I'll
take good care of these fellows."

"You worried about those two that cut out?" Art
asked him as they led the horses back toward the
stable.

"No, hell no," Cullen lied. "Those boys are already
a long way from East City and wearin' out a couple of
horses. Jake's just been kinda nervous lately, so he
might not behave himself."

"I'm pretty good with nervous horses," Art said,
well aware that Cullen was concerned for his safety.
He found it amusing that the big solemn man had a
soft spot in his grim bearing.

"Well, Jake's different. Let's hold up here a minute.
Wouldn't hurt if I took a quick look before we go waltzin'
in the front door. Stay right here, I'm gonna walk
around to the back of the barn." He handed Art the
reins he was holding and left before he could protest.

* * *

Inside the stable, Riley Pitts and Jeb Dickens sat in the dark tack room, counting on the possibility that Cullen McCabe might bring his horse to the stable. Riley had held out for a long time, thinking the best option for him and Jeb was the one that had first occurred to them naturally. And that was to ride hell-bent for leather away from East City while they had a chance to escape. Jeb was just as convinced they were passing up a golden opportunity to make a move that would set them up as key members of a new outlaw posse. The final decision was made when Jeb was so sure of his plan that he flat refused to go. "You go ahead on," he told Riley, "and no hard feelin's. Maybe you'll be back when things are like they're supposed to be again in East City."

Riley had just stood there, looking at his friend for a long moment before giving in. "Ah, hell, Jeb," he had said. "We've been partners since we was old enough to hold a gun. You wouldn't know your right boot from your left one, if I weren't there to tell you. I'm afraid if I leave you here by yourself, you're liable to shoot yourself in the foot. Hell, maybe you're right, so we'll wait here awhile to see if anybody does show up. Then we'll cut outta here like we oughta done in the first place."

"I knew you'd come to your senses," Jeb crowed. "It just takes longer with you than it does with most folks."

Now, the better part of an hour had passed since they had fled the hotel with still no sign of anyone approaching the stable. "Damned if it ain't dark as a whore's heart in here," Riley commented. "There ain't no light a-tall comin' in that little window." There was a lantern sitting on the workbench at his elbow, so he said, "I'm gonna light this lantern and turn it down real low. I'll set it on the floor and that oughta give us enough light so we don't bump into somethin' in here." When Jeb started to question the wisdom of that, Riley said, "Can't nobody see it from the outside." He lit the lantern and turned it down until it was almost out. Then he set it down on the floor, over in a corner. "See, that helps a little, and nobody can see that from the front of the stable."

"You reckon one of us oughta go set up by the back door of the barn?" Jeb wondered. They were presently standing on either side of the small window over the tack room workbench. It was the same window that Cullen and Art had looked out to see Shep Parker and Shorty Miller bringing their horses back to the stable after the shooting of Ace Brown.

"Ain't nobody gonna be bringin' their horses in the back door of the barn," Riley replied. "This is the best spot right here. We can see anybody comin' in the front of the stable, and we've got the protection of four walls in this little room, if anybody's lucky enough to shoot back. They'll have to lead their horses right by this window, if they're gonna put 'em in a stall."

"When he comes walkin' in here with his horse, which one of us takes the shot?" Jeb asked. "I'm thinkin' the man who shoots Cullen McCabe is liable to carry that story with him wherever he goes. Might be a heavy burden to tote." As soon as he said it, Riley laughed, knowing his friend as well as he did.

"You're tellin' me you wouldn't give your left ear to be that man?" Riley japed. "And be that famous gunfighter that shot Cullen McCabe?" He chuckled again.

"I'll tell you what, we'll both shoot him at the same time. Nobody'll know which one of us killed him, so we'll both be famous."

Jeb laughed with him. Then, after he thought about it for a minute, he asked another question that occurred to him. "You know, I never heard of Cullen McCabe before we came here to East City. You ever hear of him?"

"No, I never have," Riley admitted.

"The way Micah is always talkin' about him, and Shorty and Leroy, too, I just thought we hadn't heard of him over in Arizona Territory before. He might not be anybody at all, just a thorn in Micah's ass."

Riley could see that Jeb was genuinely disappointed. And he couldn't help thinking they could have been miles away from here by now. "Ah, what the hell, we'll both shoot him, anyway. It'll sure as hell tickle Micah."

"Hush! Somebody's comin'!" Jeb whispered. They both leaned across the workbench to get as close to the side of the window as they could, squinting to see through the open shutter.

"Can you see 'em?" Riley whispered back. "I don't see a damn thing." It had gotten considerably darker since they first selected the tack room as their ambush site.

"No, I can't, either, but I heard a horse snort," Jeb insisted.

"That don't surprise me," Riley countered, "since we're settin' in a stable full of horses."

"No, damn it, I'm tellin' you I heard a horse snort out there. There's somebody comin' to the stable—or they're just sittin' out there somewhere in the dark."

"Well, we ain't got much choice now," Riley said. "We'll just sit here and wait till they show up."

As Cullen had expected, the back door to the stable had been left unlocked, so he slipped inside and knelt against the side of the last stall. He waited there for a while until his eyes adjusted to the deep darkness inside the building and he listened. No sounds reached his ears but the infrequent nickers from the horses. When he could see a little better, he moved forward between the stalls, stopping again to listen when he was about twenty feet from the tack room door. He knew that was the best way to make a quick check for an ambush. From the little window in the tack room, he could see if there was anyone waiting in the front of the stable. After another pause, he was about to move again when he heard something that didn't come from the horses. In a crouch, ready to move forward, he knelt back down to listen. There was nothing for a half a minute, and then, there it was again. This time he knew what it was. It sounded like whispering. And it came from the tack room. He knew then that someone had the same idea he had, to cover the entrance to the stable from the vantage point of the tack room.

He didn't have to guess who it might be. There were only two people it would be. He had been wrong when he thought Dickens and Pitts would run when they had the chance. Being extra cautious now, he eased forward again to see if the tack room door was closed. *Damn*, he thought when he found that it was. He was going to have to figure a way to get them out of there. If it wasn't Art's barn and stables, he'd let all the horses out again and set the place on fire. The thought of Art caused him to worry that he would not wait for a signal, and in a little while, he'd get tired of waiting and lead their horses on into the stable. Anxious to head that off, he backed away to the door again.

As soon as he was out the back door, he ran a wide circle back through the trees to where Art was waiting. "Cullen?" Art called out softly when he saw him coming through the shadows.

"Yeah, it's me," Cullen answered. "We've got us a little welcomin' committee waitin' for us in the tack room. I expect it's those two young men I thought were halfway to Kansas by now. Least, I think it's two in there, unless it's somebody talkin' to himself."

"I swear," Art said, "I'da thought they'd have better sense than that—to wait around to try to shoot somebody. It's gonna get crowded in that little cell room back at the jail."

"We've gotta figure a way to get 'em outta there first. And that ain't gonna be easy. That room's a regular little fort." He thought for a few seconds. "I'll see if I can separate 'em, get one of 'em to come out if I can. Course, I'd like to get both of 'em outta there, but one might make it easier to get the other one out. As long as there's two of 'em in there, they can watch the window and the door."

"How you gonna get one of 'em out?" Art questioned.

"I'm gonna get the horses in the stalls stirred up—see if that'll do it. Here's what I need you to do. Tie the horses here in these trees and you take your rifle and find yourself some cover where you can watch the front of the stable. If they make a run for it that way, it'll be up to you to stop 'em." He figured that would give Art a part in the action without him thinking he was just trying to keep him safe.

"You can depend on me," Art responded. "I'll be ready for 'em."

"I know I can," Cullen said. He started to leave, but stopped and went back to his horse to take the coil of rope from the saddle. "Never know when some rope might come in handy," he said, and left to return to the rear door of the stables. Once inside again, he repeated his first entrance, and when his eyes were adjusted again, he moved forward to the position where he had first heard the whispering. He wanted to confirm that both Riley and Jeb were still in the tack room. It took a few moments, but eventually he caught the sound of a whispered exchange. Satisfied, Cullen moved back into the stalls, looking for something to use as missiles. He hit the jackpot in a couple of the stalls. Thankfully, since Art was not there to clean out the stalls, there were convenient piles of horse turds to pick from, most of them dried and hard. He grabbed a bucket from a nail in a pole and filled it with the drier road apples. Then he climbed up on the stall rails where he could lob pellets into several stalls.

His first few throws at the horses' hindquarters made them stir around a little, but the more he threw, the more nervous the horses became. Pretty soon the other horses began to respond to the stirring around of those being constantly pelted.

Inside the tack room, Jeb and Riley suddenly stopped to listen. "What the hell is that?" Riley wondered when he heard horses moving around. "Somethin's got after the horses."

"Maybe a fox or a skunk or somethin' has got in the stable, lookin' for somethin' to eat. They'll quiet down in a minute, or I'll go see about it," Jeb said. So they waited, but the confusion in the stalls only got worse with snorts and whinnies coming to their ears in the tack room. Before long, the two men in the tack room could no longer ignore it. "I'll go," Jeb volunteered. "Somethin' might be after our horses."

"You be careful," Riley warned him. "There might be somebody back there."

"I will, but if there was somebody back there, they woulda had to come by the window." He thought for a moment, then added, "Unless that back door ain't locked."

"Maybe you oughta take that lantern with you," Riley said.

"Druther not," Jeb replied. "If there was somebody in the stalls, they'd see me comin' if I'm holdin' a lantern." Slightly amused by Riley's concern, he said, "Move that keg of nails over against the door, just in case, and I'll knock three times when I come back. All right?" He went out the door then, smiling to himself when he heard the sound of the nail keg rolling up against the door behind him.

Out in the alleyway between the stalls, Jeb moved very slowly toward the back stalls, where most of the disturbance seemed to come from, waiting for his eyes to adjust to the darkness. The process was slowed considerably due to the faint light that the lantern had provided in the tack room. Almost to the back door, he could see nothing that would indicate anyone was in the stable but himself. Completely unaware of the ominous figure that had stepped out of a stall as he passed by and was now behind him, walking step for step. Jeb stopped when he reached the door. "Damn, it was unlocked," he muttered softly, the words barely out of his mouth when he was suddenly locked in a powerful embrace. His arms were pinned to his body by one powerful arm wrapped around him, while Cullen's other hand clamped over his mouth. Like a mountain lion surprising an unsuspecting rabbit, Cullen lifted the slighter man off his feet with his right arm and pushed him on through the open door. Outside, Cullen rode him to the ground to land on his belly. And before Jeb could realize what had attacked him, Cullen pulled his hands behind his back and tied them together. When Jeb started to yell, Cullen slammed him with an open hand to the back of his head, driving his face into the dirt, effectively muffling any sound Jeb tried to make.

Sitting on the middle of Jeb's back, Cullen used his skinning knife to quickly cut Jeb's bandanna off his neck, not wasting time to untie a knot. He stuffed the bandanna in Jeb's mouth, then quickly cut a length of rope to hold it in place. With that done, he roped Jeb's feet together and tied them to his hands. When he had him all trussed up like he wanted, he said, "You had your chance to run, but you didn't have enough sense to take it. You damn fool, I wouldn't have come after you. Now, I'll see if your partner wants to come with you."

With far less caution now, Cullen walked back to the tack room and knocked three times on the door. Almost immediately, he heard the keg of nails moving back to its original position beside the door. Riley opened the door, and when he did, he found himself facing a dark figure that looked twice the size of his partner. He realized too late that the shadow had a pistol aimed at his belly. Too stunned to react, he took a step back and Cullen matched it with a step forward to keep his .44 only a foot from Riley's gut. "Are you gonna take this the easy way, or are you gonna die here tonight?" Cullen asked, and before Riley could answer, he reached over and pulled the shocked outlaw's gun from his holster.

"I'll go quiet," Riley quickly replied.

"Turn around," Cullen ordered, and when Riley did, Cullen pulled his hands behind his back and trussed him up like he had with Jeb—with two variations. He didn't gag him and he tied his ankles, but with a short length of robe between them—hobbled like a horse—so he could walk, but he couldn't run. "All right, let's go get your partner." With his hand on the back of Riley's neck, Cullen guided him out the door and down the alleyway to the back door. "Which one are you?" Cullen asked. When Riley told him, Cullen told him the same thing he had told Jeb. "You two shoulda run when you had the chance."

"I told him that," Riley felt the need to say.

Outside the door, they found Jeb lying close beside it. Cullen guided Riley a few feet beyond that and told him to stop. Then he holstered his .44 for only a few seconds while he reached down, picked Jeb up like a sack of potatoes, and threw him over his shoulder. "All right, Riley," he ordered. "Start walkin' toward the front of the stable." Riley did as he was told. When they were approaching the front, Cullen called out to Art, "We're comin' out, Art! Hold your fire!"

Art stepped out from behind a tree. "Come ahead on, I got you covered," he sang out. Then he stood, astonished, as he watched Cullen approach, herding one of the outlaws in front of him and carrying the other one on his shoulder.

Art watched, totally amazed, as Cullen unloaded Jeb, almost gently on the ground. "Keep your eye on this one," Cullen said, nodding toward Riley, "and I'll untie his partner, so I don't have to carry him to the jail." While he was at it, he removed the bandanna from Jeb's mouth. "We might as well leave the horses tied right where you got 'em and walk these two to the jail first."

"I swear," Art said, "you boys sure shoulda run for it when you had the chance."

"I told him that," Riley said again. Jeb wanted to answer him but was still spitting dirt out of his mouth.

"Well, damn," Micah grunted when he saw Jeb and Riley marched into the jail by Cullen and Art. The two young bank robbers from Arizona were the last chance he had hoped for. After he heard they had escaped, he told Shorty and Leroy that there was still a chance they might not see the inside of the Ravenwood jail. He was especially hopeful when McCabe sent all the volunteer guards home to celebrate. With only McCabe and the deputy left to guard them all night, and the possibility they might take turns sleeping, Riley and Jeb had a good shot at springing them. If not during the night while they were in jail, they might decide to wait in ambush on the ride to Ravenwood in the morning.

"We got two more for you, Deputy," Art announced to Beau. "That oughta 'bout do it. You've got the entire East City marshal's posse right here in this little jailhouse. Don't look so dangerous now, do they?"

"These the two that ran out the back of the hotel?" Beau asked Cullen. "I didn't think there was any chance of seeing those two again. Where'd you find them?"

"Yep," Cullen answered. "They were set up down there in the stable, waitin' to ambush us when we brought the horses in." He looked over at Moran, standing near the front of the cell. "You ought not be too hard on 'em, Moran. Looks like they had it in their minds they were gonna set you free. We had to trick 'em to get 'em outta there."

It was too much for Moran to keep his mouth shut. "You'd better hope and pray I don't get set free, McCabe. 'Cause, if I do, you're a dead man."

"Good to know," Cullen responded. "If I see you out walkin' on the street somewhere, I'll cross over to the other side to avoid gettin' killed."

When they got the two new prisoners untied, Cullen and Art stood by with weapons drawn while Beau unlocked the cell and put them inside. When he was finished with that chore, he nodded to Cullen to follow him and walked outside the marshal's office. Art followed Cullen out. When he figured they were out of earshot, Beau told Cullen what was on his mind. "Two of us escortin' Moran and two others on horseback isn't much of a risk, but I'm thinkin' five prisoners are a little harder to handle. I'm not sayin' we can't do it. But as dangerous as Moran is, I think it wouldn't hurt to be a little more careful."

Not sure what he was getting at, Cullen asked, "What have you got in mind?"

"Well, I saw a jail wagon parked behind Jim Farmer's stable," Beau said. "It's been settin' there for a while now and it looked to be in good shape. I don't know who it belongs to. My guess is the Rangers, or the army, but I think it wouldn't hurt to borrow it for this little trip tomorrow—make it a lot easier on us. And I think everybody wants to make sure Micah Moran makes it to that jail in the morning."

"Sounds like a good idea to me," Cullen said right away. "You're sure right about how important it is to get Moran to court."

"I expect we can delay our trip a little while in the morning and I'll ride over to see if Jim will let us borrow it," Beau suggested.

"Hell," Art spoke up, "I'll go over and get it tonight and drive it back here in the mornin' in time for breakfast. Jim won't mind. If he does, I'll take it anyway, and a team of horses to drive it."

"You sure you don't wanna wait till mornin'?" Cullen asked. "It's way past suppertime."

"Yeah, I'm sure. I'm stayin' at the house with 'em now. Rena will fix me somthin' to eat before I go to bed." Art walked back to the horses with Cullen. He stepped up into the saddle and headed to Ravenwood, while Cullen took care of the horses.

CHAPTER 19

As Art had promised, he showed up before Lizzie had finished cooking breakfast for the five prisoners and Cullen and Beau. By the time everyone had eaten, they were more than ready to climb into the jail wagon, having been motivated by the condition of the one slop bucket. Even with no door on the front of the jail, there was very little ventilation to help with the odor left after Lizzie's red bean soup for supper the night before. The main culprit was Leroy, who had mixed his soup with too many parts corn whiskey. It resulted in a complete evacuation remedy for constipation, much to his fellow inmates' distress. Cullen and Beau were fortunate to retreat to the porch out front. When Art arrived, Cullen asked him who took care of the jail as far as cleaning up and so forth.

"Moss Turnipseed did the cleanin' when Ace Brown was deputy," Art said. "Buck Casey said that Moss quit when Ace got shot and he didn't know if he was gonna keep the job when Molloy took over. Anyway, Moss didn't show up while I was in jail. Buck said Moss ain't been back since the door got kicked in."

Cullen looked at Beau. "You might wanna remember

that name. You never can tell, you might end up in this office."

"If I do, there's gonna be a helluva lot of fixin' up to do on this place," Beau replied. Cullen was satisfied that Beau didn't flat out quash that idea.

When all was ready, the prisoners seated in the jail wagon, Tom Loughlin, Floyd, Lizzie, Wilma, and Mabel came out to watch their departure. Even though the hour was early, they were joined by a couple of prostitutes from the hotel next door, as well as some of the town's early-rising merchants. A dark, angry Micah Moran, once mighty ruler of the town, sat scowling in the front of the wagon—like his fellow passengers, his ankles locked in irons and attached to a long chain. Buck Casey, who was not about to miss Moran's last parade out of town, was there to wish them a pleasant trip. Driving the team of horses, Art Becker sat up tall, beaming with pleasure, undaunted by the knowledge that Moran would murder them all if he could get free. Cullen and Beau rode along beside the wagon, one on the right, one on the left, as Art drove the horses toward the wide creek that served as the county line. As far as he was concerned, it was a short ride that was a long time coming, and cause for celebration.

On the other side of the creek, they followed the road to the town of Ravenwood. Art drove the wagon down the main street of Ravenwood and pulled around behind the courthouse that housed the jail on the bottom floor. He pulled the horses to a stop before the door to the jail where the jailer, David Rakestraw, stood waiting. With him, Marshal Tug Taggert and guard Pete Caster were ready to help

take the prisoners into custody. Sharing many of the
sentiments of the townsfolk of East City, Tug Taggert
hoped he was witnessing a new day in the development
of the twin towns—in spite of the county line that
flowed between them.

"McCabe," Tug Taggert stepped forward and greeted
Cullen as he dismounted. "This is David Rakestraw and
Pete Caster. They'll be takin' care of our guests, right
through the trial and sentencin'." Both men stepped
forward to shake hands with Cullen while Taggert
continued, "McCabe is a special agent from the
governor's office and largely responsible for cleanin'
out that mess of outlaws in East City."

"I had a lot of help," Cullen said. "I think the folks
in East City just decided it was time to take back
their town. They might even be ready to be a part of
Ravenwood."

Unnoticed by Cullen, Art Becker, upon hearing
Taggert's remark, bolted upright in the driver's seat
of the jail wagon and turned at once to stare at Cullen.
"Well, I'll be go to hell," he muttered aloud, but not
so loud that anyone could hear. He was afraid he
couldn't wait to talk to Cullen about what he just
heard.

"I'm pretty sure Judge Raven will be tickled to hear
that," Marshal Taggert replied in response to Cullen's
remark. "And after we get these boys tucked away in a
cell, I'll be goin' to tell the judge they're locked up."

That served as Art's signal and he jumped down
from his seat, hurried around to the back of the
wagon, and unlocked the door. Then he stood back
while the prisoners climbed out of the back of the
wagon. When they were out, Cullen, Beau, and Taggert

all stood with weapons drawn to watch as Art unlocked each prisoner's ankle clamp. Almost swelling with pride for having a part in the transport of the prisoners, he went quickly down the line. Last to be unlocked, Micah Moran could not maintain his stony silence. "You little rat," he growled softly. "I shoulda hung you right away." Art said nothing in return but responded with a wide smile and a nod.

The five prisoners were marched into the jail through a set of double doors, past a small reception area, then through a reinforced door that led to the cellblock where they would be held until split up and put in two separate cells. When the cell doors were all locked, Taggert said, "I'm goin' to let the judge know they're here. I'd like you and Beau to go with me," he said to Cullen. "I know he'll surely wanna talk to you." Cullen figured as much.

Taggert and Beau waited in the reception area while Cullen went back outside with Art. "Taggert wants me to go talk to the judge with him, so I won't be goin' back right away," Cullen told him. "So if you're headin' back to East City, don't think you gotta wait for me."

"That's all right, Special Agent McCabe," Art responded with a grin too big for his face to contain. "I'll go take Jim's wagon and horses back to him, then I'll wait and go back to East City with you."

"Hey," Cullen said, "don't be fooled by that special agent crap. I reckon that's just somethin' Taggert thought up to keep anybody from lookin' into the men I shot. Hell, before you know it, they might wanna keep me in jail for murder."

"Right," Art replied, still with the grin on his face,

"whatever you say. But I'll still wait to ride back with you. I'll meet you right back here by the jail."

"All right. I don't know how long I'll be, though."

He went back inside and he and the two Ravenwood lawmen went up the back stairs that led to the courtroom above the jail. Cullen followed them through the empty courtroom, then down a hall to the judge's office, where they were met by a clerk in the outer office. He asked them to wait while he informed the judge of their arrival. *Pretty fancy for a judge*, Cullen thought, *almost as ritzy as the governor's office.* Maybe, he thought then, it was because the judge was also the mayor, plus he had donated the land for the city. In a few minutes, the door to the judge's office opened and Harvey Raven came out to greet them. "Come right on in, gentlemen." He turned around then and led them back into his office. After an introduction to Cullen, Raven invited them to sit down. "Marshal Taggert has told me how busy you've been on the other side of the creek, McCabe. And I have to say, you sure have made some progress. I understand these five men you brought in today are all that's left of the Micah Moran posse. Is that a fact?" He waited for Cullen to confirm that, then continued. "Well, I'll say job well done. We'll schedule a trial for all five of them right away. I'm going to need you at the trial, of course. But I'd like to have someone from the town of East City, too, as witnesses to the unofficial hangings and killings. Can you suggest who that might be?"

"Well, sir," Cullen responded, "right off hand, I'd say probably the mayor, Abe Franks, and maybe Joe Johnson. He owns the general store. They've both seen their share of the lawless men that have been flockin' there."

"That should be all we'd need, since we've got a man in custody here who attempted to kill Marshal Taggert. Sam Polek's his name and he's willing to testify that Moran sent him and two other men to kill the marshal. That's enough for a death sentence for Moran right there."

"He was a hardcase for a while there," Taggert interrupted. "But he changed his tune in a hurry when he found out Moran was out of business and he might escape a noose if he testified against him."

"That's right," Raven said. "He refused to give his name, but the marshal was able to find out who he was." He paused then to say, "Good work, Marshal Taggert." Taggert winked at Cullen as the judge continued. "There's another important issue to discuss and it prompts me to ask you a question, Mr. McCabe. What's going to keep East City from continuing its old lawless ways as an attraction for outlaws all over the territory?"

Cullen shrugged and said, "I don't know if anybody can guarantee that won't happen. But the only way it has a chance of changin' from its old reputation is to put a good man in the marshal's office and for the town to back him up. There'll still be the lawless drifters hittin' town for a while, till the word gets out that the marshal in East City won't let 'em stay. But I think the town council over there is ready to support a good, honest marshal right now."

"Any chance you might be that marshal?" Raven asked.

"No, sir, no chance. I'll be movin' on as soon as the

trial is over." He nodded toward Beau. "You've got what I think is a pretty good man for that job, if your marshal doesn't mind losin' his deputy right after he finally got one."

Beau immediately sat up more upright upon hearing that and gave Taggert a questioning look. Taggert smiled back at him. "What do you say to that?" Raven asked the marshal.

"I'd say he'd make a good one. The short time I've had him, I figured he was strong enough to be more'n a deputy." He chuckled then and added, "I thought he might bump me outta my job, if he stayed here very long." He looked back at Beau again. "I don't know if he wants that job or not, but I think he can handle it."

With all eyes on him now, Beau did well to hide his excitement. "I reckon Marshal Taggert knows I'm ambitious," he stated calmly. "But I believe I am qualified to do the job, and I would be determined to make East City as safe a town as Marshal Taggert has made Ravenwood." His response brought smiles all around.

"That sounds like the solution to the problem, then," the judge said. "There is only one little hitch, though. It ain't our problem. We can't appoint a marshal for East City. Their town council has to do that. And with the troubles we've had in the past, they might be too much to reconcile."

"If you want my opinion," Cullen volunteered, "I think the town council is ready to take that step, and I think they're in a hurry, to boot. Of course, you and Mayor Franks and maybe the council members will have to meet and work together. But I don't think there's a likely candidate for the marshal's job in the whole town of East City—no one I think could handle it, anyway. I expect they'd be glad to hire Beau. He's already made the arrest of the five we just brought over here, so they've seen that he can get the job done."

"We need to arrange that meeting as soon as possible," Raven said. "Can you talk to Abe Franks to see about scheduling it?"

"I'll suggest something better," Cullen replied. "Art Becker drove the jail wagon over here. He's a member of the town council, owns the stable over there. How 'bout we have Art go to the mayor and talk about meetin' with you? I'll go with him, but that way, at least the suggestion would come from a member of the East City council."

"Excellent idea," Raven said. "I'll wait to hear from you."

They filed out of the judge's office and went back downstairs. When they walked out of the jail, Taggert couldn't resist japing his deputy. "So you're talkin' about quittin' on me, are you? Ain't been settin' in the deputy's chair long enough to get the seat of your pants warm, and already talkin' about leavin'. I knew I shouldn'ta let you and McCabe work together—put big ideas in your head."

"Ah, come on, Tug," Beau japed, "you know you've been tryin' to figure out how to get rid of me from the first day." Getting serious then, he thanked Taggert for his recommendation, then turned toward Cullen. "I appreciate what you said in there, McCabe. If I happen to get that job over there, I'll do my best not to disappoint you."

"I wouldn't have said it, if I wasn't sure you're the

man for the job," Cullen said as Art came around the corner of the courthouse on his horse.

He pulled up beside Cullen's bay gelding. "You ready to go?"

"I reckon," Cullen answered, and stepped up into the saddle. "Art and I will go straight to the hardware store to talk to Abe Franks and I'll let you know how that turns out, and you can tell the judge," he said to Taggert. Taggert nodded his understanding.

On the way back to East City, Cullen explained to Art why he wanted him to go with him to see Abe Franks. "Kinda makes it more a request from a member of your own town council, and not folks in Ravenwood tellin' you what you oughta do." Art understood and was more than happy to go with him. Cullen could see how pumped up Art was becoming to be involved in almost every phase of the takeover of their town. *He might get to feeling so important that he'll get up the nerve to pop the question to Hortense Billings,* Cullen thought. He had to smile when he pictured it.

Abe glanced up to see Cullen and Art walk in his store. Cullen was aware that it was the first time he was met with a friendly smile from the usually serious hardware man. He guessed it was a friendlier feeling covering the whole town since Micah Moran was carted unceremoniously out in a jail wagon. He was aware that it was a day that many of the people there thought would never dawn. "We got some things we need to talk about," Art announced, before Cullen had a chance to speak. So Cullen let him go on with it.

"What things is that?" Abe responded.

"Now that we've got rid of the outlaw trash down at the Cork and Bottle, it's time to talk about the future of East City." Not accustomed to such serious talk coming from Art Becker, Abe glanced at Cullen, questioning, but Art continued. "Me and Cullen have been talkin' to the mayor of Ravenwood and I think it's time the two towns had a little meetin' to decide how we're gonna get along together. And Judge Raven said he thought that was a fine idea. What we need, first of all, is a strong, honest marshal, and me and Cullen have found a good man for the job. Ain't that right, Cullen?" Cullen nodded, indicating that it was so. Art went on. "Might not be a bad idea to hire a deputy to help him, too."

That caused Cullen to raise his eyebrows. Art had come up with that one on his own, but he had to admit it might be a wise decision at that. Having evidently run out of words at that point, Art simply held his hand under his chin, pretending it was a knife. Then he made a slashing motion like a man slitting his throat, to signify he was done talking.

It was not until then that Cullen spoke. "Art's pretty much covered what we came to tell you. The point is, Ravenwood is ready to help East City get back on its feet, now that Moran is gone. The man Art said was a good prospect for marshal is well qualified to do the work you need. You've already met him, Beau Arnett. He was the arrestin' officer. Course, it's up to you and the council to decide if you wanna offer him the job. So if you think it's worthwhile to meet with Judge Raven, he's ready to talk whenever you say. I told him I'd let him know what you decided."

Abe didn't answer right away. He was still somewhat astonished by Art's aggressive civic interest, a quality never exhibited before in any council meetings. The downfall of Micah Moran's posse of outlaws had happened so fast that there had not been time to examine the concepts of the actual arrest and imprisonment. Abe could not now deny a feeling that Moran should have been detained in the East City jail, tried by a jury of East City citizens, and executed by hanging in East City. Instead, a law officer from an adjoining county came to this town and arrested the felon, then took him to that county for trial. It was difficult for Abe not to feel that Ravenwood was once again trying to dictate East City's business. He said as much to Cullen.

Cullen heard him out, expecting that might be Abe's reaction. "I understand why you might feel that way, Mr. Mayor," he said. "That's why Art and I came directly to you to explain. I think I oughta tell you right off that Mayor Raven made it plain to us that he only wants to cooperate with you on the arrest of Moran. And I'm sure he'll turn him back over to you folks, if that's the way you have to have it. But the fact is, right now, we don't have a jail suitable to hold five prisoners." He glanced at Art and said, "And I reckon that's my fault. But Ravenwood has a secure jail, and they have a judge. And he wants me to tell you that he expects to involve you in Moran's trial, as well as the other four's trial."

"Of course, I'll have to talk to the rest of the council," Abe said. "But the fact of the matter is we need to take some action fast. And in my opinion, it's time to call off this feud with Ravenwood, so you go ahead and tell Raven that I'll meet with him. And the sooner, the better," he added. "Just let me know when and where. I'll see if I can round up the rest of the council for an emergency meeting right now."

"I reckon I can help you with that," Art volunteered.

CHAPTER 20

After leaving the hardware store, Cullen mounted up again to take the word back to Judge Raven, while Art stayed behind to get the word to as many of the other five council members as he could. When Cullen arrived at the courthouse in Ravenwood, the judge was conducting a trial for a man accused of cattle rustling. When the judge's clerk whispered in his ear that Cullen McCabe was waiting to deliver Mayor Franks's message, Raven called for a short recess and went to his office immediately to talk to Cullen. It was an unmistakable sign to Cullen that Raven was anxious to come to an agreement. Cullen left the judge's office with a request for a meeting in O'Sullivan's Saloon the following morning at ten o'clock.

"That'll work fine for us," Abe said to Cullen when he delivered the message. "Tell him it's a deal. We look forward to meeting with him." When Cullen started to leave, Abe stopped him. "And, McCabe, I'd like for you to be here, too."

"Yes, sir," Cullen replied. "I'll be here. I'll tell him to bring Beau Arnett along, too, just in case you wanna talk to him." He left then to go back over the creek to deliver Abe's confirmation of the meeting. "It's gettin' on about time to eat something," he said to Jake as they crossed the creek once again. "I might as well visit the dinin' room at the hotel and have myself a good meal." He had considered going to Hortense Billings's boardinghouse, since he was planning to take his room back until the trial was over. But he knew Annie was not in the habit of fixing a big noontime meal, and he felt like celebrating with a full dinner today. Things were going along better than he could have expected when he first arrived.

After dropping off his message at the courthouse, he went to the hotel dining room, expecting to find Tug Taggert there, since his office door was locked when he rode by. Beau was with him and they both waved him over to join them. Marcy Manning caught him in time to remind him of the "no-weapons policy" before he got far. "Mr. Cullen McCabe, if I remember correctly," she greeted him as she took his arm and guided him back to the weapons table. "We're glad you came back to visit us."

"Me, too," he said. "I hope you've got something good to eat. What's the special today?"

"Roast beef with mashed potatoes and gravy," she answered, "and I recommend it."

"Sold," he said, and continued on to the table.

"Heard you were already back earlier this mornin'," Taggert said when Cullen sat down.

"Yep, I've been ridin' back and forth over that creek all mornin'. Abe Franks said okay to the meetin' and it's set for ten o'clock tomorrow mornin' at O'Sullivan's in East City. And that's the last of my final announcements, so it's up to you folks now."

"I reckon Judge Raven will be schedulin' that trial as soon as he can," Taggert said. "He'll have to give everybody time to get ready for it, I expect."

"Accordin' to what he told me just now, he's plannin' on goin' to court day after tomorrow," Cullen replied. "He said the trial is just a formality for the sake of showing every man, no matter how evil, deserves a day in court. He said, if he wasn't here, Beau and the folks would probably have hanged him in East City when he arrested him."

"I reckon we'd best get some ropes ready, Beau," Taggert said. "He gonna try 'em all at the same time?"

"He said there'd be two separate trials. Moran's gonna be tried by himself because the charges against him are worse than the four gang members." Cullen shrugged. "I expect those two young boys will most likely to just get some prison time in Huntsville. Maybe Shorty and Leroy might get a rope, though."

"What are you plannin' to do after this, McCabe?" Taggert was interested to know. "You gonna hang around awhile?"

"I'll hang around till the judge says, *Guilty, death by hangin'*, then I'll be in the saddle and gone," Cullen answered him. "I've got a place down south of Austin that always needs some work, and I've been here longer'n I figured I'd be." The meal was finished with Cullen saying, "Well, I'll see you at the meetin', Beau." He left them with that and headed back to East City.

"What's the matter, Moran?" guard Pete Caster asked. "Ain't our food good enough for you? You ain't ate half of it. Maybe you're used to fancier grub than we serve here."

Micah Moran placed his plate and fork on the pass-through in the cell door, but kept his coffee cup. "I ain't finished with my coffee yet."

"I don't reckon you're enjoyin' your little stay in our establishment, are you?" Caster continued, having nothing better to do. "I heard you had some setup over there across the creek, owned the whole damn town." He smirked and added, "Well, you ain't gonna have to put up with these poorly accommodations very long. They'll be hangin' you pretty soon."

"That's what I hear," Moran said. "You heard right about me ownin' the town. I did, all right." He shook his head sadly. "It's a damn shame, though, all that money . . ." His words trailed off and he shook his head again.

"All what money?" Caster asked, always interested to hear about money.

Moran just stared at him for a long moment before answering. "It's just a damn shame," he lamented again, "all that money. And I was fixin' to leave this part of the country. I had more than I coulda ever spent in my lifetime. And then to get arrested before I could leave. Just a damn shame."

"How much money are we talkin' about?" Caster asked.

Moran cocked his head back, as if suddenly wary of talking too much. "Well, I don't know if I should . . ." He paused for a few moments, then shrugged. "Hell, I don't reckon it'll hurt to tell you, if you'll keep it to yourself." He nodded toward the cell at the end where his posse was. "I don't want them to hear us.

They might not understand how hard I worked for that money."

Itching to find out how much he was talking about, Caster asked again, "How much was it?"

"Caster, ain't that your name? Well, Caster, if I told you, you wouldn't believe there was that much money in the world. Ain't no need to tell you, you can't get it, nobody can, now that I'm locked up in here, waitin' to die." He hung his head sadly. "It's just a damn shame."

"Don't nobody know where you kept it?" Caster asked.

"Hell, no. I wasn't about to tell anybody where that money's hid." He paused and looked right and left to make sure he wouldn't be overheard. "Caster, I'm talkin' about six hundred thousand dollars. If those boys down in the other cell had known about that money, I'd be a dead man right now. I shoulda left when I had half that much. Half was more than I'd ever need." Another shake of the head and he repeated, "Just a shame. Nobody will ever see that money."

"Seems a shame to take a secret like that to the grave," Caster remarked, "when somebody could use it." Moran was right, that was more money than Caster could imagine.

Moran cocked his head back as if wary. "That's my money. I ain't gonna tell anybody where I hid that money—give it to somebody for doin' nothin'." He paused to let Caster think some more about that much money, then he pretended to be thinking out loud. "It'd be different if I could buy my freedom with it. I'd spend half of it in a minute, if I could do that.

But I can't, so the money's goin' to the grave with me."
He could almost see the wheels turning in Caster's
head as the guard thought about what he could do
with half of that money.

"Hell, you must think I fell off a turnip wagon,"
Caster said. "There ain't that much money in Texas."

"Well, there's gonna be that much money buried
under Texas and it's gonna stay there 'cause I lied,
cheated, and stole to get that money," Moran declared.
"And I ought not even told you about it. How 'bout it,
you think I could have another cup of coffee?" he said,
as if done with the subject.

"I reckon so. Gimme your cup." Moran stuck it
through the bars.

He watched Caster as he left the cell room. *He's
thinking hard about it*, he thought. *I'll know for sure, if he
comes back with more coffee.*

It wasn't long before Caster came back, and he got
a reception from the four prisoners in the large cell at
the end of the row when he passed by with a full cup
of coffee. "Hey, Guard," Leroy Hill said, "how 'bout
bringin' us some of that coffee?"

"Ain't none left in the pot," Caster answered. "You
had your coffee with your dinner." His response left a
stream of complaints and cursing in his wake, which
he ignored.

"Why, thank you kindly, Caster," Moran said most
graciously as he took the cup through the bars.

Caster remained there for a couple of minutes
before speaking. "I was thinkin' about what you said
about all that money you got hid."

"Is that right? What about it?"

"You know, you said you'd be willin' to split it with
somebody who could get you outta here alive."

"Yeah, I reckon I would split it with somebody for my freedom," Moran declared. "You know somebody who might be able to do that?"

Caster lowered his voice to almost a whisper. "I could do it, if it was worth my while, but how do I know you ain't japin' me?"

"I guess you don't, but I'm a desperate man. I ain't got time to play games with somethin' as important as my life. If I thought you could really help me get outta here, I'd be glad to make you a rich man for the rest of your life, unless three hundred thousand ain't enough for you to make it on. It'll sure as hell do me. I can tell you that."

"Maybe you could tell me where it's at, so I could go get it and have it ready when I get you outta here. That way, I'd know for sure you were levelin' with me. I could have a horse waitin' for you and we'd split the money and both say good-bye to this town."

Moran smiled and shook his head. "I swear, Caster, you must think you're takin' a fool for a partner. You open up that strongbox and see all that money, you might forget your way back to the jail. It'd be awful temptin' and nobody would believe me if I said we had a deal." He let the simple guard sweat that for a couple of minutes while he sipped his coffee. "I reckon I can understand you wantin' some kind of guarantee that I'll pay up. I'll tell you what I'll do. I've got the key that unlocks the strongbox where that money is waitin' to be dug up. I'll let you hold on to it until we get away from this jail and go get the money." He reached in his pocket and pulled out the key to his room in the Cork and Bottle. "Here it is. I'll let you carry it now. That oughta let you know I trust you to get me a horse and a gun belt and a shovel. As soon as you get me outta here, we can go get the money. That's all I need. When we dig up the money, I can buy anything else I need." He watched Caster beginning to sweat with his indecision and he prodded him a little more. "Long as you've got this key, I can't get into the box. If you don't come through with your end of the deal, you don't know where the box is buried." He paused a minute, then acted as if to return the key to his pocket.

"Wait a minute!" Caster exclaimed. Then glancing right and left in case anyone was looking, he held out his hand and took the key. He immediately balled his fist around it so no one could see it. "It's a big key," he remarked foolishly.

"It fits a big strongbox, partner," Moran replied.

"I'll be seein' you, partner," Caster returned.

The meeting at O'Sullivan's went as Cullen had hoped it would. The representatives from both towns were ready and anxious to work with one another to increase the development on both sides of the creek, hopefully to combine it as one big city eventually. It ended with handshakes and wishes of good luck. Abe asked Beau Arnett if he would stay awhile afterward to discuss the job opening at the marshal's office. Afterward, all members of the council voted to offer Beau the job and he accepted on the spot. Acting on Art Becker's earlier proposal, Buck Casey was offered the deputy's job, depending upon Beau's approval. Buck said he would accept the position as long as he could continue his blacksmith business. Beau allowed as how he could work with that, since he mostly wanted a deputy as backup when he needed one. Cullen suggested to Beau that he might want to talk to Hortense Billings when he was ready to move over to this side of the creek. The only thing left was the trial of Micah Moran the following morning and then it would be "so long" for Cullen, who was more than satisfied with the success of this assignment for the governor.

When the meeting broke up, Cullen and Art went back to Hortense Billings's boardinghouse for the noon meal, seeing it was already close to noon. She and Annie were expecting them. Annie promised she would fix something special to celebrate the liberation of East City. So Cullen and Art left Abe Franks and Joe Johnson in a discussion with Tom Loughlin regarding the operation of the Cork and Bottle from that day forward. They decided to board up the hotel next door. It was actually owned by Micah Moran, so there was no one to object to the closing of what was actually a whorehouse, except, of course, the whores, who would be hard pressed to find gainful employment or be forced to leave town. This didn't apply to Wilma and Mabel, who were defined as *saloon girls*.

Nine o'clock the next morning the courtroom was filled with spectators who wanted to get a look at the ominous outlaw marshal who had turned East City into a haven for outlaws and a hell for honest citizens of that small town across the creek. At approximately five minutes after nine, David Rakestraw and Pete Caster escorted a sullen and smirking Micah Moran up the back stairs from the jail and into the courtroom. Caster made direct eye contact with the prisoner only once, and that was when he unlocked his cell, but it served as confirmation that he was still of a mind to arrange his escape.

At roughly ten minutes after nine, Rakestraw, who acted as the court bailiff, called out, "All rise." Judge Harvey Raven walked in from a side door. As Raven had told Abe Franks and Marshal Taggert, it would be a very short trial. There would be no lawyers involved. He would question the witnesses himself and present the case to the twelve-man jury, selected from Ravenwood citizens. He called as witness Art Becker, who testified about his false arrest, sham trial, and sentence to hang. After Art, he called Sam Polek, who testified that he was a member of Moran's posse and Moran sent him to Ravenwood to murder Marshal Tug Taggert. The only change of expression on Moran's face came when Polek testified. He openly scowled at him, but Polek merely smiled back. Raven then called upon Abe Franks and questioned him about the harassment of the merchants and the shootings in the streets.

When Raven asked the foreman of the jury if they had reached a verdict, he said that they had and they hadn't needed to leave the courtroom to reach it— guilty of murder in the first degree. The judge went right on into the sentencing of the prisoner. "He shall be hanged by the neck until dead, tomorrow morning at six o'clock. Court adjourned."

Cullen watched as Pete Caster and David Rakestraw got Moran up from his chair. As they walked him by Cullen and Art, Moran broke his silence long enough to curse Cullen. "I'll see you in hell, McCabe."

"Lookin' forward to it," Cullen answered, as Moran's guards roughly pulled him away to disappear into the stairs leading down to the jail reception area.

"Damn!" Art exclaimed. "I swear, I believe I could feel the hate comin' outta that man. If looks could kill you, that look he gave you woulda done the job."

"I reckon he's got reason to want me dead," Cullen responded. "It's kinda the same way I feel about him." He didn't express it, but the reasons came to his mind, the cruel murder of the whore Lila Blanchard, and Roy Skelton, then the senseless attempt to do the same to Art.

"Well, we'll get here bright and early in the mornin' to watch the bastard swing," Art said as everybody filed out of the courtroom.

"I reckon," Cullen replied. As far as the job was concerned, it was finished, and there was no real need to watch the hanging. He could start back to Austin right away, but he personally needed to see Moran dead before it would be finished. "I'll leave Jake in your stable tonight and we'll ride over here in the mornin'. We can tell Annie she won't have to fix breakfast, then after the hangin', we'll eat breakfast at the hotel dinin' room. I'll pay. Whaddaya say?"

"That sounds like a dandy idea," Art responded. "We'll have to tell Annie the cookin' weren't as good as hers, though."

"McCabe." Cullen turned when he heard his name called and saw Judge Raven coming toward him. The judge offered his hand and said, "It would be highly remiss of me not to thank you for your part in what took place here today. Of course, Marshal Taggert told me about your reason for being here and I intend to write Governor Hubbard to let him know we appreciate his response to our requests."

"'Preciate it, Your Honor. Hope everything works out for you folks on both sides of Walnut Creek." He turned to leave, only to be met with the wide-eyed grin on Art's face. "Let's just keep this between you and me, Art. Ain't no need to say anything about it to anybody else."

"Right," Art beamed in response, "just between me and you."

Outside the courtroom, Cullen found Tug Taggert and Beau Arnett waiting for him. Several men from East City, led by Abe Franks, including Buck Casey and Cary O'Sullivan were also eager to talk to him, but waited until he had finished with the two Ravenwood lawmen. "Art says you're planning to leave for Austin just as soon as the hanging's over in the morning," Abe Franks began. "We're thinking it's not right for you to just up and leave without a chance for the people of East City to thank you for what you've done for our town. So . . . Cary, here, is inviting the council to a celebration at his saloon tonight, and you are officially summoned to attend, right after supper."

It was possibly the last thing Cullen wanted, but under the circumstances, he felt it would be downright unappreciative to decline. So, he thanked them graciously and said he would certainly be there. That business settled, Abe and Cary O'Sullivan climbed aboard Cary's buggy and the others took to their saddles for the short trip back across the creek.

CHAPTER 21

Although Pete Caster had agreed to provide Moran an opportunity to escape, he was still not sure he could go through with it. The thought of three hundred thousand dollars was almost more than he could comprehend. What were the chances he would be hunted down and made to pay the penalty? He had no morals to trouble him. He had stolen before. His only concern was getting away with it. He had set the escape plan in action, two horses tied behind the work shed behind the jail. As Moran had requested, there was a gun belt with a .44 revolver hanging on the saddle horn of one of the horses and he had propped a shovel against the wall of the shed. Even so, he was still undecided whether to go through with it or not and he tried to imagine how large a stack that much money would make. He stuck his hand in his pocket and squeezed the key Moran had given him, thinking of the life he could lead with such wealth.

Supper was served early at the jail, so the cook and his helpers wouldn't be so late in cleaning up the kitchen. Ted Preston, the night guard, had already checked in and was drinking coffee in the kitchen, shooting the breeze with the cook, as was his usual habit. "Go ahead and drink your coffee," Caster said. "I'll pick up the last plates." He went back through the reception area, which was now deserted, and hurried through the door to the cell room. *It's now or never*, he was thinking, still trying to make up his mind.

When he got to Moran's cell, he found him standing at the door, waiting for him. Detecting the look of uncertainty in Caster's face, Moran was immediately concerned. "You're takin' a step to becomin' a wealthy man, partner. Nothin' but the good life after we step outta this place."

Caster hesitated one last time, then decided he deserved the good life. He took the key to the cells from a hook inside a cabinet on the wall near the door, his movements catching the curiosity of the four prisoners in the double cell. When he walked back to Moran's cell, he handed the key to him to placate his guilty feelings. That way, he could always tell himself that he didn't unlock that cell, Moran did it. And Moran did it quickly. In a couple of seconds, he unlocked his cell. "Hurry!" Caster urged, now fully committed to the escape. "The night guard's in the kitchen. He'll be checkin' in here in about five minutes!"

"Right," Moran replied, and started for the door to the reception area. "Unlock that door!" Caster ran ahead to do it.

"Hey! What the hell's goin' on?" Shorty Miller blurted when he saw Moran and Caster running toward the door. "You goin' to get hung now?"

"Not tonight, boys. Not ever. Here, come on out and join us." He tossed the cell key into their cell, then he and Caster went through the door to the reception area. "That'll be enough to keep your night guard busy for a little while. Who else is here?"

Already panting nervously, Caster fumbled with the outside door from the reception area. "David Rakestraw's in his office on the other side of the kitchen," he said.

"Good, lock this door," Moran commanded, then with a laugh, said, "We don't want no prisoners to get out." Once outside, he looked right and left while Caster locked the door. "Where are those horses?"

"Behind that shed yonder," Caster said, and led the way.

"Damn, Caster, you did a good job," Moran said when he saw the two horses behind the shed, saddled and ready to go. The first thing he did was grab the gun belt and strap it around him. "What kinda weapon you got here?" He drew the weapon, a single-action Army Colt .45 with a four-and-three-quarter-inch barrel. "This'll do," he said, and checked to make sure it was loaded. Seeing the shovel leaning against the wall, he said, "Here, I'll take that. Let's get goin'." Caster put a boot in the stirrup and prepared to step up, never knowing what hit him. The first blow with the shovel landed against the base of his skull, knocking him to the ground. Thinking he had been shot, he struggled to get on his knees, only to be knocked down again. "There ain't no money, you damn fool," Moran gloated. When Caster still tried to roll over on his back, Moran continued to swing the shovel until there was no sign of life left in the unfortunate guard. "I killed a lot of men," Moran said, standing over him to be sure. "But you're the first one I ever killed with a shovel. I woulda shot you, but I didn't want anybody to hear the shot."

With time precious now, he quickly looked the horses over to see which one he preferred. He picked the one Caster had planned to ride, a dun gelding, primarily because it had a much better saddle. Leaving the dun tied at the shed, he led the other horse a few yards away then gave it a slap on its rump, causing the horse to trot away. After it realized it was free, the horse continued on toward the street. Satisfied the horse was going to continue in that direction, Moran set out in the opposite direction, thinking that whoever chased him wouldn't know which tracks to follow. He rode the dun behind the buildings on the main street until coming out on the street at the south end of town. With no sign of anyone after him so far, he reined the dun back and rode out the south road.

It made no difference to him if he left Ravenwood from the north end or the south end. He had but one intention, and that was to circle back to East City. He had a powerful score to settle with East City, but foremost was his passionate desire to kill Cullen McCabe. When he thought about it, he decided it was lucky that the riderless horse ran north. It meant that he would circle back to come in the south end of East City. Consequently, it would be easy to check on Hortense Billings's house first, before he even got to town. If things continued to go his way, maybe he would find McCabe there. He had no thoughts beyond killing the man he held responsible for destroying the gang of ruthless outlaws he had assembled and ruled over. He knew he would never be whole again until he had this man's blood on his hands. Only then, could he storm back into East City and take back everything that had been taken from him.

* * *

"Enjoyed the party, boys," Cullen announced. "But if I'm gonna get up early in the mornin', I expect I'd best get along to the boardin'house and get to bed."

"What's your hurry, Cullen?" Buck asked. "It ain't every day we get to celebrate the hangin' of as big a crook as Micah Moran."

"I reckon that's true," Cullen answered, "but I'd like to bite off a big chunk of that ride back to Austin after it's done. And I don't wanna be totin' a head that's throbbin' like a toothache."

"I'll go with you, Cullen," Art spoke up. "You still gonna take your horse to the house tonight?"

"Yep, I'll just leave right from the house. After the hangin', I'll ride back to the stable with you and pick up my packhorse."

"I expect I'll call it a day, too," Abe Franks declared. "Six o'clock in the morning comes pretty quick."

"Looks like Judge Raven coulda called it for tomorrow afternoon just as easy," Buck complained. "Reckon he wanted to make sure Moran caught the early train to hell?" That brought a chuckle as Cullen and Art said their good-nights.

"I still ain't figured out why that man decided to take on Micah Moran and the whole damn posse," Buck wondered aloud, watching Cullen as he went out the door.

While Art did a few little things that needed doing before he locked the stable for the night, Cullen saddled Jake. Waiting for Art to finish up, Cullen took a look at Jake's shoes. "I ain't been payin' enough attention to you these last few days, have I, boy?" He stroked the big bay's neck. "I think you're gonna need some new shoes not long after we get back."

"You've been livin' with nobody but that horse for too long," Art joked when he came out the back door and heard Cullen talking to Jake. "Does he ever talk back to ya?"

"Jake can't talk, but sometimes he'll write me a note," Cullen came back at him.

"You can ride on ahead, if you want, I'll be along," Art said.

"I'll walk. I ain't in a hurry. I'll lead Jake on that narrow little path, as dark as it is."

"Might be the smart thing to do," Art said as they started out on the path, leading their horses. "It gets dark as hell in these trees at night, but I've walked it so many times you'd think I could make it with my eyes closed."

"If I'da thought about it, I mighta told you to lead the way, but it ain't so dark that I can't . . ." That was as far as he got before the muzzle flash ripped the darkness in front of him and he heard the sound of the pistol shot at the same time he heard the impact of the bullet against Jake's breast. Taken completely by surprise, he tried to react as quickly as he could, as a second and a third shot thudded into Jake's shoulder and side. Desperate, he yelled for Art to take cover while he tried to pull the startled horse to the side of the path. With one loud scream, the bay gelding stumbled and fell, never to get up again. Still the shots rang out, pausing only a few seconds when the shooter quickly reloaded. Cullen could feel the burning anger scorching his veins as his assailant continued to shoot, hitting the dead horse again and again. It was too much for Cullen to take. He jerked his rifle from the saddle sling. Something told him that somehow it was Micah Moran. He had killed Jake, and he would pay for it, come hell or high water.

"Stay down, Art!" he yelled as he rolled over into the bushes beside the path. Then standing up, he plunged through the thick juniper bushes, firing at the muzzle flashes as fast as he could pull the trigger and crank in another cartridge. With bullets flying around him now, Moran concentrated his fire at the new target provided by Cullen's muzzle blasts. No matter how many times he fired, Cullen kept coming for him, his rifle blazing shot for shot, impervious to the hot lead flying all around him. Moran was forced to back up, unable to stop the infuriated maniac charging him.

With no thought other than total vengeance, Cullen advanced a step at a time, cocking and firing with each step, ignoring the impact of a slug in his shoulder, then another in his side. Advancing and firing at the pattern created by Moran's muzzle blasts, nothing could stop him from doing what he was determined to do. Until, finally, his target of muzzle flashes went out, leaving a darkness that hovered over the form of Micah Moran, lying facedown in the weeds beside the path. Two handguns lay empty a few feet away. There was still a flicker of life in the body, for Moran struggled to pull himself away from his executioner. Cullen jammed his boot into the dying man's side and rolled him over on his back. Then he held the barrel of the Winchester 73 only inches from his forehead. "Don't shoot no more," Moran gasped painfully. "I'm done for."

"You no-good piece of shit," Cullen snarled. "You went too far when you shot my horse." He pulled the trigger to send Moran to join the rest of the evil spirits in hell. Completely spent from the fury of his rage, he took a step backward and flopped down to sit beside the body. This was how Art found him.

It was several long minutes before Art realized the shooting was over. So stunned was he by the sight he had just witnessed, that he had never thought about firing at Moran, himself. The image would be forever branded on his memory of the infuriated avenger charging straight into the hail of gunfire—shucking one empty cartridge after another from the Winchester—daring his adversary to kill him. He wondered if anyone would believe him when he told them of this night when Cullen McCabe walked straight into a hail of gunfire, impervious to the shots that struck him, until Micah Moran was dead.

"Cullen?" Art finally called softly, fearing he might be dead. "Are you all right?" Cullen didn't answer. So Art held back, watching the dark figure sitting motionless there, afraid that Cullen might still be in the grips of the terrible rage that had engulfed him and might, without thinking, turn upon him. "Cullen?" Art called softly again.

"He's done for," Cullen finally answered, seeming to be the same solemn man Art had come to know. "He's gotta have a horse around here somewhere. We'll have to find it and drag his body up on the hill, there." He pointed to a bluff where the creek cut around a stand of willows. "I expect the judge will want Tug or Beau to take a look at it, to make sure it's Moran. We'll also need to drag Jake away from the path, somewhere a little farther from the house, I reckon. And I'm gonna need to buy a horse from you, if I'm gonna start back to Austin in the mornin'."

Art stood there, looking at him, amazed, as he called off the things to be done. Finally, when Cullen paused, Art said, "Cullen, I'll take care of them things. First, we gotta take care of you. You're bleedin' from two wounds I can see. Have you got more anywhere I can't see?"

"No, I reckon it's just the two," Cullen answered.

"Can you walk?" Art asked. Cullen said he could and got up from the ground. "Come on, then," Art said. "We'll go to the house and fix you up."

"That you, Art?" Franklin George called out from the kitchen door when he saw Hortense's hound dog run to greet the two men, each leading a horse into the yard.

"Yeah," Art answered. "It's me and Cullen."

"What was all that shootin' back down that way?" Franklin asked. "We didn't know what was goin' on, so I've been watchin' the backyard with my shotgun ready."

"I need to get Cullen on into the house, he's been shot, but I ain't sure how bad yet," Art said.

"I don't need any help," Cullen insisted. "I've gotta take care of this horse first."

"Get on in the house and tell Annie to heat up some water," Art said. "I'll take care of the damn horses." When Franklin wanted to know how Cullen got shot, Art told him to just get him in the kitchen and he would tell him after he took care of the horses.

Franklin held the door open for Cullen, and when he walked by him, he uttered, "Damn, Cullen." By that time, however, Hortense and Annie were aware of the situation and promptly took charge of it.

"Oh, dear Lord," Hortense exclaimed when she saw his bloody shirt. "Sit down and let's take a look at it." She paused. "Or do you need to lie down?" He said that he didn't and sat down on a chair and submitted himself to the care of the two women. Franklin stood by and watched, eager to hear the story, after Cullen told him there was nothing else to fear. He didn't get the details of the shooting until Art came in from the barn, however.

Cullen's concern was the fate and the whereabouts of the other four prisoners. He was sure there was no one else involved in the ambush that had just happened. It was his guess that, if the others had also escaped, they would have been more interested in fleeing than seeking revenge upon him. For that reason, he was satisfied to wait until morning to find out. So he sat quietly while Annie and Hortense cleaned his wounds and bound them to stop the bleeding. He had been lucky—a miracle, according to Art—to have suffered nothing but minor wounds. The only one that had potential to cause a problem was the shoulder wound, where a bullet was still lodged. The wound in his side was superficial, no more than a deep crease of about five or six inches long. At Annie's insistence, he agreed to go to see Dr. McNair in Ravenwood in the morning to let him dig the bullet out of his shoulder. He figured he had to go to Ravenwood, anyway, to see what happened after he left the courtroom. As long as he was going, he decided to take Moran's body back with him. Art insisted upon going with him.

"There ain't no need for you to go," Cullen said,

"since there ain't gonna be a hangin'. I ain't hurt that bad, and you've got work you need to do at the stable. But I need your help to put Moran's body on that horse." He paused before adding, "And you need to sell me a horse."

"You can take your pick of anythin' in the stable," Art said at once. "But I'm goin' with you, or I ain't gonna sell you a horse."

Cullen smiled. "You're a hard man to do business with."

The next morning found Cullen's shoulder stiff and sore, causing him to do almost everything one-handed. Fortunately, the bad shoulder was his left one, but it fell upon Art to extract Cullen's saddle out from under Jake, helped by Moran's horse and Cullen's one good arm. Knowing Cullen as a man of very few emotions, Art could still detect obvious evidence of deep sorrow on the part of his friend as they shifted Jake's carcass around. It was not so much what Cullen said, it was more what he didn't say. Without knowing the circumstances that caused Cullen McCabe to cross his path, he had no way of knowing that Jake was all Cullen had in his life. It was obvious, however, that the big bay gelding had meant a lot to him.

They went to the stable then, where Cullen selected Jake's replacement. Art suggested the black horse, named Satan, that had belonged to Micah Moran, but Cullen chose a lively dun gelding that had belonged to Sam Polek. Art allowed that Polek was as dumb as a pinecone, but he did ride a good horse. They led the horses back along the footpath to get Cullen's saddle on the dun, then managed to load Moran's body onto

Cullen's sorrel packhorse. After a breakfast that Annie insisted they should have, they started out for Ravenwood.

In spite of the fact that Beau Arnett wanted to try to track Micah Moran as soon as it was light enough to look for tracks, Tug Taggert wanted to raise a posse to go after him. His reasoning was that he intended to hang Moran as soon as he caught him and he wanted witnesses to the hanging. Consequently, they were not yet ready to ride when Cullen and Art showed up with Moran's body. "Well, I'll be . . ." Tug started. "So the rotten dog went after you. Looks like he managed to throw a couple of shots at you."

"Nothin' serious," Cullen said. "What about the other prisoners?"

"We found 'em in the cell room, walkin' around outta their cells, but they're all back in and scheduled for trial tomorrow." He went on to tell them about finding Pete Caster's battered body behind the shed. "Hard to say whether Pete was helpin' him escape, or Moran somehow got the jump on him. Whichever it was, Moran beat his brains out with a shovel." Cullen nodded and started for his horse. "You gonna hang around for the trial of the other four?"

"I expect not," Cullen answered, and climbed up into his saddle.

Art lingered a few moments as they both watched Cullen ride off toward the doctor's office. Tug glanced over at Moran's body and commented, "He sure as hell shot him full of holes, didn't he?"

Art nodded and answered, "He sure as hell did."

A vivid picture returned to his mind of the night before and the relentless stalking by the infuriated avenger wading through a sea of angry bullets. "I'll tell you one thing, it sure don't pay to shoot that man's horse."

*Keep reading for a special excerpt of the new
Duff MacCallister western
by William W. and J. A. Johnstone*

KILLER TAKE ALL
A DUFF MACCALLISTER WESTERN

*Scotsman turned cowboy Duff MacCallister traveled far
and worked hard to start a new life in America.
And anyone who tries to mess with his dream is in
for some serious Highland justice . . .*

The cattle town of Chugwater may not look like
much to outsiders. But for Duff MacCallister and the
determined settlers who've staked their futures
there, it's a land of opportunity. That's why the
whole town is fired up by the latest news. Young
railroad developer Jacob Poindexter wants to run a
rail line through Chugwater, making it easier to
transport cattle. Everyone is on board with the
plan—at first. Duff begins to suspect that Poindexter
is only after the most valuable land and he's using
strongarm tactics to force reluctant ranchers to sell.
Things only get worse when Poindexter's hired guns
show up—and the violence really begins . . .

But Duff's got a plan of his own. With a little help
from some well-armed friends, he's going to flush
this phony out of Chugwater—and run his hired
killers out of town on a rail . . .

Look for KILLER TAKE ALL, *on sale now.*

CHAPTER ONE

Chugwater, Wyoming

Thad Gorman counted out twenty-six dollars for Bob Guthrie, owner of Guthrie Lumber and Supply. "Here's what I owe you, Mr. Guthrie." Gorman smiled. "I got a good price for my wheat, and I thank you for carrying me on your books."

"Ahh, it's all part of doin' business, Thad. Why, most of the ranchers and farmers run a tab with me." Guthrie chuckled. "And I run a tab with my suppliers. Did Sue come to town with you?"

"Oh yes, Sue and the two young'uns. They're over at the mercantile now. She's payin' off Fred Matthews and stockin' up with things we been puttin' off till we had the money."

"What about Slocum? Did he come into town also?"

"I expect he'll be in tonight. I just got paid myself so I haven't paid him yet."

"How's Slocum workin' out for you?"

Gorman chuckled. "Well, he's not the friendliest feller I've ever known, but his work has been all right."

"You were a good man to hire him," Guthrie said. "Not everyone would be willing to hire someone like

Drury Slocum, a man who had spent five years in prison."

"I guess so. But it seems to me like ever'one deserves a second chance. Anyway I guess I'd better go pick up Sue 'n the kids before they spend all my money."

When Gorman stepped into the Matthews Mercantile a couple of minutes later he was greeted by a little girl who held out a doll. "Papa, look what I have! Isn't she beautiful?"

"I suppose so, but she isn't as beautiful as you are." Gorman smiled at Ethel, his six-year-old daughter.

"Huh, there's nothin' beautiful about a doll," Jimmy said. He was Gorman's nine-year-old son. "I got me a pocket knife," he added proudly.

It took half an hour for the farm wagon loaded with purchases to reach the family farm. When they drove into the yard they were met by Drury Slocum, Thad's farmhand and only employee.

"Did you get the money for the crop?" Slocum asked.

Gorman smiled. "Drury, you see all the things we bought while we were in town. Do you really have to ask that question?"

"I'll take care of the team," he said as he began to disconnect the two gray mules from the wagon.

"Mr. Slocum, would you like to take supper with us tonight?" Sue asked.

"Nah, soon as I'm paid I'll be goin' into town."

"Look at it this way, Drury. You have to eat. If you eat with us, you won't have to spend money for food in town," Gorman said.

"Yeah," Slocum said. "Yeah, that's right, ain't it?"

* * *

An hour later Slocum came into a house that was redolent with the aroma of fried chicken, biscuits, mashed potatoes and gravy.

"Drury, are you ready to be paid?" Gorman asked.

"Yeah."

Gorman reached over to the sideboard where lay the three hundred seventy-five dollars he had been paid for his wheat crop.

"I'll be giving you thirty-five dollars," Gorman said. "The extra five dollars is a bonus."

"I'll take it all," Slocum said.

Gorman smiled. "Yes, I didn't think you would turn down the extra five dollars."

"No, I mean I'll take all the money." Slocum pulled his pistol and pointed it at Gorman.

"Mr. Slocum, what are you doing?" Sue called out, her voice high-pitched with fright.

Slocum didn't answer. He pulled the trigger, shooting Thad Gorman in the chest from point-blank range. The bullet lodged in Gorman's heart, killing him instantly. Slocum then turned his gun on Gorman's screaming wife and crying children, firing three more times.

With the four members of the Gorman family lying on the floor, Slocum grabbed two pieces of chicken and two biscuits and left the house.

Slocum was in the Wild Hog Saloon later that same evening. His plan was to be very visible in town, then when word came that the Gorman family had been murdered, he would have the alibi of having been in town. That way, he wouldn't have to go on the run. But something he overheard from a nearby table caused him to change his mind.

"It was the hired hand that did it. Mrs. Gorman was still alive when Duff MacCallister 'n Elmer Gleason stopped by to buy some hay from 'em. She told 'em it was their hired hand that done the killin'. They tried to bring her into town but she died before they could get her to the doctor."

Not everyone in the saloon knew that Slocum worked for Gorman, and those who did hadn't noticed that he was there. Slocum got up and went through the back door as if going to the privy.

He had no horse of his own, nor did Thad Gorman. Slocum had come into town riding one of the two mules Gorman owned. He had considered stealing a horse, but he didn't want to take a chance. He needed to get out of town as quickly as possible.

But the mule wouldn't cooperate.

"Get up, you worthless, long-eared galoot!" Slocum said, trying to urge the mule into a gallop.

He headed south and no matter what he did to force the mule into a gallop, it wouldn't respond. Then quite unexpectedly, the mule balked, bucked, and threw Slocum off its back. The mule decided to run then, leaving Slocum stranded on the road.

Sky Meadow Ranch

"There is someone in the mine," Wang Chow said to Duff and Elmer Gleason the next day. Wang was speaking of a gold mine, played out now, that sat at the extreme north end of Sky Meadow.

"How do you know?" Elmer asked.

"Tracks go into mine but do not come out," Wang said.

"Well, let 'im snoop around," Elmer said. "He won't find anything, and if he does, we can give him a commission for finding it."

Before Duff had built Sky Meadow, before even he and Elmer Gleason were friends, Elmer had discovered and was working an old mine that had been abandoned by the Spanish more than a hundred years earlier. Legally the mine and all proceeds belonged to Duff, but he shared the money with Elmer, and Elmer invested back into the ranch so that he was not only the ranch foreman, but a junior partner.

"Elmer, have you considered that it is nae someone looking for gold?" Duff asked in the heavy Scottish brogue that he had not lost in all the time he had been in America.

"Well who else could it be?"

"Perhaps it is the one who murdered *Xiānshēng* Gorman," Wang suggested.

"I'll be damn. That's what you was thinkin' too, ain't it, Duff?"

"Aye."

"Well then, maybe we should go have us a look," Elmer suggested.

"I'll go in first," Elmer said when they reached the mouth of the mine. "There don't nobody in the whole world know this mine better'n I do." He was justified in making such a comment since he had actually lived in the mine for almost six months.

Elmer went in first, surrounded by a bubble of

golden light cast from the torch he had lit. Duff and Wang followed, but were just outside the light.

"All right, mister, you can just stop right there!" a voice called from the darkness before Elmer.

"Who the hell are you?" Elmer asked.

"It don't matter who I am. You're in light 'n I ain't." Elmer started to reach for his gun.

"Uh-uh," the voice said from the darkness. "I already got my gun out, 'n if you pull that 'n of your'n, I'll shoot you." Slocum appeared then, holding a pistol in his hand and pointing it at Elmer. "You know who I am, Gleason?"

"Yeah, Slocum, I know who you are. What I don't know is why the hell you are here? After what you done I figured you'd be long gone by now. Hell, ever'body figured that."

"Yeah, I would be if that damn mule I stole from Gorman hadn't throwed me 'n run off. You got a horse here?"

"What if I do? I ain't goin' to let you have it."

Slocum's laugh was short and without any real glee. "You think I'm askin' you for it? I ain't a-askin'. I'm goin' to kill you 'n take it." He extended his hand and pulled the hammer back.

A bright muzzle flash lit up the mine even beyond that of the flickering torch, and the sound of the gunshot was almost deafening in the closed in area. The gun flew from Slocum's hand as Duff and Wang suddenly appeared. A narrow wisp of smoke curled up from the end of the Enfield Mark 1 pistol Duff was holding.

"We'll be for taking you in now, Slocum," Duff said.

"How you plannin' on gettin' me there? Like I said, I ain't got no horse to ride."

"You can walk, can't you?" Elmer asked.

"What do you mean, *walk*? It's five miles to town," Slocum complained.

"You don't have to walk if you don't want to," Elmer said. "We can drag you into town."

Connect with

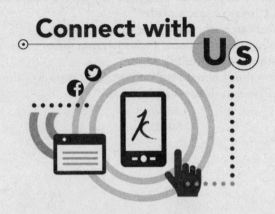

Visit us online at
KensingtonBooks.com
to read more from your favorite authors, see books
by series, view reading group guides, and more.

for sneak peeks, chances to win books and prize packs,
and to share your thoughts with other readers.

facebook.com/kensingtonpublishing
twitter.com/kensingtonbooks

Tell us what you think!

To share your thoughts, submit a review,
or sign up for our eNewsletters, please visit:
KensingtonBooks.com/TellUs.

Praise for Vicki Lewis Thompson

"Thompson continues to do what she does best, tying together strong family values bound by blood and choice, interspersed with the more sizzling aspects of the relationship."

—*RT Book Reviews* on *Thunderstruck*

"All the characters, background stories and character development are positively stellar; the warm family feeling is not saccharine-sweet, but heartfelt and genuine, and Lexi and Cade's rekindled romance is believable from beginning to end, along with the classy, sexy and tender love scenes."

—*Fresh Fiction* on *Midnight Thunder*

"Intensely romantic and hot enough to singe...her Sons of Chance series never fails to leave me worked up from all the heat, and then sighing with pleasure at the happy endings!"

—*We Read Romance* on *Riding High*

"If I had to use one word to describe *Ambushed!* it would be *charming*... Where the story shines and how it is elevated above others is the humor that is woven throughout."

—*Dear Author*

"The chemistry between Molly and Ben is off the charts: their first kiss is one of the best I've ever read, and the sex is blistering and yet respectful, tender and loving."

—*Fresh Fiction* on *A Last Chance Christmas*

"*Cowboy Up* is a sexy joy ride, balanced with good-natured humor and Thompson's keen eye for detail. Another sizzling romance from the RT Reviewers' Choice Award winner for best Blaze."

—*RT Book Reviews*

Dear Reader,

Hey, it's great to see you paying another visit to Thunder Mountain Ranch! I've had such fun with this summer's trio of books and I can't wait to hear how you like Hope and Liam's story. In case you didn't know, I'm on Facebook, Twitter and Instagram, so come find me and let's chat! Connecting with you is such a joy for me.

Here's another joy—telling you love stories featuring gorgeous cowboys! I'm sure Liam Magee will win your heart the way he won mine. He comes into Hope's life at a critical time, and the silly girl doesn't immediately recognize that he's the answer to her prayers. He'd probably be the answer to a lot of our prayers, if you get my drift...

Every once in a while an author is able to indulge herself with a story about the work she knows best—writing! Hope Caldwell is living my worst nightmare. She's a blocked writer. Thank God for Liam, who rides to the rescue even if Hope thinks she doesn't need rescuing.

Enough of the buildup—turn to chapter one and dive in! Nothing like a hot cowboy on a warm summer's night!

Joyfully yours,

Vicki Lewis Thompson

Vicki Lewis
Thompson

———

Cowboy After Dark

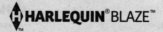
HARLEQUIN® BLAZE™

Recycling programs
for this product may
not exist in your area.

ISBN-13: 978-0-373-79903-9

Cowboy After Dark

Copyright © 2016 by Vicki Lewis Thompson

HARLEQUIN®
www.Harlequin.com

Printed in U.S.A.

A passion for travel has taken *New York Times* bestselling author **Vicki Lewis Thompson** to Europe, Great Britain, the Greek isles, Australia and New Zealand. She's visited most of North America and has her eye on South America's rain forests. Africa, India and China beckon. But her first love is her home state of Arizona, with its deserts, mountains, sunsets and—last but not least—cowboys! The wide-open spaces and heroes on horseback influence everything she writes. Connect with her at vickilewisthompson.com, Facebook.com/vickilewisthompson and Twitter.com/vickilthompson.

Books by Vicki Lewis Thompson

Harlequin Blaze

Thunder Mountain Brotherhood

Midnight Thunder
Thunderstruck
Rolling Like Thunder
A Cowboy Under the Mistletoe
Cowboy All Night

Sons of Chance

I Cross My Heart
Wild at Heart
The Heart Won't Lie
Cowboys & Angels
Riding High
Riding Hard
Riding Home
A Last Chance Christmas

To get the inside scoop on Harlequin Blaze and its talented writers, be sure to check out BlazeAuthors.com.

All backlist available in ebook format.

Visit the Author Profile page at Harlequin.com for more titles.

To every writer who's felt the pain of blocked creativity and has soldiered through it to give the world what she's got. Bravo!

1

LIAM MAGEE PULLED off the road, shoved back his hat and peered through the windshield of his truck. "That's a helluva steep driveway, Grady."

"Yeah." His brother studied the incline. "You should probably come around again and make a run at it. I'm pretty sure if you hang a right at the corner, you can circle the block."

"I know I can. I used to date a girl who lived on the next street over. Whenever we had a fight, I'd drive that loop more than a few times until I cooled down enough to apologize." He looked at the slope and calculated how fast he'd have to be going when he started up. At least it was July. He couldn't imagine why anyone would create a driveway like that in Sheridan, Wyoming, unless it doubled as a toboggan run. "You'd better check the hitch and make sure the tie-downs are tight."

"Will do." Grady hopped out and loped back to the flatbed they were towing.

Liam wasn't going to say it and upset Grady, but they were courting disaster hauling the loaded flatbed up that hill. His big-hearted brother had made a spectacular wedding present for his foster brother Damon Harrison, and he was determined to deliver it when nobody was home. He wanted it to be a surprise.

Years ago, Damon had been a significant role model for Grady—likely still was, judging from this wedding gift. Damon had been one of the older guys at Thunder Mountain Ranch, formerly a home for foster boys and now a student academy for everything horse-related.

Located a few miles outside Sheridan, the ranch had once provided a temporary haven for Liam and Grady while their mom recovered from a bad car accident. Damon's determination to become a master carpenter after high school had inspired Grady to learn a trade. He'd chosen welding, a skill that had landed him a job in Alaska working on a pipeline.

He'd come back to rejoin Liam in Cody a couple of years ago with a new dream. His recycled metal sculptures had taken the local art world by storm, and he was making money hand over fist. Liam couldn't be prouder of his little brother.

Naturally Grady had wanted to create something special for Damon and his bride Philomena. He'd welded about five hundred pounds of scrap metal into a ten-foot sculpture. Although a gallery would charge thousands for the piece, discussing the market value of his work always made Grady laugh.

He created for the love of it. When the price of his sculptures had skyrocketed, he'd asked Liam to invest the money that kept pouring in because dealing with that aspect of success wasn't his thing. Surprises *were* his thing, though, and he desperately wanted to surprise Damon and Phil.

Liam had asked some of his river-rafting coworkers to help load the gift onto the flatbed in Cody. The trailer had a tilting mechanism, so if Liam could get it up the hill, he and Grady should be able to install the sculpture somewhere in the yard. If the spot didn't suit Damon and Philomena, Grady could enlist some of the guys from the wedding party to help move it.

Grady climbed back in the cab. "Everything looks good. I spotted an SUV and a truck parked up by the house, though. Are you sure nobody's there?"

"Shouldn't be. Damon told us to meet him at the ranch, and Phil's supposed to be in town at her bachelorette shindig." Liam felt a stab of guilt. He'd been afraid the happy couple wouldn't welcome a gigantic wedding gift, so he'd secretly warned Damon that something big and metallic was coming his way. Turned out Phil was a huge Grady Magee fan, so Damon heartily approved of the gift.

Grady wouldn't have wanted to alert Damon, but Liam was used to paving the way for his kid brother, a habit he wasn't likely to break anytime soon. Damon wouldn't be surprised, but Philomena would be, and that was the compromise Liam had made with his conscience. "The women probably carpooled into town for Philomena's bachelorette party."

"That makes sense. Okay, let's do this thing."

"Keep your eye on the trailer."

"I will." Grady focused on the side mirror as they went around the block. "So far, so good."

"Yeah, but I'll really punch it the minute I see that driveway. If anything looks wonky, yell out."

"Don't worry. I will."

The driveway came into view. Liam stomped on the accelerator, and his F-350's engine roared. He would make it up the hill, by God. Grady was counting on him.

HOPE CALDWELL HAD taken her glass of white wine out to the front porch swing. She was thrilled to have been invited to the wedding and to have been asked to house-sit while Phil and Damon honeymooned. It would be a fun little vacation, her first in more than a year.

She and Phil had been close in high school, but then they'd drifted apart, so reconnecting after all this time had been wonderful. She hoped Damon and Phil would spend the rest of their lives basking in wedded bliss in this adorable cabin Phil had remodeled.

In fact, the cabin had charmed the bachelorette party guests so much, they'd changed the plan. Instead of going into town, they'd made a wine run, ordered pizza, turned on some music and settled in right here. The added privacy and cozy ambiance seemed to suit everyone as wine and laughter flowed.

Hope had been fine with all of it. Then, partway through her second glass of wine, the joyous celebration morphed into a painful reminder of her crushed and mangled dreams. She'd quietly slipped outside to regroup and put her happy face back on.

While swinging lazily and sipping her wine, she heard what sounded like a heavy-duty truck stop at the end of the drive. It sat there, engine idling, as if the driver might be scoping things out. It could be the beginning of a prank orchestrated by Damon's foster brothers, but none of them knew that the bachelorette party had changed locations.

After one and a half glasses of wine, Hope's imagination shifted into high gear. The house was filled with wedding presents. What if some bad actors knew that and were planning to rob the place? If they had inside info, they'd think no one would be home this afternoon.

Then the truck moved on. Okay, so much for that theory. Maybe the driver was just lost. But moments later, she heard the truck again, only this time the engine was cranking. *They'd gone around the block to get a faster start up the hill.* Setting down her wineglass, she raced to the door and wrenched it open. "Phil, call the cops! Someone's coming up here to rob you!"

Then she barreled down the steps toward the drive. Chances were they wouldn't run over her if she stood in their way, plus they'd realize the house was occupied. She'd heard that most burglars robbed houses when the owners were gone. Throwing her arms wide, she yelled at them to stop.

The driver slammed on the brakes, both he and the other guy looking as if they'd seen a ghost. Oh, yeah, those two had definitely been up to no good! They were towing a loaded flatbed covered with a tarp to hide the stolen merchandise underneath. No doubt they'd planned on adding some wedding presents to their pile of booty.

Fists planted on her hips, she smiled in satisfaction as the truck rolled slowly backward, pulled by the weight of the trailer.

"What's happening?" Phil's red hair swung against her shoulders as she walked quickly over to Hope. Buzzing with excitement, the other guests followed.

"I'm positive they were after your gifts," Hope said. "Did you call 911?"

"I did, but—"

"Robbers?" Edie, Phil's stepmother, stared at the truck with wide eyes. "In broad daylight?" She and Phil looked enough alike to be mother and daughter, especially because Edie had colored her hair to match Phil's.

"They thought nobody was home." Hope watched a police cruiser pull up to block the thieves' escape. Small towns usually had speedy law enforcement. "Caught in the act. That'll teach them."

Both men got out of the truck.

"Cowboys?" Lexi Simmons, one of Phil's good friends, gazed at the two guys wearing hats, boots, jeans and yoked shirts.

"Cute ones, too," someone added.

"Wait a minute." Rosie Padgett, Damon's foster mom, moved to the front of the crowd. "Those boys look mighty familiar."

"Yeah," Lexi said. "They look a lot like the Magee brothers."

"Good Lord, it's Liam and Grady!" Rosie started down the hill.

Phil gasped. *"Grady?"* She trotted after Rosie. "Are you saying I called the cops on *Grady*?"

"Isn't Grady Magee that sculptor you love so much?" Edie hurried down the drive after them.

"Yes!" Phil tossed over her shoulder. "And a wedding guest, besides! This is *so* embarrassing."

"But why would they just show up like this?" Hope observed the scene with growing dismay. She'd heard of Grady Magee. Everyone who lived in Cody had. She'd known he'd be at the wedding with his brother Liam. That probably meant one of Grady's sculptures was under that tarp and *not* a bunch of stolen goods. If they were trying to bring the tarp-covered object up the drive, it might even be a wedding present for Damon and Phil. Damn it.

"Don't feel bad." Lexi gave her a quick hug.

"Too late."

"Hey, they *could* have been robbers."

"But they weren't. And one of them is famous." Her vivid imagination had gotten her into trouble a lot as a kid, but she hadn't embarrassed herself like this in a long time.

"You didn't know that, and you were bravely defending the castle. That's admirable." Lexi smiled. "Let's go find out what they're up to."

"Okay." Heading down to meet the Magee brothers was the last thing she wanted to do, but refusing wasn't an option. She needed to apologize for interfering. She'd never met Grady, but she'd seen his picture in the paper. She picked him out as the one with collar-length brown hair.

He and his brother didn't resemble each other. The closer she came to the group at the bottom of the drive, the more familiar Liam seemed. She remembered that jet-black hair and those blue eyes from somewhere. She also recognized his warm smile.

Then she placed him. He'd stopped in a few times after dropping off his rafting clients at the hotel in Cody where she worked at the concierge desk. From his subtle flirting, she'd thought he'd ask her out eventually. Even though he was temptation on a stick, she'd been rehearsing her refusal. She had no intention of getting involved with a guy. Not now, anyway, and maybe not ever again.

She probably wouldn't need to refuse him after giving him a heart attack by standing in front of his moving truck and then bringing the law down on him. She'd be lucky if he didn't chew her out. But what in hell had he been doing delivering a sculpture when presumably no one was home?

Unless it was supposed to be a surprise, doofus. She sighed. That would explain everything, wouldn't it? But spoiling the surprise wasn't all on her, not with the party guests in the cabin this afternoon.

By the time she and Lexi had joined the gathering, the cruiser had driven away. Phil was having an animated conversation with Grady, and Liam stood there smiling with one arm around Rosie's shoulders as everyone gave

him advice about getting his truck and the loaded flatbed up the hill. Except if Hope hadn't stood in his way,
he'd have accomplished it by now.

Liam's gaze fell on them, and he brightened. "Hey,
Lex!" He moved toward Lexi, but he sent a quick smile
Hope's way as if to acknowledge that he recognized her,
too. "Grady, Lexi's here!"

As both guys converged on Lexi, Phil hurried over and
put her arm around Hope. "It's fine. They're not upset."

"I feel like an idiot."

"I know, but please don't worry about it. They're good
guys. Let me introduce you. Liam, Grady? This is my
friend Hope Caldwell. We've known each other since
ninth grade."

"Nice to meet you, Hope." Grady smiled as he touched
the brim of his hat in a typical cowboy greeting. "I have
to admit you scared the daylights out of us."

"I know, and I'm deeply sorry. I thought—never mind
what I thought."

"Oh, we're well aware of what you thought." Liam's
amused voice matched the laughter in his blue eyes.
"The cops made that clear. Hello, Hope. Good to see
you again."

"I sincerely doubt that."

"No, I mean it." His gaze held hers.

Phil blinked. "You know each other?"

"Not really." Hope scrambled to get her bearings. The
warmth in Liam's expression when he'd looked at her
spoke volumes. Instead of being upset with her, he saw
this coincidental meeting as a bonus. "Liam has rafting
clients who stay at the hotel where I work. We've seen
each other a few times because of that."

"Hope's part of the concierge staff," Liam said. "She's

been kind enough to recommend our rafting company to hotel guests."

"That's because everybody raves about the experience."

His blue eyes lit up with pleasure. "Glad to hear it! Just say the word and I'll take you on a complimentary rafting trip. Then you can know firsthand what you're recommending."

Unless she was mistaken, he'd just asked her out. Sure, it was kind of business-related, but she was getting a vibe from him that was all pleasure. Even more problematic, her body was responding to that vibe. "I, um…haven't thought about it. Maybe sometime." She cleared her throat and glanced pointedly at the flatbed with its mysterious cargo. "Do you still want to get that up the hill?"

"Yes, ma'am." He winked at her.

Her stomach fluttered and her pulse rate shot up. She'd have to be careful or this tall cowboy would slip right past her defenses.

"I've figured out it's a surprise wedding gift for Damon and me," Phil said. "And I can't *wait* to see it. Oh, my god, a Grady Magee piece on my property! Can you believe it?"

"It's the least I could do," Grady said. "After all the encouragement Damon gave me right when I needed it."

"Should I call him?" Phil held up her phone. "I know you wanted to surprise us, but now I think he should be here when you take the tarp off and set it up."

"Guess so."

Hope felt sorry for the guy. He obviously was disappointed that his grand scheme hadn't come off as planned. She glanced up at Liam. "Too bad it didn't work out the way you both hoped."

He shrugged one broad shoulder. "We tried."

"If I hadn't stood in your way, you'd at least have the trailer up there by now."

"Wouldn't have mattered. Even if we'd made it up, we'd never have been able to set up the sculpture without someone in the cabin hearing us. The flatbed makes a hellacious noise when you tilt it."

"But you were trying to accomplish something cool, and I had Phil call the police."

His dark eyebrows lifted. "So that was your idea?"

"Yeah, I told her to call the cops before I ran out to the driveway. When I saw the loaded trailer, I thought you'd already taken things from other houses and hidden them under the tarp. I'd convinced myself you were out to rob us blind."

"Some imagination you have."

"So I've been told."

He rubbed his chin as he gazed at her. "Gutsy, too."

"Not really."

"Yes, really. You believed there was a problem, so you threw yourself into the breach. What if I'd run over you?"

"I didn't think you would. Robbery is one thing. Manslaughter is another."

"I suppose, but even so, I—"

"Damon's on his way!" Phil waved her phone in the air. "And he's bringing more muscle."

Edie laughed. "I like the sound of that. This bachelorette party gets more interesting by the minute!"

2

LIAM WANTED THE flatbed up that driveway before Damon and company arrived. A guy had his pride. "If you ladies will excuse Grady and me, we'll go around the block again and mount another charge up that hill."

"We can line the drive and cheer you on," Lexi said.

Liam winced. "Much as I love that visual, you can all help by going back to on the porch so I don't have to worry about hitting somebody." He'd probably have nightmares about seeing Hope in the middle of the driveway. Fortunately he had great reflexes and good brakes.

"Spoilsport." Lexi punched him lightly on the arm. "Come on, ladies. We're relegated to the porch while the macho cowboys prove they can take this hill."

Rosie paused beside Liam. "You be careful."

"Always." He was glad to see her looking so perky. Wrangling those academy students must agree with her. She'd added some streaks of red to her blond hair, and he liked it.

She peered up at him. "You say that, but I know you run those rapids on the Snake River like a madman."

"Who told you that?"

She smiled. "I have my sources."

He didn't doubt it. Every foster boy who'd lived at Thunder Mountain Ranch knew Rosie missed absolutely nothing. If a guy got away with some infraction of the rules, that was only because Rosie had decided to let it slide.

"I'll be careful," he said. "Grady worked hard on this sculpture, and I don't want it ruined on my watch."

Rosie nodded. "Of course you don't. Also…" She paused and lowered her voice. "Hope's a sweetheart, and she meant well. I take it you aren't upset with her."

"I'm not." No, he was more intrigued. Not many people would stand in front of a truck that could mow them down.

"I'm not, either," Grady said. "The plan was wrecked, anyway, and she gave us a heads up about that, so we'll just work out a new plan."

"That's the spirit," Rosie said. "Now get moving and take it easy."

Liam scratched the back of his head. "Isn't that what you call an oxymoron?"

"Not in my world. In my world, it's the secret of life." Rosie gave them a little wave and hurried up to join the others.

Grady glanced over at Liam. "You do realize she's a Zen master in disguise, right?"

"That would explain a lot of things."

"Take my word for it. She may look like a slightly overweight grandmother, but that woman has powers and she knows how to use them."

"Then I wish she'd waved a magic wand and made us magically scoot up this driveway."

Grady laughed. "She doesn't have that kind of power. Besides, she knows it's important for us to make it there on our own. She wouldn't want to deprive us of that challenge."

"You know what? I wouldn't want her to." Liam took a deep breath. "Let's do this thing." If he was picturing Hope gazing at him with admiration after he'd hauled the flatbed up the hill, well, showing off for women was one of the perks of being a guy.

Once they were in the truck and circling the block for the second time, Grady glanced over at him. "Is Hope the blonde you told me about, the one you were thinking of asking out?"

"Yep. Small world, huh?"

"She's pretty."

Liam thought she was several notches above pretty, but if he said that, he'd give away too much. "She is."

"She seems nice. Yeah, she tried to get us arrested, but I can understand. We were a little intimidating coming up the drive full throttle."

"I suppose."

"But now that the dust has settled, you have a golden opportunity to get something started while you're both here in Sheridan."

"Maybe." Liam thought so, too, but he was still adjusting to the new reality. He'd shifted the possibility of Hope to another time and place, but then she'd appeared right in front of him, literally, and now he had to decide how to respond to that. He didn't think she was quite as glad to see him as he was to see her.

"Think about it. We're all involved in the wedding. It's the classic time for fun and games."

"Does that mean I can expect you to get horizontal with a bridesmaid?"

"Nope. Casual hookups don't appeal to me the way they used to."

Liam got a kick out of that. His little brother was grow-ing up. "But they're perfectly fine for me?"

"Hell, no. She's from *Cody*. If things work out, you could keep seeing her after the wedding."

"And if they don't work out?"

"You quit going into the hotel lobby after dropping off clients. She doesn't seem like the type who would stop sending you business."

"I'm not worried about that."

"Then what are you worried about? I've never known you to hesitate once a woman catches your eye—which she has. You winked at her. That's one of your moves."

"It is not."

"Sure it is. You give them a little wink to test their reaction, find out if you have a shot. I've seen you do it a hundred times."

"Did I ever mention that you're a pain in the ass?"

"She blushed when you winked at her."

"I know." And he'd seen a flicker of sensuality in her gray eyes. But something about her was closed up tight. He'd felt a hint of that whenever he'd stopped to see her at the hotel. The feeling was stronger today. He sensed that if he approached her like he normally would approach a woman, she'd reject him.

"I say go for it."

"I'll give it some thought."

"Okay." For no reason Liam could see, Grady was cracking up.

"What's so funny?"

"You just drove past the driveway."

"Damn it! Why didn't you say something?"

"I wanted to find out if you were as gaga over this woman as I think you are, and sure enough, you're toast."

"Am not."

"But you missed the driveway, bro. That's not a Liam sort of thing to do."

Gripping the wheel, he blew out a breath. "Means nothing."

"I beg to differ. Thank God I came back from Alaska in time to see my big brother lose his cool. When you first mentioned her, I heard something in your voice, and now that I see you with her, it's confirmed. You're twitterpated."

"I'm *what*?"

"Twitterpated. An old prospector I used to drink with loved that expression. I've been waiting for a chance to use it, so thanks."

"You make me sound like some starry-eyed fool with his tongue hanging out."

"Nah, you're not that obvious…yet. I figure we'll all be invited to stick around after we unload the sculpture, so you can engage in some casual conversation, make some inroads, get her digits so you can message her."

"I don't want to push."

"Since when is asking for a woman's phone number pushing?"

"Normally it's not, but with Hope… I don't think it's that simple."

"Only one way to find out. And FYI, the driveway's coming up again."

"Yeah, I see that. Thanks." Liam checked for traffic, but fortunately there wasn't any. He swung wide and stomped on the gas. His truck protested all the way up the hill, but they made it—along with the trailer.

When he pulled in front of the cabin and turned off the motor, he heard the women cheering as they came down the porch steps toward them. And yes, he picked Hope out of the crowd and imagined that the color in her cheeks was due to his demonstration of superior driving skills.

Grady smiled. "Sweet."

The sound of engines revving prompted Liam to glance in his side mirror. "Just in the nick of time, too. Here comes the cavalry." He drove forward a little more to make room, but two pickups were coming up, and they wouldn't both fit. He couldn't give the guys any more space without heading down the other side of the drive, and he didn't trust his emergency brake to hold all that weight. The second pickup slowly backed down to the street.

Liam and Grady piled out to greet Damon and Damon's best friend, Cade Gallagher, who had arrived in the lead truck. Cade had been the first foster boy Rosie and her husband Herb had taken in, but Damon had been added soon afterward. Consequently they shared a special bond.

Damon's brown eyes flashed with amusement as he grinned at Liam. "What a fustercluck, huh?"

"Shit happens." Liam was so glad to see his foster brothers that the screwed-up plan didn't matter anymore. They both looked tanned and fit, as if life was treating them well. "I've missed you two jokers."

"Same here." Damon gave both Magee brothers a hug, and so did Cade. Most of the foster boys had come from difficult situations, which caused them to cherish the connections they'd made at Thunder Mountain Ranch.

About that time, Rosie's husband, Herb, walked up the driveway with Finn O'Roarke. Finn towered over Herb, but the older man walked with a proud dignity that made him seem larger than life. He, too, seemed to be flourishing as a result of his work with the academy students.

He was the only father Liam had ever known, and seeing him always caused a surge of love and gratitude.

Finn had been the third boy Rosie and Herb had brought to the ranch. He, Damon and Cade had dubbed themselves the Thunder Mountain Brotherhood that first year. Some who'd arrived afterward had been jealous, but Liam never had been. Then again, he'd always had Grady.

More hugs followed, and Finn explained that his fiancée, Chelsea, had encountered some last-minute work issues. She'd be flying in the next day. Finally somebody broached the subject of the mix-up.

Phil looped an arm around Damon's waist. "We can blame everything on our cozy cabin. Once everyone was here, they wanted to stay."

"I can believe that." Damon glanced at Liam and Grady. "Still, I'm sorry the plan got messed up."

"If certain somebodies had told *me*—" Rosie paused to gaze pointedly at Grady and Liam "—I would have made sure things went as they were supposed to."

"I wanted everyone to be surprised," Grady said.

"Well, we were certainly surprised." Lexi linked an arm through Cade's. "Too bad you boys missed the excitement."

Liam noticed the affectionate gesture and was glad for Cade. He'd loved that woman since high school. Rumors continued to circulate about their eventual marriage, but Lexi's ring finger was bare.

Ring or no ring, though, her eyes were filled with love when she looked at Cade. "You should have seen Hope stare those boys down," she continued. "It was epic."

"And brave," Liam added, because Hope seemed uncomfortable with the conversation.

She glanced at him and shook her head, which made her silky blond hair gleam in the sun. "It wasn't brave.

It was stupid. What if the trailer had jackknifed and dumped the sculpture? Or you two had been hurt? I would never have forgiven myself."

"But we're fine and the sculpture's fine." Liam had the urge to wrap a protective arm around her.

"Maybe the way this turned out is even better," Grady said. "Now that we have more guys, we can do an unveiling for Phil."

"You mean just take off the tarp?" Damon gave Phil a squeeze and released her. "Yeah, let's do that. I'm eager to see it, too."

"Wait." Grady moved to stop him. "I meant get it off the flatbed with the tarp still on it, and once it's standing where it should go, *then* we take the tarp off."

"Oh." Damon paused to adjust his Stetson. "Hmm."

Liam understood the impulse behind Grady's suggestion. His artistic pride was involved, and he didn't want the crowd gathered here to see the sculpture until it was in a place of honor. But during setup, the piece could be damaged. Even worse, a person could be damaged. Liam didn't like the odds.

"Grady, I know what you're hoping to achieve," he said, "but I think we could have problems wrestling five hundred pounds of metal off the flatbed while keeping the tarp wrapped around it."

"I was a little worried, too." Herb came over and laid a hand on Grady's shoulder. "I have a suggestion, son. Since this is a wedding gift for Damon and Phil, how about if they go in the house while the rest of us set it up?"

"That's a great idea." Lexi smiled at Grady. "And while I'm perfectly willing to help, I see this as a manly bonding activity."

"Aha!" Cade shoved back his hat. "Perfect timing.

What if we make this the first official duty of the ex-panded Thunder Mountain Brotherhood?" He gazed at Finn and Damon. "You good with that?"

"Absolutely," Damon said, "but in that case, I want to be out here helping."

"We can let Grady decide if you should or not." Cade turned to him. "Here's the deal. Finn, Damon and me, we had a few beers at lunch and sat around shooting the breeze like we always do, reminiscing about all the great times we've had and the stuff we got into, and—"

"Blah, blah, blah." Damon reached over and knocked Cade's hat down over his eyes. "Cut to the chase."

"Hang on, bridegroom." Cade repositioned his hat. "I needed to set the scene. Anyway, it occurred to us that since every guy who was at the ranch is our brother, the Thunder Mountain Brotherhood should be inclusive, not exclusive. You and Liam don't have to go along with that idea if it doesn't appeal to you, but—"

"It appeals to me." Grady glanced at Liam. "How about you, big brother? Wanna be part of the club?"

Unexpected emotion tightened his chest. He hadn't thought this mattered to him, but he was incredibly touched. Tucking his thumbs in his belt loops, he rocked back on his heels and grinned. "That depends. Do I get a secret decoder ring?"

"You bet," Finn said. "Just pop one off your next can of beer, put it on your pinky and you're in business."

"Then I'm in."

"Good." Cade looked incredibly pleased with himself. "It was mostly my idea, but—"

"It was *not*." Finn rolled his eyes. "Way to hog the credit. If I remember correctly, and I'm sure I do, it was—"

"Boys!" Rosie clapped her hands. "We're getting off

track, and I want to see that sculpture. Who's going in the house with me?"

Damon glanced at Grady. "Can I stay? I can help you figure out where it should go."

"Yeah, let him stay," Phil said. "He has a good eye. I'm sure I'll be happy with the placement."

"Okay." Grady nodded. "You're right. It'll be better if one of you tells us where to put it. We won't end up having to move it later."

"Then it's settled." Rosie motioned toward the porch. "Women, inside. Men, get to work. Call us when you're ready for the big reveal."

"There's only one thing wrong with this plan, Rosie," Phil's stepmother said.

"What's that, Edie?"

"We don't get to watch all these gorgeous men flex their muscles."

That got a laugh. Liam checked Hope's reaction to the remark and discovered she was smiling. More than that, she was smiling at *him*. Maybe Grady was right. He should go for it.

3

ONCE THEY WERE INSIDE, Hope accepted with gratitude the glass of wine Phil handed her. Somehow she kept herself from knocking it back like a shot of whiskey.

"I'm organizing card games so nobody's tempted to peek out the window," Rosie said. "Who wants to play?"

"Count Hope and me in for the second round," Phil said. "We're going to take inventory of beer and snacks for the guys after they finish."

Lexi glanced their way. "Need help?"

"Thanks, but we can handle it." Phil led the way into the kitchen.

Hope followed. She hadn't offered to help organize the food and drinks, but Phil must have guessed she needed a time-out. Plus, she and Phil hadn't had a chance to talk by themselves all day. Until Phil and Damon left on their honeymoon, Hope was staying in one of Rosie and Herb's guest rooms out at the ranch.

That put her at the center of the activity, which had been great for getting to know everybody. Rosie, Herb, Cade, Finn, Damon and Lexi were all wonderful people, but Phil was the one she'd come to see.

"What did you do with your kitty cats?" she asked as they walked into the kitchen.

"Once I realized we'd be hanging out here, I closed them in the bedroom. They have food, water and a litter box. It's better if they're not part of this craziness."

"Much better."

"And if I haven't said this before, I so appreciate that you're willing to stay here after we leave and take care of MC Hammer and Nine-Inch-Nails."

"Of course! It'll be fun. So what are we doing to get ready for the testosterone invasion later on?"

Phil laughed. "No kidding. Beer is the magic potion. I have some in the fridge and more in the pantry." Phil opened the pantry door and pulled several varieties of chips from the top shelf.

"See how you do that? I've always envied your height." Phil had been the designated top-shelf gal for their crowd in high school.

"I always envied your boobs."

That made Hope laugh. "These old things? I've had them for years, but where have they gotten me?"

"Prom queen."

"Besides that. That doesn't matter."

"It does when you're seventeen."

"I suppose." Prom queen. What an empty accolade that was now. "So I assume you invited Debbie and Joan. Couldn't they come?"

"Sadly, no. I guess you didn't hear that Debbie moved to New York and Joan took a job in South Carolina. Debbie's about to deliver her first kid, and Joan was coming but she just started this job and couldn't wrangle the time off."

"That's too bad."

"I know. They both wanted to be here. They would have loved to see you."

"Likewise." She regretted losing touch with both women, but a lot of water had gone under the bridge. Maybe it was too late to rekindle the friendship. "So! What do you want me to do?"

"I'll get chip bowls if you'll put more beer in the fridge. We're well stocked, because I anticipated Damon's brothers dropping by."

Hope surveyed the cases of beer. "How much of this do you want chilled?"

"All that will fit. None of it is up to Finn's standards, I'm sure, but he'll just have to deal."

"Why's he so picky?" Hope carried a case over to the fridge and started making room on the shelves.

"He owns a microbrewery in Seattle, and he prefers his own beer. He shipped some to Rosie and Herb for the reception, but I can't buy it locally yet."

Kneeling, Hope layered cans on the bottom shelf by turning them on their sides. Phil was a lifesaver for bringing her in here to do this little chore. Working at something simple in the kitchen was perfect for calming her frazzled nerves. "It must be fun marrying into a family with so many brothers."

"It's a blast, and I haven't even met them all yet. What a coincidence that you know Liam, huh?"

"Yeah." Hope went for more beer. "Although I don't really *know* him. He's stopped in to chat a few times, but obviously I had no idea he used to live at Thunder Mountain or he was Grady Magee's brother. That was a shocker. Grady's one of Cody's most famous citizens these days, but Liam never said a word about him."

"Which gets him points in my book. He didn't try to impress you with his brother's fame."

"Maybe he wasn't trying to impress me, period."

"I think he'd like to, just not by bragging about his family connections." Phil paused to glance at her. "He seems interested in you."

"Okay, yeah. I think he is." Possibilities shimmered through her mind, teasing her with thoughts she hadn't considered in more than a year. But she didn't trust those thoughts. She wouldn't surrender to them ever again.

"And?"

"Well, obviously it's flattering. He's hot."

"No argument there. Damon's the only man for me, but I can still appreciate beauty when I see it. Liam's got that black Irish thing going on with his dark hair and blue eyes."

"Uh-huh." Hope had taken note of that—not to mention his insanely long lashes and shoulders a mile wide. He was dangerously attractive.

"You dating anybody?"

"Nope."

"It must be tough. You and Tom were together a long time."

"We were." Thinking of him didn't affect her anymore, thank goodness.

"I don't know Liam or Grady, really. All I have to go on is Damon's opinion, and he's prejudiced. I've learned that these men are fiercely loyal to each other. In most cases they couldn't depend on their biological families, but they sure as hell can depend on the family Rosie and Herb created."

Hope smiled. "So now we have a hot guy who's been through tough times and consequently sticks by the people he loves. That's a damned appealing combo."

"Don't I know it, sister. I fell for Damon like a ton of bricks. Listen, I'm not trying to matchmake, but you and

Liam will be seeing each other a lot in the next few days. It might be a perfect time to get to know him without having to play the dating game."

"True." She hadn't thought of it that way. The idea of dating completely turned her off. But she and Liam would be thrown together on a regular basis without having to plan anything. If, during that time, their relationship took a sexy turn, so what? Other people had flings, so why couldn't she?

Phil dumped the last bag of chips in a bowl. "How's the new job going?"

"It's good. I like the management, and setting up fun outings for the hotel guests has turned out to be satisfying."

"I'm glad." Phil tossed the empty bag in the trash. "What about your writing? Have you had time for that?"

Hope felt a slight twinge in the region of her heart, and then it was gone. "Not really. I could make the time, I guess, but I can't get excited about it the way I used to."

"Really? That's my most vivid memory of you, always writing something in those journals you carried around. When your short story was published in the school paper, I saved it. I probably still have it somewhere."

"Thank you for that." Hope smiled at the memory of the person she used to be. So naive. "But at some point I realized I wasn't going to write the Great American Novel, so I gave it up."

"Huh." Phil ran her hands through her red hair, which was shorter than it had been in high school. "I kind of get that, I guess. I used to think I'd be an Olympic figure skater, but eventually I realized it wasn't gonna happen. We grow up and view the world as it actually is, right?"

"Right."

"And now you're having a good time planning trips for your hotel guests."

"And you're in business with your soon-to-be husband, renovating homes that need some TLC. That must be satisfying, too."

"I love it. You look at a home that's not functioning the way it should and you figure out how to fix the dynamic through a bathroom remodel or a kitchen makeover. It changes people's lives."

"I'm sure it does." Hope thought of her extremely basic apartment in Cody and yearned for a place she could really make her own. She was saving, but not fast enough to suit her.

Phil sighed. "We need to get back to the party, but I almost hate to. It's been so good catching up after all this time."

"It has." Hope gave her a hug. "Cody isn't that far away. We need to keep in better touch." She glanced down at the almost invisible bulge that indicated Phil was pregnant with her first child. "Do you know yet if it's a boy or a girl?"

"We don't want to know before he or she is born. But I'm hoping for a girl. Damon's foster family is chockablock with testosterone. Rosie's been holding the fort with some help from Lexi and me, but honestly, we need reinforcements. I understand why Rosie and Herb decided to take only boys after they brought Cade home. Life was less complicated that way. But the ladies need more representation around here."

"Then I'll keep my fingers crossed for a girl."

"Good deal. Now let's go kick butt at some cards."

"I'm pumped. Let's do it." She walked into the living room and discovered every woman with her nose pressed against the windows.

"Hey!" Phil's shout made them turn around, and they all looked guilty as hell. "I thought we'd agreed not to watch."

"We did, dear." Edie gestured toward the window. "But we're only human, and every one of those lovely men has taken off his shirt."

"Which you wouldn't have known if at least one of you hadn't peeked." Phil crossed her arms and tried to look stern, but Hope could tell she was working hard not to laugh.

"I confess," Lexi said, grinning. "It was Edie."

Phil sighed. "Come on, Edie. I'm sure you've seen shirtless cowboys before."

"Not with muscles like theirs," her stepmother said, "and not so many all at once."

"Even Herb took off his shirt." Rosie sounded proud of that. "If I do say so myself, he's a fine figure of a man for his age. The sculpture's almost in place. Do you want to—"

"No!" Phil clapped a hand over her eyes. "I'm not looking. Grady wanted this to be a surprise, and although I may be the only one in this room who will be surprised, I'm taking the high road."

"Me, too." As a gesture of solidarity, Hope refused to look out the window, even though the prospect of seeing Liam shirtless was a powerful draw.

Rosie walked over and wrapped her arm around Phil. "I admire your ethical stand. I'm also happy to report that the Thunder Mountain Brotherhood has settled your gift in its spot, and it looks magnificent."

"Do you want a teensy-weensy hint as to what it is?" Edie looked ready to burst with eagerness.

"I do not." Phil plopped into the nearest chair. "Don't any of you dare tell me what it looks like, or give me hints, or whisper so I can hear you. Grady Magee, who is a god among sculptors, has made me—well, Damon and me—a fabulous work of art. I will not see it before its time!"

A decisive rap on the door grabbed everyone's attention, but no one moved.

At last Hope got up. "I'll get it." When she opened the door, Liam stood on the other side, holding a bandana.

He wore a wide smile. "It's up."

Everyone in the room cheered, including Hope, although she was a bit distracted by the man standing in the open doorway. He'd put on his shirt, but it hung open to reveal a chest glistening with sweat. He must have taken the steps two at a time, because he was breathing fast. Hope stared in fascination at the droplets quivering on his dark chest hair.

Then she glanced up and discovered he was looking right at her with an expression that clearly said *caught you looking.* Heat rushed to her cheeks, but she bravely met his gaze. Talking with Phil had clarified the situation for her, and if he wanted to pursue this attraction for the weekend, she was game.

"So, can we go out now or what?" Rosie asked.

Liam walked into the room. "My instructions are to blindfold Phil and lead her to the sculpture. You can—"

"Why isn't Grady doing the leading?" Rosie asked. "Or Damon?"

"Because both of them want to see her face when she takes off the blindfold, so I volunteered."

Rosie nodded. "Makes sense. Proceed."

"Thanks. You can all follow behind, but you're not supposed to say anything. You might give it away."

"Who, us?" Edie laughed. "Never."

"We'll be quiet," Lexi promised.

"That means you can't make any noises, like gasping and stuff." Liam positioned the blue bandana over Phil's eyes and tied it behind her head. "Is that too tight, Phil?"

"No."

"Can you see?"

"No."

"You're sure?"

"She doesn't want to see," Hope said. "She's been really good about not looking."

He glanced at her. "Did you look?"

"Nope."

"She didn't," Lexi said. "But you might want to skip that question for the rest of us."

"Yeah, I saw those faces glued to the window. I think we're ready, Phil. I'll hold your right hand until we're out the door. Hope, once we're out, why don't you take her left? That way she'll have support on both sides if she trips on something. The ground's uneven."

"Glad to." Maybe he'd suggested it as a reward because she'd been the only person besides Phil who hadn't peeked at the sculpture. Or maybe he liked the idea of sharing this moment with her. Whatever his reason, she was honored that he'd asked.

"I have a suggestion, Liam," Rosie said.

"What do you have in mind, Rosie?"

"Why not let us go first? Then you don't have to worry that we'll give anything away, and we get to see her reaction, too."

"Okay, that's better. Go on ahead." After everyone else had left the cabin, he looked over at Hope. "Let's give them a little lead time. Grady's excited about this moment. He's been envisioning it ever since he got the wedding invitation."

"I never in a million years expected something like

this." Phil took a deep breath. "Sure, I thought he might decide to give us something small for the coffee table, but never a large piece worth... I don't even want to think what it might be worth."

"But Grady doesn't think in those terms," Liam said. "He's astounded at the kind of money people are willing to pay for his work. He'd sell it for less, but the galleries don't want him to undervalue it and cut into their profits."

"Considering he made it for you and Damon as a gesture of gratitude," Hope said, "I'd say it's priceless."

Phil nodded. "Definitely."

"I agree," Liam said. "Ready for your special moment?"

"So ready."

"Then here we go."

Hope slipped out the door after them and took Phil's other hand. Once she was on the porch, she could see the sculpture. She swallowed the gasp that Liam had forbidden.

Damon had chosen the perfect site, a level area that wasn't blocked by trees. He and Phil would be able to see it easily from the porch swing. She knew the materials were recycled metal, but looking at the piece, no one would ever know it.

Set on a wide base, polished metal thunderclouds rose skyward. Above them soared a pair of eagles, their wingtips separated by mere inches. The image brought tears to her eyes. She blinked them quickly away, because blurred vision wouldn't help her guide Phil down the steps and over to the sculpture.

Liam didn't speak as they walked carefully toward the people grouped in a semicircle on either side of it. Grady stood on one side and Damon on the other. Hope couldn't decide which one of them looked more joyous, the creator of the piece or the man deeply in love with the woman about to see it.

"That's good," Grady called out. "She can take off the blindfold now."

Phil whipped off the bandana, gaped at the sculpture and burst into tears. "It's beautiful!" she gulped. "Oh, my God, so beautiful!" Cameras and phones clicked as everyone recorded a moment they'd all remember for years.

Phil mopped her eyes with the bandana. Then Damon came over to give her a big hug and a passionate kiss, which brought catcalls from the rest of the guys. Eventually Damon slipped his arm around her waist, and they walked over to thank Grady for what would probably be their most spectacular wedding gift.

"I'd say it's a hit."

Liam's voice startled Hope. She'd been so engrossed in the scene that she hadn't realized he was still standing beside her. "It's definitely a hit. Was that dramatic enough for Grady, do you think?"

"I'm sure. I doubt he's ever reduced someone to happy tears."

"Phil and Damon are the perfect people to give something like this to. They appreciate what goes into it more than most since they're both carpenters."

"I'm sure that's true. They seem really happy together."

"They do." She viewed their devotion the way she'd admire a rare jewel. It was a precious gift enjoyed by a lucky few but out of reach for the majority.

"I'm glad you're here for the wedding, Hope."

She glanced up at him. "So am I." Oh, yeah, he was sending all kinds of signals with those electric blue eyes. Love might be an impossible dream, but if she set her sights on lust, she wouldn't have far to look.

4

LIAM HAD NO idea why, but Hope had gone from wary to welcoming. Hell, it didn't really matter why. He had a shot, and that was the important thing.

Because everyone wanted to hang around and admire the sculpture, they'd all worked together to bring out lawn chairs, several picnic blankets and a cooler for the beer. Bowls of chips and bottles of wine had come next, and finally the party was ready to settle down near the base of the sculpture.

Liam grabbed a beer and used one of the smaller bowls Phil had brought out to scoop up some chips. Then he waited until Hope chose a blanket before walking toward it. "May I?"

"Sure. Anybody bringing chips is my new best friend." Her smile was friendly as she made room for him.

It was a smallish blanket, so nobody else decided to sit there. Or maybe people had figured out that he would like to have a semiprivate conversation with Hope. In any case, his fortune had changed for the better.

But the conversation he'd been planning was postponed while family and friends offered toasts—to the sculpture, the sculptor, the happy couple and life in general. Grady's grand gesture had been properly appreciated, and for that Liam was grateful. His brother might not care how much money he made with his art, but he cherished every kind word.

And kind words were flowing this afternoon. The toasts went on so long that Liam had to get another beer for himself and a refill for Hope's wineglass. When they emptied the chip bowl, he fetched more of those, too.

She thanked him for waiting on her. Then she smiled. "You know what? You're a pleasure to have around."

He knew that could be the wine talking, but he appreciated the comment nevertheless. And her smile made him catch his breath. She'd been subdued after the cops left, sure, but he sensed something deeper troubled her, something that had cast a shadow over her soul.

He was thrilled to see the sunshine peeking out. "I'm not such a bad guy when you get to know me."

"I'd like to get to know you, Liam Magee."

He almost choked on his beer. Before she'd seemed welcoming. Now she'd rolled out the red carpet. Talk about a dramatic turnaround. But he knew his lines. Carefully swallowing the mouthful of liquid, he held her gaze. "I'd like to get to know you, too."

"That may not be so simple. In case you hadn't noticed, we're in a crowd of people."

"I noticed." Her gray eyes were soft and dreamy, possibly compliments of the wine, but they were inviting him in. "A little quiet time together would be great, but I don't know if that's in the cards."

"You never know. It might be. Where are you staying?"

"Since the Thunder Mountain Academy students are on break for Fourth of July, Grady and I are bunking in our old cabin. It's been remodeled, but I'm sure it's not that different. It'll be nostalgic but it's not...exactly set up for entertaining."

"I'm staying at the ranch house in one of Rosie and Herb's guest rooms."

So close, and yet so far. "Then I guess I'll see you at dinner tonight."

"I'll be there." She laughed. "Along with a cast of thousands."

"Yeah, that's the thing about weddings. Lots of people." Then inspiration hit. He'd have to clear it with Rosie and Herb, but moonlit horseback rides had been one of his favorite things when he lived at the ranch. "Do you ride?" If she didn't, his plan wouldn't work. He didn't want to take a novice out on the trail at night.

"I'm an average rider, but nothing like Lexi, for example. She's amazing." She glanced at him. "I'm guessing you ride well."

"That was part of life at Thunder Mountain. We all learned to ride and care for horses. If we hadn't considered ourselves cowboys before we arrived there, we were proud to say we were when we left."

"It's really great that Rosie and Herb taught you ranch life. They're both such good people."

"The best."

"But I picked up on something that makes me curious. The other guys refer to Rosie as Mom, but you and Grady don't."

She'd been paying close attention. That was encouraging. "We call her Rosie because we have a mother and she's terrific."

Her eyes widened. "Your mother is alive and well? I thought everyone at Thunder Mountain was a foster kid."

"They were. Grady and I were temporarily in the program after our mom had a bad car accident. She didn't have any family to take over, and she had a lot of healing to do. We visited her, but she was in no shape to manage a couple of rowdy teenage boys. Rosie, who seems to know everyone in Sheridan, heard about us and invited us to live at Thunder Mountain."

"Where's your mom now?"

"At this very moment, she's on a Fourth of July paddle-wheel cruise going up the Mississippi River. She and my stepdad booked it before they got the wedding invitation. Their tickets were nonrefundable, and they've talked about this trip for years."

"Then I'm glad they didn't cancel it. So she's okay now?"

"More than okay." There was a time when it had hurt to talk about his mom. She'd tried so hard to make a life for her boys, and then a guy in a delivery truck hadn't been paying attention and she'd ended up in a coma. "She finally found a man who appreciates her. My dad obviously didn't, although I never knew him. I remember Grady's dad, though, and he was a piece of work. She was well rid of him."

"So that's why you and Grady don't look alike." Hope squeezed her eyes shut in obvious embarrassment. "I'm sorry. That didn't need to be discussed. I'm afraid I've had too much wine."

He was touched by her apology. He'd met people who thought nothing of asking rude questions about his and Grady's parentage. "Don't worry about it. You're not the first person to wonder why we don't look like brothers. Actually, Grady has my mom's coloring. Apparently I take after my dad." Years ago he'd hated that, but it wasn't something he could change, so he'd decided to accept it.

"Did you ever try to locate your father?" Then she

waved her hand as if to erase her words. "Inappropriate question. Forget I asked."

"I'm glad you asked." He smiled at her. "It means you're interested in me."

"As it happens, I am."

"So if I arranged a moonlit horseback ride tonight after dinner, you'd be willing to go?"

"Sounds like fun."

"Yeah." He gazed into her warm gray eyes. They revealed a depth of emotion that called to him. "I think it will be."

LIAM'S PLAN HAD everything going for it except the moon. After dinner at the ranch house, a rambunctious meal during which he exchanged only a few words with Hope, he excused himself to go saddle the horses. The temperature was perfect for an evening ride, but a quick glance at the sky told him he was stuck with a scrawny sliver of a moon that wouldn't give them much light.

"Want some help getting the horses ready?"

He turned back to see Cade coming down the porch steps. "Sure, thanks." They started toward the barn, their boots crunching on the gravel. "I was hoping for more moonlight."

"You may not have much of a moon, but the stars are spectacular."

"I know. I just don't want Hope to be spooked because it's so dark. I get the impression she doesn't spend a lot of time in nature."

"Then you're in an excellent position to introduce her to the great outdoors, Mister Whitewater Rafting Guide."

"But a full moon would have helped."

"A full moon always helps, but you don't happen to have one."

"So I see."

Cade chuckled. "Hey, here's a thought. Ride double. That would be cozy."

"Don't know her well enough to suggest that. Nice idea, though."

"Hey, I'm all about promoting romantic encounters for my brothers."

"Speaking of romance, what's up with you and Lexi? Rosie said Lex still has her apartment in town, and you're living in a brand-new cabin out here."

Cade sighed. "Yeah, and it's not optimal. You do know that I've handed the decision over to her, right?"

"Hadn't heard that. I live in Cody. Word doesn't always travel that far."

"Maybe that's a blessing. Anyway, last summer she turned me down flat. So I told her she has to propose to me when she thinks we're ready for that step."

"Interesting concept. Do you feel ready?"

"Bro, I feel more ready than you can possibly imagine. But she's holding off. It's been subtly suggested that I need to show signs of domesticity."

"Such as?"

"I think I'm supposed to spruce up the cabin, put pictures on the walls, stuff like that. Maybe buy a fancy holder for extra toilet paper, hang a sun catcher in the living room window. Cook some meals there. I never use the kitchen."

Liam couldn't help smiling. "For what it's worth, my mother had that kind of discussion before she agreed to marry my stepfather. They trade off cooking the meals and cleaning the house. I know you can clean. Rosie made us all do it."

"I can and I will. But I can't cook worth a damn, and choosing artwork is not my area."

"Not mine, either, but it's Grady's. Get him to help you find some stuff while he's here."

"Great idea."

"And cooking just takes practice."

Cade blew out a breath. "I suppose. I hate wasting food I ruined, but I hate not being married to Lexi even more, so I might as well burn some lasagna for the cause." He slid back the bar holding the barn's double doors. "Am I right that you and Hope have never gotten around to dating, even though you both live in Cody?"

"We have not."

"Then I guess we need to make sure this evening ride is extra special. You could take a couple of our nifty battery-operated lanterns and hang one on each saddle horn. There should be some spares in the tack room."

Liam breathed in the nostalgic mix of scents—horses, oiled leather and fresh straw. He'd missed this. "I noticed a lantern in our cabin, on the shelf where we used to keep the flashlights. How come? Don't the kids all have flashlight apps on their phones?"

"I'm sure they do. But we found out real quick that if we let them keep their phones, we'd get nowhere." Cade put the lanterns, constructed to look like old-fashioned kerosene ones, by the barn door. Then he and Liam transferred the necessary tack out to the hitching post.

"Couldn't they just turn their phones off?"

"Oh, sure." Cade handed Liam a lead rope, and they headed for the stalls. "We tried that. They'd shut them off during class, but every break they were texting and checking their social media."

"I shouldn't be surprised. I've had kids on my rafting trips carrying on because they couldn't get a signal. They've missed seeing an eagle or a bull moose because they were fiddling with their phones."

"I feel your pain. And it wouldn't be so bad if it only affected the breaks between classes, but that's not the case. They have trouble concentrating during the next class with all that junk in their heads. So now Rosie keeps all the phones at the house, and every night they get thirty minutes of phone time."

"That's strict. Do they pitch a fit?"

"You know, I thought for sure they would, but so far, no. We tested it on the first group in January, and after the shock of withdrawal, they seemed a lot less stressed. They're relieved of the responsibility of constantly updating their status."

"Bingo. Who came up with the solution?"

"Rosie, of course. She was willing to gamble that the kids would actually enjoy a break from their phones. New students are warned of the policy in advance, and nobody's canceled because of it."

"Some parents might enroll their kids just for that."

"I wouldn't doubt it." He paused in front of adjoining stalls. "If you'll take Navarre out first, I'll follow with Isabeau."

"Got it." He spoke gently to the gelding as he went inside, clipped the lead rope on his halter and walked him out of the stall.

"These two have benefitted from having the students here," Cade said as he followed with Isabeau. "Rosie and Herb weren't riding them much, and now they get plenty of attention and exercise on a daily basis."

"Looks like everybody's benefitting from the academy." He tied Navarre to the hitching post and picked up a brush to give the horse a quick grooming. "Rosie and Herb seem ten years younger. They need teenagers around."

"And as a bonus, these kids are mostly well-adjusted."

"Unlike us?" He worked through the familiar routine of saddling Navarre in the glow of the dusk-to-dawn light hanging over the barn door. Because he'd been trained years ago, he didn't have to think about it much.

Cade laughed. "Sometimes I wonder how Rosie and Herb survived those years. The crap we pulled."

"Speak for yourself."

"You were no choir boy, either, bro." Cade tightened the cinch on Isabeau's saddle, and the mare snorted in protest. "Let's not forget the fireworks you set off that damn near started a forest fire."

"But they didn't. And it was the only prank I ever tried. I wasn't constantly putting rubber snakes in guys' bunks like present company."

"Harmless fun."

"Says you. When my bare toes came in contact with that snake, I jumped out of bed so fast I whacked my head on the top bunk. Much harder and I would have been in the emergency room."

"You did have a pretty nifty goose egg. Good thing Rosie had her traditional bag of frozen peas handy."

"We went through a lot of frozen peas. We either ate them in Rosie's tuna casserole or used them for an ice pack." Resting his forearms on the saddle, he looked over at Cade and grinned. "Those were the days."

"Yeah, they were. Do you miss 'em?"

"Maybe a little, but I wouldn't want to be that age again. We were so clueless about everything."

"No kidding. Especially women." Cade grimaced. "Apparently I'm still pretty clueless in that department."

"Ah, you'll get there."

"Yeah, but I'd rather not be ninety when it happens."

"You won't be."

"Easy for you to say."

"Eighty-five, tops."

"That's such a comfort."

Liam walked around Navarre's hindquarters and clapped Cade on the shoulder. "If you get Grady to help you buy some art, and if you burn a few batches of lasagna, you might walk down the aisle sooner than that."

"Appreciate the advice, bro. Now let's get you situated for an excellent first date." He headed back into the barn. "I suggest taking a blanket along."

"I'll go with that suggestion." Lying with Hope and gazing up at a million stars sure sounded like an excellent first date to him.

Cade located a blanket in the tack room and handed it over. "You packing condoms?"

That startled a laugh out of him. "*No.* For crying out loud, Gallagher. I'm just getting to know the lady." He didn't admit that he'd thought of it and discarded the idea as being too crass this early.

"Apparently you haven't noticed the way she looks at you."

"And you have?"

"Sure. After you told me that you'd had your eye on her for weeks, I decided to spend the dinner hour watching her watching you."

"And how does she watch me?"

"Like she's buying whatever you're selling, bro."

His body tightened at the thought. "Nice to hear. Thanks for the info."

"Sure you don't want to take a couple of raincoats?"

"I'm sure. Then it'll look as if I assumed we might have sex, and that sends the wrong message."

"Your call, but don't blame me if you end up with an itch you can't scratch."

5

"I CAN'T SEE very well." As Hope bobbed along on Isabeau, she peered into the woods on either side of the narrow US Forest Service road. The extremely dark and scary woods. Any one of those shadows could be a bear, maybe even a grizzly. They'd have cubs this time of year, right? That made them more dangerous.

After several glasses of wine this afternoon, she'd convinced herself that an evening horseback ride with a handsome cowboy was a great plan. Now she longed for the cozy and very safe ranch house. Uh-oh. Something rustled in the bushes.

Liam kept moving forward, but he turned in his saddle to glance back at her. "Can you see the light on my saddle?"

"Shh. I hear something." She went very still and tried to separate the various sounds—the clip-clop of the horses' hooves, the creak of the saddles, the wind sighing through the top branches of the pines. The rustling had stopped.

No, there it was again. Just a little rustle, though. No branches breaking or stones knocked aside. Probably something fairly small like a skunk or a raccoon. In the distance, an owl hooted.

She focused on the indistinct shape of Liam up ahead on his horse, Navarre. "Sorry. What were you saying?"

"I was just going to say that if you can see my light, that's all you need. Really more than you need. Isabeau will follow Navarre, and they both have this route down cold. We could loop the reins around the saddle horns and let them take us out and back."

"What would they do if they saw or smelled a bear?"

"They'd let us know, but I—"

"How?" She pictured Isabeau turning her head and saying, *Bear at three o'clock. Check it out.*

"They'd get fairly agitated. Horses are prey animals, so they won't like it if a bear shows up."

"Or a cougar?"

"That, too."

"So they're like an early warning signal."

"They are, but I don't expect to see any predators tonight. If someone had spotted a bear or a cougar around here in the past few weeks, pictures would be on the internet. Nobody said a word at dinner, and they would have since they knew we were going out riding."

Some of the tension eased from her body. "Good to know."

"Sorry if you were worried. I should have said something earlier."

"And I should have remembered that you're an experienced wilderness guide. You wouldn't bring me out here if you thought there was a chance I'd be eaten by a bear."

"Good Lord. Were you really picturing that?"

"We established earlier today that I have a vivid imagination."

He chuckled. "Yeah, I suppose we did."

"And it's very dark out here. You can't see what might be going on in the woods. Anything could be lurking there, ready to spring. The trees are pretty close."

He turned a fraction more toward her. "Do you want to go back?"

Now was her chance to spend the rest of the evening chatting on the front porch with Herb and Rosie plus whoever else was still hanging around after dinner. All she had to do was say the word.

"Listen, we don't have to do this if it makes you nervous."

But then she wouldn't have a chance to be alone with Liam, and that opportunity might not come along again anytime soon. "I'd be lying if I said it didn't make me a little nervous."

"Then let's turn around." He wheeled Navarre in her direction.

"No, wait."

"I don't want to scare you to death." He rode toward her. "After I go past, just neck-rein Isabeau, and she'll turn and follow."

"I don't want to go back."

He stopped Navarre right next to her. On the narrow road, their stirrups were inches apart. Light from both lanterns illuminated his face, and he looked worried. "If you'll be embarrassed about showing up so soon after we left, we can cook up a plausible story."

"That's not the problem. I don't want to miss this chance to spend time with you."

"Then we'll make up a story that requires us to drive somewhere."

The light allowed her to see just how blue his eyes were. His long lashes made his eyes his most compelling feature, but his mouth drew her attention, too. She had a feeling he'd be fun to kiss. He had a little scar on the left side of his full lower lip, and she wondered how it had come to be there.

"Hope?"

She blinked. What had he just said? Oh, right. "I don't want to go through all that. Riding at night is something I've never done before, and at first I was feeling a little uneasy. Now that we've talked it through, I'm fine."

His jet-black eyebrows drew together. "Are you sure?"

"I'm absolutely sure. Let's keep going."

"I'd suggest riding side by side, but the road's a little narrow for that, and Isabeau's used to walking behind."

"Seriously, I'll be okay."

"I was planning to surprise you with our destination, but maybe I should tell you now in case you don't like the idea."

She'd seen the blanket rolled up and strapped behind his saddle. Sharing a blanket with him could be exciting or terrifying, depending on where he chose to lay it out. "I hope it's not a cave."

"No, it's a meadow, a fairly large one. Along the road, the trees mostly block the sky, but in the meadow you'll be able to see the stars really well."

"That sounds lovely."

The concern cleared from his expression. "Don't worry. I'll keep you safe."

"I should have realized that all along. You probably think I'm a real scaredy-cat."

"Not at all. Today you faced down my truck. Tonight when you got nervous, you didn't fall apart and beg me to take you back. You started collecting facts about the potential for bodily harm. I don't blame you for wanting to protect yourself. I'd rather have that than deal with someone who has no sense of self-preservation."

"Believe me, I have a well-developed sense of self-preservation." *Now.*

"All righty. Let me continue on past you and get Navarre turned around. Then we'll go check out that meadow."

"Good. I'd like that."

He smiled. "Thanks for sticking this out. I hope it's worth it."

His smile created a different kind of tension, one that was far more pleasant than her fear had been. "I'm sure it will be."

Touching his fingers to the brim of his hat, he rode on until he could turn Navarre around. Her libido was fully functioning by the time he moved into the lead and slowed the pace. Unfortunately she lost her view of his cute butt to the shadows of the tall pines lining the road.

He turned to check on her. "You okay back there?"

"I'm doing great." To think she'd considered going back. Even if he'd concocted some reason for them to take a drive, that trip couldn't possibly have been as exciting as this. "By the way, I love that Rosie and Herb named their horses Isabeau and Navarre. I was a big fan of *Ladyhawke.*"

"So were all the guys at Thunder Mountain."

She laughed. "Really? A chick flick?"

"Don't let them hear you call it that. Cowboys believe they're descended from medieval knights, you know."

"I didn't know."

"Think about it. We may not wear armor, but we sure do ride horses. We also believe we can rescue the fair maiden from the dragon who has her locked in a tower."

He couldn't know how appealing she found that image. "Have you ever been called upon for a rescue mission?"

"Can't say that I have. But I could rescue if necessary.

All of us feel that way. We used to talk about it around the campfire at night. Sure, we were young and naive, but we meant every word. Herb and Rosie encouraged us to think in those terms. They said real cowboys stand up for what's right and protect those who can't protect themselves."

"That's very heroic." She was doing her best not to be dazzled, but it wasn't easy. Sure, they were only words, but it was the way he said them that caught her attention. They were more than words to him.

"Nah, we're not heroes. Just cowboys."

"If you say so." Despite living in Wyoming all her life, she hadn't spent much time around cowboys.

"So what other movies do you like?" he asked.

"Love stories and action-adventure, mostly. Sometimes you can get a combination of the two, which is my favorite if they're well-done. How about you?"

"I like any movie where good triumphs over evil. Spare me from the weep-fests where everybody dies at the end."

"I know! I hate that!"

"What kind of stories did you used to write?"

She felt as if he'd dumped a bucket of ice water over her head. Phil had brought up the topic at dinner, and Hope had dismissed it as a dead issue not worthy of conversation. Everyone had seemed willing to let it drop.

But not Liam, apparently. *Answer him, and fast, so you can ditch this discussion.* "Love stories with some action-adventure thrown in. Amateur stuff. I never had anything published."

"Except in the school paper. You must have been happy about that."

"I was." Overjoyed. Proud as a peacock. The comments from her teachers and her friends had convinced her she would eventually be a bestselling author, maybe even make a living with her writing. "But that was a long time ago. I've outgrown all that."

"Hmm."

"What about you? Did you letter in every sport the school offered? I'll bet you did."

"Sports were a great outlet for me. Can't say my grades were terrific, though. Fortunately I had a few friends who were bookworms. They helped me pass."

"Girls?"

He laughed. "Yeah, mostly. They took pity on me."

"Oh, no doubt. I'm sure they felt extremely sorry for the captain of the football team who almost single-handedly took the school to the state championship. That's why they spent hours out at the ranch helping you with your homework."

"You must have been quizzing Grady about my checkered past."

"No, I just made that up."

"Really?" He turned around to stare at her. "You haven't been talking to Grady or Rosie or anybody about me?"

"Scout's honor."

"Wow. You weren't kidding about your imagination. Even more amazing, you nailed it, except I didn't single-handedly take us to the championship. It was a team effort all the way. We had some awesome players that year."

She smiled at that. Heroic and modest, too.

He faced forward again. "So what do you do with that supercharged imagination now that you're not dreaming up love stories with some action-adventure thrown in?"

Heroic, modest and persistent. *Damn.* "I, um…do crafts."

"Oh? Like what?"

She should have guessed he would ask. Quickly she reviewed the various half-finished projects tucked in her closet—knitting, embroidery, woodcarving and candle making. She'd lost interest in all of them, so she couldn't actually claim to be *doing* those crafts. "This and that."

"What's your favorite?"

"Don't really have one." They all bored her equally. Man, wasn't she the fascinating conversationalist tonight! "Lately I've been thinking about stained glass." It was one of the few she hadn't tried because materials and lessons were pricey, and she'd already wasted quite a bit of money on things that hadn't worked out.

"I like the look of stained glass. Grady's talked about putting a stained glass window in the loft of our barn."

"In your *barn*?"

"Our renovated barn, I should have said. The only critters living in it are Grady and me. He needed a big space for a workshop, so we bought this old barn and fixed it up. We built a couple of bedrooms in the loft, and he uses the lower floor for his work. We have a kitchen down there, too. The stained glass window would go in the loft. You could probably come up with something nice."

"I might be able to design it, but I couldn't make it. I haven't started taking lessons."

"That's okay. It's not like we would need one made next week."

She searched for some way to respond to his subtle implication that they'd stay in touch. In the end she couldn't think of anything to say that wouldn't sound ridiculous. It was too early to clarify that she was interested in only a brief affair. They hadn't even kissed.

She thought they would kiss. She hoped so, in fact. Thoughts of his mouth jacked up her pulse rate. Depending on what happened after that, she could make her little

speech and see how he reacted. Now that he was focus-
ing on her creative potential, she had even more reason
to keep her emotional distance.

He'd caught her off guard with his question of how
she made use of her imagination these days. No one had
ever thought to ask her that. Maybe they thought she
could shut off that part of her brain like turning off a
spigot. If only.

Liam lived with a full-time artist, so that probably
explained why he'd asked. He knew if Grady stopped
doing metal sculpture, he'd find another creative outlet. So would she, but she hadn't counted on it taking
so long.

While she was making the journey, though, she didn't
want anybody else involved. She'd already paid the price
for letting someone in, and she didn't care to pay it again.
What she did with her *supercharged imagination* was her
business. She shouldn't have mentioned the stained glass,
but lesson learned. If she didn't want him poking around
in her inner life, she'd best keep her mouth shut about it.

"We're almost there."

His words startled her. She'd been so engrossed in
her thoughts that she'd forgotten to be nervous about
the dense woods. But up ahead on the left, there was
a break in the tree line. That must be the entrance to
the meadow.

"After we leave the road," he continued, "the footing
won't be as even and we'll be going up a rise, but you'll
be able to see better when we're out in the open."

"I look forward to that."

He glanced back at her. "You've been a good sport,
Hope."

She smiled, even though he probably couldn't see her
do it. "Thanks."

"You'll like the meadow, even if you can't see the wildflowers." He faced forward and turned Navarre to the left. "It's been dry the past few days so we won't have to worry about mud, but there's a little ditch at the edge of the road. Let Isabeau have her head and she'll cross it just fine."

Hope loosened the reins and held onto the saddle horn to keep steady as Isabeau executed the ditch. The mare was a sweetheart. Horses had never played a part in her books, but after meeting Isabeau and Navarre, she could imagine how she could weave them into—no. *No.* That chapter of her life was over. She'd take stock of her finances and see whether she could afford to try stained glass.

Liam continued up a gentle slope as the trees fell away to create an open space. The horses' hooves crushed the grass and the fragrance rose around them, reminding Hope of summers in the park flying kites. She'd never been an outdoorsy kid, but she'd loved kites.

"This is far enough." Liam brought Navarre to a halt. "I brought a blanket if you'd like to get down."

"That sounds nice." She was touched by his respectful manner. Maybe she should have dated cowboys. The ones she'd met from Thunder Mountain Ranch were real gentlemen.

"Stay right there. I'll spread out the blanket and then help you down."

Although she was perfectly capable of dismounting on her own, she decided to go along with his suggestion. It was simple and elegant. While she waited for him, she leaned back to look up at the stars. She wasn't aware of exclaiming in wonder, but she must have.

He turned toward her in alarm. "Are you okay?"

"More than okay." She gazed at the light show above her. "That's incredible."

"I know." He walked over and held up his arms. "Ready?"

"Yes."

6

THANK GOODNESS. Liam had worried this ride had been a huge mistake, but after Hope's reaction to the sky full of stars, he relaxed. He hadn't misjudged her. She might not be used to this kind of adventure, but when it was offered, she responded to it.

She was a puzzle, and he didn't have all the pieces yet. Something didn't fit the picture she was presenting to everyone, but he'd figure out the mystery eventually. Right now they had a soft blanket waiting. He lifted her down and led her over to it.

He'd ground-tied both Navarre and Isabeau, who were old and extremely mellow. They weren't going anywhere. Hope sat on the blanket like a person about to have a picnic, except they hadn't brought anything to eat or drink.

Liam decided to set the tone. After relaxing beside her, he took off his Stetson and stretched out on his back. "You can see the stars a lot better if you lie back."

To his surprise, she laughed. "Is that a maneuver?"

"A maneuver?"

"You know, a move."

"Oh." He was getting a little tired of people telling him he had moves—first Grady and now Hope. Then he thought about the times he'd brought other women out to this meadow. She had a point. "I guess it's a move, now that you mention it." He sighed. "The truth is, I want to kiss you, and it'll be easier if you're down here instead of up there."

"So it has nothing to do with looking at the stars."

"It has everything to do with looking at the stars! First you lie on your back and appreciate how beautiful they are, and then I get to kiss you underneath their brilliant light. It all goes together."

"You sound cranky."

"That's because nobody has ever made me break it down."

"I see." She flopped down on the blanket. "Beautiful stars. Now kiss me."

"You just completely destroyed the mood."

"Are you sure?" She rolled to her side and reached over to run a finger down his tense jaw. "Last time I checked, we still had a canopy of stars arching over us."

"A canopy of stars." He turned to face her and propped his head on his hand. "Did you write that?"

"None of your beeswax."

Although she'd said it in a teasing way, he got the message. No more questions about her late great writing career. "Let's start over. How about if you lie back and look up at the stars?"

"I did that already, and you didn't pick up your cue."

"Try it again."

She sighed and rolled to her back. "Beautiful stars. Now kiss—"

His mouth covered hers before she could finish. And hallelujah, did she liven up the party. He'd thought she would. Any woman who had the guts to block the path of his F-350 as it charged up a hill would most likely be fun to kiss.

She ignited like a bottle rocket, pressing her fingers against his scalp and pulling him in deeper. He went gladly. He felt more than heard her moan, because somehow his hand had cupped her breast, and his palm absorbed the vibration.

The moan inspired him to unfasten the buttons on her shirt as he thrust his tongue into her mouth and explored the tantalizing sweetness there. She might be able to keep some of her secrets, but these he could unlock— her yearning to be touched as he unfastened her bra and caressed her silky breasts, her need to be kissed with a thoroughness that made her gasp and writhe beneath him.

Cade had told him to bring condoms just in case. Now he wondered if he'd been a fool to leave them behind. Her hot kisses and soft whimpers told him she might be willing to take whatever he offered.

Breaking away from the warmth of her lips, he braced himself above her, although he couldn't make himself give up the delicious sensation of fondling her plump breasts. He struggled to breathe. "I didn't come prepared to—"

"Neither did I."

"But I should have—"

"No." She laid a finger over his lips and took a steadying breath. "If you had, I would have thought less of you. I agreed to an evening horseback ride." She rubbed her finger over his lower lip. "That's all."

"But now my hand's inside your shirt." He continued stroking her. "Do you think less of me for touching you like this?"

"Let me ponder that question." With a soft murmur of delight, she closed her eyes.

She talked like a writer. Who else would say, *Let me ponder that question*? But he wouldn't mention it. Instead he'd focus on giving her as much pleasure as she'd allow. Beneath his gentle massage, her skin warmed, and the tempo of her breathing changed.

"Mmm...no, I don't think less of you." She opened her eyes and arched into his caress. "In fact, if you should happen to kiss me there, I wouldn't complain."

Although she was mostly in shadow, he heard the quiver of excitement in her voice. "Then maybe I will." Pushing her bra aside, he leaned down and brushed his lips over her tight nipple. Her moan of anticipation sent a message straight to his groin. In no time his already thickening cock became a steel rod.

If he had any sense, he'd stop before he ended up in agony. But the pressure of her fingertips against his scalp told him how much she wanted this. So did he, even if loving her within specified limits would be torture. Accepting his fate, he licked a circle around that quivering peak before slowly drawing it into his mouth.

His reward was her throaty cry of pleasure. She held his head to her breasts as he continued to lavish attention there. Before long she'd begun moaning and shifting restlessly on the blanket. Tension was building in him, and he knew it had to be building in her, too.

At last he kissed his way back up to her mouth and thrust his tongue inside in a blatant gesture of seduction. He couldn't give her everything, but he could give her enough. When she began sucking on his tongue, he figured she knew exactly what he was suggesting.

Ending the sensual kiss, he gazed down at her. She was breathing as hard as he was. "Will you think less of me if I make you come?"

She gulped. "Not less. More."

If he hadn't been so high on hormones, he might have laughed. As it was, he had to clench his jaw to keep his own orgasm in check. He could laugh about her adorable answer another time, when he wasn't busy unfastening her jeans and sliding his hand under the elastic of her very wet panties.

She was whimpering, so he wasted no time in foreplay. Thrusting his fingers deep into her slick channel, he pumped rapidly. She came fast, her cries filled with mostly incoherent words. The ones he did catch were earthy and to the point.

When at last she sank back to the blanket with a groan, he kept his fingers buried in her hot body as he leaned over and kissed her. He couldn't see her smile, but he could feel it. He moved his lips leisurely over hers and enjoyed the contented and lazy way she kissed him back. Finally he lifted his head. "I think you liked that."

"Oh, yeah." She sighed happily. "Solo sex isn't nearly this much fun. "

"Sure isn't."

Cupping his face in both hands, she gazed up at him. "I wish you could see me better so you'd know how happy I feel."

"I can tell by your voice."

"Thank you for…for giving me a wonderful orgasm."

"Glad to do it." He moved his fingers in a gentle rhythm. "I'd be glad to do it again."

"I think that's all I've got. You turned me inside out."

"If you say so." He didn't believe her. Their first kiss had been explosive, and he'd sensed a wealth of bottled-up emotion. Orgasms were a great way to let off steam. He was in a pressure-cooker situation himself, but it was temporary. He couldn't explain how he knew it, but he was convinced she'd been stressed for quite some time.

"You're not going to stop, are you?"

"Not unless you want me to." Curving his fingers, he listened to her breathing as he explored a little.

Her breath hitched. "That's...nice."

Ah. He'd found her G-spot. He stroked her there until she began to tremble. "Maybe you're not done, after all," he murmured.

"You have good hands, Liam Magee."

"It's a treat touching you." He leaned down again and feathered a kiss over her mouth. "I like making you come. Listening to your cries."

She laced her hands behind his neck and lifted her lips to his. "I might have sworn a little."

"I think you did." He thrust faster and circled her clit with his thumb.

"I might...swear this time, too." She gasped. "That feels wickedly good, what you're doing with your thumb. I'm vibrating from the roots of my hair to my toenails."

"That's the idea." He marveled at the way she handled words.

"Oh, *Liam*." She clutched his shoulders and lifted her hips. "I do want this. I *do*."

"And you'll have it. Come for me, sweet lady." He bore down, craving her release because she so desperately needed to let go. No telling what had her locked up tight, but maybe someday she'd trust him enough to reveal it.

"I think... I think I... Oh, yes, *there*. Do that again!"

He pressed her clit with his thumb, and she came in a rush. This time there was no mistaking her jubilant swear words or the breathless laughter that spilled out as she lost herself in the glory of letting go.

Her laughter was contagious. He couldn't remember watching a woman come and laugh at the same time, but he liked it. He liked her. A lot.

Finally they both caught their breath, and he leaned his forehead against hers. "That was fun."

"You're telling me. Epic climax. That's probably redundant."

"Probably." And there she was, throwing out those fancy words again. As writers tended to do.

"Let's relax and look at the stars."

"Okay. Sure." Easing his hand free, he lay back on the blanket. "I can't improve on a laughing orgasm, at least not without condoms."

"Just so you know, I don't usually laugh." A zipper rasped as she did up her jeans.

"Meaning my lovemaking is funny?" Maybe he should have been insulted instead of charmed.

"No! Your lovemaking is superlative."

"I like the sound of that, but please don't lie to boost my ego."

"I'm not lying." More rustling around indicated she was fastening her bra and buttoning her shirt. "You really know how to please a girl. I started laughing because it was so great it was either laugh or cry. I didn't feel like crying."

"I'm glad. That might have worried me."

"I know. Most guys don't understand happy tears."

"That's because we don't cry happy tears. We don't get that concept."

"Do you get the concept of crying, period?"

"Sort of."

She groaned. "Yeah, no, you don't. You're like ninety percent of the male population. You've been taught that crying isn't manly."

"Because it isn't. In a crisis situation, you don't want some guy sobbing when he should be busy saving the princess from the dragon."

"I agree, but once he's saved her and they're headed off to a well-deserved night of passion, that's when he could shed a few happy tears because they both survived. No one would judge."

"Wanna bet?"

"Okay, *I* wouldn't judge."

"If we're talking about your average princess, I predict she'd take one look at Sir Weepy and dump him for the nearest Sir Stiff Upper Lip."

She chuckled. "That's good. Sir Weepy and Sir Stiff Upper Lip. Can I use it?"

"For what?"

Her sudden silence spoke volumes. "For nothing. Never mind. I got carried away."

He was tempted to ask her what really happened to make her give up writing, but now was not the time. "I like it when you get carried away."

"I did tonight, that's for sure. I was only planning to kiss you."

"Well, you did that."

"And a whole bunch more." She hesitated. "I'm feeling a little selfish. It was all about me, and yet you—"

"Don't worry about it. I'll be fine."

"Are you sure?"

"Yes, I'm sure."

"Because you're Sir Stiff Upper Lip, right?"

"Um, yeah."

"And Sir Stiff Tallywhacker, I'll bet."

"What?" He couldn't help laughing. She was a riot. "Where did you get that?"

"I have a book of euphemisms. There are three pages of synonyms for *penis*."

"Good Lord. Three pages?"

"Maybe it was four. Tallywhacker was my favorite."

"I'm not going to ask why."

"I'll tell you anyway. It's the sound. It's a fun word to say. You should try it."

"No, thanks." Couldn't she see how much she loved words? How wrong it was for her to stop writing? "But while we're on the subject, I plan to bring condoms next time."

"We probably need to talk about that."

"I'm sure we do. Finding private time will be tough, considering all the wedding stuff starts up tomorrow with the rehearsal. Technically we don't have to be there, but…"

"We should go and watch. We may not be in the wedding, per se, but I think staying at the ranch makes us members of the wedding party."

"It does. And Grady and I offered to help Saturday with the final setup for the ceremony. I guess Rosie decided they needed a tent, so it'll be all hands on deck."

"Which is as it should be. I'm not about to suggest we sneak off to have sex instead of helping. I'll be with Rosie in the kitchen both days, I'm sure." She blew out a breath. "So, what can we do? Rendezvous in the barn after everyone's gone to bed?"

"That might be our only option for this weekend."

"Grady will know if you leave the cabin."

"Yeah, he will. The door squeaks. And Rosie hears *everything*. She wouldn't mention that one of her house guests left in the middle of the night, but she'd know someone did."

"I feel like a teenager with a curfew."

"Me, too. So maybe we shouldn't push it. After we get back to Cody, we won't have these issues." When she didn't answer right away, his gut tightened. "Listen, you have to know how much I want to be with you, but the barn isn't very romantic. I'd really like to make love to you on an actual bed next time."

"Liam, I don't want you to take this the wrong way."

All his senses went on alert. "Any comment that starts out with that disclaimer makes me nervous."

"A little over a year ago, I had a bad breakup."

"I'm not surprised to hear it." Some of the puzzle pieces fell into place.

"Really bad."

His heart ached for her. Such a loving, creative soul, and some slimy douche canoe had caused her pain. Maybe she stopped writing because the piece of shit had broken her heart. "Give me his name and location and I'll beat the crap out of him for you."

"He's not worth it."

"I'm sure he's not, but if it would make you feel better, I'll gladly do it."

She reached for his hand. "Thank you for that. He's a dragon not worth slaying. Stand down, Sir Stiff Upper Lip."

"Nothing worse than a knight with no dragon to slay."

"I wish it could be that kind of story, where you defend my honor and we live happily ever after. But happily-ever-after only happens in books."

"Not true. What about Phil and Damon?"

"For their sake, I hope they found their happy ending."

He might be paddling upstream on this issue. He couldn't use Cade and Lexi as an example because they were still in negotiations, and he hadn't met Finn's girlfriend, Chelsea, yet. "What about Rosie and Herb? They've loved each other for more than forty years."

"Okay, okay. Some lucky couples end up happy-ever-after, but it's rare, like winning the lottery. I don't play the lottery, and I've decided not to pursue another long-term relationship. It hurts too much to crash and burn."

"I see." So he'd been a convenient sexual release mechanism. He tried to pull his hand from hers, but she held him tight. "Hope, I'm starting to feel like the pool boy."

"You're not. You're an incredible gift after a year of misery. But I always planned to tell you that whatever happened between us could only last until the wedding was over. I'm not ready for any more than that."

He sighed in frustration. The ex must have really done a number on her if, after a year, she was still hurting. Overcoming that kind of injury with a couple of encounters in the barn could be impossible. And she'd probably refuse to go out with him in Cody because there would be no built-in parameters. "So you're leaving day after tomorrow?"

"No, actually, I'm not. I've agreed to house-sit for Damon and Phil while they're on their honeymoon. They adopted a couple of kittens, and they need someone to look after them while they're gone."

Hot damn. His odds had just improved tremendously. He felt like doing a fist pump, but he didn't want to scare her off, so he kept his tone casual. "Interesting."

"The kittens? I know. Apparently Damon's always wanted—"

"Not the kittens. I decided to take a week off from rafting and spend time with Rosie and Herb over Fourth of July. I'll be around for the week after the wedding, too."

The rhythm of her breathing changed. "I didn't know that."

"Now you do."

"What about Grady?"

"He's driving back after the wedding. Because of all

the work he put in on this sculpture for Damon and Phil, he's behind on a couple of commissioned pieces. He wants to use Fourth of July to catch up."

"He doesn't want to hang around for the holiday stuff?"

"I'm sure he'd love to, but he has obligations to the folks who've put down a significant deposit and are eagerly awaiting their creations." Liam had learned that an artist's life wasn't as fancy-free as people imagined.

"Then you'll be alone in that cabin?"

"That would be nice, but it's a home for students now. I'll move into a guest room at the ranch house so we can spruce up the cabin for the kids."

"But if Grady's leaving and taking the truck, how are you getting home?"

"Grady can fetch me, or Cade and Lexi might take me back. Lexi's been asked to give a weekend riding clinic in Cody, and she'd like to check out the venue and meet the folks before she commits to it." He paused, his heart thudding. "Or, depending on how the week turns out, I could hitch a ride with you."

And then he waited, determined not to say anything more. Two nights wouldn't make a dent in her armor, but if he had a whole week and lots of relaxed private time…miracles did happen, even if she no longer believed in them.

7

Hope gulped. "I feel as if you've led me to the edge of a cliff and invited me to jump over it with you." She turned her head and discovered he was looking at her. His face was mostly in shadow, but light from the stars glinted in his raven hair.

Liam was a beautiful man, and he wanted her. She'd thought her interest in men had died after Tom's betrayal, but Liam made her ache with longing. She shivered when she imagined spending the next week in a sexual relationship with him.

"Let's try a different image." Rolling to his side, he reached over and cupped her cheek in one large hand. "We're both on vacation, right?" He smoothed his thumb over her cheekbone.

"I certainly am. I haven't taken one since I moved to Cody, so this was the perfect opportunity."

"And I'm long overdue. The rafting company was short on guides until recently, but now they're fully staffed. So I'm on break."

"What a coincidence." She loved the subtle yet confident way he touched her. He instinctively knew the right pressure and rhythm, whether he was lightly caressing her cheek or giving her an orgasm.

"Coincidence, luck, fate. Take your pick. We both have a week off, so what if we think of it as a long-anticipated adventure, one we're finally taking the time to enjoy?"

"How in the world could this week be long-anticipated when we barely know each other?"

"We know each other better than we did an hour ago." There was a smile in his voice. "Think of how well acquainted we'll be in a week."

Dear God. The images his comment inspired made her blush. She was glad it was too dark to see.

"You're blushing."

"You can't tell that."

"Yes, I can. Your cheek just got very warm."

"Oh." It seemed she could hide nothing from this man.

"Can I take that as a sign that you're excited about the possibilities?"

"Yes." She drew in a shaky breath. "Yes, you can." Her body hummed with sensual approval of everything he had to offer.

"I'm glad."

"But that still doesn't magically transform next week into a long-anticipated adventure."

"Are you sure about that?" He combed his fingers through her hair and cradled the back of her head. "Don't tell me you've never fantasized about a wild fling with the right guy. No obligations, no promises, just good times." He drew closer. "Good sex."

"Well, okay, I have." Her blush spread along every inch of her skin. He was about to kiss her, and she couldn't wait. "I think most women do."

"I'm prepared to be that guy." His mouth settled over hers. Melting against him, she allowed herself to believe that he could be her fantasy lover, especially if he had to fill that role just for a week. A week of feeling his knowing hands on her willing body sounded like heaven. And man, he could kiss.

The hunger in that kiss and the hard length of his cock pressed against her belly reminded her that only she had been satisfied tonight. The heat of his mouth burned away any remaining inhibitions. He hadn't said what role she would take in the days that followed, but he must have a fantasy woman in mind, too. Sliding her hand down, she stroked the thick, denim-covered ridge.

He groaned. Breaking away from her mouth, he caught and held her wrist. "Don't."

"Why not?"

"I'll come. That would be embarrassing as hell."

"Not if I'm making it happen."

His breathing roughened. "I didn't bring you out here for that."

"Will you think less of me if I make you come?"

"Of course not! But—"

"Then let me." Leaning forward, she ran her tongue over his full lower lip.

"Hope…"

"Let me." She drew his lip into her mouth and sucked gently.

With a low moan of surrender, he relaxed his hold on her wrist. His breath was warm on her mouth. "It seems I'm going to."

"Good." She pushed against the solid wall of his chest. "Lie down and look at the stars."

Sighing, he rolled onto his back. "This doesn't seem heroic."

"But I'll bet it'll feel really good." She straddled his thighs and unbuckled his belt.

"I'm sure it will."

"You can't be sure." Unfastening the metal button at his waist, she carefully eased down the zipper. "I might be lousy at this."

"There's no such thing."

"That's not logical." Behind his fly, his gray knit boxers were stretched tight. It was a wonder the seams held up under all that pressure. "Everybody's bad at something. Maybe I'm bad at giving blow jobs."

"Ask any guy. Good technique is a bonus, but it's so not necessary." His breath hissed out as she pulled down his boxers and freed his cock.

Oh, my. She wasn't going to mention Tom at a moment like this, but Liam had him beat by a country mile. All this would be hers for a week. Hello, fantasy lover.

"Is…is something wrong?"

"On the contrary. Something is very right. You have a magnificent tallywhacker."

His voice sounded strained. "I thought maybe there was a problem."

"No." She glanced at his face. Even in the dim light, she could see the tendons in his neck were standing out. He was also gripping fistfuls of the blanket. "Do you have a problem?"

"Only that I think I'm going to come any second."

"Maybe I can help."

"That would be great."

Grasping the base of his penis, she squeezed hard. *"Ahh."*

"Better?" She leaned over him, her tongue poised to lick the single drop of moisture gathered at the tip.

His massive chest heaved. "Yeah. For a second there I thought I'd—" He gulped when her tongue made contact. "Hope, if you keep that up, it'll be all over."

"Not if I give you another squeeze." Circling the base of his shaft with her thumb and forefinger, she tightened her grip while continuing to lavish attention on his very fine penis. The longer she stroked and licked, the more she ached to feel him thrusting deep inside her.

But he was a gentleman and hadn't brought condoms. She understood completely. Showing up with condoms in your pocket on a first date didn't demonstrate much respect for the woman you'd invited out.

Consequently he'd suffered while giving her two amazing orgasms. She'd do well to remember that instead of wishing he'd been a little less of a gentleman. Now he deserved his reward for all that self-sacrifice. Closing her lips over his considerable girth, she took in as much of him as she could manage.

He gasped and began to shake. When she moved her head up and down, he swore. So they had that swearing thing in common. She used her tongue and her teeth and concluded from his labored breathing and the cussing that he was enjoying himself.

"Hope." He sounded desperate. "I can't wait. I'm going to…come. You don't have to…stay with me."

Yes, she did. Sucking hard, she put him over the top. As he cried out, she swallowed all he had to give. If he'd committed to being her fantasy man, she'd be his fantasy woman. For one week.

SHE MADE THE RIDE back in a sensual daze. The shadows that had spooked her on the way out had lost their power to stimulate her imagination. She had no time to contemplate a bear attack when her mind was filled with visions of rolling around in bed with a naked and aroused Liam Magee.

They'd agreed that frantic attempts to have sex in the

next forty-eight hours made no sense, though. If a golden opportunity presented itself, they'd take advantage, but otherwise they'd wait until after the wedding. Liam was fixated on making sure they had a bed next time. Now that she'd seen and touched his top-grade package, she didn't much care whether a bed was available or not.

By the time they returned to the ranch, the ranch house was dark. They rode over to the barn and dismounted under the glow of the light over the barn doors.

"You should go in." Liam kept his voice low. "I'll take care of the horses."

"That's not fair," she murmured. "I'll help. Just tell me what to do."

He seemed to consider that for a moment before nodding. "Okay. While I take off the saddles, you can bring the grooming tote out. It's a black plastic gizmo that holds the brushes and curry combs. It's on a shelf in the tack room. Can't miss it."

She found the tote, no problem. She also found an envelope tucked into it with Liam's name printed in block letters on the outside. Leaving the envelope exactly where it had been placed, she carried the tote outside just as he was taking the first saddle in. "There's an envelope in here with your name on it."

"There is? That's strange." He hauled the second saddle in before examining the note. "If someone wanted to leave me a note, you'd think they'd stick it in the cabin door." Leaning down, he picked up the envelope, opened it and started to laugh. "Oh, jeez."

"What? Who's it from?"

"Never mind." He shoved the envelope and whatever it contained in his back pocket. "You can brush Isabeau, and I'll take care of Navarre."

"All right." She picked up a brush and started in on Isabeau's dark gray coat. Curiosity was one of her failings, but she vowed not to be nosy. Keeping that vow would have been easier if Liam had quit chuckling.

She tried to imagine what would have caused that reaction. It hadn't been a note, because he'd taken no time to read it. As she replayed the moment, she remembered hearing the envelope crinkle. She recognized that crinkle.

By the time she and Liam had settled both horses in their stalls, she'd figured out the likely contents of the envelope. She waited until they'd left the barn and he'd slid the bar across the double doors before confronting him. "Was there a condom in that envelope?"

His sheepish expression said it all. "Um…yeah."

"Who—?"

"Cade, but it's not like you're thinking."

"Then the two of you didn't discuss the subject of condoms while you were out here saddling up for our ride?"

"We did discuss it."

"Ha! And I was giving you points for being a gentleman! Meanwhile you and Cade were—"

"Doing what good guys do." He gripped her arms. "If you picture us taking bets on what would or wouldn't happen tonight and making crude remarks about it, then you don't know either of us very well."

"No, I don't." And she'd pictured exactly that.

"Here's how it went. Cade wanted us to have a good first date. He suggested taking a blanket, and I agreed. Then he asked if I had condoms, and I told him I wouldn't presume to take them on a first date. He thought maybe I should reconsider because…" He paused. "That part doesn't matter. I didn't take them, as you know."

"I think it does matter, considering he left one so you'd have it at the end of our ride. Why did he think you should reconsider?"

He cleared his throat. "He's convinced you want me."

"Oh, really? Why is he convinced?"

"He's observed how you look at me."

"Oh." Her cheeks grew hot. "Well, that's damned embarrassing. I didn't realize I was telegraphing my interest to the world."

"Not the world." He drew her closer. "Before dinner I mentioned to Cade that I've liked you for a while. Cade, being protective of me, paid attention during the meal to whether you returned that interest."

"I see." She wondered how Cade would react if he knew her interest was strictly short-term. Probably not well.

"Should he have left that condom for me? Probably not, but that's Cade. He means well, but he doesn't always think how something will be perceived. He didn't want us to go to bed frustrated."

"What exactly did you say to Cade before dinner?"

"That you seemed special and I'd been meaning to ask you out for weeks."

"And why didn't you?"

His gaze searched hers. "The truth is, I had a strong feeling you'd refuse. So I put off asking to avoid what I thought would be a rejection."

"It would have been."

He accepted that with a nod. "Then my instincts were right, and as it turns out, the situation we're in now is the only way you would ever have agreed to spend time with me."

"Exactly."

"A brief affair."

"Yes. But now I'm worried you won't be okay with that."

An emotion flickered in his eyes and was gone. He

smiled down at her. "Are you kidding? What guy wouldn't be thrilled with a week of great sex with a beautiful woman?"

"A guy who wants more."

"But you don't have more to give."

"Right."

"So I'm grateful for whatever you are willing to give." He rubbed her back. "We've just begun, and you've already made me a very happy and satisfied man. FYI, you're not lousy at it. You're damned good at it, in fact. I hope we can do that particular activity some more this week."

"We can, but…" She rested her palms against his warm chest. "This won't be a stolen few days away from everything, the way I'd first pictured it. We're not on a tropical island. During the week, we'll be seeing your family, and I can't believe they'd approve of a superficial relationship that's all about sex."

"I have no intention of telling them. Do you?"

"Of course not."

"Then as I see it, we don't have a problem. We'll have our fun this week, and they can assume whatever they want about us. At the end of our time together, we'll go home to Cody. After a while, I'll announce that it didn't work out."

"You've thought this through."

"Yep. On the ride home."

"Then you really are willing to enjoy the week and end it cleanly?"

"Absolutely. I'm no fool. You're proposing a setup that's every man's fantasy."

She could either keep questioning him or take him at his word. Making her decision, she nestled closer and wiggled her hips against his. "You said the barn wasn't very romantic."

Sliding his hands down her back, he cupped her bottom. "It's not." His fingers flexed in an arousing massage, and his eyes darkened. "But then, we're not looking for romance."

"No."

"We're looking for hot, no-holds-barred, mind-blowing sex." He lifted her to her tiptoes and fit the hard ridge of his fly into the crotch of her jeans. "Right?" Holding her gaze, he thrust forward.

She gasped at the sudden jolt of pleasure. *"Yes."*

"Then the barn's as good a place as any. And it so happens I have a condom in my back pocket."

8

LIAM HAD NO intention of frolicking through a week of mindless sex with Hope and then saying goodbye, but he hadn't lied to her. If, after days of intense interaction, she could turn her back on him, he'd honor his promise and let her go without a fight. He put Ringo the barn cat into the tack room for the night while grabbing the blanket he'd left there earlier.

Then he walked back to the empty stall where Hope was waiting for him. Despite their agreement, he doubted this was the beginning of a one-week affair. His experiences with nature had given him a reverence for all connections, and he didn't make or break them carelessly. She was an artist whether she admitted it or not, and he knew from living with Grady how much emotional depth creativity required.

But if she wanted to tell herself this was all about sex, he wouldn't argue the point. Sex was a great way to connect, and he was in favor of having a lot of it. He'd wanted a king-size bed underneath them the first time they had the full-on experience. But he'd thrown down some straw before going to fetch the blanket, and that would have to do. He'd wanted the lights on, too, and all he had was ambient light from small lamps placed along the aisle between stalls.

The glow was enough for him to see her sitting on the floor taking off her boots, but not enough to gauge her expression when she glanced up. He felt a rush of tenderness that had nothing to do with lust. There were so many things he wanted to share with her. A week wouldn't even scratch the surface.

Setting her boots aside, she stood and padded over to him in her sock feet. "Give me the blanket while you take off your boots." She stood on tiptoe and gave him a quick open-mouthed kiss.

"Okay." One little kiss and lust came roaring back. He was all about efficiency. He'd just taken off his second boot when she returned and plucked his hat from his head.

"You won't be needing this, either." She hung it on the stall door.

"Are you sure? I've heard tell that some women prefer a naked cowboy who leaves his hat on for the duration." He reached for her, but she backed away.

"I'll consider that for another time. Right now I just want you naked, period."

"That can be arranged. Right now I desperately need to kiss you." He advanced toward her.

She stepped out of reach again. "How about arranging it now?"

It took him a moment to figure out what she was going for, but eventually he did. "You want me to strip?"

"Yes, I do, while I watch. I've been mentally undressing you from the first day I saw you and now—"

"What the hell? From the first day? And yet you were planning to turn me down flat?"

"Just because I fantasized about you naked doesn't mean I was ready to risk getting involved."

He rubbed the back of his neck. "You've imagined me naked from day one." He couldn't get over it.

"Why are you surprised? You'd walk into the hotel all sweaty, your damp T-shirt stretched over all those beautiful muscles you've developed from paddling a raft for hours on end. I'm sure I wasn't the only woman imagining a beefcake show right there in the lobby."

He was flattered. He'd wondered if showing up grubby and smelly might have been a turnoff for her. Apparently not. "Are you going to strip for me, too?"

She shook her head. "I promise to return the favor eventually, but tonight I'd rather have you take my clothes off after you're finished with yours."

"But—"

"It'll go faster that way."

"Good point." By the time he was naked, he probably wouldn't want to dawdle. He popped the snaps on his cuffs. "I suppose this is when I should confess that I pictured you naked from day one, too."

"I know."

"You do not." Taking off his shirt, he hung it on the stall door near his hat.

"Yes, I do. I saw that gleam in your eyes. Women can tell what guys are thinking. You tried to be subtle about it, but you obviously liked my breasts."

"I like them even better now. You feel like satin and taste like raspberries."

She drew in a shaky breath. "And you...you are even more gorgeous than I imagined you'd be. I want to lick you all over."

A jolt of desire sent him in her direction. "And I want

to kiss every sexy inch of you. Let's forget this little striptease and—"

"Not yet." She backed away and held up her hand. "Take off the rest. There's something incredibly sensual about watching a man unbuckle his belt and unzip his fly when he's got sex on his mind. I'll get to watch you do it a lot in the next week, but...this time is special."

There, she'd admitted it. She was making memories, but he wasn't going to point that out to her. Not now, anyway. And if she wanted a memory of him taking off his jeans, he'd do his best to make it a moment she wouldn't soon forget.

He couldn't see her expression very well as he slowly unbuckled his belt, but he could hear the steady sound of her breathing. He pitched his voice low. "You're right. This shouldn't be rushed."

"Exactly."

He unfastened the metal button at his waist and drew the zipper down. "No matter how much I want you, no matter how desperate I am to slide my cock into your hot body and make you come, we need to take it slow and easy. Let's draw out the pleasure. Let's make it last."

"Mmm." Her breathing wasn't steady anymore.

He distinctly heard her gulp, and although he couldn't be sure in the dim light, he thought she was trembling. He located the condom in his back pocket. "I need you to take care of this until we're ready for it." He tossed the packet in her direction, and she caught it with both hands. Obviously she wasn't about to let it go missing.

After stepping out of his jeans, he shoved down his briefs and managed to swallow a groan of relief. He'd aroused himself as much as he seemed to have aroused her. All he wanted was to take the condom back and get enough of her clothes off to do the deed.

But this time was special and he intended to make sure that she'd remember having sex with Liam Magee in the barn. "My turn," he murmured as he moved toward her.

She was definitely trembling. "I feel as if I could come right this minute."

"That would be okay." He dipped his head and gave her a kiss with a little bit of tongue as he unbuttoned her shirt and slipped it off her shoulders. Then he lifted his mouth from hers. "I'm sure that won't be the one and only climax you'll have."

"You're very good at this."

"Undressing you?"

"Driving me insane."

"Glad to hear it." He moved away and draped her shirt next to his clothes. By the time he turned back, she was dangling her bra on the tip of her finger.

"I thought I'd speed things up."

"Excellent idea." He grabbed her bra and flung it away, not caring where it landed. She was topless, and her perfection claimed all his attention. He was through playing games. "Hope, I need...you."

"Then let's cut to the chase. Put this on." She handed him the condom packet.

While he ripped it open and rolled on the condom, she shimmied out of her jeans and panties. He lowered her to the blanket and moved between her creamy thighs, but then she wrapped her legs around his and he felt her soft socks pressed against his calf muscles.

Despite the intensity of the moment, the notion made him smile. Braced above her, his cock touching the moist entrance to paradise, he looked into her eyes. "You're still wearing socks."

"Want to stop so I can take them off?"

"Hell, no." And he pushed deep into the most welcoming spot his happy Johnson had ever known.

She pressed her fingers into his back and moaned. "Good," she crooned. "So good."

"Heck, yeah." At sometime in the near future, he'd actually be able to see her face while he loved her, but it wasn't in the cards tonight. The faint glow from the lights along the aisle allowed only a shadowed view as he began pumping.

But he could hear her just fine, and she was panting and calling his name. He could feel her body clench around his cock and knew that the rhythm he'd created was going to make her come. It could make him come, too, but he decided to hold off.

This connection between them was brand-new, but it didn't seem that way. He'd known in his heart that it would be familiar. Although he couldn't explain how he was linked with Hope, he accepted that the link existed. He was supposed to be with her now, and maybe longer. She'd be the one to decide when their story would end.

For now, every stroke of his cock brought her pleasure, and in a few seconds she'd surrender to an orgasm they'd created together with the sweet friction of their bodies. He was greedy enough to want another chance to do that for her. As he'd sensed tonight in the meadow, she needed that release. The more times she allowed herself to let go, the greater her chance of overcoming her grief.

There. Her body arched upward and he bore down. Pressing her hand over her mouth to smother her cries, she abandoned herself to the sweet convulsions of her climax. And all the while he continued his steady thrusting as he coaxed her toward a second release.

She moaned. "I can't."

"You can. Stay with me."

She gripped his shoulders. "You're asking for...more than I can give."

"No, I'm not." He chuckled. "You're filled with passion. Dive into it. Wallow in it. You're safe with me." Even in the absence of strong light, he knew her gaze was focused on him.

"I believe you, Liam."

"Then let me give you joy." Sliding his hands under her backside, he lifted her so that he had a slightly different angle. Then he increased the pace, his thighs slapping hers until they breathed in ragged gasps.

Her soft wail came a moment before he felt the undulations of her climax. Closing his eyes in gratitude, he slipped the leash on his response and drove into her with a guttural cry. His cock seemed to pulse endlessly, but at last his body quieted.

Without realizing it, he'd let his head fall on her shoulder and had drifted into a semiconscious state. Her soft caresses and murmured words brought him back to reality. Startled, he lifted his head. "Damn. Did I fall asleep?"

"Not completely, but I think you were headed in that direction."

"We can't fall asleep here. We don't want Herb or Cade to come in tomorrow and find us like this."

"Considering Cade provided the condom, it would serve him right."

That made Liam chuckle. "So true, but chances are good that Herb would be the first one down here."

"That would embarrass me."

"Me, too."

"You? A big strong cowboy?"

"Actually, it would embarrass Herb, which would embarrass me. I could live with Cade finding us here, but not

Herb. He's the dad I never had, which means we have to make our way back to our beds before daybreak comes."

"I get that." She pulled his head down for a soft kiss. "Let's erase the evidence."

"In a minute." He smoothed a strand of hair from her cheek. "We need a little pillow talk."

"Just our luck we don't have any pillows."

"You are the most literal woman I've ever come across."

"I know. I drove my folks crazy."

"But you loved *Ladyhawke*. You must have known that couldn't be literally true."

"This is really complicated pillow talk, Liam. Isn't this the time we're supposed to say how much we enjoyed the sex?"

He chuckled loud enough to startle a whinny out of one of the horses. "Whoops."

"I'm glad I make you laugh."

"You do. I didn't realize you were such a kick when I used to talk to you at the hotel. You always seemed serious and quiet."

"So it really was all about my breasts. Otherwise I was kind of dull."

"*No.* I like serious and quiet, too. But laughing with you is a bonus I didn't expect."

"And the sex is pretty good, don't you think?"

"The sex is world-class. It's so good that I'm trying to imagine how I'll stay away from you for the next couple of days."

"Well…" She traced his lower lip with the tip of her finger. "I've been thinking about that, too, and I'll bet Rosie's hearing isn't quite as sharp as you remember it. Back then she was riding herd on a bunch of horny teenage boys. She might be rusty."

"She might, but I doubt it. Thinking of sneaking out and meeting me at the barn tomorrow night?"

"Only if you're willing to let Grady know what's going on. I'm sure his hearing is excellent."

"I was planning to tell him about us, if that's okay."

"Absolutely okay."

"Then midnight tomorrow night, same stall?"

"I'll be here." She touched the corner of his mouth. "When did you get this scar?"

"That, my sweet lady, is a story for another time." He gave her a quick kiss and eased away from her warmth. He would have been sadder about leaving her if they hadn't promised to revisit this spot tomorrow night.

"Then it had better be a really good story, if you're going to make me wait for it." She picked up her jeans and panties.

"It's an embarrassing story, and I want you to have a good opinion of me." He struggled into his briefs and jeans and zipped up. Too bad he didn't have a better view of her as she dressed, although a better view might get him hot and bothered again. If only they had…lanterns. He groaned.

"What's the matter?"

"We've been fumbling around in the dark, not able to see each other, and all I had to do was bring our two *lanterns* into the stall. I can't believe I didn't think of it. What an idiot."

"All your blood had drained south. You couldn't be expected to think of anything."

"Sure, but…did you?"

"Yes, but when you didn't bring them with the blanket, I was mostly glad. It meant I couldn't see you quite as well for the stripping part, but overall, having dim light for this first time was better. Kinder."

He stopped fastening his shirt and walked over to her. Bracketing her cheeks with both hands, he looked into her shadowed face. "Hope, are you shy?"

"I didn't used to be, and I won't be next time. But it's been a while, and like I said, my last relationship was… unpleasant. You're my first lover since then. I've discovered that I still love sex, especially with you, but being allowed to ease into intimacy really helped me relax."

Liam's jaw tightened. "Did he hurt you?"

"Not physically, if that's what you're thinking."

He was comforted, but not by much. "Words can leave scars, too. Is he in Cody?" If he could get a name, he just might pay the jerkwad a little visit.

"No. When we were together, we lived in Cheyenne. But he's left the state, which is fine with me. He's not worth worrying about."

He is if he's standing between us. But Liam didn't push for more information. He had a week to let her tell him what had happened. Unless she did, they'd never get past it.

She slipped her arms around his neck. "What I'm saying is that if you want to bring the lanterns into the stall tomorrow night, that would be more than okay."

"I'd like that." He shoved thoughts of her ex away so he could concentrate on the present and the bright promise of the woman he held in his arms. On Hope.

9

THE BARN BORE no sign of their presence by the time Hope walked out into the night with Liam. They kissed once more but made themselves stop before heavy breathing set in. He headed toward the cabin he shared with Grady, and she mounted the steps to the ranch house's front porch.

What a night. What a man. She did feel safe with him, partly because he was so kind, but mostly because he'd agreed that this affair would last only a week. She didn't have to worry about things going bad. They wouldn't have time to mess anything up.

As she crossed to the front door, she briefly wondered if she'd been locked out. Probably not. Rosie would have checked her room and discovered she wasn't home yet. Judging from prior conversations, locking doors wasn't a big priority around here, anyway.

She started to open the screen door just as a light came on inside the house. Her instant response—anxiety—passed quickly and left her laughing at herself. She was twenty-seven years old, and she wasn't about to get in trouble for staying out too late.

But she'd feel guilty as hell if her host or hostess

couldn't sleep because they were worried about her. Opening the door, she called out a soft "Hello?" so she wouldn't startle whoever had turned on that light, which she could now see came from the kitchen.

Rosie poked her head out from the kitchen doorway. "Hope!"

"Please tell me you aren't up because you were worried about me."

"Heavens, no. You were with Liam. He wouldn't let anything happen to you."

"That's very true. So…a midnight snack?"

"Sort of. Herb's snoring like a band saw, and I decided to come in here and have a little decaf laced with Baileys. After a couple of cups I can sleep through anything. You're welcome to join me, but you probably want to turn in."

"I'd love to join you. Let me make a quick trip to the bathroom first."

"Okay! See you in a minute." Rosie beamed at her, obviously pleased to have company.

Hurrying through the living room and down the darkened hall, Hope ducked into the bathroom that had been designated for her use. Fortunately she'd left her toiletries in there. One look in the mirror told her she'd made the right call. Bits of straw were stuck in her hair, her lipstick had been completely kissed away and her shirt was buttoned up wrong.

But Rosie might not have noticed, because the living room had been fairly dark. Either way, Hope began to reassess the plan to keep her involvement with Liam a secret, especially from Rosie. That seemed unfair to her hostess. Confessing the situation to Rosie would eliminate any worry about sneaking around.

Once she felt presentable, she returned to the kitchen,

where the scent of brewing coffee reminded her of her parents' house in Cheyenne. She'd had a few late-night chats with her mother over cups of decaf, but her mom hadn't added Baileys to it. Hope had visited her parents a few times since leaving, but she'd avoided those late-night chats. She wasn't ready to discuss why she and Tom broke up. She might never be ready.

"Did you have a nice ride?" Rosie took a couple of generously sized mugs from the cupboard. Her definition of a *cup of coffee* was probably more like three.

"We had a great time." She debated how best to explain her situation. "Liam and I have discovered that we're...that we have a lot in common, so we..."

"Sweetie, say no more." Rosie turned toward her. "You have a little romance going on. Am I right?"

"Well, yes." She wanted to be as truthful as possible. "Kind of. But we haven't declared undying love for each other or anything. We're just..."

"Physical attraction is nothing to be ashamed of."

Hope laughed. "I can see why those boys all love you."

"I was a lot tougher on them when they were teenagers. Didn't want any unplanned babies showing up, but they took that lecture to heart, thank goodness. Now they're healthy young men, so of course they like sex."

"Um, yeah." Hope's cheeks warmed.

Rosie gazed at her and smiled. "Ah, I see how it is. But you don't have a particularly great setup for spending time alone, do you?"

"Well, there's the barn." The minute she said it, she wished she hadn't. Rosie didn't need to know where they were getting it on. She had to be aware only that Hope would be leaving the ranch house in the wee hours to spend time with Liam...somewhere.

"That won't do. That won't do at all."

"Please don't worry about it. This is our problem, and we'll figure it out." And now she was probably beet red. Terrific. "It's only a temporary inconvenience, anyway. After the wedding, I'll be staying at Damon and Phil's."

"So you will." Rosie seemed cheered by that thought. "And Liam's staying on for a bit. Perfect. But I can understand why having him visit you here would be a little awkward."

Hope groaned. "This is becoming way too embarrassing. I just wanted to alert you to the fact I'll be slipping out of the house late at night."

"And that's very considerate of you." Rosie poured the coffee and a considerable amount of Baileys into each mug. She handed one to Hope. "Drink up. It's easier to have this kind of discussion if you're slightly toasted."

"Makes sense." She took a sip, and then another. "This is delicious."

"Glad you think so. Not everyone is enamored of my favorite drink. Finn's special lady, Chelsea, loves it. Others may be pretending enthusiasm to please me."

"I'm not faking it, Rosie. This hits the spot." She took another long swallow.

"Shall we go out on the porch? It's kind of fun to be out there all by ourselves. Us and the owls."

"Sure, why not?"

"Hang on a sec. I'll put the rest of the coffee in a carafe. You take the bottle of Baileys."

"I'm in." Moments later she was settled in a cozy chair on the porch with a comforting drink and a comforting friend. "I just have to say, I love this ranch."

"So do I. Last summer I thought we'd lose it because we loaned money to a friend who couldn't repay us. But my boys came to the rescue with moneymaking ideas, and here we are with a flourishing academy for teens who want to learn about horses."

"That's awesome, Rosie." Hope sipped her coffee. "It would make a great story."

"Want to write it? Phil told me you're a writer."

"*Was* a writer. I don't do that anymore." She took an extralarge gulp.

"Can you just give it up? I thought writing was something you were born to do."

"Maybe for some. Not for me." She finished off the contents of her mug and handed it to Rosie. "Hit me."

"You've got it, girlfriend." She poured more coffee into Hope's mug and added enough Baileys to get a sailor drunk.

"You gave me too much."

"You don't have to finish it. The boys gifted me with a case of the stuff last summer when they thought I was gonna go toes up."

"What? I didn't hear about that!"

"I was stressed about losing the ranch, and everyone thought I'd had a heart attack. Turned out it was a reaction to the thought of giving up Thunder Mountain. I'm fine now, by the way."

"Good." Hope sighed and leaned back in her chair. "What a scary thing."

"It's called broken heart syndrome. Behaves exactly like a heart attack, but in most cases you make a full recovery in a matter of days."

"Amazing." She remembered having chest pains a year ago. She'd dismissed them. "Guess you need to hang on to this ranch, huh?"

Rosie nodded. "And not just for me, but for all the boys we took in. Herb and I thought we were providing a temporary home for them. Not so. They look to Thunder Mountain, and to us, for their security, their sense of self."

"That's quite a responsibility."

"It is, but there are rewards, like watching Liam find someone like you. Which brings me back to the problem at hand. We have Grady and Liam in one cabin and Finn and Chelsea in another. The newest cabin will be the backdrop for the wedding since building it brought Damon and Phil together. That leaves one more. I'll give you the key."

"You really don't have to do that."

"It's more civilized than the barn. The bunks are singles, so it's not perfect, but pull a couple of mattresses down on the floor. That'll work."

"If I hadn't ingested a fair amount of Baileys, I'd be horrified by this discussion."

Rosie laughed. "But you have, so you're not."

"No, and since I'm fairly smashed, I'm going to tell you the truth about Liam and me, because you deserve to know. We're not in it for the long haul, or I'm not, and he agreed. We'll have fun this week. End of story."

"Is that so?" Rosie didn't sound particularly upset, maybe because she didn't believe Hope.

"I mean it. After my last boyfriend, I vowed never to get serious about another guy."

"I don't blame you, honey. Most men are wonderful, but if you get a hold of a bad one, he can sour you on the whole lot. You have a good time this week."

"If you think Liam's going to change my mind, he won't. Riding off into the sunset with the love of my life has been permanently scratched off my to-do list."

"What a colorful way to put it! Are you sure you're completely done with writing?"

"Done with writing, done with the happily-ever-after dream."

"Hmm." Rosie sipped her coffee.

"You don't believe me."

"What I believe or don't believe isn't important. But I'd feel better if you and Liam were tucked into a cabin instead of making out in the barn. That could get nasty."

"Like straw in my hair?"

"I wasn't going to mention it, but since you did…"

"All right. I'll take the key. And thank you."

HOPE SLEPT LATER than normal the next morning, but remarkably she didn't feel any effect from the Baileys. When she walked into the kitchen, she found Rosie, Lexi and Phil's stepmom, Edie, slicing, dicing and cooking food that was probably for the rehearsal dinner.

Rosie glanced up from a steaming pot and smiled. "Good morning, sunshine. Sleep well?"

"Too well and too late. What can I do to help?"

"We'll put you to work in a little bit," Edie said. "Grab some coffee and I'll scramble up a couple of eggs if Rosie can spare me a burner."

"You can tuck in right here." Rosie moved over. "And there's juice in the fridge, Hope. Help yourself."

"I can scramble the eggs."

"Nope, nope, we have a rhythm going." Edie backed her off. "Get some coffee and juice. Shoo."

Lexi stopped dicing ham and grinned at Hope. "Just do as you're told. Life's easier that way."

"Now there's a smart girl." Edie scooped up a handful of ham chunks from the bowl beside Lexi and dropped them into her skillet. "Thanks. That'll go nice with the eggs."

While Edie joined Rosie at the stove, Hope hovered

by the coffeepot. "I feel like a prima donna, but thank you." Sipping coffee would give her an excuse to gaze out the window. But although she took her time pouring and spent a while sipping, she saw nobody.

They were probably down in the meadow, setting up for the rehearsal. Having a wedding in front of a log cabin hadn't made any sense to Hope until Phil had explained it. Last summer when Thunder Mountain Academy was in the planning stages, the decision had been made to add a fourth cabin to the three that had housed all the foster brothers years ago. Phil and Damon had met while working on the new cabin, so it was significant to them.

"The guys and Phil are setting up the tent," Rosie said. She'd obviously guessed why Hope had been staring out the window. "They all ate earlier."

"Sorry I'm such a sleepyhead."

"No problem," Edie said. "Right, Rosie?"

"No problem at all. Hope kept me company last night. We had a little bit of coffee and Baileys."

"Oh, did you, now?" Lexi raised her eyebrows. "Have you found a new convert for your favorite beverage?"

"She has," Hope said. "I'm ready to join the coffee and Baileys club."

"Have at it." Lexi shook her head as she continued to dice up ham. "It's not for me, but when Chelsea gets here, you'll have a quorum."

Hope gazed at her. "How can you not like it? It's like coffee on steroids."

"Believe me, I tried for Rosie's sake. I know how she loves that concoction, but it doesn't work for me."

"For me, either." Edie came over with a plate full of eggs and a fork. "But if you were up with Rosie drinking coffee and Baileys, you need this. Now sit."

Hope decided to do as Lexi had advised and follow directions. She sat and began eating her delicious eggs.

"I'm glad Phil's down there with the guys," Lexi said. "I hope she keeps an eye on Cade."

"Why?" Mention of Cade immediately made Hope think of the condom he'd left. She wondered if Lexi knew he'd done it. "Is he likely to pull a practical joke?"

"Oh, he's capable of that, too, but mostly I hope he doesn't accidentally compromise the tent setup. We don't want it coming down in the middle of the ceremony."

"He means well," Rosie said.

"I know he does, but that cowboy's about as handy with tools as his cat, Ringo." Lexi turned toward the gray tabby curled in his bed in the corner of the kitchen. "I take that back, Ringo. You're probably better at it than Cade. I love that man, but I swear he doesn't know a hammer from a hockey stick."

"I do so!" The screen door banged, and boots clomped across the living room floor. "I also heard you say you love me." Smiling, Cade walked into the kitchen and straight over to Lexi. "And in front of witnesses, no less. Any day now you'll get down on one knee and ask for my hand."

Lexi chuckled. "You'll make me do that, too, won't you?"

"You bet I will. I want this proposal done right. Whatcha got there?"

He reached toward the bowl, and she smacked his hand. "Nothing for you. Did you have a reason for coming in to bother us, or did they banish you from the work site?"

"I'll have you know I'm the official messenger from the tent crew. They're about to set up that latticed arbor thing we talked about as a backdrop for the ceremony, and we'd like both moms to come give us an opinion. Some of the guys are worried it'll blow over if we get a good wind."

Edie blinked, sniffed and then fanned her face with her hands.

Hope left the table and rushed over to her. "What's wrong? Are you worried about the weather?"

"N-no." She sniffed again and wiped her eyes carefully as if trying not to smudge her mascara. "It was when he said *both moms*. That got to me, being included in the mom category."

"Aw." Hope wrapped an arm around her shoulders. "That's sweet."

"I so want Phil to think of me as her mom, even if I'm really not."

"I'm sure she does think of you as her mom." Hope had no idea if that was true or not, but it seemed like the right thing to say.

"You are her mom in every way that counts." Rosie came over to give Edie a hug, too. "She told me how thrilled she is that you love Damon and are excited about this wedding. She isn't into clothes shopping, so—"

"Tell me about it!"

"She said you were a lifesaver when she had to pick out a dress."

"She did?" Edie dabbed at her eyes again. "That's… that's so nice to hear. I thought it was a chore for her."

"It might have been if you hadn't been there to help."

Cade stood there shifting from one booted foot to the other, looking uncomfortable. "So, uh, does that mean you two can come out and take a look at the arbor thing or what?"

"Yes." Rosie winked at Hope. "We'll all come out. The more, the merrier."

Hope appreciated that suggestion more than Rosie could ever know. She was like a schoolgirl with a crush when it came to Liam. If Cade hadn't shown up, she would have found some excuse to go out and check the progress on the tent.

But as they all trouped outside, she thought about Edie's emotional reaction to being accepted as Phil's mom. Hope had a loving mother, and she'd taken that blessing for granted. In the past year, she'd shut her mom out. Talking about the breakup wasn't her favorite thing, but her mother must be worried about her.

After the week with Liam, she'd go home and give both her parents a clearer picture of what had happened. They knew only that she'd stopped writing, quit her job in Cheyenne and moved to Cody. They had to have figured out that the breakup had prompted her behavior, but she'd confided nothing.

Yet they hadn't pestered her for details. That must have taken loving restraint, something she hadn't fully appreciated until now. They'd raised her, educated her and loved her unconditionally. They deserved better.

Lexi and Cade teased each other the entire way to the meadow. Hope got a kick out of it. She thought they probably belonged together, but Lexi wasn't ready to commit. Hope was on her side. A woman had to be absolutely sure that she'd found the right guy before handing him her heart. Or her cherished manuscript.

10

LIAM HAD SPENT most of breakfast waiting for Hope to appear. Eventually he'd had no choice but to leave the ranch house where she was sleeping *right down the hall* and help his brothers and Phil put up the wedding tent. Distracted as he was, he wasn't sure how much use he'd been.

He'd tried to be quiet as he slipped into the cabin the night before, but Grady had woken up, anyway. They'd talked for a while, and Grady had offered to switch places with Hope and take her room in the house, but that seemed a little obvious. Liam wanted to be with her, but he'd rather not turn it into a drama involving everyone.

Still, he hungered for a glimpse of her. Knowing she was nearby but not within touching distance drove him crazy. Any second he expected her to magically appear. And then what? How should they act toward each other?

When Cade had been sent up to the house to fetch the two moms, Liam had wondered if Hope would come along. Fortunately she had. Cade, Rosie and Edie led the parade with Lexi and Hope following.

Liam's body tightened with yearning as she came closer, her golden hair shining in the sun. Had he seriously promised to walk away after a week if that was what she wanted? He could taste her kiss and feel the warmth of her body. His cock twitched at the thought of how effortlessly he'd slid into her heat.

Yeah, sure, she'd said all those things about not wanting a commitment and making a clean break, but she couldn't possibly mean it. And if she had meant it then, she wouldn't continue to think that way after they'd spent several hot nights together. He held on to that belief as she stepped into the meadow.

This morning she wore a crisp white blouse tucked into a pair of jeans that looked newer and not as soft as the ones she'd worn on the ride. They might pose a greater challenge for him to take off. Then he realized he was thinking about undressing her when they'd all gathered to discuss the placement of a white wicker archway. Time to dial it back.

If he'd had any sense, he'd have kept his distance, but instead he walked over to her and Lexi. "Good morning."

Her gray eyes and soft smile welcomed him. "Good morning to you, too."

"How did you sleep?" He'd tossed and turned. Every waking moment had been filled with thoughts of her lying in that guest room bed alone. He should have told her to leave the window open. He knew how to take off those screens.

"Like the dead." She told him about her drink and chat with Rosie.

"Sounds like fun."

"It was." She edged away from the group endlessly debating whether the arch should stay or go, and whether any stabilizing would make it look ugly. "I told her we're not serious about each other and all we want is a temporary fling."

He laughed. "You're kidding me, right? You didn't really say that."

"I did. I felt obligated to let her know what's going on."

He blew out a breath and forced himself to calm down. "I know what that's like. I've had many discussions with her, and she has that effect on a person."

"There's more" Motioning him closer, she spoke in a near whisper. "She gave us a key to the unused cabin so we don't end up conducting our wild affair in the barn."

"You told her about the barn?"

"She knows we don't have a lot of options until after the wedding."

He glanced over at Rosie talking with the others. "Do you think she disapproves?"

"If she does, she didn't let on."

"Because she knows me better than that."

"Oh?"

Damn. Wrong thing to say. He met her questioning gaze. "This isn't the best time and place for this discussion."

"I was thinking the same thing."

He turned toward the group. "Hey, guys. Hope and I are going for a walk. Be back in a few."

"We'll still be here, haggling over this arbor," Damon called back. "Either that or we'll have decided to turn it into firewood for the cookout tonight."

"I'm sure you'll make the right decision, bridegroom." Liam glanced at Hope. "Let's see how the forest service road looks in the daytime."

"Okay." She fell into step beside him.

He took her hand but didn't say anything more until they'd gone through the gate and had started down the dirt road. "Look, just because I've never done something like this doesn't mean I can't. For one thing, no woman has ever suggested it." He shrugged. "Maybe I'll discover a week of sex with no commitment is right up my alley."

"Or maybe you and Rosie both think a week with you will change my perspective."

"Are you completely closed to that possibility?"

"Yes."

"Really?" He looked over and noted that her jaw was rigid and her gaze was focused on the road ahead. "I guess you are."

"I'm not in the market for a steady boyfriend, so if you're going into this with an agenda, we need to call it off now." But she didn't pull her hand away, which was encouraging.

"I wouldn't say I have an agenda, but I'm not so sure we'll finish up the week and be sick of each other."

"We probably won't be."

"So what would be the harm in tacking on a little extension?"

"That would ruin the whole concept. One extension would lead to another, and then you'd want us to start living together."

"Maybe you'd want that, too."

"No. Never again."

He sighed and drew her to a halt. "What did that dirtbag do to you, Hope?"

She stared at him with a mutinous expression. "I don't want to talk about Tom. It's a closed book."

"I do want to talk about him."

"You're asking a lot. I haven't even told my parents the whole story."

He took a deep breath of the pine-scented air. "I'll leave it up to you, then, but hearing about the issues will help me understand why you feel so strongly about being totally on your own. Then we can permanently drop the subject if you want to."

"We can?"

"Yep."

"So we'll never mention this again and go on with our original plan for the week?"

"Yes, ma'am."

"And this will be just between you and me."

"That goes without saying."

"All right, then. I guess that's only fair." She slipped her hand from his and began to pace in front of him on the dirt road "We were best friends, buddies, both of us in the creative writing program. We shared books, our fledgling attempts at novels, meals and eventually a bed."

He did his best to block that last image.

"It was cheaper to live together, so we did. We talked about marriage, but both sets of parents expected a big deal, and we didn't want to take the time to plan it. After graduation, I got a job in the college admissions office and wrote in the evenings. Tom waited tables at night and wrote during the day. We each had a computer, but if one went on the blink, we shared the other one."

"Doesn't sound like you spent much time together, though." He was convinced the story ended with Tom cheating on her when she was at work.

"Oh, we found time to be together." Her pacing became more animated. "We spent hours talking about our writing projects. I finally finished a book I'd started writing my sophomore year. It was the first in a series, and I'd plotted out three more. He was after me to either submit or self-publish, but I didn't feel the manuscript was ready. He'd read it and said it was good. He got very impatient with me."

Liam's pulse rate shot up. Here it came. She'd lied about the physical abuse. "Is that when he hit you?"

"No." She turned toward him, and her face was expressionless except for her eyes. The tortured agony in those gray depths was painful to witness. "That's when he took my manuscript and self-published it as his."

He gasped. "And you didn't sue his ass?"

"I had no case. My word against his. He took all of it and erased everything on my computer that was in any way related to it—my notes for the rest of the series, my character charts, everything. All gone." She swallowed. "All gone."

"What about your friends? Didn't you tell them about this project? Couldn't they have testified that you'd written it?"

"That's the irony." Her mouth twisted in a bitter smile. "He was the only person I trusted with the details. He was paranoid about people stealing his ideas, and he made me paranoid, too. Friends knew I was writing something, but I wouldn't talk about it. Only to him."

"That's evil." His body vibrated with anger. "What's his last name?"

"I'm not going to tell you."

"He shouldn't be able to get away with this, damn it!"

"Maybe not, but he did. So now you know, and we can permanently drop the subject like you promised."

Fists clenched in frustration, he gazed at her.

"You did promise," she said quietly. "Ready to go back now?"

"No, I'm ready to break the guy's face."

A gleam of approval flashed in her eyes. "I used to want that, too, but I'm over it. What's done is done, and I can't change what happened, so the best thing to do is forget about it and move on."

"Except that you haven't."

"Yes, I have. This is the most thought I've given Tom in months. I have a new life in a new town. I've moved on."

"But you aren't writing anymore, and you only want a man around for a temporary affair. Is that what you call being over it?"

She lifted her chin. "That's how I've chosen to handle the situation. And *now* can we permanently drop the subject?"

"Yes." He rubbed the back of his neck. "Sorry. I just didn't expect it would be something that horrific."

"In the grand scheme of things, it's not. It's just a book."

Just a book. The dismissive way she said it sent chills down his spine. He wanted to argue the point, but he'd promised to drop the subject. He needed to stop making promises he later regretted.

He'd expected to find out this Tom slimeball had betrayed her with another woman. It was a crummy thing to do, but common enough, unfortunately. And not so difficult to get past, given time to realize you were better off without such a person.

But *this.* Being Grady's brother had taught him so much about the creative process. Last year someone had made a crude copy of one of Grady's sculptures and had put it up online as a Grady Magee original. Grady had gone ballistic. He had taken legal action, and the perpetrator wouldn't be trying that again.

What Hope had suffered was far worse. She'd lost something she'd spent years working on, and it hadn't simply disappeared because of a computer glitch or a natural disaster. Instead, the one person she'd trusted with her precious work had stolen it and taken credit for her creation. It was mental rape.

He wanted to find the asshole and make him sorry he'd ever been born, but he couldn't do that because he didn't even have a name. Barring that, he wanted to tell other people so they could share his outrage. Grady would be beside himself. But Grady wouldn't hear about it, because Liam had promised not to tell.

Hope touched his arm. "Sorry you asked?"

"No." He blew out a breath. "I needed to know."

"You look really upset."

"I'll be okay." He wasn't convinced that she would be, though, and that bothered him a lot. He'd never had someone he completely trusted betray him.

Yeah, there'd been a few little incidents. In high school he'd found the girl he was dating kissing another guy. Another supposed friend had stolen his ID and used it to buy beer, but that was the extent of his experience with betrayal. Small potatoes compared to what Hope had endured. He could imagine how Tom's actions would affect every close relationship she had from that moment on.

"We should go back." The upbeat lilt in her voice sounded forced. "The others must think we've gotten lost."

She was right, but he didn't want to go just yet. "I don't know how you feel about this, but I'd like to kiss you before we leave. It might not make you feel any better, but it sure would cheer me up."

She smiled. "I'd never turn down a kiss from you."

Not this week, anyway. He didn't say it, though. Instead he pushed his hat to the back of his head and drew her into his arms. She came willingly, but there was a reserve about her now, a stiffness that hadn't been there before.

When he looked into her eyes, he saw a hesitancy that tore at his heart. "Are you sorry you told me?"

"Yes."

"Why?"

"Because you must think I was stupid."

"No! I don't—"

"But I was stupid! What idiot would allow that kind of thing to happen?"

"Not an idiot. A loving, trusting—"

"Fool. There were signs that he was capable of this and I ignored them. He stole wineglasses from the restaurant where he worked. He figured out a way to cheat on a semester final and bragged about it to me. There were other things like that, and he always justified his actions. The restaurant owner was a cheapskate, and the professor's grading system was unfair. I should have seen this coming."

"Hope, it wasn't your fault. He took terrible advantage of you."

"Because I let him." The despair in her voice was the saddest sound he'd ever heard.

"It's not your fault." Leaning down, he placed soft kisses on her forehead, her cheeks, her nose and her chin. "Not your fault," he murmured over and over between kisses.

Finally she groaned and cupped his face in both hands, holding him still. "Kiss me for real, cowboy."

"Love to." And he settled his mouth firmly over hers. The moment he did, she relaxed, wound her arms around his neck and nestled against him. Ah. This was more like the woman he'd made love to in the barn.

Thank God they'd established that intimate connection. She might still believe their attraction was based on sex, but he knew it was so much more. Sharing the pleasure they'd found had the power to heal if she'd let it. Their private times together could be a place of refuge as they navigated whatever rough waters this week might bring.

She aroused him with breathtaking ease. Seconds into their kiss, he was hard and wishing they could enjoy some of that private, healing time right now. Lifting his head, he gazed into her flushed face. "I want to drag you into the woods and have my way with you."

"I know." All her hesitation was gone, and her eyes sparkled with excitement.

"And you like knowing that, don't you?"

"Yes. It makes me feel powerful."

"Good, because you are." He'd be happy to let her demonstrate her power often in the next few days. Talk about win-win.

"We can't really go off into the woods now, though."

"Not this time. But let's keep it in mind for the future."

"Believe me, I will. Okay, one more kiss for the road." She traced his lower lip. "You still haven't told me how you got that scar."

"A woman bit me." Capturing her mouth again, he kissed her with passion, but also with the tenderness she deserved from any man privileged to hold her. She'd granted him that privilege for the next week. He'd thought that would give him plenty of time to break through the walls she'd built. Maybe not.

11

HOPE DIDN'T HAVE another moment alone with Liam for the rest of the day, and she decided that might be for the best. Her emotions were all over the place and she needed time to regroup. She sincerely wished the subject of Tom hadn't been raised, but she also realized Liam deserved to know why she'd demanded a deadline for their relationship.

She'd heard confession was good for the soul, but hers felt battered and bruised after bringing that awful episode out of the mental closet where she'd stashed it. He'd said she wasn't over it, and she hated discovering he was right. Life had been so much easier during months of self-induced amnesia.

While talking about Tom with Liam, she'd struggled to stay in control of her negative emotions. His hot kisses had helped enormously, but she couldn't indulge in that distraction when there was work to be done. Fortunately the bustle of preparations for the rehearsal and the rehearsal dinner provided protection. She cooked, cleaned and helped set up without anyone noticing that she wasn't particularly chatty.

All the focus was on the wedding, thank goodness.

FREE Merchandise is 'in the Cards' for you!

Dear Reader,

We're giving away FREE MERCHANDISE!

Seriously, we'd like to reward you for reading this novel by giving you **FREE MERCHANDISE** worth over **$20** retail. And no purchase is necessary!

It's easy! All you have to do is look inside for your Free Merchandise Voucher. Return the Voucher promptly...and we'll send you valuable Free Merchandise!

Thanks again for reading one of our novels—and enjoy your Free Merchandise with our compliments!

Pam Powers

Pam Powers

P.S. Look inside to see what Free Merchandise is **"in the cards"** for you!

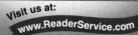

YOUR FREE MERCHANDISE INCLUDES...

2 FREE Books **AND** 2 FREE Mystery Gifts

FREE MERCHANDISE VOUCHER

❏ Please send my Free Merchandise, consisting of
2 Free Books and **2 Free Mystery Gifts**.
I understand that I am under no obligation to buy
anything, as explained on the back of this card.

150/350 HDL GKAW

Please Print

FIRST NAME

LAST NAME

ADDRESS

APT.#   CITY

STATE/PROV.   ZIP/POSTAL CODE

NO PURCHASE NECESSARY!

HB-516-FMH16

The debate over arbor/no arbor had continued through lunch until Herb had finally mentioned that besides potentially blowing over, the problematic structure would obscure the view of the cabin.

Finn had to leave to pick up Chelsea at the airport, and everyone else, including Hope, pitched in to decorate the front of the cabin. They made a wildflower wreath for the door and covered the windowsills with greenery and wild berries. Damon climbed up on the roof and attached more greenery along the roofline. The cabin took on the look of a fairy dwelling.

By the time they declared it complete, Finn had returned with Chelsea. She was a bundle of energy with turquoise streaks in her blond hair. As everyone crowded around for hugs, Phil made sure to introduce Hope.

You'll like her, Phil had said earlier, and Hope could see why. A year ago Chelsea would have been exactly the kind of person Hope gravitated to. Not anymore. Being friendly but maintaining a low profile was the name of the game. She wasn't about to get chummy with that fascinating woman and risk saying something unintentionally revealing. Chelsea was a member of the creative tribe Hope had resigned from.

If Hope had still been writing, Chelsea would have made an interesting and stimulating friend, much as Phil, Debbie and Joan had been. She'd kept seeing all three during her college years until Tom's paranoia had turned girls' nights out into exhausting efforts not to let a writing secret slip. Later she'd been too embarrassed to contact them and admit what had happened. What she'd allowed to happen.

The habit of keeping secrets was hard to break, though. She was still doing it with everyone except for Liam. He glanced her way whenever they happened to be in the

same area helping with preparations. Each time, he looked
a little worried, but then his expression would shift and
he'd give her a warm smile.

Their supposedly carefree fling wasn't so carefree
now, was it? The idea had seemed doable at first. Other
couples managed it, so why couldn't they? Belatedly she'd
figured out that a no-strings affair might sound good in
theory. In practice it wasn't all that easy to pull off with
living, breathing people who had feelings.

And oh, boy, did she have feelings. Thanks to Liam,
she realized how much she'd been muting them. No, she
couldn't blame it all on him, either. The wedding was part
of the problem. She'd been having some trouble manag-
ing her feelings during the bachelorette party, which was
why she'd escaped to the porch.

Her muddled state of mind that afternoon could explain why she'd overreacted to his truck speeding up
Phil's driveway. The combination of a wedding and Liam
had jerked her out of a soft-focus, pastel view of life into
a world of intense color and excitement.

She couldn't say she was sorry. She loved the sex. But
she wasn't so crazy about the other emotions coming at
her. Putting a time limit on this affair had been smart.

Eventually the preparations wrapped up as the designated hour for the rehearsal approached. Showers were
taken and clothes were changed. Hope had brought an
off-the-shoulder blouse and a flowing skirt for this special night. Knowing this was likely what she'd be wearing
when she met Liam in their cabin hideaway, she dressed
with extra care. She would have loved to put on the high-
heeled sandals that matched the outfit, but flats made
more sense for tromping through soft dirt and grass.

She'd save the sexy shoes for next week when she
was staying at Damon and Phil's cabin. Maybe once the

wedding was over and she wasn't viewing a happily-ever-after in the making, she might be able to recapture the spirit of a fantasy fling. Per Liam's promise, they wouldn't be discussing Tom again.

While she regretted having told Liam everything, because it had changed the dynamic, she also felt closer to him than to anyone else in the wedding party. They shared a secret. She recognized now that shared secrets could be dangerous, but nothing about Liam felt that way. Rosie had echoed her feelings the night before when she'd said, *I wasn't worried. You were with Liam.*

Hope walked down to the meadow with Rosie, Herb and the minister from Sheridan who had driven out for the rehearsal. Hope was charmed to discover that the minister Phil and Damon had chosen with some help from Rosie was a woman. To the casual observer, Rosie might appear to be a traditional wife and mother, but she was obviously ready to challenge stereotypes at every opportunity.

Once in the meadow, Hope left Rosie and Herb to do their thing, and she took a chair under the tent in the second row on the bride's side. The tent was big enough for only two small sections of folding chairs. Artificial turf had been laid down as an aisle runner, and a larger piece had been placed in front of the cabin, where the ceremony would be held.

The summer day had stayed pleasantly cool, and she could smell wood smoke from the nearby fire pit, where the rehearsal barbecue would take place. Liam and Grady had started the fire an hour ago and had covered it with a large wire screen to contain any flying sparks as the logs were reduced to embers perfect for grilling.

Everyone with a role in the wedding was in attendance except Finn. Damon had chosen Cade, Finn and Herb

as co–best men. Phil had asked Rosie, Edie and Lexi to
share the "of honor" category. Edie and Rosie were matrons of honor and Lexi was maid of honor. Phil's father,
Karl, a balding guy who had a perpetual grin on his face,
would walk her down the aisle. He'd arrived from Cheyenne two hours ago.

Hope kept watching the cabin next to the decorated
one. That was where Liam and Grady were staying, but
neither of them had come out yet. Working with the fire
must have made them late getting cleaned up. She'd de-
liberately chosen a seat with a vacant chair on either
side so when they did arrive, Liam could sit next to her.

Then she was distracted by Cade making a megaphone
of his hands. "Hey, O'Roarke!" he called. "You're holding up the show!"

She turned around in her chair and looked across to
the cabin where Finn and Chelsea were staying. It was the
first one ever built and the one Finn, Damon and Cade
had shared when they'd lived at the ranch. Chelsea and
Finn stood on the cement stoop, having a discussion.

Chelsea's dress was stunning and sexy—midthigh
length and made of a shimmering material that contained
every color in the rainbow, including a turquoise shade
to match her hair. But her shoes were the real attention
grabber—turquoise stilettos. Hope wondered how Chelsea would navigate the meadow.

She didn't have to. Suddenly Finn scooped her up
in his arms. Amid whoops and hollers from Cade and
Damon, he carried her across the grassy area and set her
on the artificial turf. She gave him a quick kiss before
walking carefully down the aisle toward Hope.

"I could've made it," she said as she sat down. "I told
him that, but he was determined to show off his manly
muscles."

Hope laughed. "It was a fun show. Now I wish I hadn't been so chicken about wearing my heels. You look fabulous."

"You, too! With that outfit, you should wear a flower in your hair. It's a very romantic look."

"I haven't worn flowers in my hair since college." Since before she'd met Tom. She used to do fanciful things like that, she realized, and gradually she'd stopped. He'd been a master at stifling those silly impulses with an eye roll or an almost imperceptible shake of his head.

"There's a clump of yellow daisies growing right over there." Chelsea pointed to a spot just beyond the tent. "Go pick one."

"I don't need to—"

"Come on. If you don't, I will."

"Oh, no, we can't have that. You'd cancel out Finn's noble gesture."

"Then you go. That outfit just cries for a pretty yellow daisy in your hair. Look, there's a daisy pattern in the material of your skirt! I just saw that. Now you have to do it."

"Okay." Smiling, Hope left her seat and walked over to the patch of daisies. Picking one reminded her of childhood summers spent lying in the grass, scribbling in a notebook, making up stories. She brought the flower back and handed it to Chelsea. "I don't have a mirror."

"I can do it. Hold still." Chelsea tucked it gently behind Hope's ear. Then she leaned back with an approving smile. "Perfect."

"It doesn't look silly?"

"No. It looks artistic. Are you, by the way? Phil said you were friends in high school, but that's all I know."

"I'm not artistic, but I'm sure you are! Marketing must be a fun job." A good offense was the best defense.

"I love it. Something new going on every day. I have to stay on my toes, which is how I function best. You're working in Cody, right? For one of the hotels?"

"I am. Good company. Terrific opportunities for advancement."

"Sounds as if you love your job, too. What's the best part?"

"Having people come back from their excursions bubbling over with enthusiasm. That's a great feeling." She wondered if her nose would start to grow. Sure, she enjoyed helping people have a good holiday experience, and it was gratifying when they were pleased with the trips she'd set up or the restaurants she recommended.

Bottom line—she liked her job, but she didn't love it. She could leave it without a backward glance. She'd never admitted that to herself until now. This wedding and Liam were making her question everything about her new and quite orderly life.

And at last, here came that gorgeous man who was so wonderful and so worrying at the same time. He wore snug jeans, polished boots, a white shirt open at the collar and a black Stetson. Sharp. Sexy. Grady looked pretty good, too, but she barely noticed. She couldn't see anyone but the man with the piercing blue eyes.

He took the chair on Hope's left, and Grady settled down next to Chelsea. After everyone said hi, Grady and Chelsea picked up the discussion they'd been having this afternoon about marketing his sculptures in Seattle.

Liam smiled at Hope. "How'd you know I'm a sucker for a woman with a flower in her hair?"

"I didn't. The flower is all Chelsea's fault. She insisted I needed one." The scent of his aftershave enveloped her, reminding her of lying in his arms on a blanket under the stars. Last night had been filled with nothing but mutual attraction. She longed to return to that simpler time.

"I don't know that you *need* one. You're beautiful without it."

"Pretty words." But they made her heart race.

"Pretty lady." He reached over and ran his forefinger around the flower's petals. "You don't need this to look great, but I love what it says."

"I picked a talking flower? What are the chances?"

He grinned. "I know. I haven't seen a talking flower in a long time but you definitely have one right there. It just whispered to me that only very sexy women go around putting flowers in their hair."

"You can't believe everything you hear from a daisy."

"I believe this one."

Next to her, Grady and Chelsea chattered away about gallery possibilities and shipping options, which left her with the perfect opportunity to talk with Liam. She gazed at him, a man she'd had sex with the night before, a man to whom she'd revealed her darkest secrets only hours ago.

When they were truly alone, they seemed to have plenty to talk about. Or if they weren't talking, they were kissing, or…best not to think about that now. She couldn't think of anything to say. Under the circumstances, small talk seemed dumb.

He regarded her with amusement, as if he understood her dilemma and shared it. "Think it'll rain?"

"Hope not." And there they were, stuck talking about the weather. If they'd been strangers, she'd have asked him about his job the way Chelsea had asked about hers. "What's your favorite thing about taking people out on a rafting trip?"

She'd obviously startled him with an out-of-the-blue

question. But after a moment, he came up with an answer. "It strips away the nonessentials."

"Like what?"

"They show up with the gear we require, but it's the baggage you can't see that weighs them down. They begin the trip thinking about whether stocks or bonds are a better deal. They're having an internal debate about whether to sell their house or remodel it. They're wrapped up in the current political drama or the prospects of their favorite team. Then they get out on the water, and none of it matters. They're living in the moment, maybe for the first time in their lives."

She stared at him in astonishment. "That's a great answer."

"It's a great question."

"I was only trying to—"

"Fill an awkward silence. I know. But when you're creative, when you're curious about people and what makes them tick, you naturally come up with stuff. Like I said—awesome question."

"That's ridiculous. Anyone could have thought to ask you that."

He held her gaze. "No, Hope, they couldn't, and they don't. Nobody's ever come up with that question. Grady might if he didn't already know the answer. We've spent hours talking about why we love what we do."

"What does he love about metal sculpture?" The question was instinctive, but the minute she'd asked it, she wished she hadn't.

"Being allowed to use his imagination. Bringing something into the world that didn't exist before, at least not in that form. Because he uses recycled materials, the individual pieces existed but not in that configuration."

Writers recycled words in the same way, gathering

them up and stringing them together to make something new. She felt him watching her, gauging her reaction. She wanted to look away and hide the turmoil he could probably see in her eyes, but that would be the coward's way out. She and Tom used to talk about the joy of bringing something into existence. "That's great."

"It is. I love talking to him because he's a creative thinker." He hesitated and his expression softened. "So are you. It's a special—"

"I believe we were talking about Grady."

He shrugged. "Then forget I said it."

"Like I can." But she'd been the one who'd stumbled into this messy topic, so she couldn't really blame him.

"Maybe you shouldn't forget it. "

"Liam, I—"

"And that's all I'm going to say on the subject, because I don't want to argue." He smiled. "I'm a lover, not a fighter."

She took a deep breath. "I'm not going to say anything more, either."

"About anything?"

"That's right. Talking will only get me in trouble."

"I don't know who you're in trouble with, but it sure as hell isn't me."

"I'm not in trouble *with* anyone. I'm just in trouble, period."

"Why is that?" His blue gaze searched hers.

She swallowed. "Until yesterday I thought I was doing fine, and now I'm pretty sure I'm not."

He reached for her hand and gave it a squeeze. "Don't panic. You *are* doing fine."

"Easy for you to say. You're not the one with her stomach in knots." She couldn't believe she'd admitted that, but it was too late to take it back.

He stroked the palm of her hand with his thumb as he looked into her eyes. "Am I part of the problem?" His voice was laced with concern.

"You are, but it's a combination of things, including the wedding. I didn't realize it would affect me to see how happy Phil and Damon are together, but apparently it does."

"I can't fix that, but I can fix my part in all of this. I'll admit I've poked my nose in your business, and I have no right to. Apparently I can't help myself, so the best thing is for me to back off."

She tightened her grip on his hand. "Please don't."

"I don't want to cause you any more stress."

"Sometimes you do, but—"

"Seriously, Hope, we should rethink the plan if I'm making you more anxious. The last thing I want is—"

"You didn't let me finish."

"Sorry."

"It's okay." She lowered her voice. "You're desperate to help me, and I appreciate that so much. But I'd be lying if I denied that you cause me stress. You make me think about things I'd rather not."

He sighed. "I know."

"That's the bad news. But the good news is…"

"What? Give me some good news, because I'm feeling like a real jerk right now."

"The good news is that you're the best stress reliever I've ever met."

12

LIAM DIDN'T FEEL particularly noble for accepting Hope's flattering statement as a reason to continue their affair. But she was right. Good sex was a time-honored stress reducer, and apparently he provided that for her. She wanted him to keep on providing it until they both returned to Cody.

She'd hinted that she was a little envious of Phil and Damon, and as Liam watched the rehearsal, he felt an unwelcome jab of envy, too. They made it look so easy. Yet Liam knew the relationship hadn't been easy at all. Damon had told him how he'd stubbornly clung to his belief that he was destined to live alone, and he'd almost lost Phil as a result.

People became damaged in so many ways. Liam counted himself lucky that his irresponsible dad had taken off before he was born. Grady's dad had stayed a little longer, but their mom had kicked him out just in time. If that loser had been allowed to stick around, he and Grady would have been messed up for sure. Instead they'd been protected by their fierce mother, and when she'd been laid up, unable to do the job, Rosie and Herb had stepped in. Hope's parents might have tried to keep her safe, but they hadn't counted on a creep like Tom. They also didn't know what Tom had done to her, and that was a damn shame. She'd denied herself their comfort.

So now her temporary sex partner—he couldn't consider himself anything more—was the only person who knew what she'd been through. And he wasn't supposed to talk about it. He wouldn't, either, first because he'd promised and second because talking about it caused her stress.

But he had a problem, and it wasn't a small one. He'd watched Grady blossom and knew that a creative person needed a satisfying outlet. His brother craved time alone in his studio, and Liam's rafting schedule gave Grady that. When Liam arrived home after a week away, Grady was always glowing with a sense of accomplishment and eager to show off his progress. Grady without his sculpting wouldn't have been the same person.

Hope had abandoned her writing, so where was that bottled up creativity going? She'd mentioned some crafts, but he didn't get the feeling she was into any of them. He pictured her imaginative urges building like a pressure cooker about to explode, or worse yet, festering and destroying her zest for life. He couldn't accept that a person who'd worked on a book for years could suddenly shut down the whole operation.

If he'd been a different kind of man, he could have dismissed those worries and simply enjoyed the sex. Chances were good that a fair amount of her frustration would be channeled into getting it on with him. He was willing to relieve her stress, but he wasn't willing to siphon off her creativity.

He'd read a book that claimed each person contributed a unique gift to the world. His was introducing folks to the Zen of the wilderness. Grady's was welding recycled metal into beautiful works of art. What if Hope's was writing stories to capture a reader's imagination? She was denying her gift.

He was still holding her hand when the rehearsal ended. "I think that went well."

"You do? Really?" Grady stood and offered an elbow to Chelsea, who laughingly waved him off as she carefully made her way over to the carpeted aisle.

"Everybody seemed to be having a good time," Hope said.

"That may be so." Grady caught Chelsea by the elbow when she stumbled on a wrinkle in the carpet. "But they have no idea who's supposed to be in charge of the ring."

"I'm sure they'll work it out," Hope said. She'd made no attempt to free her hand as they walked behind Chelsea and Grady.

"Then they should draw straws," Grady said. "It's nuts having three guys all be the best man."

"They get points for originality, though." Chelsea gave in and clutched Grady's arm as she wobbled along on her stilettos. "I've never been to a wedding with three best men and three matrons of honor. I mean, two matrons of honor and one maid. In any case, I like the idea that Phil and Damon thumbed their noses at traditional roles. That bridal hierarchy never appealed to me in the first place."

"Me, either," Hope said. "If you have several good friends or cherished relatives, why be forced to elevate one to the privileged position?"

"Exactly." Chelsea glanced over her shoulder and exchanged a look of solidarity with Hope.

"Yeah, I can see that," Grady said. "And I'm all for shaking up the status quo, but you need a plan or you have chaos. Hey, Chelsea, here comes your one and only." He called out to Finn. "I've done my best to keep her upright, bro. In return she's promised to talk me up at a primo Seattle art gallery."

Finn laughed. "Sounds like a fair exchange."

"I hate to admit it," Chelsea said, transferring her hold from Grady to Finn, "but these shoes are a pain in the tuckus."

"Yeah." Finn put a supportive hand around her waist. "But they're sexy as hell."

"Assuming that she doesn't fall on her tuckus," Grady said. "That would really sabotage the sexy."

Chelsea gazed up at Finn. "Grady's right, so it looks like you'll have to keep a tight grip on me throughout the evening so I don't fall."

"And you know how I'll hate doing that." Finn's adoring expression telegraphed exactly how far gone he was.

And now Liam envied him, too. He'd never had that reaction to happy couples until today. Maybe he'd become too invested in someone who had no intention of sticking around.

"Yeah, helluva job to be saddled with, O'Roarke," Grady said. "Come on, everybody. Let's go get us some eats and drinks. I smell steak on the barbie."

"Great. I'm starving." Anyone hearing Hope's comment would have assumed she was ready to party.

But Liam thought she might be faking it, so as they walked over to the fire pit, he gave her hand a squeeze in a show of support. Her return squeeze was enough to activate his protective instincts, and after years of watching over Grady, he knew how easily he slipped into that role. The trick might be slipping back out at the end of the week.

Grady's wire mesh over the fire had worked like a charm, and the resulting coals were perfect for grilling. Cade, Damon and Finn had appointed themselves cooks for the evening, and Herb was the bartender. Liam offered to help, but he was directed to a bench, where he and Hope were given their beverage of choice and ordered to stay put.

"You can be on cleanup duty after dinner, bro," Cade said.

"Be glad to."

"I can help clean up later, too," Hope said.

Cade grinned at her. "I appreciate the offer, but the guys are gonna handle it. By the way, that flower looks real nice in your hair."

"Thank you." Her cheeks turned pink.

"It does look great." Phil walked over and sat on Hope's other side. "Reminds me of the old days. You could always tell when school was almost out for the summer because a bunch of us girls would pick wildflowers and put them in our hair. It was fun."

Hope laughed. "They weren't always wildflowers, either. Remember sneaking into Mrs. Eddleston's yard?"

"Yes! And then we pooled our babysitting money and bought her four rosebushes because we had an attack of conscience." She glanced at Liam. "Just to let you know we weren't really bad girls."

"Thanks." Liam grinned at her. "I was worried."

"We probably could have just asked for the flowers." Hope turned to him. "But we were afraid of her. There was this rumor going around school that she'd done away with her husband and buried him under the rosebushes."

"Which we found out wasn't true," Phil said. "My dad overheard me talking about it and told me they got a divorce. Apparently Mr. Eddleston was very much alive and living in Idaho. So we bought her the rosebushes. And Hope wrote a song that we all sang when we presented them."

"Oh, my God, I forgot about that song."

"Really? I might still be able to sing it."

Hope turned bright red. "No, don't."

Liam went on alert. "Phil…"

"Trust me, Liam. It's adorable. Mrs. Eddleston loved it. We all did. Besides, I was in choir. I'm a good singer."

"Yes, you are," Hope said, "but it's not a good song. Don't sing it."

Liam opened his mouth to protest again, but then he glanced at Hope and changed his mind. She was still blushing like crazy, but her gray eyes sparkled with excitement. This might not be a bad thing, after all.

"I'm the bride," Phil said. "I get to do what I want." She cleared her throat. "Here goes."

"Noooo."

Phil ignored her. "In your yard we came creeping, with you soundly sleeping, our sharp pruners flashing, then off we were dashing, to—"

"Stop, stop!" Hope giggled and covered her face with both hands. "This is beyond embarrassing."

Phil smiled and finished the song. "To places here and there, with your flowers in our hair." She drew out the last note and ended with a flourish as everyone clapped and cheered. Standing, she took a bow and then gestured to Hope. "Composed by our very own Hope Caldwell at the tender age of fifteen! Bravo!"

Hope groaned. "It's a good thing this is the eve of your wedding, because if it wasn't, I would *kill* you."

But Liam noticed there was no bite to her words. Sure, she was embarrassed, but she also seemed pleased that Phil remembered the song all these years later. She'd lost the novel she'd spent countless hours writing, but this cute little song had survived.

Whether intentionally or not, Phil had rocketed Hope

back to a time before her dreams had been crushed. Even better, she still enjoyed being recognized for something that she'd created. It was a start.

Phil leaned down and gave her a hug. "Forgive me?"

"Oh, sure." Hope gazed up at her with a placid smile. "But you might want to check around your place after you get back from your honeymoon. I'm not saying I'll put salt in the sugar bowl or a big rubber spider in your cupboard, but I'm not saying I won't, either."

Phil chuckled. "I'll keep that in mind." She glanced over at Liam. "She may seem sweet and innocent, but I could tell you stories."

"I'll bet." Getting a glimpse of the mischief-maker Hope used to be showed him even more clearly how Tom had affected her. He wondered if Phil saw the change and had decided to remind Hope of that girl of fifteen who'd written a song about stealing flowers. If so, good for Phil.

The meal went late and the cleanup even later.

While Liam worked with his brothers at the barbecue site and then in the kitchen, Herb and Phil's dad shot pool, and Hope sat on the front porch chatting with the other women. Rosie had made a big pot of coffee and opened a new bottle of Baileys. Liam wondered if the planned rendezvous in the vacant cabin would be happening after all.

The ladies were still going strong when the guys finished in the kitchen and joined them on the porch. Liam came out the door in time to hear Edie say, "I like mine nice and thick."

"I don't mind so much if they're thin." That was Chelsea. "But I hate it when they're limp."

"That's the worst," Hope said. "Give me thick and firm any day."

Cade spoke before Liam had a chance. "What in *hell* are you ladies talking about?"

Lexi stood and walked toward him, smiling. "What do you think we're talking about?"

"I'm not about to take a guess after what I heard." He turned to Liam. "You want to?"

"Not me." He glanced back as Finn, Grady and Damon filed through the screen door. "Apparently the discussion out here on the porch is a debate about thin versus thick, and nobody wants limp. Any of you want to venture a guess as to what they're discussing?"

Finn laughed. "I know exactly what they're discussing."

"Yeah." Damon rubbed the back of his neck. "Me, too. Blame it on the Baileys. And we're having a wedding tomorrow, so I guess it's only natural that talk would turn to—"

"Fries," Finn said. "They're talking about fries. Chels, am I right?"

"You're right."

Lexi sighed. "You're no fun, O'Roarke. I had the rest of them going."

"Sorry about that, Lex. Chels and I had this discussion earlier because I was thinking of changing up the pub fries at O'Roarke's. We decided I should leave them thick."

"I thought it was probably fries," Cade said.

"No, you didn't." Lexi put her arm through his. "Let's head back to my place, cowboy. Maybe we'll cook up some fries."

Cade surveyed the group on the porch. "That's code for sex, in case nobody picked up on it."

Lexi gave him a swat on the arm.

"We picked up on it," Damon said, rolling his eyes. "See you two in the morning."

About that time, Karl and Herb finished their pool game and came out to the porch.

"He skunked me," Karl said.

"But you put up a good fight." Herb clapped him on the shoulder.

"Very gracious of you to say so." Karl beamed at everyone. "It's been a great day, but I'm bushed." He looked over at his wife. "Edie, think we can talk my future son-in-law into meandering back to town and hauling us along with him?"

"Sounds like a fine idea."

Damon laughed. "I'm in. Phil, you ready to wrap it up?"

"Sure." Phil stood. "But wait! Isn't it bad luck for you to see the bride the night before the wedding?"

"How about if I promise to keep my eyes closed?"

"That works, but I'd better drive. Goodbye, all. See you tomorrow."

The crowd was dispersing, and Liam's hopes rose in proportion to the number of people exiting the area. At last Chelsea finished her Baileys and coffee and was ready to walk back to the cabin with Finn. She'd borrowed a pair of flip-flops from Rosie after growing tired of dealing with her stilettos, which she'd tucked into a borrowed tote.

Earlier Liam had explained the vacant cabin setup to Grady, who seemed to be finding the long trail of goodbyes amusing. "Guess I'll turn in, too," he said. "Coming with me, bro?" His grin said he knew the answer.

"In a minute." Liam propped a hip against the porch railing. "It's a beautiful night. Almost hate to go in."

"It's beautiful, all right," Herb said, "but it's been a long day. I'm off to bed. Rosie?"

She swallowed the last of her drink. "It's time. You

and Hope enjoy the porch. Herb and I used to sit out here for hours when we were younger. Before we had the boys." She stood.

"And I was one of those boys." Liam walked over and hugged her. "I've said it before, but I don't know what Grady and I would have done without you and Herb."

"You would have survived." Rosie gave him a tight hug back. "You're both very strong."

Liam looked down at her, and his heart swelled with gratitude. "But for two years, we didn't have to be strong. You gave us a soft place to land."

"It was our pleasure."

"Absolutely," Herb said. "You and Grady were great to have around."

"And as long as we're getting nostalgic and sentimental," Rosie said, "this might be a good time to ask if you think Grady could make me a sculpture sometime."

"Absolutely! Do you want one? I'll bet he has no idea or he would have done it by now."

"I'd love one. I didn't want to bring it up to his face because I know he's busy, and I don't want him dropping everything to do it."

Liam nodded. "I could see that happening. He's behind now because he spent so much time on Phil and Damon's."

"And I don't want to insult him by offering to become a paying customer."

"He'd have a fit if you did that. Tell you what. I'll try to gauge when I think he's caught up and then mention that I think you'd love one. How's that?"

"Excellent. It doesn't have to be huge like Damon and Phil's, but maybe he could come up with a little something. I would cherish it."

Liam was touched by the request. "I know you would."

He gave her another hug good-night, and Hope stood so she could do the same. Then Herb and Rosie went inside, leaving him alone with Hope. Finally. He gazed at her, not wanting to come across as some raging bull even though he felt like one. "Do you want to sit on the porch for a while?"

Smiling, she reached in the pocket of her skirt and pulled out a key. "What do you think?"

13

HOPE HAD WAITED impatiently for this moment, and she wasn't about to waste a single second lounging on the front porch. Judging from the way Liam grabbed her hand and hustled her down the steps, she doubted he was interested in a moonlight chat, either.

During the rehearsal she'd regretted not wearing her sexy heels, but she'd chosen exactly the right footwear for this speedy trip to the cabin. Her daisy had long since wilted and been discarded, but she didn't think Liam cared now whether she wore a flower in her hair or held one in her teeth, for that matter.

She arrived with her heart pounding and her breathing labored, but that wasn't because they'd race-walked down here. The promise of what they were about to enjoy would have been enough all by itself. She moved forward to unlock the door.

Tugging on her hand, Liam pulled her back. "I need to go in first," he murmured. "Give me a minute or two." He took a key from his pocket and shoved it into the lock.

"Rosie gave you a key, too?"

"I asked Cade for his."

"Why?"

He opened the door and stepped into the dark interior of the cabin. "You'll see." Leaving her standing alone on the wooden stoop, he closed the door.

Because the floorboards creaked, she could hear him moving around doing something. She didn't think he was pulling mattresses off the bunks because she would have heard them thump to the floor. Since he had a key, maybe he'd sneaked in sometime this afternoon to set up the mattresses.

That could explain why he and Grady had been late to the rehearsal. Grady would know all about this rendezvous, so he might have helped. Heart still beating wildly with anticipation, she shivered as a cool breeze touched her overheated skin. The wait was driving her *crazy*.

After what seemed like forever, he appeared in the doorway, a broad-shouldered silhouette of a cowboy outlined by glowing light. He reached for her hand. When he spoke, his voice was husky, as if he'd been going a little crazy, too. "You can come in."

She stepped inside the cabin and gasped. The cabin had been transformed from what was essentially a dorm room into a romantic bower brimming with wildflowers and greenery. At least twenty votives in glass holders cast their flickering light over the bed positioned in the middle of the floor.

Although the bed likely had been created using two bunk mattresses, a set of dark green king sheets made it look luxurious and inviting.

The creative setting left her speechless. The romantic in her longed to melt into the ambiance and savor it with the man who'd helped put it all together. But the cautious side of her wondered about his motives.

"Do you like it?" he asked.

"Of course I do. It's amazingly beautiful, but…"

"It's over the top. I was afraid of that, but when I walked in here earlier today, it seemed so uninspiring. I said something about it to Grady, and he helped me improve the situation."

"Does Grady think that we're serious about each other?"

"No, I swear he doesn't. I made it clear from the beginning that we're just having some fun."

"Then why would you go to this much trouble? Don't get me wrong—I love the way it looks—but it took effort."

"Not as much as you might think, especially with Grady directing traffic." He blew out a breath. "Look, I promised to be your fantasy lover for the next week. This cabin didn't fit my image of a fun place to have sex. I know Rosie meant well, but even that empty stall in the barn seemed more exotic than twin mattresses thrown on the floor."

She finally understood and was overcome by a wave of tenderness for the tall cowboy standing in front of her. "You take your promises seriously, don't you?"

"Yes, ma'am, I do."

"This arrangement is definitely over the top, but that's what fantasies are supposed to be, right?"

"That's what I always thought."

"Then close your eyes. I want to create a fantasy image for you."

"You're doing a good job of it, standing there in the candlelight."

"That's nice to hear, but I can do better than this. Close your eyes."

"All right." Crossing his arms, he closed his eyes, which emphasized just how long and luxurious his lashes were.

"And no peeking." She began to strip.

"Hey, I don't cheat." He said it with a chuckle as if to soften what might be taken wrong.

"Sorry." She tossed her skirt and blouse over the back of a desk chair. With candlelight focused on the bed, the bunks, desks and chairs were almost lost in the shadows. "I have a bad habit of assuming people will."

"Understandable." The twinge of anger in his voice was so mild as to be almost nonexistent.

But she recognized it all the same. She'd become adept at reading moods while living with Tom, a temperamental and unpredictable man. She glanced over and noticed a muscle twitch in Liam's jaw.

Yet his anger didn't make her stomach churn the way Tom's had. Instinctively she knew that he wasn't upset with her for suggesting he might peek and spoil the surprise. Instead his anger was directed at the man who had made her so suspicious. Even though Tom's name hadn't been spoken, he'd become part of their interaction.

She didn't want that, but she wasn't sure how to guarantee it wouldn't happen. She'd been with Tom for a long time. He'd left his mark. Taking a deep breath, she vowed to push him out of her mind and immerse herself in the pleasure Liam offered so freely. She left her bra and panties with her other clothes and padded over to the bed.

Tossing back the top sheet, she stretched out on her side and propped her head on her hand. She wanted to be able to see his expression when he saw her. "You can look now."

He opened his eyes slowly at first, and then they widened and his lips parted. His sharp intake of breath was the loudest sound in the room. Then he swallowed. "Wow." That single syllable, delivered in a near whisper, conveyed a wealth of meaning.

She heard awe and appreciation, desire and eagerness. All good things she hadn't experienced in a very long time.

His chest heaved as he took his time. His gaze traveled slowly and ignited heat along its path. Her nipples tightened and her belly quivered. When his attention lingered at the apex of her thighs, moisture rushed to that tender spot, and her body trembled.

She licked her dry lips. "Was this the fantasy you had in mind?"

"I want you so much I can barely breathe."

"Then come and get me, cowboy."

"Oh, yeah." He tossed his hat to the floor and began ripping off his clothes.

She'd never seen a cowboy discard his hat so carelessly. Or pull off his boots with no regard to where they landed. His clothes ended up in a heap on the floor.

From this angle, she had a view of his pride and joy that could have been intimidating if she wasn't so wet and ready. He yanked open a desk drawer and took out a condom, which he'd obviously made handy this afternoon.

She imagined him preparing this seductive hideaway, and lust swept through her already tingling body. "Put your hat back on," she murmured.

He held her gaze as he finished rolling on the condom. "Okay." He located his black Stetson and settled it on his head before sliding into bed next to her. "Does that work for you?"

"Uh-huh." She gulped for air as he rolled her to her back and moved over her. Talk about a fantasy.

"You realize a hat gets in the way if I want to kiss you."

"Do you want to?"

"Yes. I love kissing you."

"I love kissing you, too." She ached for him in a way she'd never ached for a man before. "You can kiss me after."

"After what?" His smile was the second sexiest thing about him.

"After you take care of business."

"Like this?" He slid his thick, warm cock in deep.

"Exactly like that." She looked up into blue eyes that had turned navy with passion. The hat thrilled her, too. That might be shallow, but she was living out a fantasy, and fantasies were by definition shallow. "Now move it. Please."

"I was hoping you'd ask." He withdrew slowly. "But I don't think we should rush this, do you?"

Rushing sounded like a wonderful idea, but she had her pride. "Of course not."

"We have plenty of time." He eased back in and stayed there for a delicious moment. "We've both waited for this all day, so we should take our time and enjoy being together."

"Mmm." His fullness inside her was setting off shock waves that would soon result in a climax, whether he moved or not. "I'm ready to come."

"I see."

"So I'd appreciate it if you'd—"

"Sure thing." And he began to thrust.

Oh, heaven! Oh, glorious, electrifying perfection! She rose to meet him and dug her fingers into the flexing muscles of his firm butt. She had the fleeting thought that cowboys had firmer butts than writers. Then she forgot to think at all. She came, and she belatedly hoped the windows were closed because she wasn't quiet about it. Once again she probably swore.

Gradually his motion slowed, and she became aware

that she'd had a climax but he hadn't. She gathered enough air into her lungs to attempt speech. "What about you?"

"I held off."

She looked into those incredible eyes. And the hat. She'd never forget the hat. "So gentlemanly!"

"So practical. You're going to come again."

"I don't—"

"Hey, we've been through this. You can do it. I, on the other hand, am likely to be out of commission for a while once I let go. So get with the program, pretty lady. You're doing it with a hat-wearing cowboy. Make the moment count."

She stopped caressing his butt even though that was lovely, and cradled his face in her hands. "Hear me, Liam Magee. You are not just a hat. You're a man I greatly admire. Got it?"

He chuckled. "Are you making memories, Hope?"

"Memories? What are you talking about?"

"Never mind." He began to stroke with a controlled intensity. "Just come for me. We'll sort it out later."

She couldn't resist his seductive rhythm. Sexual tension built with an inevitability she was beginning to associate with Liam. He seemed to know how to coax a response from her no matter what. If she thought about that too long, she'd become alarmed.

So instead she abandoned herself to the erotic sensation of his talented cock bringing her to another shattering orgasm. This time he shared the experience, which made it far more satisfying. His deep groan, his shudders and the rapid pulse she absorbed in the depths of her body felt right.

Mutual climaxes were special, and she hadn't had all that many of them. She'd never considered the bonding that happened when two people enjoyed this pleasure simultaneously, their bodies linked together as spasms rocked them.

With sudden insight, she realized Tom had been stingy about sharing the moment with her, as if he couldn't allow himself to be that vulnerable. The minute thoughts of him intruded on her amazing experience with Liam, she pushed them away. They didn't belong here in this beautiful setting.

Gradually their breathing quieted, and Liam pushed himself up on his elbows to smile at her. "Nice."

"Uh-huh." He was still wearing the hat. Looking up at him, she knew this image would live in her memory forever, no matter how temporary their affair was.

"That was a first for me," he murmured.

"Climaxing at the same time?"

"No. Climaxing while wearing my hat."

"Oh." She had no business being jealous. At least she had the distinction of being the only woman who'd insisted on the hat. "I can't speak for you, but I found it memorable."

"Good. Can I take it off, now? My head's hot."

She laughed. "That's not the only part of you that's smokin', cowboy."

His reaction was adorable. He blushed. "Thanks."

He laid the hat beside the mattress, brim up. "Wish I didn't have to move, but I do." He brushed a kiss over her mouth. "Condoms aren't the most romantic part of a fantasy." He eased away from her and crawled out of bed.

"Rosie said she taught all her boys to be responsible."

"Oh, she certainly did." He returned and stretched out beside her.

She rolled over to face him. "You realize she expects us to end up together."

"Yeah." He combed her hair back behind her ear. "Does that bother you?"

"I can handle it. She's not my foster mother. What about you?"

"I want to have sex with you until neither of us can see straight."

Tension curled within her as she looked into the intense blue of his eyes. "I see."

"I hope so." He rubbed the pad of his thumb over her bottom lip. "You've offered me a chance most guys would kill for. You were skittish at first, but now you seem like a woman ready for anything."

She vibrated with excitement. "I am."

"So am I." Holding her mouth open with his thumb, he closed the distance between them and gave her a kiss that left no doubt how ready he was.

14

LIAM HAD NEVER been in a situation quite like this, and he found it liberating. Hope had asked him for a sexual adventure and nothing more. In the long run, he wanted it to become something more, but in the meantime, she needed an uninhibited lover to help release the tension of all she'd been through. At first he'd thought of her issues as a handicap, but now he saw them as an asset.

Compared to her ex, he could do no wrong. She was eager for the escape from reality that he could give her with plenty of sex and multiple orgasms. That excited him. *She* excited him. Providing what she needed should be no trouble at all.

Thrusting his tongue deep into her mouth, he tasted surrender. Her soft moan told him she was willing to give him whatever he asked. His blood heated and his cock swelled. He touched her, fondling her breasts, sliding his hand between her thighs, arousing her until she trembled with need.

So did he. He'd had the foresight to grab several condoms and dump them beside the mattress. Maybe they'd use them all. He had no idea. But they were about to use another one. He lifted his mouth from hers and gulped for air. "Roll onto your stomach."

He wanted her. Wanted *this*.

As he put on a condom, she did as he'd asked and lay with her arms out and her legs spread. Her golden hair was tousled, and her skin glowed with the moisture of arousal. Heart pounding, he moved over her and combed her hair aside to kiss her nape.

She shuddered. "I need you again," she murmured.

"I need you again, too." The ache in his balls was almost more than he could stand. Slowly he trailed kisses down the length of her back. Then he bracketed her hips in both hands. "Lift up."

Sliding her knees forward, she raised her sweet ass, and he almost came. But he clamped down on that urge so that he could lean down and kiss her bottom. The urge to take her nearly overwhelmed him, but he wanted to taste her first, to nibble and nip the smooth, perfect curves and listen to her quick gasps of pleasure. Inhaling, he drew in the rich aroma of a sexually aroused woman.

Moaning, she lifted even higher. Her blatant invitation shattered his restraint. Grasping her hips, he straightened and probed her channel with the tip of his cock. She was slick and hot.

She quivered. "Please."

With a guttural cry he barely recognized as his own, he drove forward and she came, wave upon wave of contractions that tore groans of pleasure from her throat. When her spasms slowed, he continued to thrust steadily, the breath hissing through his teeth as he fought against the orgasm that demanded release. *Not yet, not yet, not yet.*

Then he felt her tighten, heard the change in her breathing. "Again," he murmured.

"Yes."

Her triumphant reply galvanized him. His thighs slapped hers ever faster. He was going to come. Very soon. Quickly sliding his hand over her hip and between her legs, he cupped her drenched curls. The cabin filled with their harsh breathing as he slipped one finger into her sensitive cleft.

As if he'd touched a live wire, she erupted. Her climax triggered his and he pushed deep, anchoring himself as his body shook and his ears buzzed. She might have been swearing, but he'd been temporarily deafened by the roar of his blood and the pounding of his heart.

Gradually they untangled themselves, and he got up to toss the condom in the wastebasket. When he returned to the bed, she was sitting up.

She glanced at him and smiled. "That was intense."

"No kidding." He climbed in and sat facing her. Terrific view. Her breasts moved seductively as she worked the tangles out of her hair with her fingers.

"Great," she said.

"Uh-huh." She had outstanding breasts. A man lucky enough to see her naked every night would be a lucky SOB. Hard to imagine some idiot throwing that privilege away.

"Sweaty."

"Goes with the territory." He noticed a bead of moisture caught in the hollow of her throat. "Hold still." Leaning in, he licked it away. Then he moved along her collarbone, tasting her salty skin. "Lie back and I'll give you a tongue bath."

She caught his head and made him look at her. "And we both know where that will lead."

"Maybe, maybe not." He grinned. "I might be out of ammunition. You never know."

She glanced down at his cock, which was already responding. Meeting his gaze, she lifted her eyebrows.

"I can't explain it," he said with a shrug. "I touch you and up it goes. That hasn't happened since I was seventeen."

"Very flattering."

"Makes me feel pretty damn good, too. Judging from my recovery rate, I have a real shot at being your fantasy man."

"I never doubted it."

"Thanks." Smiling, he brushed his thumb over her nipple. "Lie back," he murmured. "Let me lick you all over and see where that takes us." He cupped her breast and began a gentle kneading motion.

Desire lit her gray eyes, and her breathing quickened. "Like there's any question."

"You're right, there's not. My tongue and your body are an explosive combination."

"And I would love every minute of it. But...but I—" She closed her eyes. "Damn, that feels good."

"Think of how great my tongue is going to feel." He drew closer and settled his mouth over hers. Kissing her softly, he started easing her to her back.

To his surprise, she put her hands on his chest and pushed. He lifted his head. "Hope?"

"We need sleep." Her voice was soft and breathy as she rubbed her palms over his sensitized skin. "I should go."

"You don't seem very sure about that."

"Because you have awesome pecs. And you're a great lover, damn it."

"You say that like it's a bad thing." He nibbled on her bottom lip and enjoyed the feel of her hands on him. He wouldn't mind if she moved them a little lower.

"It is if I fall asleep in the middle of Phil and Damon's wedding."

He stopped nibbling and looked into her half-closed eyes. "Are you worried about that?"

"Aren't you?" Her hand wandered south, and she wrapped her fingers around his now very erect buddy.

"Didn't think of it."

"Me, either. I expected we'd do this once, maybe twice."

"I see. Now that we're heading into round three, you're wondering if you're in for a marathon that lasts until dawn."

Her breath caught. "Could you really keep going that long?"

"When you're holding my cock, I feel like I could go all week."

"I know that's an exaggeration." She fondled him as she held his gaze.

"I'd be happy to test it."

"I have an idea."

"Me, too. If you keep that up much longer, you'll be able to guess what it is."

"Can you reach a condom?"

He leaned back and grabbed one off the floor. "Am I putting this on or are you?"

"Me." She held out her free hand. "But we need to make a pact." She tore the wrapper open with her teeth.

"Name it." He tightened both fists and held his breath as she began rolling on the condom.

She snapped it into place and put her hands on his shoulders. "Stay right where you are. I'm climbing aboard."

"Works for me." Oh, man, did it ever. When she braced her knees on either side of his hips and began sliding down that fire pole, he felt his eyes roll back in his head. He just prayed he wouldn't come right away. She was the one moving and he wanted time to enjoy the visual, although watching her would likely put him over the edge.

Once she was firmly ensconced around his rigid cock, she massaged his shoulders and gazed into his eyes. "You look happy."

"If I was any happier I'd be airborne." He cupped her bottom in anticipation. Oh, yeah.

She smiled. "I'll keep you from flying away."

"Or maybe we'll both have liftoff."

"Speaking of liftoff, don't make me come twice this time."

He squeezed gently, loving the feel of her beneath his fingertips. "Well, shoot, where's the fun in that?"

"I mean it. When I come, you come. Saves time."

"This is an exercise in efficiency?"

"Yes. We each get one more orgasm and then we leave this cozy cabin so we can get some sleep. That's the pact we have to make."

"Or what?"

She narrowed her eyes. "Are you gonna give me trouble, Magee?"

"No, ma'am. I never give pretty ladies trouble. Just orgasms."

"Then why did some woman bite you?"

"We shouldn't be talking about this when my cock's buried in your—"

"Sure we should.

"I was kissing her when she came."

"And she *bit* you?"

"She came really hard. Said she got carried away because it was the best…well, never mind."

For a woman who claimed she didn't want to get involved, Hope didn't seem to like hearing any of this. She appeared jealous, which made no sense.

"Do you still see her?"

"Sure. She's one of the rafting guides."

"Do you still…"

"No. She's married to one of the other guides now." And damned if Hope didn't look relieved.

She touched the scar. "Does her husband know how you got this?"

"He hasn't heard it from me. I'm guessing she wouldn't mention it."

"I'm guessing not, either." Leaning forward, she gave him an open-mouthed kiss.

He might be imagining it, but the kiss felt a little possessive. And a lot sexy. She sucked on his tongue as she began rotating her hips in a tight circle. Their discussion had taken his mind off coming, but he was right back to it now. Squeezing her soft bottom, he groaned and thrust upward.

Lifting her mouth away from his, she took a shaky breath. "Easy, cowboy," she murmured.

"I thought you wanted this over quick."

"Not that quick." Her breath was warm on his face. "I want to make sure I get my ride." Using his shoulders for balance, she eased upward.

He decided it was no coincidence that she paused at the exact point where her nipples were within licking distance. "Stay like that for a minute."

"I thought I would."

"Maybe two minutes." He cradled a breast in each hand and paid attention to both. When he began to suck, her core muscles clenched. He could make her come this way, but then they'd be done. So he went back to licking and massaging. Again he felt the constriction of her impending climax.

He leaned back and gazed up at her. "If I keep this up you're going to—"

"I know." She gulped. "And I said only one, but—"

"Rules were made to be broken." He drew one tight nipple into his mouth and rhythmically sucked as he pinched and squeezed the other.

Trembling and gasping, she dug her fingers into his shoulders and claimed her release. Somehow he managed to hold off, although with her tremors massaging the tip of his cock and her breast filling his mouth, that wasn't so easy. Still, the idea of breaking her rule gave him extra motivation.

He continued to kiss her breasts as she recovered enough to stop digging her fingers into his shoulders. He loved the weight nestled into his palms and the incredibly soft texture of her skin. He tried not to think about the day he wouldn't be allowed this close, the day she called a halt to everything.

He'd been arrogant to think he could change her mind, especially in a week. But he did find her jealousy fascinating. There was no other word for the way she'd reacted when he'd explained why he had the scar.

With a sigh of pleasure, she sank down onto his cock again and looked into his eyes. "Thank you for being flexible."

His burst of laughter apparently surprised her, because she blinked.

"Sorry." He brushed her cheek with the back of his hand. "It's just that nothing about me is flexible right now. I'm stiff all over, especially the part of me that's intimately connected with you."

Locking her hands behind his neck, she leaned back. "Would you say, then, that you're thick and firm?"

"Very."

"We weren't just talking about fries tonight."

"I know."

"Liam, thank you for indulging me in this fantasy. Some men would tell me to go to hell, but you didn't."

"I can't imagine any man stupid enough to tell you to go to hell."

"I can." And she began to move, treating him to the incredible sensation of her sliding up and down his very thick and firm cock.

"Yeah, well, too bad for him." He wondered if that jerk had ever appreciated her. Unlikely. But for the next week, the only time he'd been given, he'd appreciate her to the depths of his soul. "I'm here and he's not."

15

HOPE HAD WORRIED she might be wired, but she slept better than she had since Tom left. She could tell by the angle of the sun that she'd stayed in bed longer than she ever had at home. Apparently Liam-induced orgasms had a beneficial effect.

While she showered and dressed, she naturally thought about that tall cowboy. Judging from the mutual pleasure so far, ending the affair after a week wouldn't be easy on either of them. She'd likely still see him when he picked up or dropped off rafting clients.

She'd set up the rules, which meant she could break them just like she'd broken one last night. They could keep dating after they returned to Cody. And then what? Nothing ever stayed the same, so they'd either get sick of each other and break up, which would suck, or they'd get more attached and move in together.

That was the part making her stomach churn. She couldn't face the idea of bringing another person so close, at least not until she figured out who she was and where she was going. She used to know, but she didn't anymore.

Talking with Chelsea had made her realize that her current job was only a placeholder, something to pay the rent and buy groceries. And she *really* didn't know what to do with her spare time. Maybe stained glass would turn out to be the exact thing she needed. But if her job wasn't fulfilling, then she should probably start there and figure out what she really wanted to do to earn money.

Adding a man to the mix wouldn't help. He'd have suggestions. Men always seemed to have suggestions, at least the ones she'd known. This was something she needed to work through on her own.

She'd miss Liam after this week was over, and not only because of the sex. He was good company and a compassionate friend. But despite agreeing to a short affair, he was at heart a long-term kind of guy.

A week while they were both in Sheridan didn't bother her conscience too much. Chances were he wouldn't find his perfect partner this week. If she had any inkling that a wedding guest could be that person, she'd back away immediately. Really she would.

She walked into the kitchen hoping to find Liam there, but once again she was disappointed. Chelsea sat at the kitchen table eating breakfast and chatting with Rosie but otherwise the kitchen was deserted.

Rosie and Chelsea greeted her with smiles and comments about how rested she looked. She was glad she'd insisted on leaving at a somewhat reasonable hour last night so she hadn't walked into the kitchen looking like a zombie. Rosie wanted to fix her some breakfast, but she insisted on doing it herself.

"Then I'll make another pot of coffee," Rosie said. "This is the quiet before the storm, so we should sit and enjoy it."

"I hope that's not literally true." Chelsea left the table to peer out the kitchen window at the clouds hanging over the Big Horn Mountains, then checked her phone.

"Looks like a few showers midday but it'll clear by four, which is perfect timing."

"So where is everybody?" Hope cracked two eggs into a small frying pan.

"Last-minute errands in town," Rosie said. "Liam and Grady offered to pick up the cake and flowers. Herb and Finn are getting the matching vests for the four guys. They had to order them from a place in Jackson, and they didn't show up until late yesterday afternoon."

"I saw a picture," Chelsea said. "They'll be stylin'. I like a man in a vest."

"You and me, both," Rosie said with a chuckle. "Anyway, I already had my hair done, but Edie's doing Lexi's and Phil's while Damon, Cade and Karl are... God knows what those men are up to. I told them not to drive out here and pester us because they'd only get in the way."

"Obviously I decided to stay here and keep Rosie company," Chelsea said. "It gave us a chance to talk."

"Oh!" Hope turned, the spatula in her hand. "Am I interrupting? I can eat on the porch."

"You're not interrupting a thing," Rosie said. "Chelsea was just filling me in on how well Finn's doing."

"With his microbrewery?" Hope dished her eggs and got a fork from the silverware drawer.

"O'Roarke's is doing well," Chelsea said, "but the key thing is that Finn is learning how to balance ownership of the business with having a personal life."

"Chelsea's teaching him that." Rosie grabbed the coffee carafe and a mug for Hope from the counter. "He'd turned into a real workaholic, but he's a lot better since he and Chelsea moved in together."

"That can change things." *For good and bad.*

"I wasn't even sure if it would work." Chelsea added cream to her coffee. "Thank goodness it did. We've talked about making it official, but we're both really busy, so we have to find a good time."

"I wish you'd have the wedding here," Rosie said, "but I know your folks are in Washington."

"They are, plus a whole bunch of relatives." Chelsea leaned over and squeezed her arm. "Nothing says we can't repeat our vows in a small ceremony at the ranch."

Rosie's blue eyes sparkled. "I would purely love that."

"So would Finn. So would I, in fact. I adore this ranch." She turned to Hope. "It's your first visit, right?"

Hope nodded as she ate. "It's been great. Seeing Phil after all this time and then being able to meet everyone here has been wonderful. I'm so glad she invited me."

"Well, of course she would!" Chelsea laughed. "You stole flowers together. You're bonded for life!"

"We're lucky Mrs. Eddleston was the forgiving type." Hope picked up her coffee.

"She'd have to be made of stone not to melt when she heard that song," Rosie said. "If four girls appeared on my porch and sang to me, I couldn't have stayed mad at them, either. And it's not like I was a pushover."

Chelsea smiled at Hope. "I asked Phil if you'd written other songs and she said no, but that you were always writing something—stories, little plays, poetry. And you told me you weren't artistic." She gave her a mock frown. "You were holding out on me."

"Not really." Hope kept her tone light. "I don't do any of that now."

"Why not?"

Hope shrugged. "The well ran dry."

"That's too bad." Chelsea gazed at her with a speculative look in her eyes. "You mean like writer's block?"

"Something like that."

"What a shame."

"The world has more than enough writers," Hope said with a chuckle. She glanced over at Rosie. "Not to change the subject, but I never did ask you whether you, Edie and Lexi are coordinating your outfits for the ceremony."

"We most certainly are. Can't have the men outshine us."

"You should see what she's wearing," Chelsea said. "Go get it, Rosie. It's fabulous."

Rosie left the table and hurried through the living room.

Chelsea leaned toward Hope. "I'm sorry."

"For what?"

"I didn't handle that very well. I shouldn't have asked you why you stopped writing. I don't know you well enough to ask such a personal question, and I apologize."

The concern in her voice had the oddest effect on Hope. Her throat closed, and tears spilled out of her eyes. Good God, was she *crying*?

"Oh, Hope." Chelsea covered her hand and squeezed.

Drawing in a sharp breath, Hope raced out of the kitchen and nearly collided with Rosie. "Be right back!" she called as she ran down the hall. "Got something in my eye!"

She was breathing hard by the time she closed the bathroom door, leaned against the sink and battled tears that she couldn't let fall. What the hell was wrong with her? But deep down she knew. Being here was bringing up issues she'd foolishly thought she'd dealt with.

Liam was making her feel things again and Chelsea, being creative herself, sensed that Hope was struggling after losing her outlet. Chelsea's soul-deep understanding of Hope's hidden pain had nearly caused a meltdown.

This was not the time or place. Her high school friend was getting married in a few hours, and Phil didn't need any drama on her special day. Getting involved with Liam had been a mistake.

But ending things would only make them both miserable at a time when everyone was supposed to be filled with lightness and joy. Hope vowed to hold it together, although now Chelsea had seen a crack in her facade. With luck, Chelsea wouldn't discuss that with Rosie.

Blotting her eyes with a towel, she took several deep breaths and inspected herself in the mirror. She was flushed and her eyes were a little red, but that could happen if you got a foreign object lodged in your eye.

Chelsea and Rosie were laughing about something when she walked into the kitchen, which was a good sign that Chelsea hadn't said anything to make Rosie worry. "So where's this dress?" Hope asked.

Rosie stood and held it up. "Ta-da!"

"I *love* it." Hope didn't have to fake her response. The lace dress was a combination of Victorian and Western, with a high neck and graceful lines. "Do you have boots?"

Reaching under the table, Rosie produced a pair that looked as if they buttoned up the side but in fact had a hidden zipper. "The women had all this picked out months ago," Rosie said. "The guys waited until the last minute to order their vests."

"They're embroidered," Chelsea said, "so they all look like riverboat gamblers. At first they were going to wear coats, but the women nixed that idea. Coats would be hot and besides, we like how the vests emphasize their pecs."

"Perfect. I can hardly wait. This will be a beautiful wedding."

"As long as we don't end up with a thunderstorm." Rosie folded the dress over her arm and picked up her boots.

"It wouldn't dare," Chelsea said.

"I'll be back in a flash," Rosie said. "I hate to make you both work, but we need to organize the hors d'oeuvres before the men get back."

"That's what I'm here for," Chelsea said.

"Me, too." Hope glanced at Chelsea after Rosie left the room. "Did you tell her—"

"Of course not. It was my fault that you got emotional. You have everything locked down for this event, and I respect that. I'm so sorry that I upset you."

"Obviously I still have some things to deal with."

"I know." Chelsea met her gaze. "I wish to hell I wasn't leaving tomorrow. I have no idea what happened, but I think you need a friend."

Hope swallowed. "I think so, too." She hadn't realized until this weekend that she'd denied herself close friends because they might probe too deep. But she needed friendship. Everyone did.

"Come to Seattle if you can get away. We have room, and it's a mellow city. Lots of creative vibes there."

"Thanks. I'll consider it." She gave Chelsea a quick hug. Then she sniffed and stepped back. "Too bad it's too early for coffee and Baileys."

"Is it? The sun's over the yardarm somewhere!"

LIAM HAD BEEN entrusted to carry in the multitiered wedding cake, which was protected by a specially designed box. He and Grady had argued who would carry it into the house. Liam maintained that it was more like a sculpture so Grady should be in charge. Grady had insisted that his sculptures wouldn't be crushed if he dropped them, while Liam was used to balancing a raft full of tourists. Yeah, maybe he'd dumped one or two, but he'd retrieved them quickly. His record was impressive.

Besides, Grady had held the boxed cake on his lap all the way from Sheridan, which he claimed was his valuable contribution to the effort. Not once had any portion of that tiered cake box touched the dashboard. They'd kept the AC on freeze to make sure the fancy decorations didn't melt.

While Liam didn't want the responsibility of carrying in the cake, he accepted it because—bottom line—he was the oldest and he was used to being in charge of things. Grady had that much right. So Liam maneuvered up the porch with Grady in the lead like a seeing-eye cowboy. They'd left the flowers in the truck for now because the cake was the major deal. One slip and it was all over.

They had a bad moment when the toe of Liam's boot caught on the bottom step, but he didn't go down. Even more important, he kept the cake level. He decided if he ever got married, there would be no cake. Cupcakes, maybe. Damon, of course, had to have the traditional wedding cake with the cute little bride and groom on the top. Liam had that embellishment in his shirt pocket.

Once he was on the porch, he could hear country music coming from inside the house and women laughing. Sounded as if somebody had decided to get this party started.

"I'll hold the door open," Grady said.

"I'd appreciate that." He had to turn sideways, but he got the box through the opening. Grady directed him toward the kitchen, where the music was playing.

He heard Rosie cry out, "The cake!" but he couldn't see a damn thing over the top of it.

"Put it on the kitchen table for now," Rosie said.

"But where's its final resting place?" Liam didn't want to put it down in one spot and then watch some well-meaning bumblehead try to move it.

"On the pool table," Rosie said. "You got here a little sooner than I expected, and we don't have it ready. Hang on. Hope, Chelsea, Grady, help me set up the cover and tablecloth."

Liam stood in the kitchen with the tiered box blocking his view while a current country favorites blasted in his ears. He could smell coffee and...Baileys? Surely not this early. By his calculations it was only a little past noon.

"Okay, that does it." Rosie appeared by his side and took his elbow. "I'll guide you into the rec room. Be sure and step over the sill."

"I remember about the sill. Tripped on it a few times. Have you already busted out your favorite drink?"

"A little bit." Rosie laughed. "It's a celebration, after all. Okay, you're almost there. Easy does it. You're at the pool table. Put it down. Gently...gently...there!"

He set down the box with more relief than he felt bringing a raft up on shore with everyone still aboard.

"Nicely done."

He turned to face Hope, who stood holding a coffee mug and wearing a saucy grin. "Having a good time?"

"The best." She took a swig of her special coffee. "I love this ranch."

"Good, because I love it, too." But he couldn't help wondering how loving this place fit in with ditching him at the end of the week. She'd effectively be cutting herself off from Thunder Mountain Ranch. Was she contemplating an extension of their relationship? He'd cautioned himself not to wish for that, but when she stood there smiling at him, her gray eyes filled with laughter, he did wish for it. Oh, yes, he definitely did.

16

THAT BRIEF EXCHANGE of smiles was all Liam was able to share with Hope for the next few hours. Although the wedding wasn't until four, guests started arriving early. Ty Slater, a former Thunder Mountain foster boy, drove up from Cheyenne with his fiancée, Whitney Jones. Liam and Grady hadn't seen Ty in years and they'd never met Whitney, so they had plenty to talk about.

Close on Ty's and Whitney's heels came Brant Ellison, the gentle giant of the Thunder Mountain boys. He'd just finished training a new foal for a rancher up in Montana. On his way back through town, he'd stopped to pick up his girlfriend, Aria, and her brother Josh. Josh was recovering from a riding accident and used a cane to get around, but Liam didn't think the guy would need it much longer.

Rosie had mentioned Aria because she owned Lucy and Linus, the mare and colt Rosie and Herb were boarding. Brant had spent a couple of weeks training Linus from birth, and clearly the big guy had fallen hard for Aria. Last Liam had heard, Brant was constantly on the move training foals, but Aria didn't seem to mind his frequent absences, and she obviously adored him, too.

Liam could remember a time not so long ago when none of the guys from Thunder Mountain had been seriously involved. That seemed to be changing. It made sense, though. Most of them had reached an age when thoughts turned to settling down.

Even he'd started thinking about it. He and Grady had discussed what they'd do if one of them found the right woman. Their shared apartment in the barn above Grady's workshop wouldn't work anymore. But no use worrying about it yet. He'd be foolish to expect something real to develop with Hope.

In the middle of all the talk about weddings and engagements, Herb and Finn walked in with the vests, which everyone had to admire. Next Damon, Cade and Karl showed up with a plan to shoot pool until they had to get dressed for the ceremony.

Liam personally kept them from moving the cake, which they'd been fully prepared to do. Muttering "Over my dead body" under his breath, he redirected the action by setting up a game of horseshoes in the side yard. Soon everyone drifted outside to play or cheer on the contestants.

After a quick buffet lunch with wine, beer and Baileys, the party was in full swing. Everyone was there except the bride and two of her attendants, who planned to arrive by three.

Liam wondered if he was the only one keeping an eye on the weather. Come to think of it, he was the most likely since weather was critical in his line of work. When Damon beat him at horseshoes and moved on to the next challenger, Liam rounded the house for a better view of the dark clouds hanging over the mountains.

A moment later Herb joined him. "What do you think?"

"Depends on whether they stay there or not. Chelsea said her weather app predicted Sheridan would be clear by four."

"The guy on TV said the same thing."

"I've learned to take those predictions as an educated guess."

Herb chuckled. "Wise man."

"Do you and Rosie have a plan B?"

"Sort of. Rosie has her heart set on this sentimental idea of seeing them married in front of the cabin they built last summer. The new rec building would have been a safer choice."

"Yeah, it would." Liam understood Rosie's preference, though. The rec building had been built early last fall. It stood back behind the cabins and doubled as a classroom during the day and a place for the teenagers to hang out in the evening. Although it was extremely useful, no one would call it charming.

"That's my plan B." Herb scratched his jaw. "But we'd have to get it ready in the next hour if we had any chance of being done by four. I doubt Rosie would go for that. Damon and Phil wouldn't be happy about it, either."

Liam took another look at the thunderheads. Lighting flashed inside one of them, which was pretty but didn't increase his confidence that the storm would pass by harmlessly. "How many guests are coming?"

"Should be a total of twenty. Eight are already here."

"Any more of the Thunder Mountain guys?"

"No, unfortunately. We let them know about it, but they had issues of one sort or another and couldn't make it. Phil had some people she wanted to invite, anyway, and apparently it's nice if you have a good balance between the groom's guests and the bride's guests."

"I wouldn't know about that. Never studied wedding etiquette."

"Not my area, either, but it's Rosie's for sure. Anyway, the others should start arriving around three-thirty or so."

"So what is it, now? About three?"

Herb glanced at his watch. "On the dot." He turned as an SUV swung into the circular drive in front of the house. "And here comes the bride."

Herb wasn't the only one who'd noticed the SUV with Edie at the wheel and Phil and Lexi inside. As they got out, Rosie ran over with Hope, Chelsea, Whitney and Aria close behind. In a flurry of bags, boxes and laughter, the women unloaded the SUV. Then they all headed for the house.

Herb smiled. "Rosie's waited so long for one of her boys to get married here. It's great to see her so excited."

"They all seem pretty excited." Even Hope, he thought. Good. She seemed to be having fun, so maybe she was keeping her demons at bay.

"Guess that means it's time for the rest of us to put on our party duds." Herb glanced at the clouds again. "Do they look closer to you?"

"Yep. They're moving this way." The wind picked up. "Wow. They're coming in fast, Herb."

"Damn."

"Look, before we change clothes, we could all work together and get the chairs into the rec building. We might have time to add some greenery and flowers to make it look a little nicer."

Herb rubbed the back of his neck. "Rosie would hate the idea of moving the venue."

Lightning zigzagged across the sky, and Liam automatically counted the seconds before he heard the crackle and boom that followed. "She might hate it, but we don't have a choice. Even if we could hold the ceremony this very minute, I wouldn't like our chances of finishing before it hits. And lightning is damned unpredictable."

"Then let's get Damon and go talk with Rosie and Phil. I want a consensus before we move anything."

"Okay. It can't be a long debate, though. We don't have much time."

"I realize that. But when you've been married as long as I have, you don't make this kind of decision without consulting your spouse. You'll understand that better someday." He started toward the side lawn at a rapid pace.

"Assuming I find somebody as perfect for me as Rosie is for you."

Herb didn't break stride. "Rosie thinks you already have."

"She's wrong."

"Son, have you forgotten the number one rule around here?"

Liam grinned. "Rosie's never wrong?"

"That's the one."

"I haven't forgotten. I'll keep my opinion to myself."

"Doesn't matter if you do or not. And I should warn you, she has a sixth sense about these things."

"Hmm."

They reached the group playing horseshoes, and Herb paused to allow Damon to finish his throw. Another ringer. The guy was deadly at this game, but Liam had known that when he'd set it up. The groom should be allowed to dominate the competition on his wedding day. Besides, the cake was safe.

"I hate to break this up, Damon," Herb said, "but I need you to come with me into the house."

"We should all go and get changed," Cade said.

"I volunteer my cabin for any of you who want to

avoid the chaos in the house," Finn said. "Chelsea told me she'd be getting dressed with the rest of the women, so there's only me in there."

"Don't any of you change clothes yet," Liam said. "Let's wait and see whether we have to move chairs into the rec building."

Damon groaned.

"Look at the sky, bro."

He glanced up and swore. "I was hoping this wouldn't happen."

"Sorry." Liam squeezed his shoulder.

"Damon and I are going in to consult with Rosie and Phil," Herb said. "Everybody else hang tight until we have a plan. Except for you, Liam. You're the weather expert. Come in with us and make your case."

So he'd get to be the Voice of Doom. Great. But Herb needed backup, and keeping people safe was what Liam did.

Herb headed down the hall to summon Phil and Rosie to the living room. The sound of a muted argument drifted from the hall to the living room.

Liam glanced at Damon. "You're with me on this, right? It would be a mistake to try and hold it outside as planned."

"I'm with you," Damon said, "but I hate that the original idea is ruined. That cabin really is special to us."

"Didn't you and Phil work on the rec building together, too?"

"Yeah, sure. But it's not nearly as significant. Although I'm proud of it, there's nothing about it that makes you go, 'Wow, that's awesome.' So I—" He stopped speaking as Herb came into the room with Rosie. "Where's Phil?"

"Half-dressed." Rosie didn't look happy. She wore a

lacy, high-necked outfit, and her feet were bare. "She didn't want you to see her like that."

Damon laughed. "It's not like I've never—"

"That's not the point. How's she supposed to blow you away if you don't get the full effect?"

Damon sobered. "She blows me away every single time I look at her."

"Aww." Rosie's expression softened, and she padded over to pat Damon on the cheek. "I'm going to tell her you said that."

"Please do."

"Okay, but we have something more important to discuss," Herb said. "Liam thinks—"

"I've appointed myself as Phil's representative." Hope came down the hall wearing a Winnie-the-Pooh bathrobe. She was barefoot, and her hair looked as if someone had been pinning it up but made it only halfway around. She held up her phone. "I'm supposed to text her the details of this discussion as it happens."

Until that moment, Liam had convinced himself he could walk away from her when the time came. But as he looked at her standing there in that bathrobe with her hair partly fixed because she'd offered to relay information to her friend, he lost his heart.

Rosie was right. He'd found a woman he could love for the rest of his days. He'd probably known that from the first time he'd walked into the hotel lobby in Cody and spied her behind the concierge desk. She might shoot him down at the end of the week, but until then, he'd give her all he had and pray it was enough.

Herb took a breath and looked squarely at Rosie. The man was not a coward. "We can't have the ceremony outside at four. It's too dangerous."

"It can't be that bad!" Rosie hurried to the window and looked out. "Oh."

"If we move fast," Liam said, "the guys and I can have the chairs in the rec building before the storm hits. Then, if everyone gets changed quickly, we should all be able to make it in there before it starts raining, and we can have the ceremony when it was scheduled. Somebody would need to be stationed on the porch to direct the other guests to drive straight to the rec building, but—"

"Hold it." Hope held up her hand. "Let me text all that to Phil."

"And add that I'm not in favor of Liam's plan, although I don't have a better one." Rosie turned from the window. "Damn it. I knew we had the potential for a storm, but I was convinced that by some magical intervention, this wouldn't happen."

"Well, it has," Herb said. "I'm sorry, Rosie, but I don't see an alternative."

"I don't like the alternative." Rosie folded her arms. "I don't want us all throwing ourselves together and then running into the rec building like we're racing to a storm cellar. That's not elegant, and I—"

"Slow down," Hope said. "I'm texting as fast as I can."

"I don't like it, either," Damon said. "Could we possibly have it here, in the living room?"

"It'd be better than the rec building." Rosie glanced around. "But we'd be packed in like sardines. That's not elegant, either." She turned to Hope. "Has Phil texted back?"

"Nothing I can repeat in mixed company."

Damon laughed. "That's my girl." He glanced around. "The rec room in the house?"

"That's not much better than the living room," Liam said. "We'd still be crammed in there, and I don't think you're supposed to have the ceremony while everyone's staring at the cake."

Rosie shook her head. "None of this sounds right to me. I'm not sure what to do."

"I have an idea." Hope glanced up from her phone. "It might not be any good, but—"

"We're looking for every possible alternative." Liam held her gaze and smiled. He could see the wheels turning, and it thrilled him that she was using that creative brain of hers.

"Okay. I think we need to let go of the idea that the wedding will take place at four o'clock. Nobody really cares about that. It's what's printed on the invitation, but that doesn't matter."

Rosie nodded. "I see where you're going. What about the ten people who aren't here yet?"

"We text them right now and tell them to wait for our signal."

Rosie brightened. "I doubt they've left yet, and they wouldn't want to drive through a thunderstorm, anyway. And we can take our time getting ready."

"Exactly." Hope smiled at her. "When the storm's over, we'll go out to the meadow. It might be a little wet and muddy, but the air will be fresh, and you know how wonderful everything smells after a good rain."

Rosie came over and gave her a hug. "I love this idea."

"Me, too." Damon smiled. "Eliminates all the stress. We can work with Mother Nature instead of against her. But we should find out what Phil thinks."

Hope's thumbs moved rapidly over her phone. Then she waited. Finally she looked up and smiled. "She loves it."

"So we have a plan." Herb looked relieved. "I'll tell

the guys. We should get a move on if we want everyone back in the house before the storm hits."

"We'll make it," Liam said.

Herb nodded. "Yeah, guys, don't take long."

"And the women are nearly ready," Rosie said.

Hope gestured to her bathrobe and hair. "Contrary to what it looks like."

"Great bathrobe, by the way," Liam said.

"Thanks. How do you like my hair?"

"It's…different."

"Diplomatic answer. Fear not. It's only half done. Edie will finish it up for me."

"Then I guess we're set." Herb went over and gave Rosie a quick kiss on the cheek. "Any idea what we should do while we wait out the storm?"

"Are you kidding?" Rosie lifted her eyebrows. "We should party, of course!"

Liam glanced at Hope. When she met his gaze, her eyes sparkled in triumph. She'd avoided a wedding disaster by thinking outside the box. Now if only she could do the same with their situation, this week wouldn't have to end in misery.

Everything had to work out. After introducing him to a sexy, intelligent, creative woman with great taste in bathrobes, surely fate wouldn't be so cruel as to snatch her away again.

17

Hope had come up with a plan, but she realized that it had one major flaw. When she returned to the bedroom and everyone started congratulating her, she looked at Phil. "There's a problem. You're not going to want to hide back here while everyone else parties in the living room."

"You're right." She shrugged. "It's okay. I'll just go out there. No big deal. I don't need a grand entrance."

"Yes, you do." Hope surveyed her friend's confection of a dress, which mirrored the Victorian look of the others with its high collar, but the bodice had been designed with a cutout beneath the collar that dipped low enough to reveal a little cleavage. The dress was classy and sexy, just like the bride. "We can't have you wander into the living room with the rest of us. You need to knock that cowboy's socks off."

"I know what to do," Edie said. "We'll make sure everyone's gathered in the living room and facing the hallway, but we'll station Damon where he gets the best view. We'll put some music on and you can be the last one to walk out."

Phil grinned. "Okay, I like that way better."

Rosie zipped up her boots. "I'm ready. I'll find a good tune."

"Just don't use the wedding march," Phil said. "Damon insisted we play it at the actual wedding, so I don't want to preempt that moment."

"I agree. We want something else. I'll come back to let you know when the men are gathered."

Lexi glanced up from the hand mirror she'd been using to apply her makeup. "You know what? We should *all* make an entrance, one by one, and lead up to the grand finale, which will be Phil."

Edie clapped her hands. "Yes! I like it!"

"And I know just the music." Rosie's blue eyes gleamed with excitement. "I'll play Faith Hill's 'This Kiss.'"

Chelsea smiled. "You do realize a person can't just walk sedately down the hall to the beat of that song."

"I know." Rosie grinned. "I thought we'd dance."

Chelsea gave a little whoop of joy. "This is going to be so fun." Then she glanced at Phil. "Not more fun than your actual wedding, of course."

Phil laughed. "I don't care if it is. I'll love thinking back on how the storm turned my big day into a total riot. Just so you all know, I'm a crappy dancer. Hope can testify to that."

"Uh, well..."

"Come on. I was terrible. I can sing but I can't dance. Remember those slumber parties where everyone tried to teach me?"

"Yeah." Hope smiled. "You were pretty bad." Nostalgic images came flooding back—dancing in Phil's bedroom in their pajamas, eating ice cream at two in the morning, pillow fights followed by pledges of undying friendship.

"Still am bad, but I don't care. This will be epic. Thank *goodness* you came to my wedding. It's like old times."

Hit by a wave of emotion for the second time today, Hope could only nod.

"Are you okay?" Phil asked.

But Hope dashed out of the room. She took refuge in what was no longer her private bathroom, but thankfully it was empty. Dragging in several deep breaths, she dabbed at her eyes. This time she'd have to go back in and confess her real reason for bolting like that. An excuse that she had something in her eye wouldn't wash.

Squaring her shoulders, she returned to the bedroom. Conversation immediately stopped, and everyone became very busy. It would be embarrassing enough to make the speech in front of the women she'd come to know in the past few days, but she didn't know Whitney or Aria at all.

"Sorry. Small meltdown," she said with a tiny smile. "I used to have great times like this with Phil and our other friends when we all lived in Cheyenne and I've… I've missed those times, and them, terribly."

"Aw, sweetie." Phil moved toward her, arms extended.

"No, Phil!" Her laughter was choked with unshed tears as she backed away. "You'll wrinkle your dress."

"I don't care."

"I do." Edie stepped between them. "That dress wrinkles like you wouldn't believe. And I give good hugs, too." She wrapped Hope in her arms.

Somehow Hope kept from breaking down at that sweet and protective gesture. She hugged Edie back and sniffed as she eased away. "You do give good hugs. Thank you."

"She really does," Phil said. "The day we went dress shopping in Jackson, we weren't finding anything, and I was beside myself. Edie gave me a big hug and convinced me to try one more place. That's when we found this one."

Edie swallowed. "Watch out. I'm liable to start bawling, too."

"Buck up, ladies." Chelsea came over and grabbed one of Edie's hands and one of Hope's. "Edie, you have to finish your job on this girl's hair, and she needs to ditch Winnie-the-Pooh and put on that sexy green number hanging on the closet door. The show must go on." She winked at Hope. "Got it, girlfriend?"

"Got it." She had the feeling that of everyone in the room, Chelsea understood her best. A trip to Seattle to visit Chelsea and Finn might be a very good idea. But if she broke off her relationship with Liam, would she still be welcome?

Rosie left to get Faith Hill's song ready to roll, and everyone else put final touches on hair and makeup. Edie finished Hope's elaborate updo and gave her a mirror so she could see it from all sides.

"Gorgeous," Lexi said as she came over to admire it. "Want to steal a couple of flowers from my maid of honor bouquet to tuck in your hair?"

"No!" Hope laughed. "My flower-stealing days are over, thank you very much."

"You need some flowers in that hairdo," Phil said. "Steal some from my bouquet."

"Definitely not from the bride's bouquet! Talk about a bridal etiquette fail."

"Then let me give you some." Lexi went over to the bed where the flower boxes lay.

"She can have a couple from mine, too," Edie said as she added one more hairpin. "Great idea. Flowers will make this arrangement sing."

"No, really." Hope started to get up from the stool where she'd been sitting while Edie worked on her hair. "Don't mess with your bouquets."

"Sit down and let me do this." Edie pushed gently on her shoulders. "It's a work of art, and flowers will be the finishing touch."

"It's pointless to argue," Phil said. "She made me hold perfectly still for this, and I'm a fidgeter." She pointed to her hair. Although it was shorter than Hope's, Edie had managed to weave white satin ribbons through it in an intricate design. "But it was worth every tortuous minute. She really is an artist."

"You'd better believe it." Edie chuckled. "Which means I get to be temperamental."

"Okay." Hope sat down and let Edie tuck flowers into her hair. "But I don't hear any singing from either my hair or the flowers."

"Then allow me," Phil said.

"No, wait! I didn't—" Too late. As Phil entertained Whitney and Aria with the flower-stealing story and song, Hope realized how she'd craved the company of funny, loving women whose gentle teasing let her know they cared. Tom had robbed her of that, too.

By the time Rosie returned with the news that the men were in the living room drinking beer and trading insults, the women had decided on the order for their entrances. Aria and Whitney drew straws to see who went first, and Aria got the lead position. Chelsea would be third, followed by Hope, Lexi, Rosie, Edie and Phil.

"Herb will start the music when I text him," Rosie said, "but he doesn't know what we're up to. It's turned up pretty loud, and I made sure Damon has a good view of the hallway." She glanced around. "Ready?"

Phil nodded. "Let's do it."

Rosie texted Herb, and a moment later, Faith Hill began to sing. Aria went out, and the rest of them crowded into the doorway to see what she'd do.

"Nice," Lexi said as Aria danced her way down the hall. "Okay, Whitney. Go."

Whistles and cheers greeted Aria as Whitney followed a short distance behind.

"That girl has moves," Edie said with an approving nod. "We have talent in this group. You're up, Chelsea."

"Don't expect talent from me." But Chelsea put a sexy wiggle and a shimmy into her routine that made the fringe on her dress vibrate seductively.

"Your turn, Hope." Lexi gave her arm a squeeze. "Go get 'em, tiger."

Hope didn't think of herself as a terrific dancer, either, but they'd formed a team, and she couldn't let them down. The cheers and applause that Chelsea had received were still going on as she began dancing down the hallway in her green sleeveless dress with a revealing slit up one side of the skirt. If no one noticed that slit, the dress was fairly conservative. If they did, then wowza.

She had seconds to decide which way to go. She thought of the effort Edie had put into her hair. She thought of the subtle challenge Chelsea had thrown out with her knowing wink. She thought of fun-loving Phil, who was ready to go for it despite her lack of skill.

She thought of Liam, but he definitely wasn't the reason she would put her heart and soul into this hallway dance. She'd do it to demonstrate solidarity with the rowdy women who had committed to boogying their way into the living room. That was more than enough to make her hips move in time to the rapid beat.

The response from the men standing in the living room was gratifying, and she couldn't help noticing Liam's delighted grin. But Chelsea, Aria and Whitney went nuts, stomping and yelling out a whole chorus of woo-hoos.

They quickly exchanged hugs and high fives before turning to give Lexi the same reception.

The five of them formed a cheering section for Rosie, who performed the cutest little dance step ever. Then Rosie joined the group. She yelled, *"You go, girl!"* when Edie pranced out with moves nobody had expected, except maybe her husband, Karl.

Then Phil appeared, and the throng of women outdid the guys with their shouts and whistles. Phil gyrated down the hall with enthusiasm and the wild hand movements of a nondancer. She hadn't improved a lick since high school. At the entrance to the living room she paused, spread her arms, looked straight at Damon and belted out, "This is as good as it gets, cowboy!"

Everyone laughed except Damon, who walked toward her, cupped her face in both hands and murmured, "Nope. It gets better every damn day." As he kissed her, the response from everyone watching was deafening. It nearly drowned out the crack of thunder, but everyone noticed when the lights went out. Good thing Rosie had plenty of candles on hand.

As the guys came over to offer their congratulations to the ladies, Liam approached, still grinning. "That was amazing."

"Yeah," Hope said, "amazing I didn't fall down. It's been a while since I danced, let alone in heels."

"Ready to take a seat while I bring you a drink?"

She glanced around. Seating was in short supply. "I can stand."

"We brought in some kitchen chairs. Maybe... Ah, there's an empty one. I'll snag it for you."

"Okay." She'd worn the sexy sandals, and they weren't the most comfortable shoes in the world. She settled onto the chair with a sigh of relief. "Thanks."

"I'll be right back."

Giving in to temptation, she unbuckled her shoes and slipped them off. Much better. She wiggled her toes and wondered how the trek to the meadow would go.

Herb whistled for attention. "I'm sure you're all listening to the rain and thinking about mud."

Bingo.

"I've been talking with a few of the guys, and we've decided that when the time comes, we'll drive everyone to the meadow. Having everyone stroll down there was a nice idea until the storm came along."

"Thank you!" Hope called out.

"The bride especially thanks you," Phil added. "I may be wearing boots, but they're wimpy ones."

Liam came back holding a steaming mug in one hand and a bottle of beer in the other.

"Did you hear that?" Hope asked. "About driving to the meadow?"

"Much better." He glanced down at her bare feet. "Although mud can be fun if you're not wearing shoes."

"I will be wearing shoes. This was for temporary relief." She took the mug he handed her. "Thank you."

"Rosie brewed the restaurant-sized pot, but without electricity it'll be cooling off fast." He settled on the floor at her feet. "I'm pretty good at giving foot massages."

"But then you can't drink your beer."

"I can drink beer anytime."

She gazed into his mesmerizing blue eyes, wondering if that was a subtle reference to the temporary nature of their relationship. She wouldn't put it past him.

Setting down his beer, he took her right foot into his lap and began to knead her instep. She moaned softly.

"Better not do that," he murmured. "It reminds me of when I recently heard that sound."

"Sorry. It feels really good, though."

"That's the idea." He nodded toward the mug she clutched in both hands. "Drink up. It could be a long night."

She sipped the coffee and tasted Baileys. "You spiked my coffee."

"I thought you'd want me to."

"I did. Thank you." He was doing a good job of anticipating her wishes. Drinking coffee laced with Baileys while getting a foot rub from a handsome cowboy didn't suck. "Does the power go out often?"

"It does, actually."

"Do they have a generator?" She put great effort into keeping her eyes open when she really wanted to relax against the chair and give herself up to Liam's foot massage.

"They do, but they save it for emergencies, like when it's forty below. This isn't one of those times."

"Sure isn't."

"If we need to, we can gather up the battery-operated lanterns from the barn and the cabins."

"You could have used a couple of those last night."

"I considered it." He circled her heel with the pad of his thumb.

In her relaxed state, she immediately thought about where his thumb had been during last night's sexual adventures. Then she wasn't quite so relaxed. "I like candlelight better."

"I figured you for a candlelight kind of woman." He worked on the ball of her foot and slid his fingers through the spaces in her toes. "And a Winnie-the-Pooh fan."

"I've had that bathrobe a long time. Since high school. I must have looked fetching in my Pooh bathrobe with my hair half-done."

"Yes, ma'am, you did."

Outside the storm raged, and inside the party grew livelier, but in this cozy corner she and Liam seemed set apart from everything and everybody. Smiling, she glanced down at him. "I love cowboy manners. Thanks for that little white lie."

"It wasn't a lie. You looked cute and huggable."

"Nice of you to say so."

"But now that your hair's done, you don't look cute anymore."

"You don't like it?" She felt the twinge of a familiar pain.

"I love it. You look hot."

The pain receded. "That's Edie's doing. I don't usually wear it up."

"Why not?"

"It's extra trouble and it looks better down." She heard an echo of Tom's voice.

"Depends on what you're going for. When it's down it's more touchable, but sweeping it up off your neck like that creates a different kind of sexy, like you're royalty or something, and I'll have to work harder to get you into bed."

"Is that so?" Her body tingled. "Liam Magee, you really are a silver-tongued devil."

"I'm not."

"My BS meter just flipped over to the red zone."

He shrugged. "So don't believe me. But when your hair's up and all that soft skin is exposed, I have the urge to nibble on you until you surrender to my charms."

"I see." If he was trying to arouse her enough to make her squirm, he was succeeding beautifully.

"You were really something, dancing down that hallway."

That made her laugh, which relieved some of the tension. "Oh, I was something, all right. Something you'll never see on *So You Think You Can Dance*?"

"Make fun if you want, but you were sexy as hell."

"All the credit goes to the slit in the skirt."

"That was nice, but you have a certain way of rotating your hips. I almost swallowed my tongue."

"Really?"

"Yes, ma'am." His blue eyes gleamed with lust. Holding her gaze, he reached for her other foot. "Thanks for taking off your shoes so I could have a good excuse to touch you. If I thought I could get away with it, I'd probably have my hand under your skirt by now."

"Liam." Cheeks hot, she glanced around to gauge whether anyone might have heard him.

"They're not listening to us. The storm is making everyone shout to be heard."

"But you're not shouting."

"I don't have to. You're reading my lips, same as I'm reading yours."

He was right. She hadn't even known she was doing it. Watching his mouth move was such a pleasure, anyway. That little scar was an irritant because it reminded her that he'd had great sex with someone else. But it was also a turn-on, a tangible sign that he could make a woman lose her mind enough to draw blood.

Searching for a different focus, she dropped her gaze to where he was using his strong fingers to bring intense pleasure to her feet. She'd experienced the joy of his talented hands on other parts of her body, parts that were warming up at an alarming rate.

She took a sip, but the warm drink and the hot cowboy were a lethal combination. "You should probably stop doing that."

He glanced up at her and kept stroking her instep. "Is there a problem?"

"Yes."

"Can I do anything to help?"

"Not at the moment."

His beautiful mouth curved in a seductive smile. "Later, then?"

"Later." She took a shaky breath. "Definitely later."

18

IN THE PAST, Liam hadn't been particularly concerned about whether a woman craved his body or not. If she did and the feeling was mutual, then great, they'd enjoy the fun while it lasted. If he lusted after someone and she didn't feel the same, he walked away.

But now, for the first time in his life, he was prepared to use everything at his disposal to convince Hope she couldn't give up their sexual pleasure at the end of the week. A week wasn't long enough to create the kind of bond he longed for. Two weeks probably wouldn't do it, either, but if he could get her to extend the deadline once, she might extend it again.

He'd figured out that she didn't know what she wanted long-term. But he was afraid if she shoved him out of her life after a mere seven days, he'd lose her forever. She might not realize they were meant for each other, but he was presumptuous enough to believe they were. Maybe he shouldn't put so much emphasis on her Winnie-the-Pooh bathrobe, but he couldn't seem to help it.

His mother had read those stories to him and Grady when they were little, and he'd never forgotten the characters. He'd identified with Owl, who always seemed to know what to do, but he'd also identified with Christopher Robin, who looked after all of them. He knew he wasn't Pooh, but he'd always loved that bear—trusting, joyful and naturally creative.

After seeing Hope in that bathrobe, everything had clicked into place. Once upon a time she'd functioned like Pooh. Then she'd met Tom, who'd sucked every bit of that optimistic joy out of her. Liam wanted to help her regain that joy because when she did, she'd find herself. She might also decide they were right for each other.

But he couldn't expect her to hear that explanation, agree with it and fall into his arms. So he was willing to use sex to give her a reason to hang around until the light dawned. The foot massage hadn't been planned, but he'd grabbed the opportunity. As long as he could keep touching her and reminding her of the pleasure to be found with him, he might buy a little more time.

She insisted they leave their private corner and mingle. He agreed that was a good idea considering how tight his jeans had become during that foot rub and sexy discussion. But thanks to that, they were both thinking about their rendezvous tonight, and this time they could play until dawn if they wanted to.

The storm cleared as the sun began to set. While Rosie notified the other guests that they could head toward the ranch for the ceremony, Cade and Brant volunteered to feed the horses and check out the meadow. The resulting report made everyone groan.

"The tent's gone," Cade said. "Probably over in Campbell County by now. The chairs are tossed around and muddy, and the decorations on the front of the cabin blew off. The artificial turf stayed put, I guess because we weighed it down with rocks on the corners. It's wet, but it's there."

Damon wrapped an arm around Phil's waist. "It won't be quite the ceremony we'd envisioned." He gazed down at her. "I'm sorry."

Phil didn't look devastated, though. "Let's forget about the chairs and have everyone make a circle around us while we say our vows. We don't need the tent, anyway. We'll get married in the glow of the sunset."

"Instead of a circle," Hope said, "how about a heart with you two and the minister at the point in the middle?"

Liam's own heart tightened. A woman with this much romance in her soul couldn't possibly be happy with a string of temporary lovers. Not telling her that was going to take some restraint.

"Oh." Edie fanned her face and sniffed. "Now I'm ready to bawl again."

Rosie gave her a quick one-armed hug. "No time for that, lady. The guests are on their way. We need to move it."

Rides were arranged, and the guests wore the most practical footwear they had on hand. Rosie and Herb loaned out all the spare rain boots in the closet, and Liam was glad to see that Hope got a pair. Music turned out to be the easy part. Liam backed his truck into position near the meadow, and Aria's brother, Josh, who would have had some trouble navigating the muddy terrain, anyway, offered to sit on the tailgate and keep the tunes coming.

The other guests drove straight to the meadow, and all had worn boots. While Phil and her attendants waited in the SUV parked at the end of the artificial turf aisle, Hope organized the heart shape so that those who would have been sitting on the bride's side formed the left curve and the groom's guests formed the right curve. She created a gap for the maid and matrons of honor and a break at the bottom for Phil, her dad and her attendants to walk through.

Liam watched in admiration and looked forward to finding a place beside her and holding her hand throughout the ceremony. But as the guests divided into two groups, he realized that she'd be on one side and he'd be on the other. They'd be separated. Or maybe not. She was moving to the end of the line on her side.

He quickly switched places with the last person in line on his side. He managed it seconds before Josh started the music. Hope glanced at him with raised eyebrows, and he grinned at her before turning to face the procession coming toward them.

Nobody tried to dance down the rain-slick turf, but from their expressions of joy, they would have if it hadn't been dangerous. Liam had attended a few weddings, most recently one for the woman who'd given him the scar on his lip, but he'd never felt such tenderness toward the participants. Made sense that he'd be emotionally attached to this ceremony, though. These were his people in a way other friends never would be.

Lexi walked toward them in her lacy dress that was so different from the jeans and T-shirts he remembered from years ago. She'd always been riding, working in the barn or teasing the guys, Cade most of all. She'd had an excuse to hang out at Thunder Mountain because her parents, who were standing on the groom's side, were Rosie and Herb's best friends. But she'd mostly been there because of Cade.

Next came Rosie, looking happier than he'd ever seen her. Not every man was lucky enough to have one great mom, let alone two. That, combined with Herb's loving guidance, had more than compensated for not growing up with a dad in residence.

Edie looked radiant, too. She'd become Phil's stepmother only a few years ago, but judging from the way
she'd thrown herself into the wedding plans, they'd
formed a true mother-daughter bond. Last came Phil,
holding firmly to her father's arm. Every time Liam had
seen Karl in the past couple of days, he'd been laughing
and joking. Not now. He was obviously too manly to cry,
but he was blinking rapidly and his jaw was set.

After they entered the heart-shaped ring of wedding
guests, Liam stepped toward Hope to close the opening.
Lexi, Rosie and Edie took their positions in the upper left
curve of the heart, and Karl placed Phil's hand in Damon's before claiming his spot in the right-hand curve
beside Cade and Finn. He discreetly thumbed the moisture from his eyes.

The minister surveyed the guests. "Let us all join
hands as we surround this couple with the love of family and friends."

Liam took the hand of the woman on his right and
was about to grasp Hope's when she beat him to it. Slipping her soft fingers through his, she met his gaze, and
there was no mistaking the yearning in her eyes. Maybe
she hadn't completely given up on happily-ever-after.
He tightened his grip. If she hadn't glanced away, he
might have spent the entire ceremony lost in her tender
expression.

Instead she directed her attention to where Phil and
Damon stood with the minister. As sunset painted the
landscape in shades of pink and orange, everyone took
on that glow, but it seemed centered on the couple standing in the middle of the heart.

The words of the ceremony were familiar to Liam, but
the emotions they churned up were not. Until meeting
Hope, marriage had been a vague concept, an event that

would happen to him in the distant future. Yet something had clicked in his brain from that first moment with her.

When he'd talked to Grady about what they'd do if either of them fell in love, he'd been picturing Hope as a likely candidate. Hearing Damon and Phil make those age-old promises with Hope so near, her fingers laced through his, had a powerful effect on him. He couldn't know whether she was feeling that, too. Logic told him she wouldn't want to admit it.

That was okay. He could be patient for the next few days. But he was really glad he'd shuffled the order of the lineup so he could share this with her. It might be something to build on.

The ceremony ended, Damon and Phil flinging themselves into each other's arms and kissing with an abandon that brought whistles and cheers from the guests surrounding them. Then they joined hands and started toward the SUV as Josh pumped up the volume on the recessional. Liam had to let go of Hope because the happy couple needed an exit.

Traditionally the maid and matrons of honor were supposed to pair up with the groomsmen and parade down the aisle, but Karl broke with tradition and hurried after the bride and groom.

"They need a driver!" he called out as he followed them to the SUV. He hopped in, started the engine and off they went.

Edie stood with Finn at the end of the aisle of artificial turf, staring at the departing vehicle. "First of all, that's my car he's driving, and second of all, where are they going? There will be no reception waiting for them at the house. We're all here!"

"But it was dramatic," Rosie said, laughing. "Come

on. Let's load up and move on out. We won't be too far behind them."

In the confusion that followed, Hope ended up riding back with Lexi and Cade. Liam and Grady were the last ones to leave the area. Once they'd made sure no one else needed a ride, they closed the tailgate, climbed in the truck and drove toward the house.

"Nice wedding," Grady said.

"Different. I liked it."

"Me, too. I noticed you got next to Hope."

"Yeah." Liam blew out a breath. "You might as well know this. I think she's the one."

"Does she think you're the one?"

Count on Grady to cut to the chase. "She doesn't believe in such things anymore."

"Why not?"

"I can't say."

"Oh, boy. I thought I'd be the one to pick a complicated woman. I figured you'd end up falling for one of your outdoorsy rafting ladies. A straight shooter."

Liam glanced over at him. "Turns out that I ended up falling for someone as complicated and creative as you, little brother."

"Then God help you."

"I could use some divine intervention, so if you have any pull in that department, please use it."

"You're not kidding around, are you?"

"No. I know what I want to happen, but convincing her that it's the right thing won't be easy."

Grady settled back in his seat. "I knew all along that this temporary fling business wasn't your idea. That's not you."

"It's not her, either."

"Then why did she set it up that way?"

"I can't say."

"Maybe you can't say, but I'm getting the picture. She's let you into her confidence and into her bed, but not into her heart."

"Thanks."

"Am I wrong?"

"No." Liam found a parking space near the house and turned off the motor. "Like I said, there are issues."

"I can see that." Grady unsnapped his seat belt and turned to him. "I can also see that you're in danger of having *your* heart sliced and diced, big brother. Maybe you should drive back with me tomorrow and forget about playing house with a woman who's not smart enough to see that you're the best there is."

Liam smiled. "Thanks, Grady."

"I feel the urge to tell her so."

"Please don't."

"I wouldn't really, at least not at this stage, when she might still come to her senses on her own. But if she ditches you, I'll have to give her a piece of my mind."

Grady's loyalty touched him. "I'm not so smart, either. A smart guy would go back with you tomorrow, but I have to see this through. Otherwise I'll always wonder if I'd given up too soon."

"Hmm." Grady drummed on the dashboard, something he tended to do when he was thinking. "I get that. Whenever I hit a rough patch with a sculpture, I have the same thought. I could ditch the idea, and I'm so tempted, but then I might be haunted by the possibility that I gave up when I was on the verge of a breakthrough."

"Exactly."

"See, I work with metal and you work with people, but the concepts are not that different. I try to bring out the beauty in the metal, and you're digging for the beauty in the souls of your rafting clients."

"Or in this case, a wedding guest."

"Right." He punched him lightly on the arm. "Go with your gut, bro. Every time I've done that, my sculpture is so much better."

"Good advice." Liam opened the driver's side door and climbed out of the truck.

"Hurry!" Hope stood on the porch in her green dress and purple rain boots. "They took the box thing off the wedding cake and—"

"Messed up the cake?" He and Grady walked faster. "Please don't tell me they messed up that cake."

"They'd better not have," Grady muttered. "Not after all we went through to get it there."

"The cake's fine," Hope said. "But they can't find the cake topper. Do either of you know where it is?"

Liam clapped his hand over his shirt pocket, but of course he hadn't been wearing this shirt.

Grady stopped and glanced at him, eyebrows lifted.

"I put it somewhere." Liam tried not to panic. That topper had been important to Damon. "Somewhere safe."

"Mentally retrace your steps," Hope said. "You'll remember."

"God, I hope so." He scrubbed a hand over his face. "It was in my shirt pocket when I set the cake down on the pool table." Then he'd turned around to find Hope. Her smile had made him forget everything else.

"Right." She walked down the steps and came toward them. "I don't remember you taking anything out of your shirt pocket."

"I didn't. Then Ty and Whitney drove up."

"And Brant and Aria," Grady said. "And we had lunch. Did you still have it then?"

"Pretty sure I did. I'd sort of forgotten about it, in fact."

"How about when we cleaned up and changed clothes? You would have noticed if you'd still had it in your pocket, right?"

"It wasn't there by then."

Hope frowned. "I hope it didn't fall out."

"The pocket snaps shut." He continued to review the course of events. Karl, Damon and Cade had shown up to play pool, and he'd stopped them from moving the box... "That's it!" Impulsively he grabbed Hope and gave her a quick kiss. "I know where it is." He turned to Grady. "When they wanted to move the cake, I remembered I still had the topper. I got out the horseshoes and tucked it behind the set of checkers in the game closet."

"Hallelujah." Grady smiled. "Gonna give me a kiss, too?"

"Maybe not."

"I have photographic evidence that you kissed me once upon a time."

"Yeah, yeah." Liam grinned. "When you were about ten days old and looked like Yoda."

"An awesome baby, I was," Grady said in his gravelly Yoda imitation.

Hope laughed. "Nice."

"An awesome brother, he is." Grady tilted his head toward Liam.

"I know."

Grady started to say something else, and Liam cut him off. "We'd better go unearth that critical doodad so we can get this party started." No telling how far Grady planned to take his little riff or how pointed his comments would become. Liam had always been protective of his little brother, but he hadn't realized until now that Grady felt exactly the same about him.

19

THROUGHOUT AN EVENING filled with belly laughs and happy tears, Hope kept remembering Grady's words. *An awesome brother, he is.* She watched Liam joking with his foster brothers. Love shone in every teasing exchange. The first time he'd walked into the hotel lobby in Cody, she'd seen a handsome man. She still adored his blue-eyed, dark-haired gorgeousness, but now she saw so much more—kindness, loyalty and fierce protectiveness.

Grady shared those traits, and his comment had been meant as a warning. If she hurt Liam, Grady would shun her. Rosie and Herb wouldn't be happy with her, either. She might be politely welcomed at Thunder Mountain Ranch because of Phil, but she would no longer be accepted the way she was now.

She hadn't set out to hurt Liam but quite likely that would happen. He'd switched places before the ceremony so he could be with her. That had nothing to do with sex and everything to do with his growing affection and his not-so-hidden agenda. He was falling for her, and he wanted more than a week's fling.

Not surprising. Anyone seeing him surrounded by his friends and family would recognize a man secure in his identity, a man ready to share his life with someone special. Their paths had crossed when he was looking for something she couldn't provide. She should clarify that and she'd talk with him later on tonight. She'd broach the subject before they got naked. After that, rational discussion would be impossible.

But her plan didn't turn out to be as workable as she'd thought. She didn't want to discuss it while he drove them down to the meadow. The road was slick and muddy and he needed to concentrate.

He suggested leaving her boots in the truck so he'd be the only one tracking mud in. She went along with the idea even though she thought he was looking for an excuse to act manly. She didn't miss the significance of being carried over the threshold, especially after they'd spent the entire day focused on wedding traditions.

The inside of the cabin was pretty dark, but Liam didn't seem worried about illumination tonight. Kicking the door shut, he lowered her to the mattress. "I need you." His voice was rough, but his mouth was gentle as it captured hers. And his experienced hands made short work of taking off her clothes. He had her out of her dress in no time, and her panties went sailing…somewhere.

Apparently he'd rather kiss her than take off his shirt or his boots. As that kiss became more urgent, he finally moved away long enough to accomplish the bare minimum. His belt buckle clanked and his zipper rasped before the crinkle of foil told her he'd located a condom. Breathing hard, he snapped the latex in place.

The denim of his jeans brushed her open thighs, and his first thrust lifted her off the mattress. Then he held very still as he gulped for air. "Don't move. Don't move or I'll come."

Her heart pounded with excitement. No man had ever wanted her this much. "Go ahead and come."

"No." He swallowed. "I'll get it together in a second." Taking a shaky breath, he leaned his forehead against hers. "I've been wanting you…ever since we left last night. I wanted to be here, deep inside. I couldn't think of anything else. It's been…a very long day."

Slipping her hand beneath his shirt collar, she rubbed his neck. "I'm sorry."

"My own damn fault. I tried to think of other stuff." Slowly he eased out and back in. "But this was always in the back of my mind." Raising his head, he began a slow rhythm. "It's a wonder I remembered where I put the cake topper."

She laughed. "Good thing you did."

"No kidding." He leaned down and feathered a kiss over her lips. "I like being inside you when you laugh. But mostly I just like being inside you."

"I like that, too." She wrapped him in her arms and closed her eyes. So good. If only she could be the woman he needed in his life.

Rocking forward until he filled her, he paused. "I can hear you thinking."

"No, you can't." She lifted her hips to lock him in even tighter. Now wasn't the time for discussion.

"What's on your mind, little lady?"

"You." Sliding both hands under his shirttails, she cupped his ass and began a slow massage.

He groaned softly. "What else?"

"Orgasms."

"I wish I believed that."

"Believe it, cowboy." She wiggled against him and he gasped. "Believe it and make me come."

"Ah, Hope." But he began to move. Gone were the

lazy strokes. He grasped her knees and pushed them toward her chest, pumping with deadly accuracy. Delicious pressure built as he quickened the pace. "How's that?"

"Good." She began to pant as her climax drew near. "Come with me."

"But—"

"Please." She moaned as he shifted his angle slightly, increasing the friction. "I love it when we come together."

"Me, too." He took a ragged breath. "You're close."

"Yes...*yes.*"

"Let go," he murmured. "I'm right behind you."

Surrendering to the rapid thrust of his cock, she spun into an orgasm filled with light and warmth. She knew it so well now that she didn't even need to swear. Glorious. When he joined her there, his body shuddering against hers, she held him tight as joy and gratitude washed over her. No matter what happened, she would remember this moment forever.

DESPITE GIVING HOPE exactly what she'd asked for, Liam couldn't shake the feeling that the other shoe was about to drop. He took care of the condom in the dark and stripped off the rest of his clothes, but then he searched for one of the lanterns. "I think we could use some light."

"Not yet."

He didn't like the sound of that. "I like being able to see you when we..." He started to say *have sex,* but the description was all wrong. Yet if he said *make love,* she was liable to read something into it.

"I know you do. But for now, let's leave it dark."

"How about the candles? They give off a softer light."

"Not right now, okay? Come back to bed. We need to talk."

His chest tightened. "Ominous." But he climbed back

into bed with her and gathered her close. "You're still wearing your bra. I never took it off you."

"That's okay. Listen, I—"

"I want to fix that." Reaching behind her back, he unfastened the hooks and pushed the straps down over her shoulders.

"I'm trying not to think about why you're so good at disrobing a woman. You've obviously had lots of practice."

"Some." He smiled as he finished taking off her bra and dropped it on the floor beside the bed. "Jealous?"

"Yes, and I'm ashamed of myself. I'm not allowed to be jealous under the circumstances."

"But if you change the circumstances, you can be as jealous as you want." He drew her back into his arms and sighed with contentment. Her warm, silky body nestled against his was heaven. He didn't feel like talking. More of what they'd just enjoyed would beat talking all to hell.

"I don't want to change the circumstances."

Damn. Apparently he'd made no progress whatsoever. Good thing he had several more days to work with. "Okay. Forget I mentioned it."

"I can't, just like I can't forget that you orchestrated it so we could stand together and hold hands through the ceremony."

"No biggie. I just felt like watching it while I was with you instead of standing between two of Rosie's former coworkers."

"To quote you, I wish I believed that."

"It's true." He rubbed the small of her back and felt tension there.

"I'm sure it is. But I don't believe that was your only motivation."

She was right. He'd been going for significant mo-

ments, memories that would bring them closer together
emotionally. And he'd been caught doing it. Now what?

"Your silence speaks volumes."

"Okay, I wanted us to share that experience in case
someday we wanted to look back on it…together."

"Oh, Liam." She sighed. "What have you told Grady?"

"Nothing about Tom or what happened between you
two."

"I wasn't asking about that. You promised and you'll
keep your word. What did you say about your feelings
for me?"

She'd backed him into a corner. "Look, before I tell
you what I said to Grady, please know this. I'm a big boy.
I can handle the situation."

"By *handling the situation*, do you mean convincing
me that we should be a couple?"

Apparently he hesitated a second too long.

"You do! I knew it!"

"Is that so bad? We get along great, in bed and out of
it. Why not give it a try?"

"Because I'm not ready for that and might never be. I
have to figure out who I am and what I want from life before I let another person in. I have no idea how long that
will take, and it's something I need to do alone. Becoming
involved with you or any man would derail the process."

He knew he shouldn't say what he thought about that
little speech, so he kept quiet and continued to massage
her back. That might have been pointless, because her
whole body had gone stiff as a board.

"Liam, please tell me you know what I'm talking
about."

Oh, God, she really was going to push it.

He knew his next words would screw things up, but if

he couldn't be honest with her, they had no future anyway. "Yes, and I think it's bullshit."

"What?" She scrambled away from him.

"We need light." He left the bed and stumbled around until he located a lantern on a shelf. He turned it on low before setting it beside the bed.

She was sitting up with the sheet clasped protectively over her bare breasts. Her elaborate hairdo was coming down, and a couple of the flowers had fallen onto the pillow. "If that's the way you feel, maybe I should get dressed and go back to the ranch house."

His heart sank. "If you want to go back, I'll drive you, but at least give me a chance to explain."

Her gray eyes glittered with anger. "Why should I?"

"Because I'm not trying to hurt you. I'm trying to help."

"Oh, yeah, I've heard *that* before."

"Please."

She blew out a breath. "All right. Go ahead."

This was so damned important, and he'd never been a wordsmith. He thought of all the conversations he'd had with Grady about self-knowledge and nurturing that creative spark. "You say you don't know who you are, but I think you do, deep down."

Her chin lifted. "Oh, really? What gave you that great insight?"

"Several things. Partly your bathrobe."

"My *bathrobe*?"

"You've held on to it since high school. How come?"

"It's cozy."

"And it also belonged to the girl who wrote a little song to apologize for stealing flowers. I'm going to take a wild guess that you did a lot of writing in that bathrobe."

Her eyes flashed in defiance. "Well, I don't anymore. I've moved on."

"You're a writer, Hope. It's what you were meant to do."

"That's not true!" She leaped out of bed and began putting on her clothes with jerky, uncoordinated movements.

"But it was so important to you!"

"Must not have been or I'd have kept doing it, wouldn't I?"

"Not if it hurts."

She met his gaze and for one brief moment let him see the agony there. "I'm done with writing. That's all there is to say."

"I don't know about writing, but I know about sports injuries. When I used to get injured I had to rest my arm or my leg, but then I'd gradually start using it again. That hurt, but it was the only way to get back to normal."

Her defiant mask slipped back into place. "Nice story. Doesn't fit. I don't want to go out on the field again, Coach. I have zero inspiration. The well's dry."

"I don't believe that. He took one book. You have dozens of books still inside you."

"How can you know such a thing? Like you just admitted, you're not a writer!" Her body vibrated with rage. "That one book was the basis for a series of books. I had it all figured out with a whole cast of characters, and it's gone. Gone!"

"So what?" He got up and pulled on his briefs and jeans.

"So *what*? Now I know you can't possibly understand. He took work I'd labored over for *years*. I can't just start over!"

He gazed at her. "Yes, you can. I know you can. He

stole that project, but if you give up writing, you've allowed him to steal your entire creative life."

Quivering, she stared at him in silence. Finally she cleared her throat. "And I thought you were kind. I thought you were compassionate. But you're not, Liam Magee. You're just like Tom, who wanted me to fit into a certain preconceived mold. Well, I'm not doing that. Do you hear me? I'm not doing that!"

Her words cut deeper than he'd ever imagined. "Hope, please. I'm not asking you to be what I want. I'm asking you to be yourself."

"To use your word, bullshit!" She raced for the door and jerked it open.

"Hey, I'll drive you!"

"Never mind!"

"Damn it, you're barefoot!" And so was he, but he charged out the door after her anyway.

"Leave me alone, Liam!" She ran through the muddy grass.

He ran after her, slipping and almost going down. But he caught her and pulled her into his arms.

She resisted and beat on his chest as tears poured down her cheeks. "Let me go! I hate you!"

"Hope…" He stared helplessly at her tears, knowing he'd made her cry. All he'd ever wanted was to bring her joy.

She gazed up at him, her cheeks wet and her hair a tangled mess. "Let me go."

He relaxed his grip. Slipping out of his arms, she turned away and started toward the house. But he had one more thing to say, and this might be his last chance. "I love you."

She paused.

For one heart-stopping moment, he thought she might come running back to him.

Apparently that only happened in the movies. She didn't turn around, but she did respond. "Tom used to say that, too." Then she continued walking.

Yeah, but I mean it. He let her go because she'd told him to. He felt hollow inside and knew he was in for some rough times. But he'd said what was in his heart, every bit of it. What happened next was up to her.

20

STUPID BATHROBE. Here Hope was, spending a lazy week in Phil and Damon's cabin, the perfect place to lounge around in her favorite piece of clothing in the world, and Liam had ruined it for her. She couldn't put it on without thinking of him.

But she wasn't about to get rid of it. Finally she decided that wearing it was the best way to desensitize herself to the association with Liam. Besides, the kittens loved it, especially when she sat on the floor and let them romp around her. She first thought of doing that on the Fourth, when she'd wanted to distract them from the sound of fireworks.

Fireworks could frighten animals. She wouldn't have gone to the celebration anyway because Liam might have been there. Instead she'd closed all the windows to mute the noise and had concentrated on entertaining the kittens.

That night they'd come up with a routine. The solid black one, MC Hammer, would go crazy over the sash when she twirled it for him. The black tuxedo, Nine-Inch Nails, preferred to hop onto her lap and knead his tiny claws into the soft fleece. When Hammer got tired of batting at the sash, he'd leap on Nails, and they'd wrestle until they rolled onto the floor. Then the whole thing would start over.

They made her laugh, thank goodness. Crying and swearing upset those little fluff balls more than fireworks, so she only did that on long afternoon walks. That was when she'd rehearse what she'd like to say to Liam if she ever had the opportunity to give him a piece of her mind.

On her third day of house-sitting, she woke up with a brainstorm. She'd go old school and write him a letter. She didn't know his snail mail address, but he'd be at the ranch until the end of the week. If she mailed a letter to Thunder Mountain this morning, he'd get it before he left.

All through breakfast and during her floor time with the kittens, she congratulated herself on coming up with the letter scheme. She imagined him reading it and realizing that he'd had it all wrong. He'd curse himself for indulging in amateur psychoanalysis and messing up what might have been a fun week. Sweet revenge.

Oh, and she'd make damn sure he understood that he was no longer welcome to stop and chat when he dropped off rafting clients. Mister Know-It-All could stay in the van from now on and keep his opinions to himself. She wouldn't be there much longer, anyway, but until she found a better position, she wanted him to stay the hell away from that lobby.

Once the kittens conked out for their morning nap, she found some stationery and stamps. Phil wouldn't care if she borrowed them, and she'd replace them before she left.

The living room coffee table was adjustable, and she brought it up to desk height. Pouring herself a cup of coffee reminded her of sharing coffee and Baileys with Rosie. That was likely over.

The morning after the wedding, she'd packed up before dawn and waited in the kitchen until Rosie had come in to start breakfast. Explaining that she and Liam wouldn't be seeing each other anymore had been tough.

Fortunately Liam hadn't shown up to make it worse. She suspected he'd waited until she'd driven away before making an appearance at the house. He also might have asked Grady to hang out with him in their cabin until she was gone.

Rosie hadn't seemed angry about the news and had hugged her goodbye, but she'd looked sad. Her loyalty was to Liam, as it should have been. Hope didn't like the idea of ending her relationship with everyone at Thunder Mountain, but she understood now that it had been inevitable. Imagining herself as a part of the clan had been a fantasy.

Within minutes of beginning, she'd filled both sides of the first sheet and had to get more paper. Oh, well. So it would turn out to be a long letter.

Two hours later, her fingers had begun to cramp, and she had ten pages front and back. A *really* long letter. But she didn't want to leave anything out. Belatedly she realized that she could probably download Phil and Damon's printer specs to her laptop.

Since she had more she wanted to say, she might as well type the rest of it. Postage on this sucker would be a lot, but it felt great finally to get out all the things she'd been thinking for two days. More than two days, actually. These were thoughts that had been rattling around in her head for months.

She'd given him a lot of backstory so he would understand exactly how wrongheaded he'd been. Wave a magic wand and poof, she'd be off and running. Nonwriters didn't get it, so in a way she forgave him. But he'd turned her bathrobe into some kind of symbol, and she wasn't sure if she'd ever forgive *that*.

Opening up a document on her laptop felt weird, but in a good way. She hadn't used her computer for anything besides email and the internet in a year. The blank page sat there waiting to be filled with more pages for Liam to read.

Sometime later her stomach growled, and she quickly opened a bag of chips. She'd be finished soon and could fix herself a regular meal. Except she couldn't seem to end the letter. She'd decided to explain the premise of her series so Liam could see how intricate it had been and why she didn't have the heart to start over.

Hammer and Nails woke up, and she paused long enough to feed them. She was still wearing her bathrobe, so she plopped down on the floor and went through their familiar routine again. "You guys are the cutest things ever," she told them. "I don't know why I don't have a couple of kittens. Probably because my apartment doesn't allow pets. I need to fix that."

They both stopped playing for a second and stared at her with their huge kitten eyes.

"I know! My life has been boring as hell, hasn't it?"

Nails took that as an invitation to jump into her lap. Hammer followed, tackling him. They wrestled and fell off on the floor, like always. For some reason, Hope found it more hilarious this time. She was still laughing as they scampered away and played chase around the living room.

Moving might mean paying a penalty for breaking the lease, but she'd do it and rent a place that would allow pets. Maybe she should find a new job first and move somewhere close to work. Yes, better plan. Once she'd finished this letter, she'd go online and look for job openings.

The kittens settled down, and she returned to the couch to discover she'd finished the chips. Man, it was dinnertime! She wouldn't get the letter mailed today after all. Opening a bottle of wine Phil had left for her, she poured herself a glass and got out a can of mixed nuts. She'd cook dinner the minute she finished the letter.

But something about the description of her series caught her attention. A character she hadn't done much with initially seemed full of possibilities now. Why hadn't she seen that before? He had such an interesting back-story that he could be a main character. She could change his name and alter his appearance a little so he'd be different from the character Tom had stolen.

For the heck of it, she opened a new document and typed a revised description of him. Then she wondered what he'd be doing in the first scene. What if it was a battle scene and he was fighting next to his best friend, a spunky woman? What if she got wounded, and…

Hours later, when both kittens crawled up the side of the couch and into her lap, she glanced at them in surprise. Oh, right. Hammer and Nails, her charges for the week. Slowly she returned to reality—Phil and Damon's house, an empty bottle of wine, an empty can of mixed nuts, and *fifteen pages of a story*?

As the kittens scampered over and around her, she stared at the evidence on her laptop. Against all odds and in spite of all her loud protestations to Liam, she was writing.

LIAM FIGURED THAT CADE, Lexi, Rosie and Herb had organized the poker game to take his mind off Hope. He appreciated the effort, but it wasn't working too well. He kept losing track of the cards and screwing up his bet.

They'd spent the past three days getting ready for the next session of Thunder Mountain Academy, which would begin with students arriving the next day. He'd thrown himself into the preparations with a vengeance. He'd worked so hard that Rosie had taken him aside and given him the "many more fish in the sea" talk.

Funny, considering only days ago she'd thought he and Hope were soul mates. He'd listened, nodded and assured Rosie that he would continue to search for the love of his life.

But he'd found her. She just didn't know it. Maybe she never would have that realization, and he'd have to live with the consequences. But he was counting on a few days of solitude to give her clarity. Solo treks through the wilderness always helped him see things differently.

He was holding three aces when someone knocked on the front door. A premonition made him throw in his hand. "I'll get it."

Heart pounding, he walked quickly through the living room, and there was Hope standing outside the screen door, clutching a handful of papers. He could barely breathe as he reached for the door. "Want to come in?" His voice sounded pretty ragged.

"No. Come out, please."

He didn't need to be told twice. Once on the porch, though, he wasn't sure whether to touch her or not. He wanted to grab her, but that could be a mistake.

She was breathing as fast as he was. She looked as if she'd dressed in a hurry in a T-shirt and jeans, and although her hair was combed, she wore no makeup. She shoved the pages at him. "Here."

He took them. "What is it?"

"The..." She swallowed. "The first chapter."

He stared at her in bewilderment. "Of what?"

"My new book."

"Your new...you *wrote* this?"

She nodded. "This afternoon. Tonight. I started out writing you a letter and then it just happened." Tears glistened in her eyes. "Liam, you were right. I'm a writer."

With a shout of joy, he swept her up in his arms and swung her around, although he kept a tight hold on those precious pages. The screen banged, and everyone came running out to see what was going on. When he saw them standing there, he figured they'd been in the living room, eavesdropping, but he waved the papers anyway and made the announcement. "A book! She's started a book!"

They surrounded Hope, gave her hugs and showered her with congratulations. She looked as if she'd won the lottery. He stepped back and watched, his heart full of love for her. He'd wished for a breakthrough, and here it was.

Then she turned toward him, took the pages back and handed them to Rosie. "Could you please move these inside? And don't bother reading them. It's a rough draft. I printed them out as physical evidence for Liam, but it's a first chapter. First chapters always change."

"But can I read it?" Rosie held the pages as if they were breakable.

"If you want." She glanced at Cade, who still had cards in his hand. "Did I interrupt a game?"

"Yes," Rosie said, "but that's okay. Want to come in and join us?"

Liam held his breath.

"Well, sure, but I was wondering if I could borrow Liam for a few minutes first."

All four of them fell over themselves assuring her they didn't mind and she could borrow Liam for as long as she wanted. Everyone else went in, but as sounds of rejoicing drifted out from the kitchen, Liam prayed they weren't being premature.

Her back ramrod straight, Hope faced him. "I don't know how to say this."

"Take your time." He was a wreck. She'd found her writing vibe. That didn't mean she'd changed her mind about being with him. But it might mean just that.

She dragged in a shaky breath. "A year ago a man took something very precious to me." She met his gaze. "And you, Liam Magee, have given it back."

"I just gave you a nudge. You did the rest."

"But that nudge made all the difference." She hesitated. "And I wasn't very appreciative at the time. Now I know that you did it out of love."

He clenched his hands at his sides. "Yes, ma'am."

"I love you for that." She took a step toward him. "But I also just plain love *you*."

He closed his eyes as the breath whooshed out of his lungs. "Thank God."

"And if you don't kiss me this very minute, I might die."

Opening his eyes, he saw her standing there smiling and knew he was the luckiest SOB in the universe. "Can't have you kicking the bucket." He gathered her close. "You have a book to finish."

"Not just one." She wound her arms around his neck. "Some cowboy told me I have dozens inside me."

"Smart man." And a smart man would hold this woman to his heart and never let her go. As his mouth found hers, he vowed to do exactly that.

Epilogue

DELIVERING A SCULPTURE to a client in Buffalo, Wyoming, provided the perfect excuse for Grady to swing up to Sheridan and help Cade pick out artwork for his cabin. They'd talked about it during the wedding festivities, but they'd run out of time to drive into town. Apparently Cade needed to demonstrate more of a nesting instinct before Lexi believed he was ready for marriage.

She was in Billings conducting a riding clinic, so she'd never have to know that Cade had brought in a consultant. Grady had suggested they meet at the Sheridan Art Barn, a recently opened artists' co-op on the outskirts of town. He had no trouble spotting it. The converted barn had been painted deep purple.

Cade was leaning against his truck as Grady pulled in. "Sure do appreciate this, bro," he said as he walked over to Grady's truck.

"No problem." Grady hopped down and grinned at him. "It'll be fun."

"Easy for you to say."

"It will be." Grady punched him lightly on the shoulder. "Buck up, pardner. You been in there yet?"

"Not me! This is foreign territory for this ol' boy. Thank God that Liam suggested you help me."

"What's your budget?" They walked together toward the open double doors.

"I have some cash and I also brought plastic. I guess my budget's whatever my credit card limit is."

"We're not going to max out your card. I'm sure we'll find some good stuff that's reasonable." He paused next to an easel holding a sign listing the artists' names. "Hey, Sapphire Ferguson's part of this. We went to school with her and her sister."

"Yeah." Cade peered at the easel. "I don't remember her very well but her sister is a different story."

"Amethyst."

"Yep. I was blown away by her performance in the school musical and I remember thinking she was hot, too. Which I never told Lexi, by the way."

"I should hope not." But Cade was right that Amethyst had been the flashier of the two sisters.

Grady had thought Sapphire was more interesting, though. She'd been into art back then, too—delicate pottery that had sometimes shown up in the school's display case. Her mom had been the art teacher, maybe still was. If he hadn't been so damned worried about his manly image in those days, he would have taken Mrs. Ferguson's class.

"Are you cowboys coming in or still thinking about it?" A woman stood just inside the doorway. Her long auburn hair was pulled back on one side to show off an earring of turquoise feathers that dangled almost to her shoulder. Her sleeveless yellow blouse displayed a fair amount of cleavage, and she'd woven a colorful sash through the belt loops of her snug jeans.

Grady wasn't about to ignore an invitation from a

beautiful woman. "We're coming in." He walked through the door, and once his eyes made the adjustment from sun to artificial light, he was able to see the color of the woman's eyes. They were bright turquoise. "Sapphire?"

She gasped. "Grady?"

"Yes, ma'am." He touched the brim of his Stetson and tried not to stare. She was *nothing* like he remembered. Back in high school she'd had short hair and worn flowered dresses and almost no makeup. This far more dramatic Sapphire had on eye makeup, and her glossy lipstick was fire-engine red.

"I've been hoping I'd run into you sooner or later! You've done very well for yourself."

"Thank you." That kind of comment always made him a little skittish, so he shifted the focus. "You remember Cade Gallagher."

"Of course I do." She smiled at Cade. "I heard you were back."

"Back to stay this time," he said, "which is why we're here. I have a cabin that needs artwork."

"You've come to the right place. We have some wonderful local artists. Oils, watercolors, pastels, mixed media, fabric art, you name it."

"What about you?" Grady had a hard time imagining that this new version of Sapphire made dainty little teapots.

"Still doing pottery. Love it. Although my style's changed quite a bit."

"I know what you mean. I've noticed how different my newest pieces are from what I was doing a year ago. I—" He caught himself. He wasn't here to have a discussion about art while Cade stood around twiddling his thumbs. "Anyway, we'd better start looking."

"*I'll* start looking." Cade clapped him on the shoulder. "I'll yell for help when I get stuck."

"No, I'll come with you."

Cade was already backing away. "I'm caught up in the spirit of adventure. You wouldn't want to spoil that, now would you?"

"Guess not." Grady laughed. "I'll be there in a few."

"I take it you're supposed to advise him on what to purchase?" Sapphire looked amused.

"He thinks he doesn't know anything about art."

"I don't!" Cade sang out as he continued down the aisle. "But I know what I like!"

"Then you'll be fine!" Sapphire called after him. She turned back to Grady. "As long as he's giving us a chance to talk, I might as well tell you about the great idea I just had."

"What's that?" Several interesting possibilities came to mind.

"Next month we're doing a charity event here at the barn."

That wasn't one of them. "Oh?"

"We'll all spend the evening putting the finishing touches on our current project and invite the public to watch. There'll be a silent auction for those works. Would you be part of it?"

He wasn't going to tell her what he'd been thinking the moment he recognized her. It had nothing to do with charity and everything to do with getting to know her better. Much better. That was impractical on many levels, and so was this request.

Besides being up to his neck in commissioned work, he needed to carve out time to make something special for Rosie in the next few weeks. Liam had passed on her request for a sculpture and he wanted to fill that request

ASAP. The charity event might be only one evening, but he'd need to allow several days to set up his workspace and make enough progress that he could finish it during the event.

She sighed. "Okay, it was a long shot, but I had to ask."

"I'll do it."

"You will? Really?"

"Sure."

"Oh, Grady, this is huge." For a moment she looked as if she might hug him.

He would have been okay with that.

But instead she took a deep breath and gave him a brilliant smile. "Thank you."

He might have spent a lot more time gazing at that wonderful smile if Cade hadn't yelled out that he was in desperate need of advice. Grady excused himself and went to do the job he'd promised. Cade ended up with some great stuff at a reasonable price.

Before they left, Sapphire gave Grady the date and time of the event, and they exchanged email addresses so they could work out the details. He and Cade loaded everything in the passenger side of Cade's truck as Sapphire stood in the doorway, watching.

"A charity event, huh?" Cade said in a low voice. "What's the charity?"

"I have no idea."

Cade seemed to find that hilarious. "Gonna ask her what it is? She's right over there."

"Don't need to."

"Because it doesn't matter, does it?" Cade grinned at him.

He didn't bother confirming. Cade already knew the answer. "See you at the ranch." He walked over to his truck. Before getting in, he gave Sapphire a wave. She waved back. She was still in his rearview mirror as he drove off, so he tapped on the horn as a last farewell.

He'd have to work his ass off to make up the time he'd lose while participating in an event to benefit some unknown cause. But as he pictured Sapphire Ferguson standing in the doorway, gazing after him, he had a strong feeling it would be worth every late night slaving over a hot blowtorch. That woman was dynamite.

* * * * *

*Sparks are flying between Grady and Sapphire!
Read their story in COWBOY UNTAMED,
the next book in Vicki Lewis Thompson's
THUNDER MOUNTAIN BROTHERHOOD series,
coming August 2016 only from Harlequin Blaze!*

*Sculptor Grady Magee wants one thing:
Sapphire Ferguson. She's sworn off artists, but how
can she resist a man who creates art out of scrap—and
one with cowboy swagger to boot?*

*Read on for a sneak preview of
COWBOY UNTAMED, the third story of 2016 in
Vicki Lewis Thompson's sexy cowboy saga
THUNDER MOUNTAIN BROTHERHOOD.*

"Lady, you and I generate a lot of heat. You can head home to catch up on paperwork, but that's not going to change anything."

"Maybe not." She shoved her hands into her pockets and clutched her keys as a reminder that she was leaving. Just because he thought her surrender was inevitable didn't mean he was right. But she could feel that heat he was talking about melting her resistance. "I need to go." She started to turn away.

"Hang on for a second." He lightly touched her arm.

The contact sent fire through her veins. "What for?" She turned back to him and saw the intent before he spoke the words.

"A kiss."

"No, that would be—"

"Only fair. I've been imagining kissing you ever since I drove away three weeks ago. If you don't want to take it beyond that point, I'll abide by that decision." He smiled. "What's one little kiss?"

A mistake. "I guess that would be okay."

"Not a very romantic answer." He drew her into his arms and lowered his head. "But good enough."

The velvet caress of his mouth was every bit as spectacular as she'd imagined. If she stuck to her guns, this would never happen again, so it seemed criminal to waste a single second of kissing Grady Magee. She hugged him close as he worked his magic. She'd figured the man could kiss, but she hadn't known the half of it. He started slow, tormenting her with gentle touches that made her ache for more.

When he finally settled in, she opened to him greedily, desperately wanting the stroke of his tongue. Kissing him was exactly what she'd been trying to avoid, but when he cupped her bottom and drew her against the hard ridge of his cock, she forgot why she'd been so reluctant.

Wouldn't a woman have to be crazy to reject this man? Wrapped in his strong arms and teased with his hot kisses, she craved the pleasure he promised.

Taking his mouth from hers, he continued to knead her bottom with his strong fingers. "Still think we should nip this thing in the bud?"

Don't miss COWBOY UNTAMED
by Vicki Lewis Thompson, available in August 2016
wherever Harlequin® Blaze® books and ebooks are sold.

www.Harlequin.com

HBEXP0716

Reading Has Its Rewards

Earn **FREE BOOKS!**

Register at **Harlequin My Rewards** and submit your Harlequin purchases from wherever you shop to earn points for free books and other exclusive rewards.

Plus submit your purchases from now till May 30th for a chance to win a $500 Visa Card*.

Visit **HarlequinMyRewards.com** today

MYR16R1

Love the Harlequin book you just read?

Your opinion matters.

Review this book on your favorite book site, review site, blog or your own social media properties and share your opinion with other readers!

JUST CAN'T GET ENOUGH?

Join our social communities
and talk to us online.

You will have access to the latest
news on upcoming titles and special
promotions, but most importantly,
you can talk to other fans about your
favorite Harlequin reads.

Harlequin.com/Community

f Facebook.com/HarlequinBooks

Twitter.com/HarlequinBooks

P Pinterest.com/HarlequinBooks

HARLEQUIN®

A *Romance* FOR EVERY MOOD™

**Stay up-to-date on all your
romance-reading news with the
Harlequin Shopping Guide,
featuring bestselling authors, exciting new
miniseries, books to watch and more!**

The newest issue will be delivered right to you
with our compliments! There are 4 each year.

Signing up is easy.

EMAIL

ShoppingGuide@Harlequin.ca

WRITE TO US

HARLEQUIN BOOKS
Attention: Customer Service Department
P.O. Box 9057, Buffalo, NY 14269-9057

OR PHONE

1-800-873-8635 in the United States
1-888-343-9777 in Canada

Please allow 4-6 weeks for delivery of the first issue by mail.

HSGSIGNUP